The black leather ring of his collar

is perfectly showcased in the field of bleached cotton. Of everything in Kyle's possession, and out of every instrument of sexual pleasure and torment in the house, and there are countless, this is the one out of them all that he dreads the most. And that Ben has taken it from the shelf in the closet and placed it there for Kyle to see means that Ben wants him to wear it. If Kyle wears it, all of his rules and preferences are dissolved. Only Ben's rules stay in effect. Ben is Master.

For a small, yet intense moment, Kyle is truly scared.

I could say no, he thinks. And he's tempted to. But to do such a thing when Ben has made it so clear that he wants this would be close to a declaration of war. It's not Kyle's place to question Ben. That's their arrangement. Of course, Kyle's consent is a key element in their play, but after a year and a half together, tension has grown in their relationship. Ben knows that Kyle is unhappy. He hasn't said as much, but it's there, and Ben can sense it. If, on top of that, Kyle starts to deny Ben the indulgence of being Master and slave, Dominant and submissive, there would be no going back. There would be *A Problem.*

Aware that he's probably overanalyzing things, Kyle grips his head, rubbing the heels of his hands into his eye sockets, taking a deep breath to calm down.

You could still say no, his conscience whispers to him.

Also recommended...

You may also enjoy these other Forbidden Fiction works:

The Charming by J.A. Jaken

Clayton MacAllister had it all, but the shadow of a past love blinded him until life was slipping through his fingers. Just as Clay is ready to give up on the idea that he might ever be happy, a charming stranger steps into his life like a blessing — or a curse. (M/M+)

http://forbiddenfiction.com/library/story/JAJ-1.000046

Don't... by Jack L. Pike

"Don't... open me." Three simple words that tease Jack, taking him places from his dark past. For Jack, BDSM is a way to resist his worst impulses. Yet, the stranger calling himself The Unknown seeks to use that to seduce him. As Jack slips further down into the abyss, two men hold the power to save him. Will it be Gray, the Master who knows Jack's every secret? Or Jan, the first man to give Jack a reason to hope? With deadly ghosts coming out to play, Jack may lose everything, even his life. (M/M)

http://forbiddenfiction.com/library/story/JP2-1.000134

From Temptation

Lynn Kelling

ForbiddenFiction
www.forbiddenfiction.com

an imprint of

Fantastic Fiction Publishing
www.fantasticfictionpublishing.com

FROM TEMPTATION
A Forbidden Fiction book

Fantastic Fiction Publishing
Hayward, California

© Lynn Kelling, 2012

CREDITS
Editor: Rylan Hunter
Cover Design: D.M. Atkins
Cover photo: KrisCole at Pixmac
Production Editor: Erika L Firanc
Proofreading: JpH323, Kel Draves

SKU: LK1-000026-02 FFP
ISBN: 978-1-62234-077-4

Published in the United States of America

DISCLAIMER

This book is a work of fiction which contains explicit erotic content; it is intended for mature readers. Do not read this if it's not legal for you.

All the characters, locations and events herein are fictional. While elements of existing locations or historical characters or events may be used fictitiously, any resemblance to actual people, places or events is coincidental.

This story depicts fictional BDSM; it is not intended to be used as an instruction manual. It contains descriptions of erotic acts that may be immoral, illegal, or unsafe. The characters are not models for the Safe, Sane and Consensual forms embraced by most current practitioners of BDSM. The author takes license with the use of BDSM for dramatic effect. Do not take the events in this story as proof of the plausibility or safety of any particular practice.

For those who have doubted their bravery.
Have Faith.

Contents

Chapter 1

Good Intentions

With a head full of intentions, Ben opened his home's unlocked front door and felt the change in air pressure, the chill. He brought it in with him, wind whistling around his legs, tugging at the end of his long coat before he could get the door closed again.

As he turned, he caught sight of a figure out of the corner of his eye. "Oh! There you are," he said in surprise. It was Kyle, sitting in the living room, facing the television with a beer in his hand, still dressed in dirty work clothes. Kyle always changed and showered as soon as he was home from work. It was unlike him. His hands were scrubbed clean, Ben noticed, but a smudge of dirt ran under one cheekbone. The TV was off, a darkened monolith that Kyle stared at blankly.

The house was warm, but for Ben, the chill lingered. He hesitated before taking off his leather gloves and removing his coat. Kyle said nothing, no hello or greeting of any kind. Maybe he hadn't heard Ben enter, sunk too deep in his thoughts to notice. He didn't even glance Ben's way, just took a sip from the bottle and kept staring straight ahead.

"Hey," Ben said more sharply to get Kyle's attention.

It worked. Kyle's head slowly craned around. Vibrant, sky-blue eyes caught him.

"Look what the cat dragged in," Kyle remarked, giving Ben a one-over. Then he turned back around again to face the TV.

"That's funny," Ben replied, though he didn't smile or laugh. "C'mere, smartass."

Frustration was in the command, more than Ben wanted it to be.

Before, months ago, he would have been able to play this another way, to coax Kyle sweetly, seducing him with the idea, but things had changed. Kyle only looked at Ben these days like the blood was still staining his hands, a red scream that drowned everything else out.

But the training held. Ben's submissive dutifully set down his beer, and stood. His back cracked as he stretched it. Gaze lowered, Kyle circled the couch, walked right up to Ben, and dropped to his knees. His hands clasped loosely behind his back, he tossed his golden blond bangs out of his eyes, and he waited.

Ben asked, "How was your day?"

Ben reached out and raked his fingers through Kyle's shining, silken hair. Tugging gently on it, Ben drew his slave's head back to get a better look at him. Kyle kept his gaze lowered. He was wound tight, anticipating maybe many things at once.

"Long. Fine," he answered. "Thank you, Master."

"No shit? You look like something I scraped off my boot. I should have you get cleaned up before we do this, but I'm feeling impatient."

Kyle glanced quickly up at Ben's face, then away again. It was enough, though. That brief look let Ben see the questions that had been stirred. Kyle was wondering why Ben was home early, and why he evidently was home early specifically because of Kyle. He wouldn't dare ask outright though, not unless given permission first.

That smudge on Kyle's cheek irked Ben. He rubbed a thumb at it, but it was stubborn.

"Don't worry, kitty, it's *good* news," Ben smiled. "Stand up. Relax. Drink your damn beer if it'll help get rid of that pissy look on your face."

The tension drained almost instantly out of Kyle upon realizing this wasn't going to turn into anything sexual. That reaction, of course, only served to aggravate Ben.

Kyle grabbed his beer. They headed into the kitchen and stood by the island in the center of the room.

"What's up?" Kyle asked.

"Plans for a new video," Ben said. "Trace and I came up with the idea. It'd be a piece of cake for you, but we think it'd sell really well. Diadem could use an influx of cash. We want you to star in it because of how much experience you have, but we're trying to line up someone else, too. That's kind of been the hiccup."

"Wait. What?" Kyle froze. "You're not the Dom?"

"No, it'd be me," Ben explained. "The idea is to have two submissives doing things to each other. I'd watch, but not interfere except to keep the subs in line. It'd be voyeurism for the audience, voyeurism for the Dom. Sounds good, right? You always get off on that shit. But see, this other guy, also a sub, he needs some convincing to go through with it. We need you to talk to him, explain that it's no big deal. Everyone will enjoy themselves; we'll all get off, get paid and win in the end."

Kyle had turned his back to Ben. After downing the rest of his beer in one shot, he threw the bottle at the recycling bin where it landed hard and smashed, loudly.

"Hey!" Ben scolded.

"It's been months since I've done any videos," Kyle said without facing him, his voice tight and thin. "You need to ask me before assuming I'm game for whatever you guys think up."

"I'm asking now."

"No, you're *telling* me. I've been really busy with work ever since they made me foreman."

"I know that—"

"I'm tired. I don't need the money like I used to. You really think I have the time or energy for this shit? It's not going to play well on camera."

"Will you look at me, for Christ's sake? I'm over here," Ben snapped, tired of talking to the back of Kyle's head. "And what's with throwing the fucking bottle?"

Slowly, too slowly, Kyle faced him. His hands were on his hips, which spoke of defensiveness. His eyes were too wide, though, too angry and not completely focused on Ben. Tense energy crackled around him like the threat of lightning.

"It's not like it was, Ben. The timing is bad. Someone else would do a better job."

"There is no one better than you, and you know it. You're the pro. Look, if it's weird for you to do this with me, then we'll get Trace, or Micah, and I'll just handle filming."

"Because it's so much less weird for me to submit to your best friends while you've got a camera pointed at me," Kyle said snidely.

There was no leniency in Kyle's arguments. It was like there were stone walls erected around him, which Ben could knock himself against as long as he liked. There was no getting through to the other side.

He scrambled for bait, something to lure Kyle out. There was always something — something forbidden, secretly desired, that Ben could offer as reward.

"Okay," Ben murmured, thinking, searching. "Okay, if you don't like including friends or strangers, how about we just use people you're familiar with? We could ask Dare to be the second sub. You two have gone at it before under direction, and you got off on it, hard — "

Kyle bolted from the room before Ben could finish the sentence, his boots landing heavily on the wooden floor as he stomped away.

"Hey! Get the hell back here!"

He chased after Kyle, and saw him yank a coat from a hanger. The closet door slammed shut, hard enough to rattle the frame.

"I'm talking to you!" Ben yelled.

"*Fuck off!*" Kyle screamed, suddenly red-faced with fury. His keys were sitting on a table by the front door. Scooping them up, Kyle yanked the door open. Wind howled in Ben's face, moaning with the promise of a storm.

"Will you calm down so we can talk about this — "

But Kyle had already left. The screen door slapped closed behind him as he headed for the driveway, his car's headlights flashing as he unlocked it with the fob.

"*Kyle!*"

Gusts of air touseled Kyle's blond hair wildly, pushing him around on the path as he rushed to get behind the wheel. He must have heard Ben's shout but ignored it. Helpless, confused, Ben could only stand there and watch as Kyle drove away.

It was hours before Kyle came back. Past midnight he snuck inside and crept to bed.

The following morning, patiently, Ben waited for Kyle to wake up and get ready for work. As Kyle was finishing a meager breakfast of a banana and coffee, Ben confronted him with only good intentions, hands raised to show he meant no harm.

"Look," Ben said. "I don't know what I said to piss you off last night. I thought this would be something you'd *like*. I'm trying to make this shit *better* between us, but how am I supposed to do that when you won't talk to me? Tell me what the issue is, and we'll fix it. Hey! *Hey!*"

Ben caught Kyle at the door, just as he was about to bolt again. He grabbed Kyle's arm to keep him there.

Shaken with overwhelming emotion that Ben was startled to witness, Kyle growled, "*Stop trying.*"

His arm began to slip from Ben's grasp. Briefly their hands interlocked. With tears in his eyes that Ben couldn't claim to understand, Kyle gave his hand a brief squeeze. Pulling free, he fled Ben like he was being chased, like there was nothing Ben could do to save him. Not anymore.

"Is there anything in particular you want to talk about today? Anything on your mind?"

Kyle glares at her, his expression deliberately masked, unreadable. The air that surrounds him is that of one who has had more than enough of life's trials. Tired, worn thin, a mean glint is the only thing that stirs behind his gaze as he struggles with his own hostility. Something has happened since they last met. Kyle knows his shrink wonders what it is, but doubts she'll ever find out the truth.

Sophia O'Malley has been Kyle Roth's psychiatrist for almost five years. A while back, he stopped coming to see her and gave no explanation why. Now, suddenly and also without explanation, he's back. This is their fourth appointment in less than two weeks. Just as with the others, he's in an uncooperative mood.

"Kyle? We're on your time. I would like to help, but if you have nothing to say...."

"I've figured something out. Actually, I've figured out a lot recently, but let's start with this. When I talk, people don't listen. They don't hear what I'm saying, and it's pissing me off."

She waits for him to continue, and when he doesn't she prods him with, "Tell me more about that. What are you trying to tell them?"

Clenching his jaw, he gazes out the window, tinted to keep out the glare of the sunlight. It makes everything that should be vibrant dull, murky and overcast. It's appropriate, he thinks. *My life is like that, seen through a film that screws everything up.*

"It's been like that for years. I tried to tell Darrek something really important when we were in high school. You know, I don't even remember when I first met him. He lived close by. It must have been, like, early grade school. Anyhow, fast-forward to senior year. My parents were gone, like usual, so he was crashing at my place. I'd gotten my hands on this sweet bottle of rum. He wouldn't touch the stuff. Too afraid of gettin' a whoopin' from Daddy Dearest if he happened to smell it on Dare's breath."

The old anger washes over Kyle briefly, built up from too many years of having to witness, helplessly, his best friend's torment at the hands of an abusive bastard of a father. He tries to push past the emotional response before it can get too muddled and drag him down. It's the reason why Kyle usually tries not to think about that era of his life. It's a black hole, ringed with teeth, chewing him up from the inside out.

So much pain — pain that began it all, the profound damage that Jerry Grealey caused his little boy. It planted the seed. Kyle wonders, not for the first time, how a man could be such a cruel father to an innocent, trusting child. Didn't Jerry know that once you nurture a taste for pain and perversion, that is what will be sought?

Clearing his throat, Kyle tries to ground himself to the present once more. "Anyway, like I was saying, I got hammered and he didn't. And I guess it gave me some courage to say things that I'd been too scared to talk about before." He sharply blows out a breath and scowls. "If he'd just *listened* to me, maybe things didn't have to happen like they did! People wouldn't have gotten hurt! Fuck...."

"Hey," Sophia says soothingly. "Kyle, talk it out. You need to give me a little more than that."

Tears shine, unshed, in his eyes.

"Tell me what you said to Darrek?" she asks softly.

He laughs mirthlessly. "God, I was such an idiot," he sneers, then considers it and, a moment later, adds, "Maybe I'm still an idiot."

5 Years Earlier

Long before Kyle got wasted on rum, before the bottle had even been opened, Darrek confessed that he needed input on whom to ask to prom. He was at a loss. Karen, who Darrek had been dating for almost a month, broke up with him to date someone from the crew team instead. Luckily, Darrek had options. There were more than a couple of girls who were happy to go to prom with a towering, handsome, bright-eyed goofball. But Darrek didn't want just any girl; he wanted the right girl. So, naturally, he asked Kyle for his opinion.

All night long, Kyle talked Darrek out of asking person after person for a plethora of reasons — personality quirks, tendency to gossip, tendency to be a raging slut, tendency to *not* be a raging slut. The arguments started off rational but as the rum kicked in, they spanned out widely, until Kyle forgot what they were talking about in the first place, only aware that there was a reason why he needed to convince Darrek that the female species was bad for him.

"Women," Kyle said seriously, pointing a finger at Darrek's nose as Darrek struggled not to break into laughter at his best friend's intoxicated gravity. "Let me tell you what I've learned about women. They're easy. Right? They tend to look for a few basic things." He started to tick them off on his fingers. "Companionship; someone who understands them, on more than a superficial, I-like-pussy level; someone who knows what a clitoris is. You with me so far?"

Darrek stifled his grin and frowned, nodding. "Yeah, man. I'm with ya."

"Good," Kyle said approvingly, clapping Darrek on the shoulder. "Throw in an element of danger—a kinky little somethin' some-thin'—show you give a half-a-shit about them, and you're golden."

"No, you're a douchebag."

"Whatever. Women like douchebags. Douchebags tend to have money and power and lots of good stuff. Follow me."

"Okay, I'm following you, but I'm putting on my hazards and looking for someone, preferably in a uniform, to get you help."

Darrek locked eyes with Kyle, who flipped his shaggy blond bangs back out of his blue eyes, looking just as he always had, like the typical American jock pretty boy. But Darrek knew Kyle's out-ward appearance was misleading, that though he looked innocent enough on the outside, there was darkness and pain buried under-neath.

They were leaning over the kitchen's island, in the center of the room. The only light came from the full moon shining down through the skylight above and, in slanting, pale shafts, through the large windows overlooking the back yard. Kyle squinted at the im-plication that he didn't know what he was talking about and replied, "Fuck you. My point is...."

"There's a point?"

"*My point is,*" he powered on, talking over Darrek, "What's in it for me?"

"Um, a relationship? Happiness? Sex?"

"No, you're wrong. You get that stuff on their terms. What about *my* terms?"

"You have terms?"

"Yes! I want someone who can pull me out of my own head. I want someone who's always a step ahead of me. I want... I want someone who not only gets how fucked up I am, but is so much more intense themself that every day, every single fucking day is... an adventure. The scariest things I can think of? I want a taste of that, not enough to hurt me permanently, but just a taste so that I can develop a tolerance and get stronger from it. Women can't give you that shit. And the ones that can are way too out of control to deal with in any capacity."

"Wow. You are such a horse's ass. All of this coming from the guy with how many girlfriends?"

"Not that many. Like, five. 'Cause, I mean, hey, if you can't beat 'em, you can at least stock up on extras."

"It's amazing that Darrek never figured out the truth beneath what he had already determined was pure bullshit, before I *told* him the truth. He must have just chalked it up to arrogant tunnel vision brought on by too much rum. But after I told him I'm gay, he still didn't get it. Not really. Besides Darrek, though, no one ever got it — got *me* — until I met Ben. Ben saved me and then he annihilated me. No one has ever loved me more and no one has ever hurt me like he has. Maybe that's a good thing. Then again, seems like everyone I know is out to hurt me."

Sophia stops scribbling notes and sets her pad and pen aside. Folding her hands in her lap, she leans forward and tells her client, "I'm worried about you, Kyle. It's good that you're getting this stuff off your chest, but if you want me to help, you have to stop speaking in riddles and be plain with me."

Kyle smiles, then chuckles, recognizing his cue to leave. He stands and grabs his jacket, slinging it over an arm. It's been a long day and it's time to get out of there, whether the clock has run out or not. He came here right after work, directly from the construction site, and now he's spent and just wants to get cleaned up and have a beer. "Thanks, Dr. O'Malley. Catch you later?"

"Same time next Tuesday," she sighs. "Think about what I said."

He waves, his back already turned, as he opens the closed door and moves through it, feeling better for what he's said, even if he said it to the wrong person.

Chapter 2

Out of Options

When Kyle gets to his car, he thinks of all of the things he wanted to confess to his shrink but didn't, and can't. With all of the time he's been spending in his own head lately, there's a heck of a lot accumulated in there — realizations like heavy fruit weighing down the branches of his soul. He thought visiting Dr. O'Malley would help. And it did, to some extent. But it's not enough.

It hasn't been enough for precisely eleven days.

About a year ago, Ben, along with some of the other Dominants at Diadem — the private BDSM club where they work — had managed to locate the man who had repeatedly and routinely raped fellow Dominant, Gabriel Hunter, since he was a boy. At Diadem, Gabriel worked with submissives like and including Kyle. And Kyle pegged him as the coldest one of all. But the coldness stemmed from hidden personal turmoil. Ben, along with Trace and Micah, sought to enact revenge for Gabriel's suffering. They found Harry, the pedophile who preyed upon Gabriel, all the way down in Texas. And then? Then they carved him up, cutting the names of the boys he'd scarred into Harry's arms; cutting a stark warning into his face too, thereby scarring him in turn.

Kyle thinks their vengeance to be sort of beautiful. It's also intensely awful.

Ben did that. Kyle's Ben. During, and after, Kyle was sworn to secrecy. Luckily, Kyle can do secrecy. He didn't breathe a word to his best friend, Darrek, Gabriel's partner and submissive, nor to Gabriel himself. Kyle gave them that gift, then he shut off. He was done, at least on some level. Ben went to a place with Harry that

Kyle couldn't follow, and ever since, Ben has felt very far away. Kyle wants to reach him, but he doesn't know how.

For most of a year, Kyle was lost. Knowing things that Darrek and Gabriel didn't—terrible, horrible, wonderful things—and enduring the distance with Ben, it pushed Kyle farther and farther away from all of them. It might have continued on like that. Friendships and relationships might have died quietly.

One conversation with Ben was all it took to derail Kyle entirely. He was coasting along, miserable but functioning, until Ben suggested that Kyle participate as a submissive in a new video for Diadem.

Sitting in his car, outside of his shrink's office, Kyle's mind starts to go there, putting him back in what was supposedly the safety of his own house, having his lover, his partner, his Dom put him in the scariest position Kyle could imagine. A complex emotional response, strong and awful, rises like bile, so he slams his head back, hard, against the headrest.

Stars burst across his vision. His train of thought slips sideways; instead of in his own car, Kyle imagines he's in a crappy old Camaro beside the high school's football field with the lights so bright they hurt his eyes. Deliriously, as his head spins, it occurs to him what he should have said to Dr. O'Malley during his appointment.

I should have spelled it out for Darrek and just confessed that the reason I was ranting like an idiot about women was because I was too busy getting regularly sucked off by the tight end of the varsity football team in that rank old Camaro. The tight end's name was Walter, of all things. A freckle-nosed, barrel-chested kid with braces and an impressive lack of a gag reflex. It's a miracle he didn't do some major damage with that mouth full of metal wires, but then again, I've always gotten off on the thrill of imminent personal injury.

It's getting bad again, he realizes. When it used to get bad, Kyle would turn to the Exacto knife in his art kit. The only way to feel better was to bleed the pain out. Then, when he moved away and started a new life, Kyle needed more than knives. He began submitting regularly to Ben at Diadem, sometimes with Gabriel or Trace helping to take Kyle apart. That wasn't quite enough, either, so he'd started using. He'd take anything he could get his hands on—didn't matter what. He usually didn't even ask what was in the drugs he would ingest, snort or inject. Ben started to call him on it, though. He'd punish Kyle for using and forbid him from continuing. Kyle would try to sneak a hit now and then, but Ben always seemed to know or figure it out. Eventually, Ben helped Kyle free himself from that particular addiction.

Head throbbing dully, Kyle tries to remember if he has any blades in the trunk or under the seats.

Darrek and Gabriel come home this week, Kyle's mind whispers to him. Ben's a persistent bastard. He'll probably invite Darrek over and talk him into the idea of fucking Kyle on camera, maybe hurting him a little to add some spice. Or maybe after Kyle takes Darrek's cock, Kyle will get to hurt *him.* Darrek loves watching Gabriel's old Diadem videos. There's a good chance he'd be game. Then it would be Ben *and* Darrek versus Kyle.

Uttering a low, nauseous groan that disturbs him even more as he hears it come out of his mouth, uncensored, Kyle digs his hand down in between the seat and the door, looking for something, anything sharp, and tries to remember the phone number for the guy he'd buy crack from down in the nasty end of town.

Eleven days. Only a couple left.

Darrek's gonna know. He'll talk to Ben, hear him out, take one look at the guilt-riddled terror in my eyes, and then he's gonna know. He'll remember.

After he smacks his head against the headrest a few more times, a merciless headache develops and he feels much better for it. He can do this. He's been doing this for years.

A few minutes later, Kyle parks in the driveway. Ben's truck is there. With a pang of shame, his head throbbing, Kyle realizes he was hoping Ben wouldn't be home. Itching, craving, restless, tired as he's ever been in his life, he sinks back into the seat and hesitates before getting out. All he wants is to get a beer from the fridge and sit with it on the front porch; no one to bother him, no one to answer to or disappoint, or be disappointed by.

He's not in the mood for games, but it seems like lately his whole life is one big headgame.

Kyle gets out of the car and goes inside. Ben is watching TV. His naturally curly, light brown hair, kept in a short cut, is perfectly visible from the hall. He's reclined in his favorite over-stuffed chair, his feet propped on a leather ottoman. A Minor League baseball game is playing. Not for the first time, as Kyle hangs up his keys on the little hooks on the wall by the door, trying not to make a sound, he wonders what it would be like to live with a guy who is lazy, who gets so wrapped up in sports and his beer and relaxing that he doesn't care when his significant other gets home. Maybe a grunt or a half-hearted wave of greeting would be all the interaction between them. But that's not Ben. Ben is always on. He's constantly hyper-aware, constantly ready. It can be exhausting to be his significant other.

Kyle toes off his shoes and creeps across the wooden floorboards. When he gets to the bottom of the staircase leading to the bedrooms and bathroom, his destination after a long, grimy day on a construction site, he doesn't even need to be called; he can feel Ben's eyes on him.

The rules kick in. Kyle knows how he's expected to act, and he's given a second, maybe two, to decide whether to play along or face the consequences. There are always consequences with Ben.

Kyle turns toward the living room. A wide entryway stands between them. A glance tells Kyle everything he needs to know while a knot tightens his gut.

Bowing his head, he says in a voice he knows comes across as tired and verging on irritable, "I need to take a shower."

It feels like he's wearing the collar again though his neck is bare. He used to wear it all the time, except for when sleeping. One of the more significant changes in his life of late is that he's been resisting the collar, and Ben's been allowing it, without totally understanding why. Inhaling, filling his throat with oxygen, Kyle waits for the thick leather to bite and constrict, and it doesn't. It should be a comfort. Somehow it's not.

"Come down when you're done," Ben replies.

"Yessir," Kyle murmurs automatically.

The hint of a threat is there, simmering under the order. Hating himself for it, as his id overrides his ego, Kyle starts to get hard. He climbs the steps and tries to fight back the blush that rises along the back and sides of his neck as his Master watches him go.

Once he has washed and is slightly revived, Kyle goes into the master bedroom that he shares with Ben to look for something clean to wear downstairs. He tries to focus on the moment, but memories of the past stirred up in Dr. O'Malley's office cloud everything. Darrek, his first love, his current best friend, is first and foremost in his musings. Lately, over the course of the past few months, Kyle has been making a concerted effort to think of Darrek in only a friendly manner. Things got twisted up after the foursome that happened once, spontaneously, between Ben, Kyle, Darrek and Gabriel. It made the un-crossable lines harder to make out, so Kyle redrew them, for no one's benefit but his own. Darrek, he's positioned safely in the platonic category. Trouble is, Ben doesn't know that. Sometimes, just to rile Kyle, he'll tease the sexual tension between Kyle and Darrek. And Kyle doesn't always mind. Today, though—today he would mind.

Kyle stops inside the bedroom, beside the bed. His gaze is locked to the object sitting dark, heavy and ominous in the center of the crisp white sheets.

"Balls," he groans under his breath.

The black leather ring of his collar is perfectly showcased in the field of bleached cotton. Of everything in Kyle's possession, and out of every instrument of sexual pleasure and torment in the house, and there are countless, this is the one out of them all that he dreads the most. And that Ben has taken it from the shelf in the closet and placed it there for Kyle to see means that Ben wants him to wear it. If Kyle wears it, all of his rules and preferences are dissolved. Only Ben's rules stay in effect. Ben is Master.

For a small, yet intense moment, Kyle is truly scared.

I could say no, he thinks. And he's tempted to. But to do such a thing when Ben has made it so clear that he wants this would be close to a declaration of war. It's not Kyle's place to question Ben. That's their arrangement. Of course, Kyle's consent is a key element in their play, but after a year and a half together, tension has grown in their relationship. Ben knows that Kyle is unhappy. He hasn't said as much, but it's there, and Ben can sense it. If, on top of that,

Kyle starts to deny Ben the indulgence of being Master and slave, Dominant and submissive, there would be no going back. There would be *A Problem*.

Aware that he's probably overanalyzing things, Kyle grips his head, rubbing the heels of his hands into his eye sockets, taking a deep breath to calm down.

You could still say no, his conscience whispers to him.

But Kyle knows what happens when he says no. Bad things happen, and to other people. Say no and he's the one causing someone else's torment.

With the fading light of day washing in from the window across the room, Kyle Roth gathers his resolve and says, "No," to the empty room as he reaches out and plucks the collar from the bed. He wraps it around his throat and buckles it tightly. The finishing touch is the small padlock that he snaps shut. The tiny click it makes is the punctuation to his self-made damnation.

Chapter 3
Breaking Kyle

"C'mere, kitty, curl up in my lap."

Kyle knows what that means. He unfastens the jeans he'd just put on not three minutes ago upstairs and steps out of them.

"The underwear too."

Ben, stroking his neatly trimmed beard, is again stretched out in the stuffed chair in their living room, his feet propped on the ottoman. The chair is positioned perpendicular to the television, and Ben only sits in it if his attention isn't really on the TV at all, though the television might be on and playing as background noise, like it is now. Ben is a few inches taller than Kyle, and of a slightly more thickly-muscled build, but it's not the size difference that has always given Ben the power to intimidate Kyle ever since they became involved. His striking, royal blue eyes flash darkly, hard as iron, just like his resolve and his well-learned capability to be absolutely merciless when needed. One look and a queasy tickle slithers in Kyle's gut.

Even as he straddles Ben's legs and sits carefully on his upper thighs before lying back, Kyle tries to anticipate what Ben wants. Ben guides him with his skillful hands, arranging Kyle's lean, naked body, his naturally light but suntanned skin dusted with blond hair. Kyle's head is near Ben's feet, his torso fitted in the valley made between Ben's legs. Kyle's feet are planted on either side of Ben's hips, by the back of the padded chair. He would rather have his arms at his sides, and feel like he has more control over his position, but that isn't the point, is it? The queasy tickle gets stronger as he curls his arms loosely above his head, and gets a murmur of praise from his

Master.

It's his job to lie there and bear his Dominant's ministrations silently, unmoving, lest restraints become necessary. Because Kyle has shown himself to be such an obedient, well-taught slave, literal bonds are not always needed. Not anymore. The mental play that comes into effect when they're absent has proven itself to be much more fun for Ben, as he gets to watch Kyle fight not to squirm.

They've done this before, though not recently. Kyle knows from prior experience that he may watch the TV if he wants. He keeps his eyes shut.

Guiding Kyle's knees apart until they're fallen open wide, Ben exposes him. A ripple of tension laces up and out through Kyle's body as he braces for the unknown. With a wicked smile, unseen by his captive, curling the corners of Ben's lips, he begins to touch. He caresses along Kyle's inner thighs, up the contracted muscles of his abs, and down over the cradle of his hips. Miniscule frown lines form in Kyle's brow. But as soon as they appear, Kyle tries to soothe them away. It's subtle enough to be unclear if they're part of the show Kyle is making of his resistance or if they're genuine, so they fascinate Ben. Watching those small creases carefully, he begins to play with Kyle's genitals. Starting with feather-light contact, brushing touches of his fingertips and palms, Ben takes his time. Kyle responds, thickening and nudging against Ben's hands.

After ten minutes of this, a shiver shakes him. He's grown fully erect but Ben is not giving him any form of friction toward release. Each touch remains teasing and torturously gentle. After twenty minutes, the tension has not left Kyle's body at all and the frown lines have only deepened.

Ben breaks the silence between them only when Kyle has been completely hard for long enough to cause him to be verging on desperate for relief, his shaft flushed dark, his skin glistening from head to toe with a light gleam of sweat. The jitteriness sparking in Kyle makes him visibly restless though he does not disobey or move at all. He stays still, but the fight grows to control the urge to thrust against the hand playing with his cock.

Casually, like they're sitting down to dinner and not almost a half-hour into a session, Ben asks, "How was therapy?" He punctuates the question by inserting, in one smooth stroke, his dry index finger into Kyle's anus.

Kyle hadn't seen it coming. Ben hadn't been touching him anywhere near there since Kyle had laid down. If Ben thought Kyle was tense before, he's exponentially more so once the finger enters him, probing in the most intimate of physical ways as the posed question probes Kyle's most vulnerable mental weakness. His body locks up around the digit, clamping down at the unwanted intrusion. The cords of his neck pop out. His feet flex against the chair cushion at Ben's hips. Kyle's stomach is rock-hard and his knees even twitch like he begins to close them but realizes the danger in doing so and catches himself just in time.

A scowl darkens Ben's expression, disapproving, whereas Kyle's frown shifts in tone, wariness replaced by something harder to define. Withdrawing his finger slowly, then twisting to push back in through the ring of muscle, squeezed so tightly shut that it's clear Kyle is trying to keep him out, Ben repeats this to set a rhythm.

Kyle's knees twitch again. His hands, previously limp, close into fists. It's not just Ben. It's never just about Ben anymore. It's about history, memories, nightmares, secrets. *I hate this position. I hate this position. I really, really hate it,* he repeats to himself over and over again, just to have something to hold on to. Kyle forces himself to look at Ben, needing to see that it's him and not someone else, grounding himself in the present. He hates that Ben has such a good view of him and his responses, can feel his body's reactions through his legs bracing Kyle's back, but most of all, Kyle simply hates being spread-eagle in front of Ben, especially when Ben is so clearly in the mood to exploit Kyle's most profound insecurities.

Stroking over warm, soft inner walls, Ben tells him with just a note of a threat, "Open your legs. As wide as you can. Now."

Kyle obeys but Ben can feel him breathing shallowly, in sharp, rapid inhales and exhales through his nose, his lips sealed tight.

Fully exposed to view and further probing, the long, thick finger pumping in his asshole, Kyle doesn't seem to be enjoying it, if one were judging by expression and body language alone.

Ben crooks his finger, triggering his slave's prostate gland. Deliberately, he rubs over the bundle of nerves. Kyle's breathing chokes off completely with a thick grunt. Flinching bodily, jolted, he scoots an inch or two away.

"Do I need to tie you down?"

Possibilities flash through Kyle's mind. After debating, he takes a deep breath, but a shaky one. He shakes his head with effort, trying to relax. Ben continues to finger him, but Kyle ceases to chase away from it.

"Answer the question I asked you, slave. How was therapy?"

Slave. Not 'kitty.' It's a bad sign, in Kyle's opinion, of the way this is going.

Ben triggers Kyle's prostate again, making him whimper. Fluid weeps, clear and viscous, from the slit in his cockhead as his member jumps—the one part of him not losing interest in all of this. His attention momentarily drawn there, Ben wraps the erection in a loose fist, squeezing in stationary pulses as he resumes fingering his submissive.

Kyle shakes his head once, side to side, tightly, in protest of the added stimulation and Ben can see the swallowed curses that Kyle wants to spit out at him. After a stifled moan, Kyle stutters, "F-fine, Sir. It w-was fine."

"Was it? You seem just a smidge *tense.* I mean, call me crazy...."

There it is, Kyle laments. Ben is nudging at the truth as he does the same to the nerves in Kyle's body, wracking him with the rising flames of his nerve endings' reactions. It's too much to process, the deliberate working of Ben's hands on him and in him as his questions dig and dig at Kyle's frazzled mind. He tries to keep his defenses up, but that in and of itself is dangerous. If Ben thinks he's hiding something, that's just more incentive to keep at it until Kyle breaks.

Knowing he has to say something, Kyle does, and with as much care as he can muster. "W-we talked about Darrek," he confesses around a bitten-back whine.

Ben's mouth quirks with interest, but Kyle doesn't see. "And that's why you've gotten all shy on me, huh?"

Reaching down beside the chair's cushion, where he'd wedged a tube of lubricant earlier, Ben finds it and draws it out. He flips open the cap and removes the finger stuck in Kyle's ass. He squirts

19

plenty of lube over all of the fingers of his right hand. With that done, he inserts the first two into Kyle after rubbing some of the slick around the invitingly pink opening. He slides them in slowly, and completely. Then he stops, holding them there, letting Kyle feel them filling up his ass, letting it screw with his head. On the withdraw he scissors them apart in a V shape, effectively prying Kyle open. He stays like that, watching Kyle fight not to react, or squirm or show how very much this bothers him, because Ben knows better than anyone how Kyle hates being opened up and observed. Of all the kinky techniques he's used on his boyfriend and submissive over the years they've known each other, this is the one that never fails, and the one Ben goes to only when he has no choice.

Delivering exactly the reaction Ben hoped for, Kyle's battle for self-control shows itself in an outward-radiating tremor, and a broken gasp of, "Don't."

There's a beat then, quiet and deadly, Ben says, "What did you just say?"

Fear claws at Kyle's gut. "P-please, Master. Fuck!"

Ben squeezes painfully around Kyle's dick, scissors his fingers wider apart, and more than is comfortable.

"Maybe you need the speculum."

"No!" There's real panic behind the exclamation, not defiance but anguish. It always comes down to this, to Kyle being on display, to Kyle getting the unsavory job of pacifying others with his body.

He's gonna make me. He's gonna see everything.

Ben sighs with disappointment. "You brought this on yourself. Remember that."

"No! Please, Master, I'll be good. I'm sorry!"

"Flip over."

"Sir, I'm sorry!"

"Flip over! Grab ass and pull. No arguing or I may change my mind about the speculum."

Some of the rising flush brought of Kyle's fight drains from him, leaving him paler, colder.

"Yessir."

He's going to be punished. At least he knows what to expect now. It helps him cope.

A curtain descends from that point forward, with Kyle on one side and Ben on the other, driving the problem at hand further from Ben's grasp. Regretting this, Ben grabs at the discarded puddle of Kyle's jeans on the floor beside the chair as Kyle gets up to change position. He draws the brown leather belt from the loops, whisking it free. Kyle watches sharply as this happens, getting on his hands and knees. Ben sits up straighter, doubling the belt over in his right hand, getting a good grip on it. Breathing deeply, Kyle readies himself to be struck.

It's funny, Ben thinks, as the tension dissolves and dissipates from Kyle's form. All of the guardedness, all of his fight is gone at the prospect of pain. Rubbing over the firm curve of Kyle's backside with his left hand as his right chokes up on the belt and prepares to strike, Ben wonders, *What's going on with you, huh? What is this?*

"I'm sorry, Sir," Kyle says without inflection. Bracing his shoulders on the ottoman, Kyle's face is turned to the side and he sticks out his ass. Widening his knees slightly, which are perched on the chair, straddling Ben, Kyle makes sure he's not going anywhere then does as commanded, pulling himself open. It should be hot. Ben should be getting off on it, but it looks like Kyle is on the verge of tears. It looks like this is the last place he wants to be, and Ben has no idea why.

Suddenly, Ben doesn't want to punish Kyle. All he wants is to get free of his pants and fit himself in the snug, sanity-destroying perfection of Kyle's gorgeous body. He wants to make love to him over and over again, tenderly asking what's bothering him, wresting free the truth no matter the cost to his own pride, for fear of losing the one he loves with all his heart.

"Please punish me," Kyle says through gritted teeth when Ben does nothing. He sounds impatient, but maybe that's just because he hates being exposed like he is, and wants pain as a distraction.

Snapping his wrist, Ben aims at the underside of Kyle's left cheek where his buttock meets his thigh, just under where his hand pulls at his flesh. The bite of leather into skin is loud, but not loud enough to mask the sharp gasp Kyle makes. His hole twitches closed. Ben strikes the other cheek next, then begins alternating back and forth, left and right. It hurts him much more than it does Kyle.

After ten blows, Ben pauses, rubbing over the welts. Kyle is breathing roughly.

"I'm sorry, Sir," Kyle says dutifully again. "Please give me more. Thank you."

Ben bites down on his tongue almost hard enough to draw blood and begins delivering blows to Kyle's hands where they grip at his cheeks. Each lash draws a small, stifled cry that digs and cuts into Ben, so that he effectively punishes himself as he punishes Kyle. After six of those, Kyle is shuddering and flinching reflexively away from him, so he changes target, swatting with the tip of the folded belt, a little more gently, squarely at Kyle's opening.

Moaning deeply, his lower legs flexed and feet curling up, Kyle fights to bear it and not try to escape. Ben hits him there five times then runs the belt up and down through the crease of Kyle's ass, letting him feel the friction, the threat. His skin is pink in splotches, his breathing uneven, but he's clearly happier than before, though probably not happy with Ben's choice of target. But when Ben slaps his hole with the belt five more times, he can imagine Kyle sending up a prayer of thanks that he's being whipped and not simply observed or opened up for inspection.

That's why Ben reaches out for him with his left hand, tugging briefly at Kyle's huge hard-on, then questing back, sticking out his thumb and pressing it through the pink, throbbing ring of muscle and into Kyle. He palms Kyle with the rest of the hand, keeping the thumb seated and pulling upward with it.

Just like that, the tension returns. Kyle closes down. Ben gets angry. While Kyle turns his face into the fabric of the ottoman and shouts a muffled, growled curse, Ben whips him again and again and again with the belt on the back of his right thigh. He hits the same spot repeatedly until Kyle screams and tries to twist away.

The belt falls to the floor. Ben stands up, pulling his hand free of Kyle. Quickly, he strides from the room, going to the stairs and taking them two at a time.

"No. No," Kyle moans. "Ben, please! BEN!"

When Ben returns—with supplies—Kyle's face is turned away from him. Moving a directional floor lamp closer, Ben aims the light at Kyle and turns it on. A ragged, tear-choked moan emits from Kyle, full of dread. Tremors wrack his body. Ben wraps his slave's wrists in leather cuffs and locks them together behind his back. With a length of cord, he ties them to one of the metal loops in the back of the collar, making sure there's no slack. Next is the thigh spreader. Kyle whimpers behind pursed lips as it's secured to him.

The TV gets turned off, so that Kyle knows all of Ben's attention is on him. Then, Ben returns to the chair, sitting perched on the back of it, facing Kyle and looming over him. By choosing to sit on the padded back of the heavy chair with his feet planted on the cushion, Ben gains added height and a better view. It makes Ben seem bigger than he is, and makes Kyle feel smaller, more helpless. Ben slicks lubricant over the speculum.

'Dirty boy... you want it, don't you? God knows you do.'

When Ben touches the cool tip to Kyle's hole, letting him feel the metal's kiss, a violent shudder makes Kyle jolt on the chair. He pulls on his bound wrists so hard he gurgles and chokes as the collar squeezes his windpipe.

"Use the safeword," Ben dares. "Go ahead."

Grabbing Kyle's wrists with his left hand to keep him from getting away, Ben slowly inserts the speculum. Kyle bucks forward, hard. Ben yanks him right back and begins to open the speculum, cranking it so that it gradually spreads Kyle wide. Kyle is strangling himself on the collar, so as soon as the speculum is opened to Ben's liking, he pushes on Kyle's wrists but holds him in place by the hip.

The slack on the cord connecting the collar to Kyle's cuffs is increased. Taking a hoarse, huge gulp of air, Kyle swallows down the oxygen then sobs it back out.

"Do that again and you'll be sorry," Ben warns. Kyle suspects that Ben is afraid, with good reason, that Kyle would prefer choking himself to the point of unconsciousness over enduring his punishment. "Don't fucking choke yourself."

Still gulping air, Kyle fights back another sob and turns it into a growl. He can feel Ben looking at him, at his stretched out opening, the sight of Kyle trying to clench up, but unable to with the metal leaving him gaping, his ass positioned right in front of Ben for close inspection. Ben reaches out and touches him there, fingering at his rim around where the metal enters.

Kyle holds his breath, still fighting an internal battle, his masochistic side trying to get off on it all, his guilt reminding him how worthless he is, that he deserves this, the rest of him just tired and wanting to get away. When his exhale breaks free, it comes out as an even keener sob of pain. Before Ben can react, Kyle yanks on his arms once more.

"God damn it, Kyle!" Ben shouts as Kyle chokes.

Picking up the knife at his side, Ben expertly slides the blade between Kyle's back and the cord. With a twist of his wrist he slices through it. Oxygen rushes back into Kyle's lungs as he gasps hoarsely.

"What the fuck is your problem!?"

"I hate you."

It hits Ben like a left hook, sending him reeling.

He stops touching Kyle. He drops the knife. Silence, perfect and absolute, broken only by the soft sound of Kyle crying, fills the house.

Though he could get up, Kyle doesn't. He doesn't use his safeword. He also doesn't apologize, though he does want to. It just won't come.

They stay there, frozen in place by the cruelty of Kyle's words, for a long, long time. Regretting what he said so profoundly, that he just wants to disappear and hide, it's perfect torture to be so acutely observed by the one he hurt. Kyle feels Ben's eyes on him, and it takes him apart more completely than anything else could.

After some horrible silence, the stalemate is broken at last. Flaccid and humiliated, Kyle waits for it to be done. Maybe, he thinks, when Ben lets him go, he'll be able to look at him and say what he feels, that he didn't mean it. It's someone else that Kyle hates, after all. Not Ben. Kyle holds on to that like a lifeline.

It's not pleasurable, in any sense of the word. It's only punishment. And it's effective.

But Ben isn't done. Kyle can see that he's hurt, and wants Kyle to feel hurt too. *Or maybe,* Kyle thinks, *that's just how it looks to me. Maybe I'm wrong about everything. Maybe I'm the one who doesn't understand what should be obvious.*

Ben takes in hand the prostate stimulator that he'd brought downstairs with the rest of the gear. First he wraps a hand around Kyle's completely softened member, and begins to stroke him hard.

" — Don't!"

Ben inserts the toy into Kyle. It makes Kyle jerk, coming up off the ottoman for the first time. Ben rocks the toy against his prostate, the plastic arm also pressing against his perineum, triggering the nerves from the outside as well. Fluid weeps from his slit as Ben milks him.

A thick grunt of surprise leaves Kyle and for a moment he almost wriggles to get free, but then resigns himself and endures it. "Please don't," he begs. "Please don't do this."

He's not saying it as Ben's submissive. He's saying it as his partner, and it almost works. Ben hesitates for a moment, but then perseveres. Manipulating Kyle's dick until it's erect and then jerking him off, Ben continues to milk his prostate, bombarding him with unwelcome sensation. Kyle buries his face in the ottoman and bellows into it. His orgasm is wrenched violently from him, and mostly against his will.

See that? God knows what you really want, and there's the proof.

He comes onto a towel Ben shoves unceremoniously under him to protect the furniture. After he's emptied, Ben throws the toy aside and stuffs three fingers into Kyle, the speculum still keeping him opened, and strokes his softening cock until Kyle's discomfort is clearly audible in his cries. Not once does he ask Ben to stop, though. He drowns in the hurt and invasion.

Eventually, when there isn't much left of him, Kyle feels the speculum come out. The bonds come off. The light goes dark.

"Get up."

"Ben, I didn't mean it — "

But one glance at Ben's face silences Kyle. The words die in his throat and he knows them to be useless.

Ready to kneel but reluctant to since Ben told him to get up,

Kyle bows his head, folds his hands behind his back and says meekly, "What would you like of me, Master?"

"Get cleaned up."

Swallowing around a lump in his throat, Kyle struggles to speak then manages, "We're not done, are we?"

"No, slave. We aren't."

And so, for a second time that night, he showers as Ben waits on him. Kyle makes quick work of it then goes out into the hall. He only takes a few steps then he finds Ben—standing in front of their bedroom with a pillow and blanket in his arms. He holds them out to Kyle.

"You aren't welcome in my bed. Sleep downstairs."

It feels like dying. Kyle's heart rips through his chest and, sounding pathetic in his own ears, he pleads uselessly, "Ben, I am so sorry...."

It's just part of the punishment, he tells himself, as Ben goes into the bedroom, closes the door and locks it from the inside.

It's just like when I tried to kill myself and Ben threatened to leave me, and it turned out to be part of my punishment then. That's what he tries to convince himself. But this time, he just can't do it. It doesn't feel true. It feels like the end.

Long, sleepless hours later, dawn shines bright and new. Ben is starving, and, realizing that Kyle never ate dinner the night before, emerges from the bedroom to declare the punishment finished, to forgive Kyle and fix everything.

But when he unlocks and opens the door, he finds Kyle curled up on the floor, pillow under his head, wrapped in the blanket. He hadn't slept on the couch as Ben intended. He never even went downstairs. At first Ben just stares at him in disbelief, regretting the decision to give in to his burst of temper and kick Kyle out of their bedroom. But after he stares for a minute, he sees something that scares him much more than the word "hate," flung by his boyfriend hours ago.

Along with the pillow and blanket, Ben had also provided sleep pants to Kyle. But now, Kyle is wearing something else, too. Kyle had gone downstairs after all — to get his watch. It's one with a wide leather band, which Kyle only wears when he's going out, but not to work, for fear of it getting damaged. And he never wears it to bed.

Crouching down, careful not to wake Kyle just yet, Ben peers at the band.

The bottom drops out of his stomach.

A small trickle of blood had run out from under the band and down around Kyle's wrist. It has since dried. And Ben can just make out the edges of a bandage, hidden by the watch, and just barely visible upon closer scrutiny.

Stepping over Kyle, Ben bolts for the bathroom. He scans it, but what he's looking for isn't there. He creeps downstairs, and checks the living room next.

Then, he finds it. He picks up the knife, and tells no one, "This is my fault," as he turns the blade in his hands. He had left it on the arm of the chair. Somehow the blade, and only the blade, had moved in the night to the end table. The silver gleams brightly as if recently washed and polished dry. All of the other paraphernalia litters the room, right where they left it.

Ben stares at the ceiling like he can see through it to the man curled up, fast asleep. And he has no idea what to do.

He's cutting again. And if I call him on it, maybe he'll start using again too, instead of just cutting. And if I call him on that, maybe he'll try to kill himself again. Maybe this time I won't be able to get there in time to stop it.

A contrary voice speaks up in Ben's head, arguing from another perspective. *Maybe he wanted you to figure this out. It's all pretty obvious isn't it? Maybe he just wants attention. He wants you to feel guilty for kicking him out last night.*

But, staring up at the ceiling, feeling the weight of the knife in his hand, imagining Kyle standing there, not too long ago, and using it to slice open his wrist, he can't be sure. The only thing that Ben is sure of is that this is getting away from them. It's out of control and he doesn't have the slightest clue how to fix it.

Chapter 4
Obedience's Reward

It's a gorgeous Saturday at an exclusive island resort in the Florida Keys, one specifically designed for Dominants and submissives. Darrek and Gabriel have been enjoying an extended stay as part of the celebration of their second anniversary together. Gabriel's gift to Darrek is the three-month-long trip and plenty of time to enjoy each other without distraction. Darrek's gift to Gabriel is his own physical fitness.

The end of the trip draws near and Darrek's body has undergone an impressive transformation. Gabriel gets total control over Darrek's diet and exercise regime for six out of seven days a week. Darrek has accepted the challenge enthusiastically and has worked so hard at defining muscle, slimming down and improving his cardiovascular health that Gabriel has actually had to order Darrek to give himself a break once in a while. But now, Darrek is cut. His old clothes don't fit him anymore, so Gabriel bought him a brand new wardrobe. The pants were too big around the waist, the shirts too small. His shoulders, back and chest nearly rip the fabric as it's stretched to bursting over bulging new muscles. There are inches lost on his waist and belly, though Darrek didn't even have much to lose in the first place. His glutes and thighs are much more toned and firm as well. Darrek had never really been out of shape, but doing construction gave him physical fitness of a different sort than hardcore, regular exercise and lifting weights in order to define his body in a sharper, more chiseled way.

Every day, all day—except for Saturdays—Darrek is Gabriel's submissive. Six days out of the week, night and day, unceasing,

Gabriel is Darrek's Master in every sense of the word. He controls everything Darrek does, says, eats, or wears. This freedom from choice, having every aspect of his existence tended to by the love of his life, brings Darrek a sort of peace that he didn't even know possible. Trusting Gabriel, his lover and partner, so very much, and giving himself over to Gabriel utterly makes Darrek happy. It makes Gabriel happy, too. It feels right. It gives them balance.

But there's still a lingering part of both of them, a small part but just as valid as the rest, that needs that balance flipped. Sometimes Gabriel needs to not be in control. In these times, he needs to not be in control at all, so the rules go away — every one of them.

Darrek takes the control back. They don't label it as anything, specifically. Gabriel doesn't call Darrek Master, but he does submit. He makes himself weak and vulnerable. Anything and everything that Darrek has wanted to say, have, or do to Gabriel for the other six days of the week can be had. It's his for the taking.

If he wants to lie in bed and watch professional wrestling on the ridiculously huge flat screen TV and eat ice cream all day, he can do that. But he doesn't. For the most part, Darrek continues to obey Gabriel's dietary restrictions even on Saturday. And, when it comes down to it, Darrek usually wants to indulge in Gabriel more than anything else. Having a free pass to do to Gabriel *anything* he wants is too good to ignore.

The constant surrender, constant trust, has worked wonders on their relationship. One of the reasons they decided to take this trip and agree to such a long stretch of time as purely Master and slave is that their relationship more and more has veered away from the lifestyle. The demands of work and home have taken over. They fell into a routine, got comfortable. Sex became vanilla. It was a richly decadent flavor of vanilla, but vanilla nonetheless.

So they took a leave of absence from responsibility. Gabriel closed up shop. Darrek did too. And then they left, to be together and focus only on each other and themselves.

This Saturday is the last one of their trip. There are only a few days left before they have to return home. This one they spend quietly, alone, with Darrek showering Gabriel with attention.

On their bed, Gabriel lies on his stomach with a couple of pillows wedged under his hips to tilt them at the right angle, his bathing suit tossed away onto the floor. Folding his arms under his head, he tries to relax into it as Darrek enters him. Darrek's movements start out and remain gentle and unhurried. He wants to draw it out and stave off orgasm. Lying down on Gabriel's bare back, Darrek caresses his lover's suntanned skin from shoulder to thigh, rocking in and out of the snug channel like a perfectly fitting glove wrapping his cock. Just breathing, the room quiet, a breeze floating in through the opened windows, the soft rush of the ocean's waves crashing on the beach like music, it's peaceful—heavenly. For Darrek, at least.

Darrek doesn't know what causes the change. One moment Gabriel is fine—he's relaxed, his grey-blue eyes half-lidded, a slight sheen of sweat making his gorgeous body glisten in the moonlight. He's breathing heavier than normal as Darrek's thrusts grow in strength and force, tensing up on each push so that he's not knocked farther up on the bed.

Then, just like that, everything changes.

Gabriel flinches. The fight switch in his head gets flipped; Darrek has seen it happen too many times now to mistake it. As soon as he hears the choked sob and feels Gabriel's body knot up under him, ready to squirm and get away however he can, Darrek compensates.

"Hey! Shh. Gabe, open your eyes. *Gabriel*," Darrek fills his voice with as much stern authority as he can. He stops moving, but doesn't pull out or roll off of Gabriel. Instead he holds him down, keeping him in place and waiting for the moment to pass. "You're fine. Hey!"

Much of the color is gone from his face as Gabriel makes himself open his eyes, which had squeezed shut. He stares blankly at the room, breathing with heaving, violent rips and tears. Covered in a cold sweat, the instinct to fight and escape lingers. Whenever he gives into it, Darrek holds him to the bed, pushing back on the imaginary demons. He's not trying to be cruel, but only to force Gabriel to confront reality.

Everything warm turns cold. Everything soft is hard. Next the self-recrimination will come, so Darrek moves before it can arrive. He withdraws and rolls them. Positioning Gabriel on top so that he straddles Darrek's hips, newfound confidence blooms behind Gabriel's tortured stare.

"Better?" Darrek asks, groaning as Gabriel steadies Darrek's cock and lowers himself onto it.

"Yeah, much," Gabriel nods.

"If you want to stop...."

"Shut up, okay?"

Darrek moans, silenced effectively as Gabriel begins to move, rolling his hips in tight circles, working himself up and down on Darrek. Planting his feet, holding on to Gabriel by his hipbones and guiding his speed, Darrek's senses are overtaken with pleasure. His orgasm creeps up on him and he fights it back. With his right hand, determined to keep Gabriel interested, Darrek strokes him idly, pumping his shaft a few times before letting it go, leaving him to bob and strain, unsatisfied. But whenever he begins to soften or looks to be retreating into his head, Darrek does it again, pulling Gabriel into the present by his dick.

For a while it's just sex again, and Gabriel's panic is temporarily forgotten. Darrek's face screws up against the building need to release, which only drives Gabriel to move faster. Bouncing on Darrek's dick, he gasps and moans softly, rocking into Darrek's fist in pointed thrusts whenever it takes hold.

When Darrek gets a drip of Gabriel's pre-come on the junction of his thumb and index finger and sucks it clean, Gabriel growls and dips his head to get a taste, licking the salty tang of himself from Darrek's tongue. Acting immediately, Darrek braces Gabriel with a hand to the middle of his back, and another gripping his thigh. Using where his feet are planted against the bed as leverage, Darrek fucks up into Gabriel, taking him hard and deep, almost driving the air from his lungs in his frenzy to use and plunder. Gabriel whimpers and buries his face in the side of Darrek's neck, breathing heavily, holding on to him with clawed hands. Hips slapping loudly against the firm curve of Gabriel's buttocks, Darrek comes with a long, drawn out groan and peppers Gabriel's skin with kisses, weaving his fingers through Gabriel's short, dark hair.

Once the room stops spinning, he croaks, "Sit up." He guides Gabriel upright, sitting him back up on his dick, nestled fully inside his body.

"Hands off," Darrek instructs, nodding to Gabriel's arms, which he immediately puts behind his back, out of the way.

Hard and drunk on a dark breed of lust that slithers and moves behind his eyes, there's fight there, and Darrek knows Gabriel is showing him that for a reason.

"Stay still," Darrek warns. Lightly, with only the tips of his fingers and the barest edge of the heel of his palm, he plays with Gabriel's hard-on, fondling it, tracing its outline, grazing it. It clearly frustrates Gabriel, who wants more, much more, and the battle to endure it is plain within him. But whenever he breaks and tries to rut forward against Darrek's hands, Darrek releases him entirely, waiting for Gabriel to stop moving before resuming the torture.

Head fallen back on his shoulders, then rolling forward, arm muscles bunching, thighs tensing, Gabriel clenches around the cock stuck up his ass and breathes through the frantic need to get off.

Darrek senses it coming but Gabriel does not, at all, when his orgasm hits him. With a shudder and a startled, small cry, a thick jet of come erupts from his cock, splattering hot over both of them. Making a tight fist around Gabriel's dick, Darrek tugs him through the aftershocks as he continues to shudder with each pulse, wringing out everything in him with each pull of Darrek's hand.

Aware of Gabriel's unusual silence, Darrek mutters a soft, "C'mere," and coaxes Gabriel to lie down on his chest. Gabriel's arms wind around him, anchoring to the contact. Collapsed and boneless, he's easily malleable in Darrek's arms. Watching him in the mirror positioned over the bed, Darrek pulls Gabriel's knees higher up along where they straddle Darrek's larger body. With that done, and a small tilt of his hips, he slips, wet, out of Gabriel. Another tug at Gabriel's knees, thereby pulling his ass open more, and Darrek murmurs Gabriel's name, beckoning to him.

Gabriel turns his face to Darrek, his eyes tired and haunted, but he focuses. Eyes locked, Darrek sees exactly what it does to Gabriel's expression when he presses two fingers through his throbbing opening, rubbing through the come dripping down inside. Vulnerability, heart-stoppingly beautiful and awe-inspiring, shines from Gabriel in the tilt of his eyebrows, the curve of his lips. He breathes out a soft sound then closes his eyes for good, letting Darrek draw him in for a kiss that turns deep and dirty fast. Gabriel pours some of his lingering fight into the contact, giving Darrek what he can before breaking away and hiding his face as he arches his back and reacts to the invasive touch of Darrek's burrowing, questing fingers.

"Love you," Darrek whispers, withdrawing and rubbing some of the fluid over Gabriel's rim, soothing any ache that might linger there, afraid for his lover's silence.

Long minutes later, Gabriel stiffens, ready to get up.

"Guess we should take a shower," Darrek suggests with reluctant sigh.

"Gimme a couple minutes, okay," Gabriel counters, sliding off and onto the floor. With shaky legs, he steadies himself before letting go of the bed. He doesn't look for Darrek's reaction or check to see if he is concerned at all as he retreats to the bathroom.

The door shuts. The light does not go on.

Gabriel turns on the water in the dark, hiding in the noise it makes and tries to catch his breath. Angry, hot, bitter tears sting his eyes and he wants to hit something. He wants to tear the pain out and purge himself of the evil of his past, but he can't. It's a part of him as much as anything else. He knows that.

A while later, he emerges from the pitch-dark bathroom and goes to stand at the fridge in the kitchen, lit by the fluorescent light inside and holding a bottle of water. Staring off into space, unreacting, blank, Gabriel is frozen there. Darrek's feet pad softly on the tile floor as he crosses the space, coming up behind Gabriel.

He touches Gabriel's shoulder, reading the tension in his form, the darkness of his mood, and easily catches the elbow that Gabriel instinctively throws back into Darrek's gut, having not heard him approach.

That snaps Gabriel, finally, out of his daze. Face crumpling in misery, Gabriel lets Darrek turn him, and hug him against his chest. A hitching whine of pain escapes him and he curls into the warmth and comfort Darrek gives so freely.

Darrek envelops Gabriel in the hug. He kisses the top of Gabriel's head with nothing but patience and love.

"It wasn't you; it was just triggered from nothing. Nothing!" Gabriel rages incredulously.

"Gabe," Darrek assures him. "It's okay."

"No, it's not. It's ancient history. I just want to forget it!"

"I know."

Now forgive my sin once more and pray to the Lord your God to take this deadly plague away from me. Exodus 10:17, Darrek thinks, automatically. With a grimace, he wonders where that came from and is just glad he didn't say it aloud.

Gabriel is a strong, commanding presence in Darrek's life. He has been for years now, but in that moment, he feels small and fragile as memories of rape at the hands of his stepfather flood his senses, battering him. Darrek feels the transfer of power. Gabriel relies on him, needs him. Darrek has to take some of the responsibility of control, whether he likes it or not. "I think I'm ready to go home," Gabriel admits quietly.

Darrek hugs him tighter. "Okay. Let's go home."

Chapter 5

New Scars

It's early—too early. Morning dew shines on the thin strip of grass edging the sidewalk. The car is filled with the scent of freshly brewed coffee and the slanted, hopeful light of dawn hits the windshield and fragments apart. But the warmth and slices of brightness don't touch Kyle. They wash over him, useless. In the shadows, he hides.

The pocketknife is in his hand before he realizes he's grabbed for it. Flipping it open, he automatically twists his left arm underside-up. He makes a fist. The scar from the last time he cut his wrist, scabbed over now, is scratched across the skin horizontally. Staring at the mark, he thinks about how quiet it's been the past few days. Ben has been distant, even moody. It's unlike him. And the silence makes Kyle want to scream just to fill it up.

Work has distracted both Kyle and Ben since the punishment that left Kyle sleeping on the floor in the hallway, but it's Friday and the prospect of a weekend filled with confrontation causes the knife to twitch towards Kyle's skin, wanting to bite.

"This is stupid," Kyle says rationally, like he's trying to talk some sense into himself. "You're too old for this shit."

Ever since his last appointment with Dr. O'Malley, the old itch has come back strong. He's been in so much pain—amorphous, indescribable, and hidden—that the urge to see blood and proof of his own vitality is something he can't ignore. It felt good to cut his arm with the knife Ben had used in their session. The horror from the fight had been lessened by it. He felt purged, his penance paid in blood. Now, he wants to feel that again.

The silver blade gleams, catching some of the golden daylight, shining from its recent swabbing with rubbing alcohol. He'd disinfected it earlier, at home, just in case.

Fist clenching, veins and tendons popping, Kyle thinks of what Ben's reaction might be if he found out about the cutting, and the real reason for it. He can never know. Kyle has always realized that. Ben is like an unexploded bomb; Kyle's past would be the spark that lights the fuse. The resulting explosion would be devastating. And this—the pocketknife, the cutting—would be the first step toward detonation. Because, though Kyle would do anything to keep his secret from Ben out of fear of what Ben would do to him in reaction to his sins, hurting himself this way is just another way that Kyle is telling Ben that something is wrong. He doesn't even need to say the words. The self-harm speaks loudly enough. Kyle can't self-harm without alerting Ben, but he also can't stop the urge to cut.

"You're pathetic!" Kyle screams at his right hand, at the demon in his brain whispering for—no, *demanding*—blood, demanding sacrifice. "He'll see it and he won't even say anything, he'll just...." What? He'll just what, Kyle wonders. The answer is uncertain. History argues that Ben will leave him, or at least pretend to. Experience tells Kyle that anger fueled by betrayal is more likely. But if Ben only knew the truth, and what a sick, damaged fuck he's sharing his life with, that anger might turn on Kyle and obliterate him.

"He's gonna kill me," Kyle says on a relieved sigh as the sharpened edge splits his wrist open. The invisible hand that had gripped and twisted his guts relaxes as blood bubbles slowly to the wound, which stings. The blood drips and Kyle grabs a towel he has ready just for this purpose. He catches the blood with it, before it can stain the floor of the car.

For the rest of the day, he feels better, but the evidence of what he's done is a real problem. Kyle's body is not his to fuck with, not anymore. There are rules and consequences—always—should those rules be broken. And the worse the violation of the rules, the more unthinkable those consequences are. The thing is, Kyle is willing to pay those in order to get what he wants. Today what he wanted was to bleed, an act of brazen defiance that has born pleasure and reward, a reward that Kyle clutches in the hand of his injured arm. A freshly applied bandage hides once more under the thick band of his watch, but the bloodstained towel—white cotton painted crimson—is his talisman. Even simply holding it gives Kyle strength and courage. The stark red on white is a visual shriek against everything that's wrong with his life.

Hours slide by and the workday comes to an end. The sun is setting. Everyone else from the crew is heading home to their families or their beds, but not him. Not yet. There's still a job to be done—hide the evidence. Tucking the towel under his arm, Kyle shuts the car door and heads into an alleyway beside a store lining the quaint street. No one is watching him, he sees, after glancing around. If Darrek were there—and in a day or two, he would be, for the nauseous riot in Kyle's stomach tells him so—Kyle wouldn't be able to pull this off. He'd be more closely observed by exactly the wrong person. But now? Now he's free.

Once he's in the shadows, he eyes an old brick wall to his left. It's coarse, broken and jagged in places here and there, and absolutely unyielding. It'll serve his purpose. Placing the bloody towel between his teeth, he bites down hard on it until he tastes copper. He braces himself and then acts before he can overthink what he's doing.

His arm hits the brick with force. The inside of his wrist and forearm—so recently abused with a modest pocketknife—scrape along the serrated surface, tearing up flesh as Kyle drags it purposefully. Grunting thickly into the towel, Kyle's eyes roll at the wash of heady, screaming pain. He swaddles the arm in the soft, though soiled cotton and jogs back to the car before someone can walk past and sees him standing there, bloody and guilty.

"Have you seen this shit?"

Dark-haired, olive-skinned and with haunting green eyes that speak of innate serenity and intelligence, Micah leans against the side of Diadem's main building. The disquiet he expresses verbally doesn't seem to reach past his unruffled exterior.

Diadem is privately run by himself, Ben, Micah's lover Trace, and a hard-assed woman named Sam. They employ a few other people, including a fledgling Dominatrix named Alyssa and some other recent hires, but their little quartet runs the show. For long years, Gabriel was also a part of their little group. He's since moved on from his job as Dominant, but he will always be family.

After nodding to Ben, who is sitting across the parking lot on the back of his truck and scowling down at the dirt under his feet, Micah raises his eyebrows at Trace, who has just come up beside him.

Trace is a tall, intimidating-looking man, who wears his long silver-black hair tied back and keeps a full, neatly-trimmed beard to help hide his strong, handsome features. His dark eyes peer out from under a heavy brow. Crossing thickly-muscled arms over his broad chest, Trace exhales and acknowledges Micah without bothering to look at Ben. Since he knows Micah well enough to detect carefully concealed but genuine alarm, Trace is instantly made aware that Micah expects him to fix the problem whether he likes it or not.

"Yeah, whad'ya want me to do about it?"

Shrugging, Micah stares at Ben, who seems unaware he's being observed—which is strange in and of itself. Ben always knows exactly what's going on around him. He's the most hyper alert human being Micah has ever encountered. But right now he's lost in his own head. It's wildly out of character for him. Micah has known Ben for a while; Ben used to be Micah's Dominant before Micah was trained and hired into the business himself. Never in all of that time did Ben ever look as upset as he does now.

It's a slow day, but there's still enough to keep them busy—calls to make, equipment to prep, videos and web features to finish. But, for a solid hour, Ben has been sitting outside by himself, picking at his nails and frowning at his boots.

"You think I'm his girlfriend or somethin'?" Trace growls defensively under his breath to Micah.

"I think you owe it to him to acknowledge his behavior."

"Says who? He's probably just constipated."

Micah flaps his arms in surrender. "Fine. I'll do it, then," he says. Micah takes one step forward and Trace grabs him by the shoulder, yanking him back—hard—against the siding.

"Goddamn it."

Striding directly over to where Ben is sitting, Trace unfolds his arms and tries to ignore the fact that Micah is following. When he's standing over the hunched figure of his emotional co-worker, his long shadow falling squarely over him, causing Ben to squint up at the intrusion, Trace demands, "So what crawled up your ass and died?"

"Gerbil," Ben tells him, not missing a beat. "Very uncomfortable."

Exasperated, Micah steps forward, and says, "I think he means, what's wrong? Are you okay?"

"Dandy," Ben blurts, frowning even more at the non-sarcastic concern in Micah's voice. He rips apart a leaf that he'd plucked from the truck's bed, tossing the pieces into the driveway's dirt.

"Heard from Gabe lately?" Trace tries.

"He's still in the Keys. They're flying back today."

"Oh," Trace grunts, obviously searching for what to say, which only makes them all more uncomfortable. "Trouble with the missus?"

Admiring the admittedly feeble effort on Trace's part, Micah watches Ben's reaction to the question closely. Ben becomes visibly angry, and fast. He grabs his crotch, gives it a little shake and spits, "Bite me," with enough bile to make Micah want to take a step backward.

"See?" Trace says, gesturing to Ben, glancing back at Micah. "I knew it was a Kyle thing."

Ben starts to get up. Trace pushes him easily back down. "I ain't done. Is this because Micah gave you a hummer last Wednesday?"

With a level glare of burning anger, Ben holds Trace's gaze and doesn't answer.

"That's a no," Trace says, helpfully, to Micah.

"Did you two fight?" Ben sags subtly, so Micah presses on. "Is Kyle in trouble?"

Anxiousness flickers behind Ben's eyes, then is gone, stifled.

"Fuck off," Ben says softly, ending the conversation. He pushes past both of them before they can say or do another thing.

Sighing, Trace laments, "Gabe would know what to do."

"I could call Ky—" Micah starts.

"Don't even think about it," Trace cuts in. "It's Benny's thing.

Give him space. If he ain't ready, he ain't ready."

The day dies slowly, bruising and fading to black. When Ben gets home from work around ten, Kyle is there, lying on the couch in the living room with no lights on. The house is a tomb. After swatting at a switch, the hallway overhead burns to life at a touch of Ben's finger. Kyle squints but doesn't say a word. With a scowl, Ben marches up to him and yanks the earbuds from Kyle's ears.

"What the fuck is this?" Ben demands, grabbing up Kyle's left forearm. A thick, wide bandage wraps almost the whole thing, the stark white nearly glowing in the gloom. "*What the fuck!?*"

Eyes half-lidded, face impassive, Kyle says calmly, "I had an accident at work. They patched me up and sent me home early."

Ben is already picking at the tape holding down the gauze, and a moment later, he carefully peels it back.

The whole length of the inside of Kyle's forearm, from elbow to wrist, is chewed up.

With shock, fury and fear, Ben growls, "You're quitting. You're done with that job, as of right now."

"Bullshit!" Kyle exclaims. Ben takes it like a slap.

In a low, ominous tone, Ben says, "Excuse me?"

"I'm not quitting my job, Ben!" *This isn't the way this was supposed to go,* Kyle thinks, *not at all.* "It was an accident!"

"Was it? I think the risk outweighs the benefits at this point. There's no reason for you to have a job anyway, I was allowing it only because you enjoy it, but I will not have you risking your life."

Kyle sneers, "You think construction is a fucking hobby for me?! That I do it for fun? How would you feel if I told you to quit *your* job? Huh? That would solve a *hell* of a lot more problems than me quitting mine!"

The outburst from Kyle startles Ben, who is not used to Kyle being so blunt or aggressive. With the anger fled from his voice, Ben asks, "What does this have to do with *my* job?"

"It has everything to do with it!" Kyle screams. "That fucking job means more to you than I ever will and it's ruined everything!

Some shit needs to be left alone and all you fucking do over there is stir it back up!"

Gasping for breath, Kyle wants to take it back as soon as he's said it. More than that, he wants Ben to hit him for having the gall to say it. He doesn't know how to apologize, because what he said is true and, more than that, he knows Ben can't quit Diadem. Ben *is* Diadem, and that's just how it will always be. Which leaves Kyle where? In a hopeless situation, and not just because of Diadem, but because of the constant fear that Ben will force it out of him somehow—the nightmare that Kyle facilitated.

Glancing wildly around the house where he's lived as Ben's submissive for nearly two years, every inch of the place drips memories.

"I can't do this. I can't. I give up." Smoothing the bandage back down, Kyle bows his head and takes a step toward his jacket and keys.

Ben surges toward him, his face unreadable.

"Don't touch me!" Kyle shouts abruptly, flinching back. "Just... don't."

I could keep him here, Ben thinks. *I could tie him down, make him listen, and find out what's causing his torment by whatever means necessary.* As Kyle slides his jacket's sleeve up his battered arm, and shrugs it onto his shoulder with a twinge of pain while walking to the door, Ben thinks all of the things he could say and do. He could be a bastard. He could be Kyle's Dominant. He could even be Kyle's lover, but every possibility feels like something that might make this worse rather than better. All he can think, all he can see is the chewed flesh of that arm, and the hollow, dull, rotting pain in Kyle's bright blue eyes that's been there for far too long.

Which is why Ben says nothing—nothing at all, and it hurts more than anything he has ever known.

Kyle walks out the door to the tomb and into starlight. Ben tells himself it's for the best. *Maybe I'm the poison Kyle was trying to cut out with that knife,* he thinks. *Maybe I'm the problem.*

As the sound of an engine starting cuts the air, Ben releases his frustration in a long, throat-tearing howl that no one hears. It echoes back, a mockery.

"Dammit Kyle. I will fix this," he rasps, when Kyle's headlights recede down the drive. "Once I figure out how."

There's a knock on the glass of Kyle's driver's side window, a hollow tap that jolts him from sleep.

"The fuck...? Gabe?" Wiping his eyes with his good arm, Kyle turns the key in the ignition just enough to be able to lower the window.

"Rise and shine, sleepyhead."

"What are you doing here? Don't you have some tropical anniversary trip you should be enjoying?"

Gabriel smiles at the bitter resentment laced into the question and takes a look around their surroundings. Kyle had parked in a litter-strewn public park down the street from Ben's place; near the restrooms, should he need them. "Nah, this is way more glamorous. I get to drive around looking for your sorry ass instead of recovering from jet lag. It's awesome. What the fuck is your problem, Roth?"

"I don't have a problem. I'm minding my own goddamned business and no one asked you to go out looking for me. I'm a man, not a lost fucking dog. I left. I'm fine."

"Well, see, someone did tell me to look for you and if you don't know who, then you are as dumb as you look."

Kyle slouches in his seat, hating to be stuck in it while Gabriel stands there as big as life, giving him the third degree. Groaning, Kyle curls forward, holding his face in his hands.

Gabriel demands, "The fuck did you do to your arm?"

"Kiss my ass, Sir... dammit!" Kyle curses, kicking inside of the car's door. The title had slipped out automatically. "Kiss my ass."

Gabriel laughs. "No, it's good that you know to mind your manners. I like that."

"I'm tired!" Kyle frowns, hating the honorific of 'Sir' that still sits on the tip of his tongue, ready to be said. The years of using it when addressing Gabriel, who has dominated him too many times to count, overrides everything else.

"If it makes you feel better, then fucking say it," Gabriel hisses. He waits as Kyle tries to resist. "Say it!"

"Yes, Sir."

"Very good."

The praise is like a pleasant tingle that climbs Kyle's spine to the back of his neck, then spreads up the base of his skull and around his chest. It's comforting and makes the turmoil of his emotions and his situation marginally easier to handle. Flushing with embarrassment and bruised pride, he gives up some of the fight. He opens his mouth to speak, then shuts it again when the words won't come.

"Go on," Gabriel urges. Crickets chirp in the distance, the night like a blanket draped around them.

"May I ask who else Ben called, Sir?"

Gabriel scans the car as he answers, and Kyle feels a pang of guilt as his gaze catches on the blood-soaked rag in the footwell. "Who do you think? Trace. Sam." Kyle winces with misery. "Dare is out by your old place. Trace is covering his end of town and Diadem. Micah is out by your construction site. Sam's checking motels."

"I'm gonna kill him."

"For what?" Gabriel seethes. "Caring about you?! Get out of the fucking car."

"Gabe... Sir....."

"Get out of the fucking car!"

Kyle sighs and does as he's told. Closing the driver's side door behind him, he stands before Gabriel. Eyes averted, he holds out his arm when Gabriel gestures for it. Again, his bandage is peeled back. Gabriel uses a pocket-sized, LED flashlight to examine it.

"I'm gonna give you one chance to explain this truthfully, and if I detect even a *whiff* of a lie, about anything, I swear to fuck I will coldcock you and drag you right back to Benjamin to deal with. We clear?"

Amazingly, the threat loosens some more of the knots in Kyle's chest. Some of his fret disappears. "Yessir. Um. I started cutting again, so I did this to hide the marks."

"Subtle. What the hell is wrong with you?"

"I don't know. Too much. Way too much."

With a deep exhale, Gabriel re-covers the wounds, releases Kyle's damaged arm and tucks away his flashlight. Kyle relaxes slightly but, suddenly, while pulling something else from his back pocket, Gabriel twists Kyle's arm behind his back and sweeps his leg, forcing him down to his knees.

Using the arm as leverage, pulling it up painfully behind Kyle's back, Gabriel slides a long, gleaming blade under Kyle's chin. Turning it into the skin, Gabriel lets Kyle feel the dangerously sharp edge and his eyes widen with fear. Kyle's breath comes shallow and quick, and Gabriel says with eerie calm, "What do you say, slave? Should I just finish the job? Save you the trouble?"

Gabriel twists the knife a little more, slicing skin enough to bleed, but not enough to do real damage. Kyle whimpers and fights him, trying to pull away. "Shh... be still. Don't want me to slip, or do you? This is the idea, right? You wanna off yourself? I could do it. Slit your throat. All your problems would be gone."

Kyle stops moving completely. He closes his eyes. His breath hitches and a tear slips down his cheek. For a long, quiet moment, he just feels the pose he's in, and the helplessness of it. He savors the bite of the blade into his neck, and the grip of Gabriel's hand on him, keeping him down.

"What's it gonna be?"

It's clear that Gabriel would do it. Kyle doesn't doubt it one bit.

"Live or die? Live or die, Kyle?"

The fight drains from Kyle's body. He lets go of everything, everything but trust.

"Live."

Imagining that he can hear Gabriel sigh, Kyle feels him press up even more snugly to his back. Still kneeling in the dirt, his right arm twisted up sharply by Gabriel's left hand, Kyle feels Gabriel's grip shift to his throat, his hand wrapping it as Gabriel slides to the ground, kneeling behind Kyle, their bodies flush. Kyle keeps his chin tilted up as Gabriel's left hand tightens on his windpipe, restricting his air. Both of them are breathing rougher than usual, the air around them charged with the energy of what could have been. Kyle leans into the warm solidity of his Dominant's body.

Gabriel's hand unhurriedly pushes up the front of Kyle's shirt, all the way to his collarbone, the fabric stretched across his chest. Wielding the knife, Gabriel draws it up. It flashes silver in the moonlight. Kyle grunts softly, following it out of the edge of his vision.

"Shh," Gabriel hushes, purring the sound into Kyle's ear. The knife's edge drags firmly, in a smooth curving line, under Kyle's right pectoral muscle, biting hot as it cuts. Blood oozes and drips down, thick and dark over pale skin. Kyle moans and shudders.

Dropping the knife to the dirt, Gabriel holds Kyle's form tightly to his chest with both hands as he thrums and shivers. Eventually, the fit passes. Eyes rolled up, trembling and flooded with heady gratitude, bursting with it, Kyle feels steadier than he has in weeks.

"Better?"

"Yes," Kyle sighs, his voice breaking on the word. "Thank you, Master."

"I got him. He's asleep in the spare bedroom."

"Thank Christ," Ben groans, sounding worn-out.

Standing in the kitchen of their home with his cell phone in hand, the call on speaker, Gabriel holds Darrek's gaze, lit with concern. In Darrek's hand is a crumpled paper that Gabriel had slipped him when he brought Kyle into the house, telling of suicide and an offer of mercy. Pale and shaking slightly, Darrek wants to throw the paper away, or maybe burn it, but somehow he can't bring himself to let it go.

"We'll keep him here until things smooth out. I'll keep an eye on him."

"Good. Good plan. I owe you one. I just... didn't know what to do."

"Don't worry about it. It's been handled. It wasn't something you were equipped to do, anyway. And Kyle knew that, which is why it went as far as it did."

"What aren't you telling me, Hunter?" Ben asks warily. Darrek's gaze fixes to the ceiling, like he can see through wood and sheetrock to the broken man waiting upstairs.

"Soon. It's not a conversation to have over the phone."

Ben sighs.

"Go get some sleep, Knox. But first I need your okay on something."

"What? Anything. Anything you need."

"Well, you know your boy. He responds best to a firm hand."

"Okay. It's fine," Ben admits somewhat reluctantly, almost too quietly to hear.

"You sure?"

"Yeah. Whatever it takes. Just... keep him from hurting himself anymore."

"I'm gonna hold you to that," Gabriel warns.

"I know."

Chapter 6

The Cruel Triumph of Duty

"I'm his Dominant. I need to do this, just for now," Gabriel tells Darrek.

Gabriel is pacing in the backyard, kicking at stray stones hidden in the grass, while Darrek sits on the back stoop with their dog, a golden retriever named Sierra whose head is nuzzling his lap. Scratching behind her ears, murmuring sweetly to her under his breath, Darrek averts his eyes.

He's not sure how he feels about all of this. He hasn't even really seen Kyle yet, except for the briefest glance as he was rushed upstairs to bed. Gabriel won't let Darrek near him. All Darrek knows is what was written in that note, passed hand-to-hand so that Gabriel wouldn't have to speak the words and confess what he almost did to Darrek's best friend. And now they're left in limbo—Kyle can't go home, but if he stays, it'll have far-reaching consequences.

Darrek loves Kyle. They're best friends and have been as far back as he can remember. But there's also complicated history there, given that Kyle confessed romantic feelings for Darrek not so long ago, and has indulged in a single, though intense, sexual encounter with both Darrek and Gabriel, with the permission of Ben. That was over a year ago, but none of them have forgotten. Now, fresh from their trip, having spent weeks as nothing but Gabriel's submissive, day and night, Darrek resents the fact that Gabriel is—not asking—*telling* Darrek that this is going to happen, that Gabriel is going to act as Kyle's Dom.

It occurs to Darrek to ask if he has a say in all of this, but, since he knows the answer, he shuts his trap. He's also too well used to taking Gabriel's orders without complaint. That doesn't make the resentment go away, though.

"His head's not in a good place and there's literally no one else that can help him right now."

"Trace could, Sir," Darrek mumbles, flashing an unreadable but dark glance Gabriel's way.

Gabriel stops in his tracks at the honorific, but doesn't look back at Darrek as he replies, "No, he couldn't and you know that."

Darrek knows no such thing. Sure, Gabriel has worked more frequently as Kyle's Dominant than Trace has, but Darrek suspects this has more to do with the fact that Gabriel is beginning to sound like Kyle is *his* now. It's all set and concrete in his head. Nothing Darrek could say would be able to sway him, no matter if he said it as Gabriel's partner, his slave, his friend, or his lover. Maybe it's because Gabriel knows firsthand what it is to be in such a dark place that suicide seems like an incredibly tempting escape route, and believes he knows the way back, intending to lead Kyle along the path to safety. Maybe he thinks he's the only one who knows what Kyle is going through.

"He'll stay in the second bedroom," Gabriel tells Darrek. "If he's well enough to manage it, I'll have him go to work each day."

Arguments form in Darrek's mind. Gabriel has intended to dive into his fledgling business full-force now that they've returned from their trip. That means Darrek has been forewarned that their time together will be limited for a while. Now, with Kyle demanding Gabriel's attention as well, Darrek wonders where that leaves him.

Darrek also can't help but think of the thinness of the bedroom walls. Besides the fact that the second bedroom is where they keep the bulk of their BDSM gear and furniture, there is no way that anything could happen in the master bedroom without the occupant of the second hearing every single thing. Knowing it's pure selfishness that makes him resent the intrusion into their privacy more than anything, Darrek swallows his complaints. Frowning, mood darkening, he rakes his fingers through the soft fur covering Sierra's back. She looks up at him with big, concerned eyes and whimpers.

"It's okay, girl. We'll get'cha to bed soon. I know it's late," Darrek hushes her.

Feeling the weight of Gabriel's stare, which has finally fallen solely onto Darrek, he bears it and waits. A moment later, Gabriel hooks a finger under Sierra's collar and brings her in through the house's back door. When she's inside, he closes the door behind her and turns to Darrek. Walking up to him, standing over him, Gabriel says, "Look at me."

"Yes, *Sir*," Darrek says with more of an attitude than he intended. They knew that something was off with Ben and Kyle when they were away in the Keys. Once a week, Gabriel would check in with Trace or Micah, but Ben and Kyle remained unreachable. All news of them came second- or third-hand. Darrek stopped leaving Kyle messages with the hope of having them returned. The most he ever got in reply was an abbreviated text, telling him to enjoy his vacation and not worry, everything's fine. It was never an actual call, just a text message. The same went for Ben. He'd imply or say outright that a lot was going on and they'd all catch up in detail when the summer was over. It was bizarrely elusive, for both of them.

"Do you want to help Kyle?"

Darrek sighs, rolling his eyes wearily. "Of course I do. I just... I don't know."

"This isn't about sex. This is about making him feel safe and cared for. He's my responsibility but I am going to need your help. I can't be here all the time, so when I'm not, I need you to do as I say, without questioning or second-guessing me every step of the way. You might feel like you know him better, or that you know *me* better, but what happened in the dungeons, for all of those years, between Kyle and me and Ben, that's different, and I think you can understand that."

"Yes, Master."

"Do I have your consent to do this?"

"Yes, Master."

"And if you're worried about losing our privacy, I can assure you that I have in mind more than a few solutions to that complication."

"Thank you, Master. I trust you."

"Good," Gabriel sighs, placing a single kiss to the center of Darrek's bowed head.

The next morning, overtired and waiting for the half-cup of coffee that's already in his belly to kick his ass awake, Darrek holds yet another slip of paper in hand. It's covered in Gabriel's slanted, scrawled script:

> Check on Kyle before you leave. Lilianna should arrive before you go. She's going to stay with Kyle until I get back. Ask Kyle if he's interested in going to work tomorrow. Don't mention Ben or what happened last night.

It's signed with a looped G. Gabriel had left while Darrek was still in the shower, to check out his new workspace and storefront. There was no conversation after they'd come inside the previous night. They were both too tired, with too much work to do in the morning, so they passed out as soon as they were in bed.

It doesn't miss Darrek's attention that the note is an order. Though he resents being herded around his own best friend like an idiot child, he knows the reasons are valid for Gabriel to handle things this way. If he was consulting with Darrek on what to do with Kyle, it would be jeopardizing the balance in their relationship and make things that are already wildly out of control seem that much more so. However, the intensity of Darrek's distaste for the idea of Gabriel manipulating Kyle to this extent, and being complicit in it, catches him off guard. Unable to put his finger on, or give explanation to the reasons for his feelings, Darrek gives up trying.

It makes sense that Gabriel called Lilianna for help. She's Micah's wife, she's known to be discreet and from the little that Darrek is aware of, is or was also Micah's Domme. The particulars are not something that is openly discussed, though, especially since Micah began submitting regularly, in his own time, to Trace.

Lilianna's job involves frequent prolonged travel, all around the world. She's not usually around and has only made a few appearances at dinner parties held by their small circle of friends. Darrek supposes that Gabriel made a call, found out she was available, and asked for assistance with Kyle. It was probably a more appealing option than turning to one of the men, all of whom have complicated histories with Kyle.

Eyeing the closed door at the top of the flight of stairs, Darrek carefully folds the note and slips it into his pocket. Without the faintest idea of what he's going to find when he opens that door, Darrek masters his own reactions to the situation and begins to climb the steps.

He knocks lightly, waits for a response that doesn't come, then turns the knob. Inching the door open, his towering form fills the doorway as he looks inside.

The air in the room is thick with the massive waves of tension and energy baking off of Kyle's prone form. At first Darrek's response is too keen to voice. When he does find his tongue, he groans, "For fuck's sake, Kyle."

"Screw you. Get out," Kyle says, scowling.

Kyle is lying on the spare bed, tucked up against the far wall under the heavily curtained window. Some morning sunlight slips in around the curtain's edges, but the room for the most part is dark and shadowy. Kyle is naked, or at least Darrek assumes he is. There's a sheet covering Kyle from the waist down and his chest is bare. His eyes are ringed with dark circles, and appear sunken, his frame thinned out since Darrek has last seen him. A stark white bandage covers almost half of Kyle's chest. It's taped down at the edges. Another fresh bandage wraps Kyle's entire left arm from the elbow down.

When Darrek doesn't leave, Kyle screams, his voice cracking with strain, getting hoarse, "GET OUT!"

"Do you need anything?" Darrek asks gently. "I'm headed to work. Lily's going to be here any minute, I guess. She's going to hang out until Gabe is back. Or, you know, if you want to come along with me, I can get you some clothes.... The guy that's covering for you's kind of a weasel and I'm sure the crew would rather have you there to boss them around. But if you're busy...."

"Shut up, Darrek," Kyle sighs heavily, giving up.

Kyle had become foreman over the summer. He's always been good at organizing the guys and getting things done. He's ballsy enough to handle the union reps, the old-schoolers, the fresh meat— everyone—but he's also got the skills to back it up. Given a challenge at work, Kyle can step up to it. He figures out what he needs to do, the best way to do it, and conquers it to the best of his ability. Darrek admires him for it, his perseverance and determination. It's still going to be weird to work for him, though, if he ever decides to come to work.

Kyle has been staring fixedly at the white expanse of the room's ceiling but, as Darrek watches on closely, watches *Kyle*, he closes his eyes. Darrek stares unapologetically, seeing everything, and small crinkles form in Kyle's brow. His lips turn sadly down at the edges and he's the most utterly pathetic that Darrek has ever witnessed. It should make Darrek want to back out of the room, to leave Kyle alone so that he can rest and recover, but it does the opposite. Darrek feels rooted to the spot.

"I don't want you seeing me like this. I don't want anyone seeing me like this."

"Except Gabe, right?"

That does the trick. Kyle's vividly blue eyes spring open and they lock on Darrek. The defenselessness in them, -- the sort Darrek hasn't seen in Kyle since they were little boys, almost knocks Darrek clear off his feet. It twists something in his heart and acts like a light, creeping caress over his balls. Intoxicated, Darrek tells himself that his swelling arousal is due to the lingering effects of their sexual play, instigated and mediated by Ben and Gabriel. But that was a long time ago, and now it would be inappropriate to get off on Kyle's helplessness. Kyle is his friend, and no more than that, Darrek tells himself. Smothering the reaction before he can think to examine it any closer, Darrek takes a step farther into the room. Kyle rolls his eyes and glances away.

"I'm not trying to steal your boyfriend, okay? Or your Dom. This wasn't my idea. I didn't ask for this. I kind of didn't have a choice. If the tables were turned, and you'd come to Ben for help, how would you feel, facing me?"

"We can't talk about it," Darrek says, with love for his old friend etched into the words. "Sorry. It's one of Gabe's rules."

Kyle draws a deep breath and lets it out.

Eyes determinedly averted, blushing as Darrek's gaze skates over Kyle's body, Kyle reacts to the scrutiny. It makes him visibly nervous and restless. He fidgets on the bed, shifting position. When his cock twitches under the sheet, Darrek notices and, Kyle almost breathlessly begs, "Leave. *Please.*"

But Darrek doesn't, and the tension in Kyle's body, the delicate lines forming in his brow, only grow. Darrek walks right up to the bed and folds his hand around one of Kyle's. "I'm sorry. I'm sorry you're having such a hard time. I'm here to help, too. Anything you need."

His voice is a deep vibration in the air, felt as much as heard. Darrek yearns to fix his friend, knowing he can't.

"I'm cool," Kyle admits. He lifts his other hand, closed over a small phone. "Gabe's got me covered. Don't really want to see anyone right now, so I'll probably stay in here until he's back."

"Lily's coming to watch you. Literally. You know that." The reminder is met with a brief twist of anguish that's there and gone in Kyle's expression.

"Oh yeah," Kyle murmurs.

Darrek's thumb drags in an arc, caressing over the back of Kyle's hand. It raises goose-bumps on Kyle's arm. Studying Kyle closely out of the corner of his eye, Darrek can tell that he's getting hard and a voice whispers temptingly at the back of Darrek's head that maybe Kyle'd be okay with some hand release before Darrek leaves. For a fleeting, damning moment, Darrek imagines it, fantasizing about yanking off the sheet, fondling Kyle's dick, listening to him moan....

Quickly letting go of Kyle's hand, Darrek clears his throat and crosses his arms over his chest, wondering what the hell is wrong with him.

He's so helpless... Look at him. He wants you to. That's why he's blushing like that. That's why his prick's getting stiff....

"Yeah. Okay," Darrek says too loudly, trying to drown out the devil's voice in his head. "So, maybe later in the week, you'll be up to coming with? To work? Might be a good, um, distraction."

"Sure," Kyle agrees, ready and willing to agree to anything, as long as it gets Darrek out of the room.

"Great. Okay." Darrek turns, walking back to the door. Resting a hand on the frame, he pauses, keeping his back to Kyle. "You know I love you, right? And I refuse to let anything bad happen to you."

Kyle's only reply is a soft, hurt sound. Darrek closes his eyes against it, squeezing the wood of the frame until his clipped-short nails dig in, making dents like half-moons in the wood. Confused, hard-up, and filling quickly with self-recrimination, Darrek croaks in a voice much rougher than it should be, "I'm going. You okay?"

Kyle grunts.

Not sparing another second, Darrek closes the door, putting much-needed space between him and the incomprehensible temptation beyond it.

Chapter 7

The Difference Between Gabriel's Slaves

Darrek has all day to let his guilt fester over being turned on by Kyle's weakness. He tells himself that he only liked it because Gabriel was the one to put Kyle in such a position—stripping him down, setting him up in a bed in their makeshift dungeon like Gabriel's new pet submissive. Gabriel's elusive behavior, being less than forthcoming with details and using his status as Dom as his excuse only makes Darrek fixate that much more on what all is happening that he doesn't know about.

That seems reasonable at first. It's never been a problem for Darrek to enjoy Gabriel's work, whether it's Gabriel dominating him, or Gabriel letting Darrek watch old videos of his work at Diadem. So it shouldn't really come as a surprise that Darrek is starting to get off on the idea of getting to witness first-hand as Gabriel dominates another man whom, incidentally, Darrek and Gabriel have both been sexually involved with in the past.

They are in uncharted territory, Darrek tells himself. Never before has Gabriel taken another submissive with Darrek's approval. And since Darrek has gotten a few opportunities to act as a Dom himself when Gabriel has submitted to him, surely it's natural to lean that way when confronted with a totally, seductively submissive Kyle.

Darrek's initial reaction to the arrangement—concern for Kyle's well-being, then offense at the intrusion into his and Gabriel's relationship, especially coming right off of a long period of time savoring each other in absolute privacy—is forgotten. Concern for Kyle still remains, of course, but it has shifted in tone. With solid faith that they can help Kyle find his feet again, and back to happiness with his life, whatever that means, Darrek resolves to do whatever he can to make it happen.

The day shuffles along sluggishly. Dreaming of a full night's rest in his very own bed, Darrek at last makes it home from a long day downtown. His crew, typically acting with Kyle as its foreman, is currently building a new clothing store. After hours of hanging sheetrock, sweaty and worn-out, Darrek forgets some of the drama at home and simply acts out of habit.

He gets home and parks his Tundra in the driveway, behind Gabriel's Discovery. After locking his tools in the garage, then walking around back to let Sierra out to run in the fenced yard, Darrek grabs a cold bottle of water from the fridge and downs it while standing just inside the kitchen. Sighing loudly at the meager refreshment it provides, he twists off his sweaty shirt and tosses it into the laundry room. Impatiently pushing his damp, stringy, long hair out of his eyes, he tries to tune in to where Gabriel might be.

After a moment, Darrek detects his voice coming from the living room, so he shuffles that way. Gabriel is seated in an armchair. Darrek, still running on autopilot, goes directly to him, sinks to his knees and embraces Gabriel's left leg, bowing his head and letting it rest against Gabriel's thigh, in his lap.

"I missed you," Darrek breathes in a sigh, letting the walls come down, putting himself in Gabriel's capable hands.

Fingers twist tightly in Darrek's hair, yanking on it, pulling his head back. Closing his eyes and drinking in the small pain, Darrek shivers as Gabriel's other hand scratches down over his back, along his spine and the thickly bunched muscles there, slicked with glistening beads of sweat. Gabriel tugs firmly with the hand holding Darrek's hair, forcing him closer. With a moan of surrender, Darrek lets Gabriel guide his face deeper into his lap.

Inhaling the scent of him, Darrek parts his lips and mouths hungrily over the swell of Gabriel's crotch when his face is buried there at Gabriel's urging. Kissing and licking over the line of his cock through his cotton pants, Darrek accommodates his Master's whims with pleasure. And though Darrek waits for Gabriel to unzip and allow him greater access, more than willing to suck him, salivating at the thought of it, it doesn't happen. Gabriel remains silent and stiff in the chair. Something is wrong.

"Master, let me please you?"

"So good for me," Gabriel praises. "So *obedient*. I can tell how tired you are. You've had a rough day, haven't you, my beautiful slave? And yet, here you are, giving yourself to me, freely."

"Of course, Master. Anything for you," Darrek says, dragging open-mouth kisses over the thickening line of Gabriel's flesh.

"And you don't hold it against me that we had a... disagreement... last night?"

"No. No, Sir. That doesn't matter. I just want you to be happy with me."

"Oh, I am. Believe me. Maybe our guest will learn a thing or two from your devotion and selflessness," Gabriel says slyly.

Darrek freezes. His body tenses under Gabriel's hands. His eyes widen in surprise. Lips closing tightly, the color drains from Darrek's face.

"Go on and look. You have my permission," Gabriel says.

"Sir," Darrek blurts in acknowledgement. Steeling himself, he clears his throat and turns to look over his shoulder.

It's Kyle, kneeling in the corner, his arms behind his back like they're bound there. He's wearing jeans and a short-sleeved shirt, barefoot. His face is redder than Darrek has ever seen it, and he is resolutely avoiding Darrek's eyes. Once the room's attention is now focused solely on him, Kyle shifts with discomfort. That's when Darrek sees that he's kneeling like he is because his wrists and ankles are bound together, loosely, behind him.

Darrek's gaze wildly snaps around to Gabriel, questioning.

"This is our home. Kyle knows that. You are free to behave as you always have, without consideration to my new slave. If I give you permission, it's absolutely fine. Understood?"

"Yes, Sir."

"Good. Now, I'd like to play with you for a while, but I'm not in the mood to give our guest the privilege of watching, so we're all going to go upstairs but he'll be wearing a blindfold. He'll have to be content with listening."

"Yes, Sir."

"Upstairs," Gabriel says tenderly. "Now. Crawl."

Suppressing another hard shiver, Darrek obeys, crawling on his hands and knees, slowly, across the room and up the steps.

While Darrek is ascending to the bedroom, Gabriel says, more sharply, and not to Darrek, "Slave?"

"Yes, Sir," Kyle mutters, his voice wavering and raspy, worn thin from shouting. "Thank you, Sir."

"You're welcome."

Gabriel watches him as Kyle pretends not to track Darrek's progress from the corner of his vision as his glistening, hard body flexes and moves, feline and sensual. Then he stalks over to Kyle, crouches down, and stares at him, intimidating and threatening.

"Maybe if you behave," Gabriel says, "you'll keep getting these little rewards. If you don't, I'll chain your ass up, blindfolded, gagged and spread-eagle. You won't be the spectator; you'll be an equal participant, and you know how I was nice enough to give you a catheter earlier so we didn't need to stop for bathroom breaks? Next time you won't get the cath, I'll just let you piss yourself. Think about that."

"Yessir. Thank you, Sir."

"Damn right."

A blindfold is fastened to Kyle. He's on edge, his heart racing when Gabriel unties him long enough to lead him upstairs and re-secure him in the corner of the spare bedroom. Kyle hears floor-boards creaking only feet away and exhales sharply, twisting as far as he can as he tests the cuffs hogtying him.

He wants to curl up in a ball, and can't. If he fell over, there'd be no way to get back up without help which may not come, so he's stuck there, kneeling on the hard wood of the floor. But he kind of welcomes the bruises he can feel forming on his kneecaps and shins. At least they're a diversion from the noise in his head and the sounds coming from right in front of him. The thought of listening to Gabriel have at Darrek, and of having to imagine it, makes Kyle a little crazy.

It causes him to miss Ben, to remember his lust for Darrek, his head ringing with Darrek's profession of love from that very morning. But there's nothing for it.

Earlier, Gabriel had stripped Kyle naked (blindfolding him when Kyle began to panic), laid him down on a tabletop, and carefully examined and photographed his entire body, head to toe. Gabriel had not planned to bind Kyle for that process — as he said, regretfully, to Kyle — but it quickly became obvious that it would be necessary. So he had restrained Kyle, flat on his back, to the long table in the second bedroom. When the close inch-by-inch scrutiny of his skin was completed, Gabriel had gotten a tongue depressor and looked down Kyle's throat, testing his gag reflex in the process. He'd gotten a special instrument to look in Kyle's ears and up his nostrils. He'd looked under his eyelids, at his fingernails and toenails, at the webbing in between his digits. Knowing where this was headed, Kyle was keyed up and frantic when Gabriel photographed and manipulated his genitals, looking for any mark or scratch or blemish. Then all that was left was to flip Kyle over, tie him down, wrist and ankles, and apply the same scrutiny to his back.

Kyle had smelled the latex before he heard the soft snap of it against Gabriel's skin when he put the glove on. He listened with sharpened ears as Gabriel slicked on the lube and could muffle his swallowed scream no more than he could control his violent shuddering as Gabriel probed his rectum.

When it was completed, Gabriel had told him seriously, that each time he let Kyle leave the house and away from supervision, when Kyle returned he would be subjected to the same procedure. He would not be permitted to harm himself and Gabriel would be sure to find any evidence pointing to that, no matter what means Kyle tried. And if Kyle tried to get his hands on any drugs, and Gabriel suspected as much, he threatened to start routinely pumping Kyle's stomach too.

Part of Kyle doubts Gabriel would actually go through with that, but, when he was still throbbing from the violation of the man's fingers in his ass, it was hard not to take the warning at face value.

So, Kyle is more than happy to stay alternately bound, babysat and close to Gabriel in order to avoid such treatment, until he's able to prove that he is trustworthy and will no longer try to harm himself. But, strangely enough, kneeling in the corner of the bedroom of Gabriel and Darrek's home, listening to the clink and rattle of chains, the murmur of voices, with the promise of getting to be a voyeur into their sex life, hurting himself is the furthest thing from Kyle's mind. He's absolutely fine where he is, in Gabriel's fierce care, knowing that Gabriel does what he does not to scare Kyle or fuck with his head for his own pleasure, but merely to help.

Kyle feels safer with Gabriel than with Ben. He had tried to analyze that newfound knowledge in the long hours he was left alone with his thoughts earlier that day as Lilianna set up her chair and laptop and got some work done. Lying on his new bed, Kyle dissected the reasons why Ben scared him. Initially Kyle thought that he was his own problem; his head was simply fucked, he was purely incapable of trusting someone completely and there was no help for it.

In a perfect world, Kyle would like to trust Ben completely, but Kyle's world will never be perfect. Ben will never hear Kyle's most closely guarded confessions; he's too resolute a judge, too malicious, too determined to punish those who have done evil, and turn that evil back on them in turn, to feed.

No, for Kyle Roth, it has been either suffer or die. But as the ability to suffer, and the capacity to die has been taken from him, he is forced to examine other possibilities.

Gabriel won't tear Kyle apart, like Ben would. Not in a million years. The danger in Gabriel is subtler, seductive. It's a real possibility that, unknowingly, he'll shatter Kyle's protective barriers without realizing it's happening. Even by being the Dominant of both Kyle and Darrek, the process has begun. The danger is here with them. The dance has started.

Now they only need to stumble upon the right steps and everything that Darrek has convinced himself never happened will rip open and spill in a putrid heap around them. And the beauty of Kyle's absolute entrapment is that he can't protest, or put a halt to it. He can't warn Gabriel or Darrek without giving himself away or hurting Darrek more than he already has. But since Kyle is the only one that remembers how this is supposed to play out, he sees that it is in his power, at least, to deliberately try to lead them astray. It's not much, but it's all he has left.

Chapter 8
Testing Darrek

At first Darrek simply kneels inside the doorway to the second bedroom, where his best friend has so recently taken up residence, though at the moment he is tied up in the room's far corner. Trying hard not to pay any attention to Kyle, Darrek focuses on the room's other, main purpose. It holds almost all of their fetish furniture and gear. The larger pieces are mounted, displayed on the walls, surrounding the large cross and the padded wheel to his right. The closet has been converted into lockable cabinets outfitted in trays full of toys and creams and accessories. As the unyielding wood floor grinds against his kneecaps, Darrek focuses on his breathing and shivers slightly at the feel of Gabriel's fingers twisting in his hair, scratching lightly against his scalp.

Gabriel scans the choices before him, feeling the heat bake from Darrek's sweaty, tightly muscled, enormous body at his side. His hair is silky and long enough for Gabriel to wrap it completely around his fist, which he does, pulling gently on it until Darrek's head is forced back, his neck elongated, the long line of it exposed, his throat working around a swallow.

With a sigh, as if the choice was a difficult one, Gabriel commands, "Whipping bench. Climb on."

"Yes, Master. Thank you," Darrek says with almost a smile, grateful as he is for the ability to be supported by the bench rather than be forced to stand or hang from his arms. After shedding his clothes, he crawls up to the bench. The thick, black, heavy metal frame weighs it down in its place in the far corner of the room. It has four legs and the padded surfaces are staggered at two heights, the topmost angled down at the front, up at the back. Bolted to the frame are leather cuffs, one on each of the back legs, a wide strap across the width of the lower bench, another wide strap that spans the vertical posts which are the bench's middle support, and finally a strap across the higher bench.

Darrek settles himself onto the black padded leather, wrapping his hands around the posts at the front of the bench while Gabriel straps him in. His ankles are buckled into the rear cuffs, which are pulled tight, prohibiting movement. A strap is fixed across the back of his lower legs, keeping them snug to the lower bench. The middle-backs of his thighs are hugged with another, as is his back. Gabriel tests the give, ensuring that Darrek has absolutely no range of movement. The most he can do is lift his head, move his arms and flex his feet. He's ass-up and not going anywhere for a while. The ankle cuffs keep his legs spread, and allow Gabriel room to work.

Relaxing in his confinement, Darrek watches keenly as Gabriel moves around the room, gathering supplies. By turning his head this way and that, he can almost track Gabriel, but Kyle is out of view, blocked by the single bed.

Gabriel plucks a long leather whip from a hook on the wall then goes to the cabinet while, for Darrek, the realization truly sinks in that Kyle will hear everything quite clearly. Curiosity sparks as to what exactly his Master and Kyle have been up to in his absence. Gabriel had said their arrangement was not about sex, but some part of it has to be, Darrek knows. He wonders where Gabriel touched Kyle, the pain and pleasure he's brought him, the things he's done to him.

His musings are derailed as Gabriel comes back to the bench and immediately grabs hold of Darrek by his cock and balls. A sharp exhale mostly of surprise leaves Darrek and he forces himself to un-clench and trust. Gabriel fits his slave into a contraption that Darrek has worn many times before—a black leather divider that lifts and grips the sac while it fits snugly around the base of the penis, keeping Darrek rock hard for as long as Gabriel wants. Snapping it in place, one strap fed up the middle of Darrek's sac, and another around the root of his penis, Gabriel says quietly, "No gag. I want to hear you. And if you try to be quiet, I'll be harder on you than I want to be until I'm satisfied. Understand?"

"Yes, Sir."

The smell of citrus tickles the inside of Darrek's nose, so he glances back to see Gabriel with a bottle in his hands. He's wearing latex gloves and squirting the fluid into his palm.

"Oh fuck," Darrek groans, knowing what it is, and tensing up reflexively.

Gabriel only chuckles.

"You really react beautifully for me when I use this on you," Gabriel says calmly, amused at Darrek's alarm. "And though you like to pretend you hate it, I know it's all just a fucking act."

Gripping the metal posts until the corners dig into his flesh, providing distracting pain, Darrek forgets to breathe and squeezes his eyes shut as cool fluid is rubbed over his testicles, covering them completely. Gabriel is careful to rub some under the leather straps, too. Then, fingers wrap his shaft and squeeze up it, slowly, root to tip, as the stimulating cream coats him. It's a special concoction that Darrek happens to know was perfected by Ben of all people, and is used regularly at Diadem. Gabriel has his own supply of it stashed in his personal collection. Instantly, the tingling starts, crawling over his balls, shooting into him as the nerves react. Then it climbs his shaft and Gabriel smears a huge dollup of it over his crown, making small circles over his opening with the pad of his thumb.

Darrek breathes out a shaky breath through his mouth that's almost a laugh and inhales deeply. It's not terrible, yet. It's a cold tingle that spreads and intensifies, but he knows it will only get worse, and worse and worse, growing hot, then burning. He's already fully hard, and as Gabriel pumps him slowly, Darrek can't deny that it feels spectacular. Moaning back in his throat, his hair hanging down in his face, obscuring his view, the sizzling cold shifts, blossoming into heat and Darrek's hips twitch, trying to buck into Gabriel's tight, gloved fist.

"Feels good, doesn't it?" Gabriel says with a smirk, as Darrek flushes and shudders. With his thumb, he rubs more of the clear fluid into Darrek's slit. Spreading the stimulating cream over his left hand, making sure his first two fingers in particular are well coated, he works Darrek closer to orgasm as pleasure meets pain, blending together, indistinguishable. Unhesitating, Gabriel rubs with his left hand through the crack of Darrek's ass and repeatedly over the knot of his hole, which clenches more tightly at the contact. The fluid begins to act there too, cooling, then tingling, but Darrek knows what comes next, so he moans freely in anticipation.

"Please don't," Darrek begs, his low voice roughened already, the tension audible in it.

"Don't what?" Gabriel teases as he oh-so-slowly presses with the pad of his lubed index finger at Darrek's opening. It breaches him and passes through the ring of muscle that closes like a vice around it, trying to keep him out. Darrek shudders almost violently and shifts in his bonds, but the finger slides into him, knuckle by knuckle, slicked with plenty of the cream. Instantly the delicate tissues are set alight. The burning starts almost right away and Darrek gasps loudly, fighting to bear it. Gabriel works the finger in and out, rubbing all around inside Darrek's anus, then withdraws to add more cream, pushing that into Darrek with two fingers.

"Oh sweet fuck," Darrek whines, gasping in rough, shallow breaths. He's trying, because of Kyle's presence and despite Gabriel's warning, to be quiet, but it's difficult as his genitals and anus are engulfed in invisible flames. He fights against the leather straps holding him down, his ass so perfectly presented for torturing, no way to escape, nowhere to go. "God*dammit.*"

Right near Darrek's ear, in a threatening growl, still pumping his slave's bound cock, and two fingers impaling him, Gabriel warns, "I have a long sound right here that I would love to use to get this cream farther inside your dick."

"No! Please. Please, Master."

"Then control your fucking breathing. Calm down. Now."

"Y-yeah. Yes. Yessir."

"*Now.*"

Darrek nods, and takes a deep breath, holds it, and lets it out, but as he does, a sharp yelp is startled out of him as Gabriel probes him.

"You know better than this. Is it because our slave is listening? Does it bother you that much?"

"No, Sir."

Gabriel measures the truth in this, then says, experimentally, "Should I take his blindfold off so that he can watch, then?" While posing the question he hefts a full-size black dildo, grasping it by the ribbed handle on the end and presses the head gradually into Darrek, who moans loudly, his voice wavering as he parts around the thick toy. Gabriel holds it there, steady, for a moment, with just the tip inside. "Good boy, just relax.... I know it feels too big. Gonna fuck you with it, nice and slow." Holding it by the handle, he presses it farther, watching Darrek's ass suck it in, inch by inch. Darrek tries to breathe normally as he's entered, but small lilting whimpers and gasps slip in. His skin flushes even pinker under his suntan. Gabriel withdraws the toy a few inches and Darrek groans, then pulses in Gabriel's fist as the black cock thrusts home, deeper still. "That's it. Take it. I know you can. Nothing like taking a thick cock up the ass, right slave?"

Eyes rolling back in his head, burning everywhere, Darrek is stuffed full with the fat silicone phallus. Gabriel jacks him perfectly, with little twists of his lubed hand. Darrek is wracked with sensation, but has enough sense to answer the questions, or be punished for it. "No, Sir."

"Hmm. No? No what?"

"Please no, Sir. Don't let him watch."

"Are you sure? Your cock seems to like the idea. You know, I had my fingers in him today...."

"Oh, Jesus," Darrek moans.

"I'll have to finger him again tomorrow after work, if he goes. Should I let you watch?"

Fluid weeps from Darrek's slit, dripping down through the stimulating cream, over Gabriel's fist. Twitching with lust, pressing into the gloved hand, Darrek seems right on the verge. Gabriel jabs him with the dildo, snapping his wrist. Darrek cries out. Letting go of the handle, leaving the phallus buried completely in Darrek's ass, with just the handle sticking out, Gabriel uses his freed hand to grasp the base of Darrek's bound sac and pulls hard on it. His dick is like hot iron in Gabriel's hand, proof that he's aroused by the explicit questions, by being overheard by Kyle, by the cream, by the toys, by everything. "Remember. Honesty, my beautiful slave."

"Y- yes. Please, Master."

Gabriel squeezes Darrek's testicles, left and right, in his palm and jacks him double-speed. Darrek gasps, the breaths torn violently from him as the urge to give in to a rapidly-approaching climax engulfs him, despite the knowledge that he can't with the leather straps constricting him, and Gabriel's rules prohibiting it.

"Does it hurt?" Gabriel asks in a wicked whisper behind the shell of Darrek's ear.

"Yeah. Thank you, Sir," Darrek chokes, blissful, delirious with it.

Gabriel releases him, steps back. Darrek sags, catching his breath. "Thank you. Thank you, Master. I love you."

The black handle obscenely protrudes from his body, stark and so very inviting. Unable to resist, Gabriel takes from the wall nearby one of his shorter whips, after debating whether to use the one with the barbed tips and deciding against it only because he knows Darrek has work again in a few hours. With the whip in his right hand, Gabriel grips the dildo's handle. Darrek tries to push his ass back and prohibit Gabriel from removing the toy, but bound to the bench, he's held in place as the plastic cock is pulled with torturous slowness from his body. Once the head is free, Gabriel runs the length of the toy up through Darrek's crack, then uses it to paddle his balls, Gabriel watches his slave drink down the small pain like nectar, using it to stifle his pleasure and regain control.

"Harder, please," Darrek croaks. "Sir."

Gabriel swats his balls more firmly with the dildo, and Darrek swallows a cry.

"No, what did I say? You let me hear you, or I make this less enjoyable."

Steadying Darrek, cradling his balls in a hand, Gabriel taps them with the toy with increasing strength. Then he aims only for the right side, pulling the testicle away from Darrek's body as far as it will go and smacking it directly with the dildo. A sharp, shrill cry emits from Darrek, softly, then more fully.

"That's better. Let it out. Scream for me."

"Oh god... please... FUCK... ow... god! Fuck! Ow!"

But Gabriel keeps tapping, tap-tap-tap-tapping that one side until Darrek is keening, alternately whining and growling.

"Stop!"

Gabriel stays quiet and keeps doing it. Darrek shudders, fighting harder still against his bonds. He hits the metal bar of the bench with an opened fist, then closes the hand and punches the metal with his knuckles.

"STOP!"

"Pussy," Gabriel tsks, letting Darrek's balls go, and instead, wasting no time, smoothly inserts the thick toy to the hilt, thrusting at enough of an angle to drive a startled gasp from Darrek.

Breathless, Darrek flexes the hand, throbbing now, that he'd used to punch the bench, his chest rising and falling heavily.

"Want me to fuck you myself, slave?"

"Yes, Master. Please. Please fuck me," Darrek almost sighs, latching on to the idea greedily.

"Then you let me fucking hear you. The louder you are, the more likely you are to get my cock."

"Yessir. Thank you, Sir."

Gabriel runs an open hand over Darrek's back, down the backs of his thighs, up again over his ass, collecting sweat on his glove as he does. Darrek is dripping with it. "How's that cream?"

"Fucking burns, Sir."

"Good."

Gabriel palms Darrek's ass with one hand, and with the other, grabs a huge handful of the long hair at the nape of his slave's neck, pulling hard on it so that Darrek's head is forced back. Kneading the muscle of his buttock, Gabriel is rough on him, wanting to bruise. Darrek moans, frowning, and when Gabriel pulls at the muscle, spreading his ass, watching the toy shift where it's buried, he hums with pleasure. Grasping the black handle, Gabriel tugs it out and presses it back in, fucking Darrek slowly with it.

"Please...."

"Please what?"

"Please fuck me, Sir."

"You like that?"

"Love it," Darrek moans. The toy's strokes get harder, more brutal, and Darrek moans loudly.

Holding the toy steady, with Darrek impaled on it, Gabriel draws back the arm wielding the whip and aims a direct hit to the left side of Darrek's ass. The whip bites, leaving long pink trails over the curve of Darrek's cheek and down his thigh. Darrek flinches, focused on the burning that reaches far inside his body now, and crawls like licking flames over his balls and cock, seeping down inside his urethra. But he's also keenly aware of being stuck on the end of Gabriel's toy, lodged so far inside that Darrek feels like he's choking on it. With Gabriel's fist wrapping the base of the toy, flush to Darrek's body, jabbing it impossibly farther into him in little pulses, he whips again, and again, and again.

Chapter 9

Controlled Recklessness

Small cries, let out freely, broken sweetly on the edges, purr from Darrek, making Gabriel so hard he feels lightheaded from the force of his desire. The more twisted-pleasure-tinged-with-pain that Gabriel inflicts, the better the rush that makes his head spin. The louder Darrek cries out, the more Gabriel wants to be balls-deep inside him. Darrek's ass gets pinker with each hit, but the more lashes of the whip that fall, the more relaxed he seems. His muscles unclench. His breathing evens out.

Gabriel pumps the phallus into him a few more times, with deep strokes, then removes the toy again, setting it aside. Darrek's hole is wet and rubbed red, his cheeks covered with thin, pink welts. Gabriel's mouth waters, wanting to lick and taste that, but he stifles the urge, knowing the cream isn't meant to be ingested. Drawing himself up, Gabriel gets a wide stance and delivers with full force a strike of the leather whip.

Darrek yells and flinches. He grabs the table like that will help, his feet flexed, his arm muscles knotted. The whip falls again, again, five more times, until the fire is outside as well as within, and Gabriel caresses the curve of Darrek's ass to feel its hot throbbing through the latex of his glove.

"Beautiful...."

Ten more lashes fall, most of them striking fully across the meatiest part of his ass, now a full, dark, rosy pink, and the flesh hot to the touch. Darrek had favored him with bright screams so Gabriel rewards him by gently stroking his cock back to full hardness. Darrek hums and writhes, delirious. Feeding the whip through Darrek's legs, Gabriel uses it to gently strike the underside of his cock a few times, then runs the leather over his balls as he fondles Darrek's hard-on.

When Darrek seems to have slightly recovered, Gabriel resumes whipping him, giving him ten lashes in a row. By the end, Darrek is tensed from head to toe and shouting hoarsely, sobbing softly with each breath.

"Good boy. Your ass is so inflamed and sensitive...." Gabriel scratches the abused, swollen flesh, making Darrek groan thunderously. Drawing back his hand, he spanks him with it, watching the flesh jiggle. Setting down the whip, Gabriel grabs the long black dildo again and, with a hand, pulls Darrek's hole open. The air kisses the tender flesh, and Darrek moans, pressing his ass up in invitation. Gabriel, holding him open, rubs repeatedly over his rim with the head of the silicone cock, stimulating it. He sees Darrek waiting for it, wanting to get fucked, which is why Gabriel draws it out, not giving it to him.

Eventually, Darrek resorts to begging.

"*Please...*"

Gabriel runs the ridged plastic over the swollen, wet ring of muscle, which puckers.

"Please, Master. Please fuck me...."

Gabriel spanks him, three times, as hard as he can, then corkscrews a thumb into Darrek, up to the hilt, making him moan in pure desperation.

"Tell me exactly what you want," Gabriel instructs calmly, spanking Darrek yet again, running the dildo between his legs, over his straining, bound flesh.

"You. Your cock. Fuck me with your cock, Sir. Please."

"You don't want the toy?" Gabriel asks, aligning it, feeding it inside in a steady, angled push that makes Darrek whimper gorgeously.

"Rather have you, Master."

"But you like this too. Don't you. Fucking cockslut...."

Darrek grunts thickly, as Gabriel fucks him with long strokes of the toy.

"Say it."

He grunts harder. "I, uh... I'm a... a cockslut. I'm a fucking cockslut... Sir." The last word breaks apart, shattering Gabriel's fragile hold on himself. With a sigh of surrender, he drops the dildo and yanks his pants open, freeing himself. Straddling the bench, he enters Darrek in a greedy thrust, burying himself in him with a heady moan. Sobbing with gratitude, Darrek opens to it, relaxing and letting Gabriel take as much as he wants. "Thank you, Sir. Please fuck me."

The 'please' lilts sweetly and Gabriel's hips snap, pumping into Darrek's orifice, coated with the stimulating cream which starts acting on Gabriel's cock as well, tingling, warming, starting to burn. It's exquisite. He ruts in Darrek's wet, fluttering channel, knowing he's grunting and moaning and that Kyle is listening to him, too, but Gabriel doesn't really care. Their bodies slap loudly together as Gabriel takes him, and moments later, with a shudder ripping through, empties himself into Darrek.

Still hard-up, but hovering very close to the oblivion of exhaustion and overstimulation, Darrek glances back over his shoulder as he feels Gabriel pull out and immediately start unfastening the straps holding him down. Before he's anywhere close to being recovered, Darrek hears, "Get up. On your feet. Careful now."

Darrek sways a little on his feet. Gabriel takes off the leather binding Darrek's genitals, and guides him into a pair of loose boxers. They're tugged up over his hips, covering his erection. Gabriel also pulls his own pants back up.

"Stand over against that wall. Move it."

It's clear that Darrek wants to ask why, but is too delirious to find the words or coherency, so he walks across the room silently, with Gabriel at his back.

Kyle is right where Gabriel left him, of course, tucked into the corner of the room by the foot of the bed. He hears Gabriel order Darrek, "Stand there."

"Yes, Sir," Darrek mumbles, slurring a little.

Gabriel stalks up to Kyle, not stopping until he's right in front of him, close enough to reach down and palm the back of Kyle's head. Fingers skate through the short blond hair, and pull Kyle to Gabriel, his face nuzzling the rough denim and crotch of Gabriel's jeans. Kyle moans, mouthing over the fabric as he fights for control of himself. It's him and Darrek, again, and both being controlled by the sexual whims of an older, confident, decisive man, though this one doesn't wish them true harm. It's a clear distinction between the two, but in his frazzled state, the lines blur. Exhaustion pulls at Kyle's body. The mounting mental stresses are compounded; his balls draw up tight and heavy to his body, his dick is hot, stiff and aching. And Darrek is watching. Darrek can see the proof of Kyle's desire.

It's all happening again. Ashamed of his arousal, as he was taught to be, Kyle feels scrutinized, judged, damned. Recognizing the fact that he's letting it play out the old way, wanting to push things away from that dark place, for his own sake in part but mostly for Darrek, Kyle tunes in to his caring Master. Breathing in the scent of Gabriel, burying his mouth and nose in his Master's crotch to get as close to the sweaty musk that's all him — Gabriel, no one else — Kyle grounds himself to the moment. He's knows that he's the show now. They're both watching. Kyle is hard and begging for it and that's all that matters. That's all that ever mattered. Grunting thickly as the fear slips like a cold knife into his belly, Kyle lets out a soft, scared whimper that's loud in the stillness of the house.

"C'mere," Gabriel growls with what sounds like tenderness. "It's okay."

He shifts his right booted foot, sliding it snugly under Kyle's crotch. The effect is instantaneous. Kyle's hips roll forward in greedy mindless movement, his body acting of its own accord, grinding against the freely offered source of relief.

"It's okay," Gabriel says again, holding the back of Kyle's head tighter still, feeling the heat of his breath against his thigh.

Kyle inhales the heady scent of Gabriel's come, still coating him, tinged with the citrus of the cream. It gets into Kyle's head and breaks loose some of the ties holding his mind together. Mouthing over the inside of Gabriel's thigh as he takes deep inhales of the glorious scent of his sex, Kyle struggles to shift closer, fitting his hips to Gabriel's lower leg. He grinds in tight, quick thrusts against his ankle, encased in the boot, and the friction makes Kyle swallow a groan. After the first push, his body chases for more, moving unceasingly. Squeezed between his hips and the denim of his jeans, rubbed roughly against Gabriel, his dick throbs, but each shallow drag brings him closer to climax. He feels it low in his balls, in the tingling at the base of his spine. He doesn't give in to the urge to stop just because Darrek is watching—*Darrek is watching*—all he thinks about are the wanton sounds he heard, the scent of Gabriel's come-soaked cock filling his sinuses and how grateful he is to have something solid and real to fuck and get off against.

With a grunt and a soft purr, hiding his face against Gabriel's leg, Kyle comes, hot and wet, in his pants, soiling himself. But he doesn't care because all of his tension, all of his cares expel from his body with his load of spunk, leaving him shivering with bliss. It's done and he didn't ask for it. Gabriel gave this to him. All Kyle did was take it.

Head swimming, he feels Gabriel slip the blindfold from Kyle's eyes and step away, leaving him there to recover.

Gabriel goes to Darrek, whose form is suddenly larger than life and staring right at Kyle.

"Face the wall. Spread your legs."

A few steps away from Kyle, Darrek watches from over a shoulder. When Gabriel starts handling Kyle, out of nowhere a wild shout of protest bubbles up in Darrek's throat. He almost doesn't catch it as he instinctively starts to scream for Gabriel to stop, to leave Kyle alone. What's happening to Kyle is Darrek's fault. Darrek feels the truth of that on a profoundly deep level, beneath reason and logic. Kyle's pain—all of it—is his doing, and the more Kyle endures, the more Darrek is guilty of. He wants to look away, needs to look away, for his own sanity, for self-preservation, but, like he does with Sierra when she makes a mess and he sticks her nose in it to teach her a lesson, Darrek punishes himself for getting off on Kyle's whimpers and tears by not looking away. He doesn't even blink.

The safeword 'Tundra' sits on Darrek's tongue. He wants to say it, but he can't, because he deserves this too. He wants to get off, and it's going to feel even better with Kyle watching. It's sick and wrong and that's just how Darrek wants it. Apologies, pleas, protests all mingle and blend, coming out as a rough grunt as Gabriel leaves Kyle's side and returns to Darrek.

Knowing he doesn't have permission to look, Kyle does anyway simply because he has to. It feels like the only way he can keep a handle on what's happening is by seeing all of it unfold.

Gabriel positions Darrek against the wall, his hands splayed on it as Gabriel fits himself to Darrek's back, his hips forming themselves naturally against Darrek's recently-fucked ass — Gabriel's sole property. Some of Gabriel's semen is dripping down the inside of Darrek's leg, and Kyle moans. Suspecting that Gabriel knows Kyle is staring, realizing that the whole point of this was to allow Kyle to watch, he sees Gabriel push Darrek's boxers out of the way, shoving a greedy hand in there to wrap his flushed-dark, heavy cock.

Kyle feels like the air is sucked out of the room, leaving him gaping like a beached fish as he watches Gabriel give Darrek manual release, his gloved hand pumping along the glistening-wet shaft, sweeping over the bulbous, red crown. Gabriel bites down on the back of Darrek's shoulder, seals his lips around the spot in a dirty kiss and wraps an arm around his broad chest as Darrek gasps and thrusts in sharp little pushes into Gabriel's busy hand.

In seconds, Darrek comes hard and tries at first to hold in his cry, then seems to lose control of it and lets it out, his face carefully turned away from Kyle's direction.

"That's it. Let me hear you. You did so well for me. I'm so damn proud of you," Gabriel says.

Darrek shudders, crying out, and goes boneless as the praise appears to sap what little was left of his strength. Pulsing weakly as he comes down, he tenses his arms and uses the wall to prop himself up.

"Head to the shower. I'll meet you there in one minute, okay?"

"Okay, Sir," Darrek murmurs, sounding only half there. Kyle knows where the rest of Darrek is—trapped behind the protective walls inside his head, hiding from something Darrek never wants to expose.

When Darrek is going, and they hear the door to the bathroom close, Gabriel turns his attention back to Kyle, who avoids his gaze.

"Thank you, Master," Kyle manages, feeling ashamed, feeling like less than the dirt on the soles of Gabriel's boots.

Gabriel hunches down, fishing a key from where it hangs around his neck. He uses it to unlock the cuffs hogtying Kyle, thereby freeing him.

"Up we go," Gabriel says, getting to his feet and hefting Kyle up as well, pulling him up by his arm.

"*Fuck*," Kyle hisses as pins and needles sting his half-numbed legs and arms.

"Steady," Gabriel says, holding him up. "Give it a minute. How do you feel?"

"Swell. Sir."

"Be more specific than that," Gabriel tells him warningly.

Kyle glances sideways at Gabriel's cool grey eyes and starkly dark hair, marveling at how incredibly intimidating the man is, with very little effort. It's an innate power that Kyle will never have. Calculating his reply, knowing that Gabriel always can tell a lie, Kyle says after a pause, "I'm better. I appreciate that you allowed me to listen, and that you let me, uh, you know."

"Well, you look better," Gabriel admits. "I'm going to watch you shower after I'm done helping Darrek. Then I'll get you in bed. If you want to go to work tomorrow, I'll permit that, with the conditions we've already established. Think it over. You don't have to decide 'til morning."

Nearby, the water runs in the shower. They can hear it beating against the tile and the tub. Kyle's cheeks turn pink at the declaration that Gabriel will be watching him bathe, and the promise of enduring another examination should he go to work. He wonders, dully, if this time, Darrek will be brought in to observe. They truly have come full circle. The terrible completion in that gives him a tainted kind of peace. The emotional response quickly drowns out all of Kyle's cares and worries, and for a moment, it doesn't matter how fucked up things are with Ben, or how much Kyle hates himself sometimes, or how screwed up his life is — he's just happy to have something familiar to deal with, and feels better than he has in a long time.

"Why are you doing this for me?" Kyle hears himself asking before he knows he's going to.

"Because I care about you," Gabriel frowns, like that should be obvious.

Kyle gazes at him with wonder tinged with heartache, as tears suddenly sting his eyes. Suddenly, Gabriel hugs him. Kyle is surprised greatly by this, but folds into Gabriel's embrace easily, burying his face in Gabriel's neck. "I'm tired of being scared all the time."

It's a feeling that Gabriel can relate to. Kyle knows this, which is the only reason he can admit to it. He hugs Kyle even tighter, hissing, "I know."

"Thanks for reminding me how nice it is to feel taken care of," Kyle tells him, then quickly detangles from Gabriel's arms, stepping back, folding his arms over his chest and rubbing blood back into his arms.

A brief upward glance shows Kyle how closely Gabriel is scrutinizing him, and his words.

"What the hell happened to you?"

"Shit. Shit happened. Lots of it." Kyle glances to the doorway, leading Gabriel's attention there.

Deflating a little, Gabriel runs a hand back through his hair and sighs. "Yeah, okay. Time to get cleaned up. It's late."

"Thank you, Sir."

Chapter 10
The Blind Fight Against Fear

The worst thing about sitting alone on the edge of a curb by yourself at three in the morning, for Ben Knox at least, is not the combined stench of spilled cheap beer and drying vomit, nor is it the fact that his favorite black V-neck tee shirt is probably never going to be rid of the fresh bloodstains on it. It's that there's a crusty, one-eyed reptilian stuffed animal only a few feet away, mocking him. He'd grab it and throw it somewhere out of sight where it wouldn't stare at him like that, only that would mean touching it. He'd kick it, but that would mean getting up, and the four or five punches he has taken to the stomach are making that an unappealing thought also. He has better things to be thinking about than why on Earth there would be a stuffed animal of a gecko or a chameleon, or some god-awful thing, in the gutter outside a shitty, run-down bar in the bad end of town, but he can't seem to help himself. Its presence is aggravating, and the glassy-eyed mocking leer is worse.

This is what's going through his head as he gingerly touches the tip of his tongue to where his lip has been bleeding steadily, when someone comes up behind him. Before he can snarl some sort of obscenity-laden warning to scare them off, he hears, "Your legs must be tired because you've been running through my mind all night."

That's enough to make Ben pause long enough to forget what he was going to say. Twisting slightly at the waist, wincing at the sickening twinge it causes in his gut, he squints back over his shoulder at the person addressing him.

"You've gotta be fuckin' kidding me," he groans, rolling his eyes and facing forward again.

"No? Okay, how about... was your father an alien? Because there's nothing else like you on Earth."

"Why did I call you? Why? Maybe I do have a concussion."

"Oh, hey now. That was a good one," the newcomer says, standing on the sidewalk behind Ben, a stone's throw (or a creepy toy alligator's throw, Ben thinks deliriously) from the bar's front door. "Your daddy must have been a baker, because you've got a nice set of buns."

Ben laughs despite himself, then recovers, regaining his scowl. "This must be why Trace loves to spend all of his free time playing Ping-Pong with your balls."

"Well, actually, one never can tell what exactly it will be that annoys him to the breaking point. He's a tough cookie."

"Yeah, and you're a psycho," Ben mumbles, palming his side as a hot, sharp pain flares there.

Micah tsks, "That's really the best you can do? You must be worse off than you look, and that's saying something because you look like horseshit."

"Fuck you very much."

Micah holds out a hand, saying, "Come on, big guy."

Resenting Micah's presence and snark immensely, Ben takes his hand and uses the help as he gets to his feet. He stands there glaring at Micah until he coughs up an explanation.

"Well, you did say you needed someone to 'pick you up'...."

"For Christ's sake," Ben sighs.

"Should I even ask? I probably shouldn't ask," Micah ponders, giving Ben a once-over, doing a cursory appraisal of the amount of visible blood. Ben's split lip is swollen and bloody; his eyebrow is also split and leaking more blood down Ben's nose and cheek. His knuckles are likewise bloody but that could easily be someone else's.

"Just take me home," Ben asks. When Micah doesn't so much as blink, he says, "I walked."

"From where? You live miles from here." Dismissing the question as soon as he voices it, he thumbs over his shoulder in the direction of his car. "Come on. You can crash at Trace's tonight. Someone should look at your wounds, and if I did, and fucked it up, Trace'd flay my hide, so... lucky you!"

"Fantastic," Ben says sarcastically. "Why do you think I called you and not him, asshole?"

"Tough shit," Micah replies evenly.

"Yep. It certainly is."

Twenty minutes later, they are both seated at the kitchen table in Trace's kitchen. The overhead lamp casts stark shadows down on the three men and it's too quiet, but at least there's no noise to make Ben's headache any worse than it is. Micah frowns at Ben's darkening bruises as Trace dabs disinfectant on his cuts.

They haven't asked Ben any more about why he was beat to hell and stranded at a bar, but Ben knows they're waiting for an explanation anyway. It's a verbal stalemate, as he doesn't want to talk about it with them, so the silence draws out.

"You shoulda seen the other guy," Ben manages eventually.

"Yeah," Trace grunts doubtfully. Ben frowns at the lack of confidence.

Trace's salt and pepper hair hangs around his face, his dark eyes peering out from the shadows, any expression masked by his thick beard.

"Yeah, actually. The bartender was dialing for the ambulance when the guy up and took off and went running down the street with his arm bent in directions arms don't bend in. And I think I stepped on some of his teeth when I went to sit outside and called our boy Mic, here."

"Yeah," Trace grunts again.

Ben's frown deepens.

"Any chance he'll press charges?" Micah inquires.

Ben laughs sardonically, "Not fuckin' likely."

"Why?"

"He's a drug dealer."

Trace and Micah exchange a glance.

"Oh come on. Don't fucking do that," Ben complains. "I saw that and I know what you're doing."

"What are we doing?"

Ben begins to stand. Trace wraps his thick, callused hands over the tops of Ben's shoulders and shoves his ass back down into the seat with enough force to knock some of the wind out of him.

"You ain't leavin'."

"Guess not, huh?" To Micah, Ben says, "Get me a drink."

"You ain't the boss of him," Trace says in a low growl of a warning. "And you've had enough booze for one night."

Ben seethes in quiet rage for another solid five minutes, bearing the sting of the ointment and Trace's fingers probing his torso and hands for broken bones, finding none.

"Fine! God! He was Kyle's dealer, okay? Happy?! Preventative measure."

Trace sets down the cotton swab and glowers at him.

Micah asks, "You think Kyle's using?"

"No, I think Kyle's going to go back to using. There's a difference. But if he can't get shit from the scumbags, I don't have to worry so much, do I?" He doesn't want to say any more, but now that he's started, the words come in a flood, unleashed to fill the unbearable quiet in the darkened house. "He's OD'd at least once before, and I can't be there to make sure he doesn't do it again, and I won't be able to fucking sleep if I keep worrying about it. There's only so much Gabe can do and I know Kyle. I know him better than Gabe, better than fucking anyone, and I know what he does and how he is."

The subject of Gabriel taking the reigns as Kyle's Dom is another, as yet un-broached subject, and Trace and Micah exchange another glance at the mention of it, unprompted, by Ben.

Micah asks hesitantly, "Are you okay with Gabe watching out for him?"

"Kyle needs it. I trust Gabe. That's all that matters."

"It's got to be tough, though, giving him that much power over Kyle. I mean, Gabe has Darrek, and he loves the guy, but he's a hell of a Dominant. Right?"

Ben's gaze is fixed on his lap. He hunches forward, looking miserable. "I get daily updates. Kyle's... improving." He shoots them a piercing look, daring them to question his hope.

"You'll get through this. Both of you. You belong together," Trace says to Ben, gripping his shoulder supportively.

"Yeah yeah...."

"You can't go out there assaulting people just to make yourself feel better."

Ben locks eyes with Trace, and what passes between them is so dark and intense and unsettling that Micah looks away, gazing out the window rather than being witness to such a thing.

"Won't happen again," Ben says through gritted teeth.

Trace nods once. "Bed's all yours," he says, inclining his head in the direction of Gabriel's old room. "Sleep it off, soldier."

"Sure." Ben stands with a grimace, and hobbles down the hall, into the gloom.

Standing in the shadowy hallway, messenger bag at his feet stocked with his laptop, papers, keys, and everything else he'll need to haul over to his new office space as he continues setting up operations, Gabriel is ready to go. It's early, barely dawn, but Darrek and Kyle are needed at their jobsite and it's Gabriel's duty to see them off.

Already, Gabriel has pulled Darrek aside and explained things to him. It would fall on Darrek to watch out for Kyle in Gabriel's stead, and Darrek is okay with that. Gabriel is expecting to spend long, twelve-hour-plus days getting his business in gear. Calls, both over the phone and in person, need to be made to clients. He has to set up his portfolio and ready the website. The finishing touches need to be put on the studio space, and he has to be there to receive any ordered supplies so that he's ready to work in his photo lab and also host clients, should they be interested in seeing where he works. And he's doing all of this absolutely on his own. Eventually, he would like to hire an assistant, but that can only happen once the income starts to flow in and he has the resources to do so, plus he would have to add creating job advertisements and interviewing to his to-do list.

His head swimming with all of this, there's precious little left over to manage the chaos of his personal life. Gabriel resents Ben for shoveling everything with Kyle on him at exactly the wrong time, but there's no way that Gabriel is going to be even partially responsible for anything that might happen to Kyle simply because no one stepped up to help when it was sorely needed. Who knows where

Gabriel would be if Ben hadn't done the same for him when he had nothing and no one. It's karmic payback. Gabriel knows he has to do this. There's no way around it. And Darrek has to help Gabriel out. They haven't discussed things like they should have, but Gabriel can't worry about that now. Later maybe, once things settle down, there can be damage control. After so many weeks alone with each other, as nice as it is to have some time and ability to focus on his other passion — his work — Gabriel feels guilty for having such little energy and attention for his partner.

Driven by necessity and responsibility, Gabriel puts everything else momentarily aside until he ensures that Kyle and Darrek are both fine and safely out the door for the day. Once that is accomplished, his focus can be more selfish, at least for a little while.

Standing in the shaft of morning light falling through the opened front door, Kyle restlessly fiddles with the edge of the bandage on his forearm, which peeks out from the end of his sleeve. When he woke up, roused by the sound of voices in the next room, he had lain there, lost in thought until Gabriel came to get him. He had escorted Kyle to the bathroom — noticeably cleared of any razors and scissors — and offered to shave his face for him. Politely declining, Kyle chose instead to deal with the stubble on his jaw for the time being. He was strangely comfortable with letting Gabriel watch him wash up and use the toilet. Once upon a time, he might have resented the hell out of something like that, and Kyle takes it as a sign of how much things have changed that such an intrusion of his privacy makes him feel safer.

Gabriel used to make Kyle very uncomfortable. His ability to intimidate, the power and confidence that he exudes, his standoffishness and talent at keeping others at arm's length, not ever getting too close, it all combined to make Kyle practically hate the man. That's why Kyle was so upset when Darrek began dating him. But now, when Kyle looks at Gabriel, he sees someone who was made so very vulnerable and hurt deeply for so long that a tough outer shell became necessary for survival; someone who knows nothing of the crimes his friends have committed in order to seek vengeance in his name. He also sees Darrek's lover, his confidant—a treasured position that Kyle has sought for as long as he can remember. Gabriel is a victim of abuse, but he's also strong, wise, talented, and most of all, he's a good man and a good friend. Hate has fled, replaced by love. Kyle wishes he were Gabriel sometimes. Other times, he's just glad to be in Gabriel's care.

"We'll grab breakfast on the way, whatever you want," Darrek tells him, looming tall and broad over Kyle's much smaller form.

Kyle knows it has become Darrek's job to keep an eye on him while Gabriel is working. It puts a weird spin on their old friendship, and makes it that much harder for Kyle to look at Darrek without thinking of the night before.

"Maybe this was a bad idea," Kyle says, mainly to himself. "I don't know if I can handle this, man. It's all... crazy out of control. How am I supposed to concentrate on work? What if Ben shows up? What if...?"

"Hey, you can do this," Darrek tells him, like he believes it. Kyle bites his tongue and closes his eyes. After a moment he scratches restlessly at his itchy stubble.

Someone grabs his arm, pulling the hand away from his face where the nails have left pink trails beneath the light scruff. "Maybe this will help," Gabriel says in his deep, powerful voice as he wraps a two-inch thick leather band around Kyle's wrist. It covers the edge of the bandage that he's been playing with and he likes how tight Gabriel pulls it, so that when Kyle flexes his arm, the leather bites into the skin.

"Thank you, Sir," Kyle says quietly.

"You have my cell number. If you need to come home, call me and I will come to get you. Okay? Promise me you'll eat and stay within eyeshot of Darrek all day. I've cleared my schedule this evening, so I will be here when you get home. Ben knows not to show up. I've got him under control, so don't worry about that. Now, if you can't do this, I can bring you with me to the office, but it will not be enjoyable for you. You're better off staying busy and useful. But it's your call. What's it gonna be?"

Kyle grunts, "Work."

"Good." Gabriel turns to Darrek and nods to Kyle. "Give him a hug, show him you don't bite."

"Is that an order?"

"It is, actually," Gabriel smiles.

"For Christ's sake," Kyle groans, dropping his arms to his sides as Darrek folds him up in a hug.

"Go on, hug him back. That's an order too," Gabriel smirks.

"Ben never fuckin' made me hug people," Kyle complains, slurring his words slightly and reluctantly hugging Darrek back as he fights hard against memories it triggers.

'Touch him.' The leather whistles as it slices air. It cracks loudly against skin again and again. Then the screaming. Oh sweet, merciful God, the screaming. Make it stop. Kyle touches and obeys just to make it stop.

Kyle trembles faintly and turns his face into Darrek's solidity to muffle a whimper borne of desolation.

"Yeah, well, I ain't Ben."

Chapter 11

Just a Hug

Darrek looks down at Kyle, feeling him shiver inside his arms. Caressing gently over Kyle's back—his body so much smaller than Darrek's own—Darrek feels a surge of power. A muscle in his jaw twitches as Darrek responds to Kyle's fragility with a testosterone-fueled instinct to claim what's rightfully his. Not Gabriel's, not Ben's—*his*. His Kyle.

Darrek feels the hitch of Kyle's chest as he fights back tears. It doesn't make sense for Kyle to be crying, but it wakes Darrek up. What's he doing? What the fuck was he thinking?

"This is really gay," Kyle complains softly, with plenty of self-hatred, feeling smaller than he ever has with Darrek's pumped up, hard body gripped around him. Pushing forward through time, back to reality, he wonders how much of their vacation was spent in the gym because he would swear Darrek wasn't this big before.

"No, *you're* gay. Aren'tcha, bottom boy? And we love ya for it."

Kyle squints at Gabriel as Darrek gives him an extra hard squeeze and the air woofs from Kyle's chest. Then Darrek pats Kyle's head, tousles his hair and bends down to kiss his cheek.

"Knock it off," Kyle protests, needing the touching to stop, trying to wriggle out of Darrek's crushing hold.

"You really are like a kitty, aren't you?" Darrek observes as Kyle tries to squirm out of his arms. "That's a really apt nickname."

"Dare, I swear to fuck if you say that word again," Kyle warns, eyes blazing.

"But it's true. You'll let people pet you when it suits your mood...."

"*Pet* me?"

"...and try to bolt when it doesn't," Darrek finishes.

"Nah, I'm pretty sure the name came from the way he purrs when you tickle his balls, metaphorically or otherwise," Gabriel says with a sly grin. "But that's enough of that. Dare, don't torture our slave. That's my job. Capisce?"

"Yes, Sir," Darrek sighs, curiously sounding both disappointed and relieved.

"Go on, boys. Play nice. Have a good day."

They exit the house and walk over to Darrek's Tundra. Kyle shoves his hands deeply into his pockets and ducks his head to hide his strained expression.

As soon as they've driven away, out of sight, Gabriel fishes his phone from his pocket and dials Ben's cell. It's early, but Ben has always been an early riser.

It rings four times and is answered by someone who is definitely not Ben.

"Gabey," a gruff voice says pleasantly into the phone. "How's it hangin', sweetheart?"

"Oh, this can't be good. Tell me you're answering because Ben had a really fuckin' early appointment with a client."

"Sorry, babydoll. He crashed here last night. Not really in any shape to be taking calls, even from you."

"He's smashed?"

"His *face* is smashed," Trace tells him, some of the humor evaporating from his voice. "The dumb fuck thought it'd be smart to go picking a fight with Kyle's old dealer, you know... just in case."

"Jesus wept," Gabe groans, rubbing his eyes, wishing for coffee. He goes to grab his bag, slings the strap over his shoulder and starts to lock up while he talks, just to get to work and the coffee pot stationed there that much faster. "What's the damage?"

"Eh, he's fine. Face is swollen and he's got some impressive bruises. Nothing broken. The cuts aren't even bad enough to warrant stitches, which is a shame really. Would've been fun for me to have Micah tie the bitch down so I could run a needle through him a few dozen times."

"Yeah, I bet."

"Sounds like Benny took the other guy apart, though. That was probably the rage. Comes in handy sometimes. Anyway, we're letting him sleep it off. Gave him a week's paid vacation and taking over his clients for the time being."

"Shit. I suppose that means you and Micah are pretty busy." Lilianna is unavailable for the next couple of days because of work commitments, so Gabriel is looking to arrange another sitter for Kyle, just for during the late afternoon hours between when Kyle gets done at work and Gabriel's not yet home.

Trace laughs, and Gabriel can hear the tiredness creeping into his voice. "Yes, ma'am. Why, what'd you need?"

"Never mind. Doesn't matter. I'll figure it out on my own."

Gabriel expects Trace to protest and attempt to weasel the info out of him anyway, but the sounds on the other end of the line are suddenly muffled, like Trace put his hand over the phone. There are multiple voices. Gabriel can tell that much, at least, and when the line clears, it's not Trace he's talking to anymore, but Ben.

"Hunter. How's my boy doin'?"

"He's good," Gabriel sighs. The house is now locked and he opens the door to his Discovery, sliding in behind the wheel. "He felt up to going to work today, so that's progress, I think. He's looking better too. The wound is healing. And he's lost some of that scary blankness."

"Good. That's really good. So, you want to tell me what you couldn't before? What the hell went on with you and him when you found him? Was he okay? I mean, he didn't hurt himself more, did he?"

"No, nothing like that. But he was miserable as hell. I uh, gave him the option of an easy out, but he didn't take it."

"What the hell is that supposed to mean?"

"I kind of put a knife to his throat. He cried mercy."

Ben is perfectly silent. It makes Gabriel nervous, so he quickly continues.

"He seemed relieved after that, like making that choice cleared his head a little."

"What else did you do with the knife, Hunter," Ben says in a soft, eerie growl.

"Not much. One shallow cut across the chest, just enough to release some of those endorphins."

"He let you cut him? You're not shitting me?"

"No, why?"

Ben pauses. "It's just, he hasn't let me come anywhere near him with a sharp object for nearly a year. Always uses his safeword. Every time."

Gabriel rolls his eyes wearily, but files this information away for further scrutiny. "Any idea why?"

"No," Ben says, a little too quickly. It's a lie, and Gabriel grows even more curious as to why Ben would lie to him about this.

"Sounds to me like he's scared of you," Gabriel says gently, knowing that hearing such a thing might enrage Ben again.

To Gabriel's surprise, Ben doesn't refute this or argue the matter. "When can I see him? I need to see him, Gabe."

"It's not a good time. He needs some space right now until things get closer to normal. He's just started to act like himself again. Ask me next week. I'm not trying to be a dick here."

"Yeah yeah. I know," Ben grumbles. "Keep me posted? And just make sure he stays safe."

"I swear it. I'm taking good care of him."

"I know you are. Thanks. I'll make this up to you."

"Don't sweat it. I figure I've owed you since I was seventeen. Call this reparation for saving my life and my sanity."

When they hang up, Gabriel sits in his driveway, staring at his phone for a long time.

It's a quiet but busy day. Kyle keeps the men on their crew in line and a lot gets done. The sunken, pale look to Kyle scares off anyone who might otherwise have asked where he's been, so Darrek doesn't have to step in to protect his friend's privacy. Kyle and Darrek take lunch at different times, but neither of them leaves the big empty space of the framed-out store without the other, and then only to use the portable toilets.

Quitting time rolls around at last, and Kyle won't look at Darrek as they walk to his Tundra for the drive home. Watching Kyle fidget, his blue eyes framed with golden eyelashes darting around, Darrek refuses to unlock the vehicle until they address some of the weirdness between them.

"Dude, open the door."

"No. Not until you look at me," Darrek insists.

"I think I've looked at you plenty," Kyle counters, his gaze flicking over anyway, up to Darrek's eyes and down, quickly, over his body.

Frowning, Darrek steps closer to him.

Kyle's eyes widen fractionally. "What're you doing?"

"I'd like to hug you."

"Did I not make it clear earlier that I don't enjoy hugs? Especially when my crew could be watching? Guys don't hug."

"Sure they do," Darrek says, softening his tone, closing the distance between them. He slowly backs Kyle up to the side of the truck and plants a hand on the window beside Kyle's head, leaning into him. Gently, he places a kiss to the side of Kyle's mouth. "I'm worried about you."

Breathing shallowly, in little gasps, Kyle continues to avert his eyes and frowns when Darrek doesn't move away, but stays right where he is, in Kyle's personal space.

"Me too," Kyle says almost too softly to hear.

Darrek's thumb drags back over the side of Kyle's cheek, prompting a soft noise low in Kyle's throat.

"How do I get you to snap out of this?" Darrek wonders, hooking a hand around Kyle's ear, holding on to him.

"How do I get *you* to snap out of this?" Kyle mimics. "What are you *doing*, Dare?"

"I don't know. I just... want to save you... or something...." Darrek's lips brush against Kyle's and he inhales Kyle's soft sigh. The back of his head flush to the window's glass, Kyle has nowhere to escape to as Darrek's lips close around his. Like he's pushed by an invisible hand, Darrek is driven to seek more. Kyle opens his mouth, maybe to protest, maybe not, but then Darrek is licking over his bottom lip and pushing his tongue into Kyle's mouth. Kyle moans and shoves violently at Darrek's shoulders, which only gets Darrek to grab his wrists and slam them back against the truck, pinning him there as he plunders Kyle's mouth which opens quite readily for him.

And then, abruptly, like a splash of cold water, Darrek is gone, taken three steps backward with a hand over his mouth.

He turns away from Kyle, then right back. Pale and startled, Darrek sputters, "I-I don't know what that was. I...."

"It's not your fault. We're not talking about it. It didn't happen. Dare, it didn't happen. Got it?"

"Okay. Right. You're right," Darrek nods, latching readily on to the suggestion, composing himself with effort, willing his hard-on to soften. He remembers, suddenly, the turmoil caused last time he kissed Kyle without permission, but, then again, that was before things got way more complicated than kissing. So who knows what's out of bounds now? Telling himself that's why he crossed the line, Darrek glances at Kyle and can't decide if he wants to hug him and apologize or kiss him again.

Kyle clears his throat and goes to the passenger side door. "Come on. Time to go home."

"Right. Yeah. So," Darrek says, fumbling out keys and hitting the 'unlock' button. "How about those Phillies? Hell of a game last night."

"Yeah, I wouldn't know. I was a little distracted, and kind of hogtied to your spare bed."

"Maybe Gabe'll let you use that flat-screen to watch the game tonight," Darrek says, getting in.

Kyle slides into his seat too, curling up into a ball, with his legs drawn up to his chest. "Sure," he mutters, like he's talking to himself. "First, I just have to let him examine all of my body's cavities."

Darrek makes a noise of frustrated irritation. "I'm trying to change the subject, here, asshole! Not helping!"

"Not helping what? Your stiffy?" Kyle says it distractedly. It sounds like a joke meant to lighten the mood, but the look on Darrek's face makes Kyle mumble, "Oh. Well then. Sorry. Yeah, it'd be great to watch the game. Really distracting. Distracting is good."

"Yeah it is," Darrek agrees, shifting into drive.

Chapter 12

Seduced into Complicity

"There's a problem."

Gabriel stands toe-to-toe with Darrek. Stress tightens Darrek's expression at these ominous words. They're in the garage, also not a good sign for Darrek. If what Gabriel has to say is bad enough to warrant going to another building to say it, rather than doing so in earshot of Kyle, it must be pretty bad.

Darrek clears his throat and nods with forced solemnity as he ferociously buries lingering guilt over kissing Kyle. "Lay it on me. What's up?"

"I called Trace to see if he or Micah can help out with Kyle this week. I'm going to be working late every day or else what I'm trying to accomplish with this business is going to be doomed from the start. It needs to have the majority of my attention, and there's no way around it. You know that. Hell, you've known it was going to be like this for months. But this stuff with Kyle... it's a complication I never planned to have. So, since Lily is busy I reached out, but Ben, the fucking dumbass that he is, got in a fight last night and is laid up, so everyone else at Diadem has to cover for his ass. No one can help us. And I can't let the kid go back to Ben. Not when he's in as much pain as he is. I feel like I'm the only one that can help him, but maybe that's not true. Maybe I should be asking for more help from the person who's cared about him longer than anyone."

"Gabe, wait," Darrek starts, not liking the way this is going at all.

"Hear me out," Gabriel cuts in. "You've been there for me when I needed someone to take control and get me past my shit. You're capable. And best of all, you have always been very caring with your friends. I know that you love Kyle, and that you'd do whatever it takes to save him from himself."

"That's not my issue," Darrek says, growing desperate with panic he doesn't quite comprehend, only knowing that this is bad. This is not good at all. It's not just about him kissing Kyle earlier. That's definitely a part of the reason, though. All Darrek knows for certain is that the best thing right now would be for Kyle to get away from him so that things can get back to normal, for all of them. "My issue is the history I have with Kyle. It's complicated, and you know it's come between me and you in the past."

"That was a long time ago," Gabriel says levelly. "Ancient history."

"Is it? What have you been teasing us with then, like last night? You can't expect me to treat him like a... a *client* or something. You said it yourself! I do love the guy. Always will. You're telling me to cross lines that you and Ben have warned us not to cross." His voice becomes shriller with fear as he manages to convince himself more than he does his Master. "*Please*, Gabriel...."

"Your job is a very specific one. You hear me?" Gabriel holds his gaze, the force of his will dizzying. Darrek can tell that no is not an acceptable answer, no matter what the reasoning is. "I need you to cuff him to the table after work. Then you need to inspect him for any signs he's harmed himself, and needle punctures especially. I'm going to have you videotape it so that I have it to review later, so I can correct your technique if need be."

"You say that so clinically," Darrek chuckles bitterly. "'Inspect.' You're asking me to strip him naked, tie him down, and fondle him!"

"What are you afraid of? Enjoying it? You're allowed to enjoy it, but it's more important that Kyle feels like he's got someone he trusts in charge of him. If it turns you on, I'll take care of you when I get home. It'll give me something to look forward to."

"I don't like this," Darrek says, shaking his head from side to side, arms folded.

"I get that. Will you do it anyway? For us? For my business? For our future? For Kyle's future?"

Dread is an ice-cold, unrelenting son of a bitch squeezing like a fist around Darrek's heart. But Darrek is nothing if not obedient, especially when it comes to Gabriel's demands.

"Yes," Darrek sighs, sealing his fate.

"Good. Excellent. Now, it's a good thing if you can get Kyle to enjoy the process. If he's digging it, there's less of a chance he's done anything that we would find evidence of. The more comfortable he gets with us being in charge of him, the more likely he is to open up about why he wanted to kill himself and why he's scared of Ben. I know he loves Ben, and that Ben loves him. We want to get to the bottom of this and get them back together. That's the goal."

Agreeing with that wholeheartedly, Darrek nods with vigor and begins to ready himself for the task at hand, or at least get used to the idea.

"What you need to know about Kyle, as a submissive, is that he has two things that really push his buttons, in good and bad ways. He's got an issue with being penetrated, and he's got even more of an issue with being observed in intimate ways. Both of those things make him feel like he's powerless and out of control. Kyle likes feeling in control. All the same, he gets off in a major way on anal play and feeling exposed, but it's a fine line. If he seems about to use his safeword, or *does* use it, you back the fuck off. Understand?"

"Yes."

"And again, the goal is not to get him off. It's to make him feel like he can't hide things from us, but also that he can trust us completely."

Gabriel watches all of this sink in. Darrek is staring off at the woodworking tools hanging from the far wall.

"I'll handle things tonight. We'll take him up there now, after he showers, and do this. You will watch *everything* I do. Take notes if you think it'll help, because tomorrow you'll be on your own."

Kyle emerges from the upstairs bathroom, his stomach full of dinner, his body cleaned diligently, inside and out. The urine sample Gabriel requested has been left on the counter. An internal debate tangles his thoughts, over whether he should go to see his shrink again tomorrow, and if so, what he wants to talk about there. He's not really paying attention as he wanders into "his" room, but when he gets to the center of the room, he senses an added presence besides Gabriel. Eyes flicking up, he sees Darrek standing in the shadows, leaning against the wall with his hands in his pockets.

"What's he doing here? He's not supposed to be here."

Gabriel takes Kyle by the arm and turns him around, putting his back to Darrek, and says, "Listen, I swore to take care of you, but I can't put my life on hold. There's going to be a few nights where I won't be able to make it home in time to do this, and I trust Dare more than anyone. All he's going to do is help me make sure you're safe and healthy before tucking you in at night."

Fear, fresh and strong, is like ice water pouring through Kyle's veins, chilling him from head to toe. Gabriel doesn't know what he's doing by putting Darrek in control of him like this. Before, Kyle would have loved to be alone with Darrek and have free reign to do whatever Darrek wanted of him without someone tainting it and making it into something sinful. But now it's gone too far.

There's much more of a chance of Darrek triggering repressed memories. Kyle does not want to cause that, or to witness it. Gabriel can't possibly know the dangerous situation he's creating, and Kyle can't tell him. He can tell Gabriel no more than he can ever tell Darrek or Ben. Darrek doesn't remember and Ben will never, ever find out if it's the last thing Kyle does. But the bitch of it is that Gabriel would understand. After everything he suffered at Harry's hands, he would be able to relate perfectly. This is a battle Kyle can't fight or win once it starts. His only hope is heading it off, even though, deep down, he realizes this was always coming. It's fate.

Pleading softly, lacing hidden meaning into his words, he says, "Don't do this. I am *begging* for you not to do this. Master, please...."

"I have no choice," Gabriel says with some regret. "We refuse to leave you on your own to further harm yourself. Your only other option is Ben, and I assumed you'd rather put up with Darrek."

Ben is dangerous to everyone. Darrek is dangerous only to himself. There's no choice, really. Kyle is going to be forced to let Darrek take the risk, again, and suffer any consequences should they occur. Complicity might head off the reawakening of memories that Darrek buried long, long ago. Explanation would be the worst thing Kyle could possibly do. Submitting is the only option.

Rubbing a hand up his own arm, now covered in goosebumps, Kyle trapped, damned and scared, murmurs, "I can't do this."

"You can," Gabriel says firmly. "Right now, I'm just showing him the process. He's not going to be touching you. And I will give you a reward each time you are able to do this for me. Anything you want, within reason."

Kyle rolls his eyes upon hearing this, knowing well that he's always been unable to resist an opportunity to get something he wants—almost *anything* he wants. For a long moment, he thinks it over, or pretends to try to. Ringing through his head, louder than reasoning, is misery over the whole situation, hopelessness over the course his fate has taken, and raw pain over the utter lack of safety, security and control he has in his life. He misses Ben, but Gabriel is giving him a chance to have some of that control back, and shift things in a direction that favors him. Every decision recently has been taken out of Kyle's hands. Now, it doesn't have to be that way anymore. Kyle can choose to sacrifice himself in a new way, to his desire for Darrek, to humiliation and the whims of destiny.

But he still wants no part of it. The slithering, hissing voice sliding around his brain whispers how much better he'd feel if he could get his hands on a good, sharp knife. When he uses it to open his flesh, for good this time, he'd think of Harry, the pedophile lawyer, and of Ben carving the names of brutalized children into the lawyer's body without batting an eye, then coming home like nothing happened. Nothing at all. Then he'd imagine Ben carving up others, for no one's sake but Darrek's. It'd be a pretty dream. A sweet song to savor as his life's blood seeped out.

Kyle makes a sickened, tear-choked groan and Gabriel instantly takes his face in hand, turning it up toward him. "Hey. Hey, look at me. Whatever you're thinking about... it's done and finished."

Never. It'll never be finished. When I'm dead and burning in Hell for hurting Darrek, it'll still be my torment. It'll never go away.

The hand on his cheek feels warm, solid, and strong. A tear that falls gets brushed away. Part of Kyle wants to tell Gabriel, or maybe Darrek, about Harry. The truth of what befell Gabriel's rapist might help Kyle to shed light on the creeping dark, but then Kyle would be unloading his burden on the one person trying to keep him sane and alive, and he can't do that either. Pressing his face against Gabriel's hand, squeezing his eyes closed, he breathes out a hitching breath when Gabriel folds him into a hug. Kyle holds on to him tightly, drawing strength from the embrace.

"It's no use. I'm fucked. You should have killed me. I should've let you."

Kyle wonders, *How can I ever face Ben again? But how can I go on without him? It's never going to get better. Nothing will ever be okay again.*

"Look at me, Kyle. Get out of your damn head!"

Gabriel has him by the jaw now, and there's a buffer of space between them. His granite-colored eyes are hard as stone when they bore into Kyle.

"It's not real! You know what's real? You and me, right here, right now. I'm going to make sure you're okay, and then you can watch the game. But first, I'll help you relax. I'll give you that. But only if you convince me that you're with me right now. Are you with me?"

It's funny, when Kyle looks at Gabriel, he sees two people, vastly different on the inside, the same on the outside. He sees the betrayed little boy, hurt, lost and afraid. But he also sees his Master, who is stronger than Kyle will ever be. The dichotomy makes his head spin.

"I love you."

Gabriel sighs, softening, "I love you, too."

Kyle would love for Gabriel to help him be okay, to show him how to banish the ghosts and live only in the present, without fear of people finding out what he did when he was just a little boy, and without fear of a man that's still, terribly, a part of Darrek's life. "Relax... help me relax. Like in the park?"

"That's what you want?"

This is my blood of the covenant, which is poured out for many for the forgiveness of sins. Matthew 26:28, Kyle thinks, with heartbroken surrender.

"Yes, Sir."

I have to protect him, Kyle realizes. *Gabriel can't know about Harry, and neither he nor Darrek can know about the rest. It's up to me to deal with that part of it, because it's not fair to pass that onto them. They've been through enough, and Gabe deserves better after doing so much for me.*

Steadier, with a mission and something to look forward to, Kyle regains control. He clears his throat and nods with downcast eyes. Gabriel kisses him between his eyebrows and it fills Kyle with devotion.

"Thank you, Master."

"You're welcome. Better?"

"Much."

Chapter 13

The Inspection

It starts easy. Gabriel puts on sports talk radio for Kyle to listen to as a distraction, and snaps on a pair of purple latex gloves. Kyle, wearing only a pair of boxer shorts, lies down on the mattress secured to the tabletop, scooting up so that his head hangs off the top. Rolling a cart laden with supplies closer to his side and supporting Kyle's head with his left hand, Gabriel takes a tongue depressor from the glass jar filled with them and grabs a small but very powerful flashlight.

"Okay," Gabriel says, talking to Darrek. Usually this process happens with little talk, and only some direction to coax Kyle along. It feels strange for Kyle to have Gabriel narrate his actions. "First you want to check his head for any visible injury—the skin, scalp, hairline. You're looking for puncture wounds especially."

His fingers rake through Kyle's hair, making him shiver, as he goes carefully from his ears inward, using the light to see through the blond hair to the skin. When that's done, he turns Kyle's head this way and that, feeling lightly over the skin of his cheeks, temple, neck, jaw. It's pleasant, like a massage.

"When you're satisfied, next is the internal exam. Mouth, throat, nostrils, eyes, ears."

Kyle listens to the announcers, describing plays from the Mets versus the Marlins game from that afternoon, using all his will to block out Gabriel's voice and Darrek's presence. When Gabriel touches Kyle's jaw, he knows it's the prompt to open his mouth. He sticks out his tongue and opens wide. The wooden tongue depressor slides back over his tongue, far enough that someone without the control Kyle has over his reflexes would be gagging hard. He fights against the urge.

"Say *ahh*," Gabriel says to him. Kyle complies. The depressor slides a little farther back, pushing his tongue down as the flashlight moves closer, shining down his throat. Kyle gags, eyes tearing, throat working. "Easy, easy." He recovers with effort, because the depressor is still there. Clawing at handfuls of the mattress, Kyle uses it to steady himself. "Look for any abrasions, like from corrosive liquids or any objects he may have swallowed. Then check the insides of his cheeks, gum line, under his tongue...." The depressor slides out, gets tossed into the trash. Kyle lifts his tongue when Gabriel comes back with the flashlight. Gabriel uses a few tissues to dry Kyle's eyes, nose and mouth for him. "Good. Relax." Gabriel presses gently at the tip of his nose, using the light to look up his nostrils. "Check for any powdery residue. Kyle knows that the first sign I see anything suspicious these checks will become even more invasive, so it'll be his own damn fault if that happens."

Darrek's presence is like a heavy weight at Kyle's right side, sucking the air out of the room. Knowing he's blushing, Kyle lies still as Gabriel pulls gently at Kyle's lower eyelids. "Again, puncture wounds, irritation."

"I'm not gonna fucking shoot up in my eye," Kyle grumbles. "Sir."

"Yeah, well, I trust you as far as I can throw you, slave."

Kyle turns his head sharply to the left while Gabriel shines the light in his ear, then to the other side. "All good. Okay, slide down. Get comfy."

"Sir?" Kyle hears the strain in his voice, and blushes more.

"Yes?"

He waits until Gabriel leans down closer, then whispers, "May I have a blindfold and gag? Please? And full restraints?"

Gabriel looks displeased at the request. He thinks it over, then says, "Okay. But no restraints. It'll just make this take longer."

"Thank you, Sir." Kyle's tension eases as soon as the strip of black fabric is tied over his eyes and a small leather gag is fit between his teeth, secured around the back of his head. He bites down on it and tries to breathe normally, wishing he had the restraints, too. At least this way, he can block out the sight of Darrek lurking in the corner and bite the leather to calm himself.

He can still hear everything, though. Gabriel moves away and then comes back, his voice helping Kyle track his location. "I have a whole series of photos from every night. It's your job to take new photos of him so that we have something to compare against. These are from yesterday. It's especially helpful to have these when checking his arm. You have to look really closely at the wound to make sure it's getting better, not worse."

Kyle feels the tape pull away from his inner arm. The bandage comes off and for a few minutes, Gabriel and Darrek are looking at the area, illuminated by an overhead directional light as well as the flashlight. Kyle feels Gabriel touching him lightly, turning his arm slightly.

"If everything looks good, take a few shots and then put some of this ointment on the wound and put a new bandage on." Kyle hears the click of the camera's shutter and waits as his arm is dressed. Then the camera clicks again and again and again as Gabriel takes shots of his upper body. "Okay, now just do a careful check of his upper body, paying special attention to anywhere that it'd be easier to hide marks, like the underarm, nipples, belly button...."

Kyle bites the leather hard enough to make his jaw ache as his arms are each lifted in turn and fingers quest through his armpit hair, then slide over his arms, up and down, feeling everywhere. Then they slide over his chest, press at his nipples and work downward. He feels Gabriel prod at his belly button. He's already braced for it when he hears Gabriel say softly, "You ready?" Fingers hook under the waistband of his underwear.

He grunts an assent, but can't contain a small whimper as the last and only piece of clothing left is pulled down and off of him, leaving him naked and exposed. He's half-hard just from the scrutiny, and embarrassed by it.

"Same idea, just check his legs and feet, between the toes." Kyle's legs are each lifted, fingers and palms sliding feather-light over the skin, and that feels nice too. His toes are spread one by one. The hands slide up his thighs, positioning his feet apart so that his legs are at a forty five degree angle. "So far, so good. Now, gently do an exam of his genitals." Gabriel lifts his penis, then his scrotum. Kyle bites down on the gag, wishing again for restraints. He finds the wrist shackles on the table's sides and pulls on them, his head falling back, neck elongating as he tries not to imagine Darrek watching this. But the hands poking and touching him become suddenly too much and he jerks, bodily.

"Hey, it's fine. You're fine," Gabriel tells him. "Take a deep breath. Inhale, now." Kyle breathes in as fingers comb through his pubic hair and stretch the skin of his scrotum. "Good, and out...." He exhales sharply, shakily. The flashlight clicks on and Gabriel is steadying his penis in a hand, using the fingers to pull his opening apart slightly. "Inhale. Now." Kyle yanks hard on the wrist shackles and whimpers, but inhales. "Hold it...." It goes on forever. Kyle's lungs burn. His face is so hot, the skin tight, the blood surging under it. "Let it out."

Kyle blows it out and Gabriel lets him go. "Okay. Photograph the area and then we'll move on."

Kyle moans, his breath quickening, sweating lightly, heart racing, and they aren't even touching him. It's just the small soft click of the shutter as they photograph his naked body from the waist down. "If you see anything suspicious, make sure you get a closer shot of it for the records. Document any skin abrasions."

A moment later, it's finished.

"Sit up," Gabriel tells him, taking Kyle by the arm and guiding him upright. "Now, usually I do this on the table as well and without restraints, but our slave is going to need full restraints for this part today, and when you check him tomorrow. Understood?"

"Yes, Sir," Darrek says gruffly, his voice filling Kyle's head. It makes Kyle tense and begin getting overwhelmed by the anticipation, wanting the knife, wanting Darrek to hurt him, use him, fuck him, destroy him, just to make it stop. Just make it stop.

"Do you? It's for his comfort. You aren't doing him a favor by going without."

"I get it, Sir," Darrek says with some exasperation.

"All right then. Slave, we're taking you to the bench to your right, so just come down. That's it." Kyle slides off the table. Gabriel brings him slowly a few feet away to the padded spanking bench.

"There. You can kneel, I've got you." Kyle eases down and once his knees are planted, it's easy enough to bend at the waist and fold forward on the top half of the bench.

He grunts his thanks as Gabriel secures the latches. Both of his arms are shackled to the bench's sides. His ankles are bound to the bench's feet, kept wide apart. His back is strapped down tightly. The backs of his thighs are strapped tightly against the vertical supports connecting the bottom and top bench. Lastly, his neck is wound with a collar and that is linked snugly to the bench, with little slack.

"Is the collar really necessary?" Kyle hears Darrek ask under his breath.

"Yes. And if you start arguing with me over clear direction, then we have a problem."

Kyle starts to have trouble drawing in enough breath as the panic kicks in, full force. He can feel the heat from the directional lamp when Gabriel brings it over and shines it on his backside. A small scared noise sounds in the back of his throat and it's overloud in the room. But then Gabriel is there, caressing his back and thighs, hushing, "It's okay. You're okay. Keep taking nice, deep breaths. It'll be over fast. I promise." More softly, talking to Darrek, Gabriel says, "Come on, let's get this over with."

The squeal of the cart's wheels perks Kyle's ears and he forces himself to inhale as deeply as he can, expanding his ribs until the strap across his back constricts enough to hurt.

"Do an external exam first. Take a few shots," Gabriel is talking very quietly now, like he doesn't want Kyle to hear, or rather, doesn't want to upset him any more than he is, but he can feel Gabriel pulling his buttocks apart, spreading him open and then there's the damned click of the camera as they take a picture of him like that. For a moment it feels like he has an out-of-body experience and sees himself down below while his spirit floats in mid-air. He sees himself on the bench, naked and bound, tensed and sweating, as Gabriel and Darrek pull his ass open and photograph it. Angry that he's allowed himself to be made so helpless yet again, and that he's enjoying it on some level, he moans and jerks violently on the bench, but it doesn't jostle and he can't move much. Gabriel ignores the reaction and doesn't let go. A finger circles his opening, rubbing around it. There's a pause, and Kyle imagines him slicking lube onto his fingers, and braces himself for the next part. It's still a shock when the finger touches the center of his opening and presses inside. Crying out brokenly, he tries to clench and push Gabriel out, but the finger just goes deeper, pumping in and out as Gabriel smears lube into him.

Steady and calm, unfazed as Kyle continues to sob and whimper, Gabriel says, "Use plenty of lube. He'll be tense, so you'll need it to get the speculum in place without hurting him. You're also doing a manual exam for any injury or foreign objects. It may seem like overkill, or cruel, but if Kyle hates this part of himself, it'd be tempting to injure himself here."

The finger probes, rubbing over his inner walls, reaching deeply as it can as Gabriel searches the cavity. Kyle's dick is fully hard now, and pulses, straining into the air in front of his hips when he hears the clink of metal, knowing it's the speculum being jostled against the tray when Gabriel reaches for it. A second finger is wedged through his anus and Kyle bucks on the bench, breathing roughly, growling and whining. The fingers spread and pull at the muscle, trying to work it loose.

"You need to be able to get two fingers in before trying to get this into him."

Kyle's eyes roll up in his head. He bites on the gag and pulls at all of his restraints at once, but the fingers slide in to the hilt, impaling him, and his dick jumps.

"He's going to hurt himself," Darrek says.

"If he's tied down tightly, he'll be fine. At least we'll know what the bruises are from. That's what the photos are for. Just check where the straps were. The marks should match up."

The fingers draw out of his body, slowly, leaving him wet, throbbing and looser. Kyle imagines Darrek watching Gabriel's fingers twist and tug inside him and purrs. He wishes for the fingers just a little longer, but part of him is thrilled by the prospect of the speculum, as much as he hates the damn thing. His love/hate relationship with it is exactly why Ben always loved to threaten him with it. It's both a punishment and reward. Savoring the bondage, being trapped, unable to fight back, unable to see the men using him, Kyle knows he'll never be able to look Darrek in the eye again without flashing back to this moment, but at least one of his dirtiest fantasies is coming true.

Gabriel lubes up the speculum and Kyle makes small, kitteny mews of helpless fear as they watch his buttocks clench back up. Aligning the instrument, Gabriel says, "It'll be easier if you *try* to relax, Kyle. Now, bear down so I can get this in you."

The tapered, funnel-shaped tool is fed slowly inside all the way, as Kyle pushes like he's trying to have a bowel movement. The speculum feels about four inches long, the size of an anoscope. Kyle knows Gabriel to also have a proctoscope and rectoscope, at five and ten inches long respectively, which means that he's going easy on him intentionally. As Gabriel opens the tool, it pulls him widely apart and once Gabriel has it secured, lets go, leaving the anoscope in Kyle's rectum.

A hard shudder rips through his body, and Kyle grunts through the wash of terror and pleasure in equal measure. He's suddenly lightheaded and Gabriel must be able to tell, because he caresses up and down Kyle's leg, soothingly. "Easy. Easy, baby. I know you don't like it."

Breathing heavily through his nose, Kyle focuses on the kindness in the words and the gentleness of Gabriel's touch, knowing he's not getting off on Kyle's torment like Ben does, or that bastard did, and trying to hold on to that fact.

Gabriel tells Darrek, "Feed this into him, about five inches. It'll let you see as far as you need to."

Kyle whimpers sharply and shudders again as a light is fed into his rectum an inch at a time. He tries to listen to the voices on the radio, but it's all white noise. More pre-come weeps from his dick and when he feels the light slide a little farther into his body, almost comes spontaneously, but he fights as hard as he can to keep a lid on it. Then, the light is pulled out. The speculum closes back up and is slowly, torturously, extracted from him, leaving him feeling very loose and throbbing and overheated.

His head thrums with the pounding of blood in his ears, every nerve in his body keyed up and oversensitive. The shackles are removed, one by one, and they aren't even done yet. Gabriel pulls him to his feet and Kyle knows his erection is in full view now, though he's sure Gabriel could tell anyway that he was getting off on it all while it was happening.

Right by his ear, very softly, Gabriel asks, "You want to change your request for reward? You want the knife or you want to come? Shake your head no for the knife."

Without any idea what may be passing between Gabriel and Darrek—they seem to be communicating wordlessly, Kyle pauses, knowing his answer, but shy about giving it. Then, he nods, his face aflame.

"Good boy," Gabriel praises, obviously very pleased. He rakes short-clipped nails through Kyle's hair, scratching over his scalp and tugging lightly on the hair, making him shiver with goosebumps. "There might be hope for you, yet. Come on. On the table."

Kyle lets Gabriel help him onto the thin mattress placed on the tabletop for Kyle's comfort. His wrists are shackled with care in the padded but unbreakable leather cuffs at his sides, and already Kyle knows he made the right choice.

"Bend your legs, plant 'em. There ya go." Kyle's feet are flat on the mattress, knees bent. Gabriel presses at the insides of Kyle's knees so that his legs fall widely open. "Beautiful. Stay just like that." There's a minute or so where Kyle doesn't know what's happening. Gabriel isn't touching him or talking, but he can feel the heat in the room, like someone has suddenly cranked on the furnace to full-blast. And, weirdly, he can hear Darrek breathing.

Then something—ropes, maybe—are wound around his knees, one then the other and then they're being pulled. He imagines Gabriel wound the rope under the table and is now tying it tightly. He tries to close his knees and they don't budge.

Kyle moans.

The gag is taken from him.

"Oh fuck... oh *fuck*...." he cries, trembling.

"You were so brave. We could tell how scared you were, but you did it. And I'm proud of you for choosing this over the knife. I'm so proud of you...."

He doesn't expect it, so when something touches his anus and then there's pressure—a lot of pressure—and he begins to part around something cool and hard, Kyle's feet flex. He throws his head back and cries out as the smooth dildo, not wide but a good ten inches long, is thrust in a smooth, slow stroke into his rectum. His dick jumps, hot and hard and wet. Gabriel works the toy in and out rhythmically; going so deep with it that Kyle feels it all the way to the top of his head. The room tilts and nothing has ever been this good before—having this done to him while Darrek watches. Gabriel buries the extra long dildo and leaves it there, using his gloved hand to rub Kyle's rim as it hugs the toy. His other gloved hand, the palm and fingers slicked with lube, circles his penis, guiding it up away from his body at a ninety degree angle, Kyle tries to curl forward, and Gabriel starts to jack him, double-speed. Gasping loudly, unable to find breath, Kyle sits forward as far as he can, arms tensed and knotted up, feet flexed, legs wide as Gabriel pumps him at a brutal pace. The fingers feel hot and wet as they squeeze him and pump, sliding on his shaft. It pulls whimpers from Kyle, his hips twitching up, or trying to. Then Gabriel, oh-so-slowly, begins to pull the dildo out. It feels so good leaving his body. Even without seeing, Kyle knows that Darrek is watching it come out while Gabriel tugs fast and hard at Kyle's lube-slicked, glistening, purple-red dick.

Kyle comes with a shout, coating Gabriel's hand, splashing hot in a long arc over his own body. Semen spurts on his stomach and thighs and still the toy is pulled out, then pressed right back inside. Kyle purrs.

"Good... such a good boy for us...."

"Th-thank you, Master. Thank you," Kyle rasps, wrecked and spent, half-delirious, still tingling. He's vaguely aware of lying back down, of his knees being released from the rope after he is wiped down, his genitals cleaned with a wet washcloth, his bottom wiped free of lube.

Gabriel takes off the blindfold off of Kyle, helps him sit up, then stand. "You okay?"

"Yeah," Kyle croaks.

"Good."

They cross to the bed. Kyle lies down and is covered with a sheet.

"ESPN okay?" Gabriel is cool and composed, looking tenderly

down at Kyle.

"Yes. Thank you, Sir." Kyle smiles a little, too tired to manage more. All of the supplies have been rolled out of the room on the cart or locked up, out of Kyle's reach.

"I'll be back later to give you a drink and check on you. Call if you need me."

Nodding, overwhelmed, his body tingling and alight, Kyle barely marks Darrek's absence as he slips into light, untroubled sleep.

Chapter 14

The Demon, Awakened

Five minutes later, hands scrubbed clean, tools put away to be disinfected, Gabriel comes downstairs with a profound sigh, grateful that Kyle went from near-suicidal to vibrantly alive (and vibrantly horny) in so quick a timeframe. He hadn't planned on things going the way they did, but it gives him hope for Kyle's state of mind and capacity to heal. He had asked Darrek's permission for Kyle's reward with a glance and mouthed question, so he's headed down to have a real talk with him, expecting to find him in the kitchen having a strong drink or outside playing with Sierra to blow off steam.

So, when Gabriel is stopped mid-stride in the pitch-black darkness by Darrek's broad, imposing figure in the middle of the living room, his heart skips a beat out of pure shock.

"Dare, what're you—" Gabriel starts before Darrek swallows the words, claiming Gabriel's mouth in a hungry, probing kiss. He holds on to Gabriel by the waist, backing him up to the couch as he takes his lover's breath away, pressing down on him so that Gabriel has no choice but to yield. The backs of Gabriel's thighs touch the couch-back and then Darrek's hands are impatiently yanking Gabriel's fly down, forcing the pants down on his slim hips. Gabriel grunts, frowning, but can't break the kiss, Darrek is too greedy and ravenous.

Then he's being turned, trapped between the couch and Darrek. Darrek catches his mouth again from over Gabriel's right shoulder and bending him over, folding his larger body over Gabriel's. Two fingers wriggle determinedly into Gabriel's anus and he makes a soft sound of surprise that Darrek growls at. The fingers thrust harder, burrowing as far as they can reach, but at least they're lubed and Gabriel thinks dazedly, *where'd he get the fucking lube?*

Trying to breathe through his nose, but too startled to quite manage it, he finally manages to break away, gasping, from Darrek's kiss but then Darrek's fingers twist back out of him, and are immediately replaced by the wide, blunt head of his cock. Hands pull Gabriel open and he moans as the thickness breaches him, popping through his rim.

"D-dare?" Gabriel gasps.

Darrek growls and thrusts into him, driving the air from Gabriel's lungs, filling him up with the fattened, rock-hard column of Darrek's erection.

"Oh *god,*" Gabriel moans, grabbing behind him at Darrek for purchase as Darrek latches on to the side of Gabriel's neck, sucking hard at a spot under his jaw, making Gabriel's mouth fall open wide around his wavering cry. Then Darrek's huge, roughly-callused, carpenter's hand pushes Gabriel's underwear impatiently down in front to fondle him hard while he works to bury his flesh completely in Gabriel's smaller body. "God... *dammit!*"

A car drives past the house and its headlights briefly cast light into the room. In a mirror across from them, Gabriel catches a glimpse of Darrek's face, obscured by wild, fallen tendrils of his light hair. Dark eyes, wild and fearsome, peer from shadows cast by Darrek's furrowed, heavy brow, his lips drawn back in a snarl. The headlights pass, sending them back into darkness.

With a twitch of his hips, Darrek pulls out a few inches. His right hand rubs hard over Gabriel's balls, down then up to close in a tight unyielding glove around his dick, holding Gabriel in place by it. Darrek's left hand draws back then falls, delivering a hard, loud smack to Gabriel's left butt cheek. Gabriel flinches, clenches, yelps as Darrek ruts into him, splitting him open. He draws back, does it again, another spank, another long, hard thrust, making Gabriel gulp down air. It happens a third time, a fourth, a fifth, and Gabriel's bottom throbs. He can feel the heat of Darrek's handprint on it.

Grabbing on to the couch, heart beating wildly, Gabriel is panting and dizzy when Darrek enters him fully and then holds there. That massive, rough hand kneads the muscle of Gabriel's sore left buttock, rubbing hard over the hurt, making him swallow a whine. Darrek gives him a second to recover, using it to tug on Gabriel to get him harder, stroking the blood into action, feeling him swell and thicken.

"You told me it wasn't about *sex*," Darrek growls. "Then you fingered him open, stuffed his ass full and played with his dick until he came over your fist."

"Oh fuck me... *Dare*...."

"Gabey's been a bad, *bad* boy," Darrek rasps. He squeezes too-tight around Gabriel's cock, until he gasps and writhes, then ruts in shallow grinding digs into Gabriel's rectum. Undulating in Darrek's hold, Gabriel's head tilts to the side. Darrek bites down on his neck and swipes a thumb over the head of Gabriel's dick, then begins to wriggle the edge of the nail into his slit.

Gasping, then moaning, Gabriel feels Darrek withdraw almost completely, then snap his hips. He proceeds to fuck Gabriel as hard as he ever has, beating his bottom with his pelvis, making him take the full force of his cock driving like a piston into his body.

If he was hoping that Darrek would settle down once he came, Gabriel is wrong. Darrek unloads with a hard grunt, pumps into his captive until the last drop is spilled then manhandles Gabriel onto the couch, pulling Gabriel's dazed form down over his lap. Bracing one foot against the couch so that the knee is higher than the other, Darrek holds Gabriel down over his leg, ass-up and pulls his cheeks apart with one hand. With the forefinger of the other hand he begins flicking the tender, throbbing ring of Gabriel's sphincter.

"Take your belt off. Do it," Darrek orders, needing the belt without understanding why, just that he does. The more he feels Gabriel submit, the more Darrek lets his instincts take over, blindly. He keeps flicking with the fingernail as Gabriel, fumbling, feeds the leather belt back through the loops of his jeans until it's fully removed. It takes a long time. With shaking hands, he passes it to Darrek.

Darrek rubs Gabriel's rim, and pushes through it, corkscrewing his middle finger through the clenched muscle, up to the hilt. With the finger embedded, Darrek one-handedly folds the belt over then chokes up on it. Gabriel folds his arm over his head, holding on to the couch with the other to brace himself. Darrek whips his ass with the belt, aiming for both cheeks, one, then the other, keeping his finger buried, liking the way Gabriel clenches around him with each strike. Then he whips the backs of his thighs, leaving pink lashes in the belt's wake. After pumping his finger a few times, triggering nerves, letting Gabriel feel helpless, exposed, dirty, Darrek pulls it out. Holding Gabriel down with his left arm, he gets a good grip on the belt and whips it directly across the thickest part of Gabriel's ass, holding nothing back, drinking up his cries like the sweetest wine. The skin pinks in wide stripes. Gabriel clenches at each strike. Five times Darrek whips him, without ceasing, then rubs down over the inflamed flesh, scratching the abused skin so hard that Gabriel cries out again.

"Tell me. Admit it. Admit what you are!" Darrek snarls. The words echo in his head in someone else's voice and Darrek lets his own desire for cruelty drown them out.

"I-I... I'm a... a bad boy...." Gabriel gasps. Two fingers twist all the way up into Gabriel, and he pushes back against Darrek. Darrek holds him down, fingers him, rubbing and twisting and digging, scissoring the fingers apart. A wild, long, thunderous moan rolls from Gabriel's lungs. "I'm sorry, Daddy."

Daddy....

It's perfect. It's what Darrek wanted to hear without even knowing it. Egged on, Darrek pumps the fingers in and out of Gabriel, taking him deeply, pushing his captive's legs farther apart to open him even more. Then he feels between Gabriel's legs and fondles his balls, drawn up with fear and pleasure. He gives them a hard yank and Gabriel grunts. Rolling a palm over them, then stretching them away from Gabriel's body and keeping them stretched, Darrek keeps fingering him, feeling Gabriel begin to push against each inward thrust.

"Say please."

"Please."

"Say please, Daddy."

"Please, Daddy," Gabriel moans. Darrek lets go of Gabriel's

scrotum and grabs the belt, using it to run the leather over his balls and cock while he finger-fucks him. The belt flicks, striking lightly at the sensitive flesh. Gabriel flinches.

"You deserve this punishment," Darrek fumes, living in the echo, saying things that sound so familiar he can't help but say them aloud. They're imprinted on his brain.

"I'm sorry."

"Your pecker's hard...."

Gabriel grunts, shivering. Darrek lets go of the belt. His fingers slide out of Gabriel's ass, rubbing his rim.

"Grab your ass and pull, sweetheart. Show me where a dirty boy like you wants it."

"Oh fucking *Jesus*, Dare...." Gabriel moans. He complies. Darrek draws his knee up even farther, bending Gabriel over even more sharply, and drapes an arm over Gabriel's lower back to hold him in place.

Then that arm shifts. The hand caresses over Gabriel's sore bottom, soothing. Two fingers prod at his hole, breach him slowly and hook inside. Darrek's free hand wraps Gabriel's straining cock and begins to stroke. The movements are unhurried, and Gabriel is too unsteady to be able to thrust. Darrek is in control, completely. The fingers rub deeper. The hand tugs every few seconds at his dick and Gabriel cries out with need, the sense of helplessness so familiar it's comforting in the most terrible of ways.

"You like that, don't you?" Darrek asks, teasing.

"Yes," Gabriel grunts, twitching against Darrek's lazy, measured tugging. He comes suddenly and hard. The hand pumps him faster through the orgasm, encouraging it, and Gabriel yells roughly, "*Yes.*"

Upstairs, sleep is the furthest it's ever been from Kyle Roth. Ears pricked, he wishes he had the damn remote so he could mute the television and hear better. If he gets up and manually turns down the volume, the floor might creak and give him away, so he lies there, listening to every word, every cry, every moan and whimper.

The door to his room is wide open; the living room is right at the bottom of the steps that are directly beyond his door. Kyle knows what Darrek doesn't. Memories are coming back to the surface, but not strong enough to be recognized for what they are, and Darrek is interpreting them as fodder for role play with Gabriel—Gabriel who knows just what Daddy is capable of. Scared for Darrek, and of him, Kyle is very quiet and wide-eyed as he listens. He's hard again; his body betraying his soul.

"Darrek, don't. Don't go there. You won't be able to come back," Kyle whispers a prayer that Darrek can't hear. "You're hurting him. He might not agree, but you are. Don't do this to Gabriel. *Please.*"

But Kyle is in Hell and when you're damned, prayers go unanswered and the guilty burn.

Chapter 15
Playing the Game

"What do we say?"

Gabriel folds his arms, with a wide stance to better keep him on his feet a little longer. He really should be resting and letting his body recover, but unfortunately there are other priorities to handle first.

Arms stretched wide, pulled up by chains affixed to the ceiling's rafters, impaled on the monstrous dildo secured to an adjustable pole, Darrek is the picture of exquisite discomfort. Trembling from bound wrists down to curled toes, but unable to move so much as an inch in any direction, he's coated in sweat, his eyes barely opened but locked like a sniper's sites on Gabriel. The intensity of the stare and the churning force behind it communicates clearly that Darrek is only thinking of revenge—sweet, sweet revenge—and it makes Gabriel's skin prickle with goosebumps, but fuck, he's the one in charge here. At least for now.

It's more growl than anything as Darrek says, "I'm sorry for fucking you over the back of the couch, turning you over my knee and spanking your butthole with your belt while making you call me Daddy."

The laughter explodes from Gabriel like a shot, making him fall to his knees and curl forward. Once he starts, he can't stop, becomes hysterical, wheezing for air, laughing so hard that barely any sound actually comes out.

"Ow," Darrek groans, surprised into laughter himself, but it hurts, his body jostled by it. Gabriel had also attached metal clips with small weights to Darrek's nipples, and snapped a leather hood around the base of his genitals, where he hooked on more weights, thereby pulling him down onto the pole.

"Fuck, I hope I don't piss myself again," Gabriel wheezes between laughing fits.

"Gabe! Stop making me laugh," Darrek complains, exasperated, woozy with ache and stimulation. "It fucking hurts and my dick is gonna rip off!"

This sends Gabriel into fresh peals of laughter. Tears spring to his eyes. Crumpled on the floor as he is, he takes a moment to let it pass then composes himself with effort. A full minute after he's stopped laughing, his expression serious once more, he regains his footing and says, "Okay. Say it again. I'm cool now."

"I don't believe you. Did you have to do the nipples?! Fucking Christ!" Darrek takes a deep, cleansing breath through his nose. The massive object lodged in his rectum is a little difficult to think past, but he scrambles for the words, the apology. He's not getting out of this without it.

"Okay. I'm sorry for the rough sex, for bending you over my knee, whipping you with your own belt, torturing your butthole. Oh! While making you call me Daddy. Was that everything? Gabriel?! Goddammit! *Come on!*"

"I'm sorry," Gabriel cries, hands on his knees, bent at the waist and clutching a stitch in his side. "I think it's the word 'butthole.' Say it again."

"No! Fuck you, you heartless bitch!"

Gabriel has absolutely lost it. Darrek has never seen him like this, and quietly blames himself for pushing Gabriel so far into delirious hysterics. Laughing helplessly, crying real tears, Gabriel slowly hobbles over to a small step stool and grabs it, then brings it over to Darrek.

"No, not the stool...."

Gabriel snorts and Darrek fights against the chains holding his arms, as the laughter infects him again, dangerously contagious. "Ow," he complains, chuckling as Gabriel stands on the stool to be at eye level with him, and begins to kiss him.

It quickly gets heated, Gabriel kisses the sense out of Darrek, inhales his breath, drowns him in scorching tenderness. The weighted clips on Darrek's nipples are removed one then the other. The flesh throbs as blood rushes to the hurt and still the kiss goes on. Darrek tenses his arms to keep from rocking back on the pole inside him, gasps for air between silken brushes of Gabriel's heated lips.

"My lips hurt," Gabriel says softly, and Darrek can see how inflamed and tender they look.

"My colon hurts," he counters.

Gabriel snorts, insane mirth rising behind his bright eyes.

"*Please* don't start again," Darrek says desperately. "I'm *begging* you."

Kyle is rather surprised when Gabriel walks, admittedly more than a little bowlegged, into his room a few hours later with a bottle of water. He's never seen Gabriel drunk, but this is close to it. His lips look swollen, chapped, and glisten with some sort of lip balm. His eyes are half-lidded and his skin is flushed. The funniest thing is his rumpled hair. Kyle fights back a smirk brought mainly of relief to see that Gabriel is okay. Gratefully, Kyle takes the water when Gabriel offers it, drinking a third of the bottle before recapping it.

"What?" Gabriel croaks defensively. The unusual coarseness of his voice further amuses Kyle, since he's had a chance to *hear* why Gabriel's voice is hoarse.

"Nothing, Sir. Shouldn't you be asleep by now? You look... tired. Sir."

"Yeah, well...." He leaves it hang there.

"Um. May I ask where Darrek is?"

"Lying in the grass out back with Sierra. Takin' a little breather. He sure needs it. He's been in the garage, strung up with a fist-sized dildo on a pole lodged up his ass. Fair play and turn-around and all that jazz."

"Ohhkay. Are you all right? Sir?"

Gabriel's face is a mask—cool, composed, nothing except weary. Then it breaks into a cute, heartfelt, honest grin. He laughs suddenly, wildly, like he's been laughing for hours and has only just managed to compose himself and stop. With effort, he forces the laughter back down and runs a hand back through his dark hair, mussing it even more as he clears his throat. Then he chews a little on his swollen lower lip and says, smooth and easy, "Hell yeah, I'm motherfuckin' *fantastic.*"

Kyle heard some of the kissing, but there must have been more once Darrek carried Gabriel into the garage. He'd heard the shouted, feigned protests as Gabriel insisted Darrek put him down, and that he was perfectly capable of walking despite the recent spanking. He'd also heard Darrek's grunted defiance. It did Kyle's heart glad to overhear the banter and love between them, despite the rest of what has been going on. Gabriel and Darrek truly love each other, flaws and all, and that's an amazing thing.

"That's... good?" he teases.

"You want something to eat?"

"Nah, I'm good for now. Thank you, Sir. So, um, if I may, is Darrek going to work tomorrow?"

"Work? Kid won't even be able to bear his own *weight* tomorrow."

"Then...." Kyle leaves it hang, waiting for Gabriel to catch up, but he's too dazed to detect the logical problem at hand. "I'm going to work alone? You're okay with that?"

Gabriel rubs absentmindedly at his lower lip. It takes him a second to process what Kyle said.

"Oh, damn. Huh. Well, guess you're taking a day off too, you lucky son of a bitch."

"I can't stay home for the fuck of it. I'm the foreman, Sir. We just started the job and I've already missed time without explanation. I'll catch hell."

"And you won't catch hell if you disobey me?"

Gabriel watches with some fascination as Kyle mentally rolls his eyes, but manages to stifle the actual eye-roll. A muscle in Kyle's jaw twitches. "Your wish is my command, Master. I live to please."

"Smartass."

There's a low noise, sounded from a small distance, carried on the air currents. Kyle turns his head in the direction it came from—the backyard. It was a roar, whether of exhaustion or frustration or pain, he cannot discern. "Um. Maybe you should check on him? Oh wise and benevolent Master?"

"Keep it up, slave, and you'll be the one screaming," Gabriel warns.

"You two are a little scary. You know that, right?"

Gabriel beams proudly. It's slightly unsettling. "That's what makes us so charming!"

The next morning finds Kyle, the most mobile and rested of the bunch, making breakfast, brewing coffee and straightening up the house. Gabriel and Darrek are curled up on the couch and in bed, respectively. An air of hangover-esque guilt and shame hangs like a dense cloud around Gabriel. Kyle feels it keenly as he hands over a filled, steaming mug and sets a plate of protein-rich eggs and a bran muffin in front of him on the coffee table. It's mostly his fault, Kyle knows. His presence in the house has complicated matters between Darrek and Gabriel, and their new Kyle-centric routine has done weird things to the former balance in their relationships with one another. So it is with unspoken apology that Kyle tends to his Master. And it is with a grunt and heavy resignation to his situation that Gabriel acknowledges the food without meeting Kyle's eyes.

"I've got a plate warming in the oven for when Dare wakes up," Kyle says, keeping his voice low. Gabriel's been rubbing his temples for an hour, waiting for some ibuprofen to kick in and lessen a wicked headache. "Is there anything else you'd like, Sir?"

"No. Just...." Gabriel flicks his gaze over to the kitchen. Most of the sharp utensils have been locked away, but Kyle supposes that Gabriel's not sure he got everything, and, after all, Kyle has always been a resourceful son of a bitch. "Stay in eyesight. Don't go wandering off."

Nodding solemnly, a little too solemnly perhaps, Kyle hovers nearby. "No problem, Sir." He moves over to the armchair, sets his ass delicately upon the edge of the cushion, rethinks it, slides to the floor and turns slightly to face Gabriel. With his best obedient, attentive expression, he looks up at Gabriel.

"Fucking hell," Gabriel groans. "What is it?"

"Nothing, Sir. Enjoy your food."

"Don't fuck with me, Kyle, I know you too well. That's why this is such a beneficial arrangement between us. I can detect your bullshit like a goddamned bloodhound. Just spit it out so I can eat without you looking at me like the damn dog begging for scraps."

"She's out in the yard, by the way."

Gabriel gives Kyle an exasperated look.

"Fine. Okay. I need a favor."

"What, precisely, have you done to deserve a favor?"

"Not stuck my head in the oven?"

"Goddammit," Gabriel curses. "You must love being chained to the fucking radiator, because I don't know why you'd say that unless—"

"I want to start going back to therapy," Kyle interjects, suddenly, and with surprising confidence. "Please, Master."

This startles Gabriel out of his tirade. His mouth hangs open as he mentally steers the conversation around in a wild right turn, following along with the deceptively angelic-looking man-child kneeling before him. "Shit."

"There's a waiting room. With a flat-screen and WiFi. Comfortable chairs. It'd only be for an hour. Maybe twice a week. I'd like to go today. You're home anyway, so...."

"Do you know how complicated my schedule is already without adding twice-weekly trips to your psychiatrist's office to the chaos? No. It'll have to be Dare. I need to check in at the office later. He can take you while I do that, if he's feeling up to it. And he can take you after work on the way home on the other days, too."

Thinking of how Darrek is typically one of the main topics covered in his appointments, and imagining Darrek sitting just beyond the door while Kyle pours his heart out about him, he's left torn. But what other choice does he have?

"Great. That's great. Thank you, Sir."

Rubbing his forehead, looking sideways at Kyle, Gabriel sighs.

"Starting tomorrow," Gabriel begins, speaking slowly, the words heavy, leaden and filling Kyle with dread. "Dare will be handling your post-work safety check. Just Monday through Friday. I'll be supervising via video, and I'll check on you when I get home."

Eyes widening like Gabriel had wrapped a hand around his windpipe rather than told him something he already knew, Kyle strangles on fear. Even setting aside the gigantic elephant in the room embodying all of the things from adolescence that Kyle has been dealing with and Darrek has, thankfully, not recollected, at least consciously, the fact of the matter is that Darrek kissed him, pinned him to the truck, and got hard. And now Kyle is expected to put himself in Darrek's hands? Trust him? Let him inspect his body with the thoroughness of a proctologist? Vivid images flash in Kyle's brain as he imagines it, Darrek looming over him while he's bound and helpless, and no one there to mediate. Literally anything could happen. Demons could be loosed and Kyle would be unable to do anything about it.

A small scared sob sounds from low in Kyle's throat and Gabriel sits up straighter. "Hey, talk to me. That's an order."

"What if I enjoy it? Will I be punished?"

"That's what you're worried about? I'd rather you enjoy it than panic about it not being me. Do you trust Darrek?"

It's a simple question, really.

"He would never hurt me," Kyle replies, sounding like he's telling himself, not Gabriel.

"That's right. He's your boy. He's loved you like a brother since you were knee-high. Will you let him help me keep you safe?"

"Yes, Master."

"Kyle, look at me."

Gabriel holds his gaze, staring into his wide blue eyes.

"Say it for me," Gabriel urges.

"I trust Darrek," Kyle says in a small, lying voice. He doesn't believe it for a minute, and his stomach cramps as his bladder threatens to void itself in terror. To help convince himself of the actuality of the statement, he says it again, a little more loudly, "I trust Darrek."

"Good," he says, nodding. "He makes the rules when I'm not here. He speaks for me. Understood?"

No.

"Yes, Sir."

Please... he tortured you just last night! And you let him! You enjoyed it!

"You obey him like it's coming from me. No arguments."

NO.

Wanting to cry, wanting to die, with no way out and no one to turn to, Kyle's stomach plummets, turning to lead.

Forgive me, Father, for I have sinned.

"Yes, Sir."

Dr. Sophia O'Malley is sitting up on the edge of her seat, hands folded as she perches there, like a bird ready to take to flight at the first sign of trouble. It's not exactly helping Kyle relax to see he's disturbed his shrink already, and he hasn't even gotten to the good parts.

"So...." He stares at the closed door, with Darrek waiting behind it, down the hall, his too-tall body folded into one of those small, padded waiting room seats. Darrek is well out of range of hearing but definitely not out of range of thought. "It's like this. I've been feeling really guilty and freaking out about something that happened a while ago. People... reacted to that in a plethora of different ways, depending on personality and how much of a psychopath they were."

Sophia's eyebrows scrunch. Her mouth puckers. Kyle, feeling small in his sweatshirt, cups his hands around a glass of water and stares at the edge of the bandage on his wrist, peeking out from under his sleeve. "Now I'm in the care of Gabriel, who's been one of my Dominants since forever. He never lets me out of his or Darrek's sight. Darrek is like his second in command. And if I *do* go out of sight, they check me out afterward to make sure I'm shiny and not about to OD or something again. It's a good time. And I haven't, by the way. I'm not using. Shit's weird enough as it is without drugs making it weirder."

"Does Gabriel have any professional training, or—"

"Oh, he's a professional all right," Kyle laughs, because it's funny.

"You know what I mean."

"Of course I do. I'm not a moron. People don't always realize that, but it's true. Anyway, that's not the point. I'm good with Gabe taking care of me. I can handle him. He's pretty much just got the one speed, most of the time. He got a little weird the other night, but that was probably stress or the spanking talking. Darrek is another thing, though. He, uh," Kyle sees the water in his glass ripple as his hands quiver. He sets the glass down and pulls his sleeves down to cover his unsteady fingers.

"Things have happened. In the past. Between us. Things that people don't know about, and if they did, there'd be very serious repercussions. But when I say the past, I mean, like, *way* in the past. It's been old news for a while now. I thought it was over, you know? Nothing stays buried forever, I guess. It's gotten complicated again. He kissed me. And held me down. Um...."

"He forced himself on you?" Sophia asks.

"No, it wasn't like that. And that's not the point either."

"Then what's your *point*, Kyle?"

Humming, he thinks about that before answering. "I don't know how to get things to stop speeding up so fast. That kiss. The way he...." Heat rises from the core of Kyle's body, spreading upward and out. "All I used to care about was wanting him to want me. That was what drove everything I did! And he just didn't. I was his best friend, and he loved me, but it wasn't like that. There was that moment when we kissed for the first time after I told him, flat-out, how I felt and... he got weird, right away. I left and he kept calling me, and I *knew* that if I let him come over like he was begging to, that he'd be fucking me as soon as he was through the door, and..." He takes an unsteady breath. It feels good to get this all out. Really good. "That scared me shitless. Darrek would have been capable of that, even knowing how much it would hurt Gabriel, and I hated him for that. He's supposed to be the good guy. It wasn't his fault, it was *my* fault. I kissed him first! *I'm* the bad guy. *I'm*...."

The tears catch him by surprise. One minute he's fine, the next he's choking on a sob and Sophia is there, her arm wrapped around his back, handing him a tissue. "You aren't the bad guy," she tells him softly.

It takes a good five minutes before he is able to compose himself. When he's sure that his voice won't waver if he speaks, he says, "That's not the point either."

She sighs audibly. He laughs, and it helps.

"Okay, here it is," he starts. "He's out there, right now, my *chaperone*. Tomorrow he's taking me to work and taking me home from work. Gabriel won't be there, and Darrek will be in charge of things in Gabe's place. And I know what Darrek is capable of, more even than Gabriel does. Gabriel has *no idea*. It's not my place to say no to him, but I don't even know if I want to anymore. Maybe it's still me trying to hurt Ben. Maybe I'm just curious after all this time about what would happen if Darrek did what he wants to, without rules."

"Or maybe you're still trying to punish yourself," Sophia provides.

Kyle stares at a point in mid-air, shrinking in on himself. "It's all out of control. All of it. Every part."

"Maybe you should get away from all of them. Heal yourself and put some distance there."

The side of Kyle's mouth twists up in a semblance of a grin. "Oh, it's way too late for that. This is the way it has to be."

"No, it doesn't. You're strong, intelligent, resourceful...."

He shakes his head, stands up. "This is the game. And it's all I have left. Even if I lose, I still have to play."

As Kyle and Darrek walk out of the office complex and over to Darrek's Tundra, Ben watches them from a good distance. Sitting behind the wheel of his SUV, he runs his tongue over the points of his teeth and stares with enough heat to melt the windshield's glass. He hurts everywhere, still, from the fight. The painkillers are only helping a little. But pain is inconsequential. Kyle is all that matters.

Ben wants to punch Darrek in the mouth hard enough to shatter some teeth for putting his hand on Kyle's shoulder like he is, like Kyle is *his* property now. Or maybe better than that, Ben wants to string Darrek up and show him what real pain is, when you have someone other than soft-hearted Gabriel delivering it. The fantasy stirs something deep down in Ben, wakes a sleeping monster, but he pushes it away, for now.

Kyle is far too thin, hollow and weak. He looks scared and exhausted, and Ben knows why. Kyle doesn't know how to take care of himself anymore, and Gabriel clearly doesn't know how to do it for him either. Darrek, well... Darrek is just waiting for his chance to get a piece, isn't he? Ben has known that as long as he's known Darrek. Part of Kyle wants to sacrifice himself to the curiosity of that. Kyle would lay himself out on Darrek's altar and let Darrek have at it with teeth and knives then there'd be nothing left at all when it was done. It's Ben's job to make sure that doesn't happen, but fuck if he knows how to do it now when his presence has become toxic to Kyle's mental wellbeing.

Ben's phone rings, blaringly loud in the stillness of the vehicle. "Shit," he curses, digging it out. "Yeah?"

"Where the fuck are you, asshole?"

"Running errands," Ben tells Trace, unable to mask the bile that seeps into the words.

"You stupid shit, you're spying on him, aren't you?"

"What? No? Of course not. I'd never do something like that. It'd be an invasion of privacy."

"If you want to earn his trust back, you really think being the psycho possessive boyfriend's gonna accomplish that for you? Come on, Benny. Don't shit all over what little chance you have left."

"Hey! You don't get it, all right! He's not safe."

"Bullshit. You just want to convince yourself of that so that your obsession is justified. Get your sorry ass back here, now. You hear me? Now. Or the pain you're chewing aspirin by the handful just to manage is gonna be like the fuckin' appetizer to a spectacular feast."

Ben snarls, teeth bared, and punches the steering wheel.

"Are you a little bitch or a fuckin' man?"

"Fuck you," Ben growls, and hangs up. He shifts into drive and swings out of the parking spot, foot on the gas.

Chapter 16
Brutal Love

"This is about responsibility. Not what *you* want. It's all about taking care of someone you care about, the best way you know how."

"Absolutely."

Gabriel's expression is hard, chiseled onto his face. The dynamic at play is mind-boggling to Darrek. After everything they've been through, trusting each other with the darkest details of their lives and confessing secrets hidden in their hearts, and Darrek repeatedly, routinely, literally putting his life in Gabriel's hands, Gabriel seems not to trust him. Or maybe that doubt is just Darrek's conscience talking.

"I'll keep him safe. I promise."

"This is serious. That kid is at the end of his damn rope. Think about that. You could lose him forever." Gabriel jabs a finger at the stairs, which lead to where Kyle waits.

"I love Kyle. You know that," Darrek reminds him, adding, "Sir."

"Okay." Gabriel nods, ending the conversation. "You know how to reach me. I'll try to call in a few hours on your lunch break, but either way we'll see each other tonight. Hopefully not too late."

"Good luck at work. Don't worry about us, just do what you need to do," Darrek tells him, seeing the strain all of this is taking in Gabriel. In a way, he seems lesser than — weakened. But maybe that's just a holdover from their twisted sexual encounter the other night, from which they're both still recovering. He leans down and holds the side of Gabriel's face as he kisses him, watching him frown, feeling the urgency in him.

Gabriel pulls Darrek's hand away from his face, squeezing the fingers briefly before turning and leaving the house, satchel swung over his shoulder, keys in hand and jingling as he walks away.

This is just the first day of many. They need to establish a routine, a way to make this arrangement work so that they can each play their parts without going insane. Darrek tries to make it as easy on Kyle as he can. Tackling one thing at a time—breakfast, driving to the jobsite, going to work—it happens more smoothly than he hoped it would. Kyle is overly quiet, but functioning. Darrek hardly ever lets him out of sight. When Kyle heads to the portable toilets, Darrek follows him, checking over his shoulder constantly to make sure the guys they work with aren't noticing anything out of the ordinary.

Darrek nurses his thermos, buzzing from caffeine. He wants to do a good job, and come through for both his Master and his best friend. It seems, however, that his libido is determined to sabotage his efforts. It's easy to dismiss, at first, as psychological—wanting something just because you know you can't have it. Darrek has not forgotten the punishment he received when he betrayed Gabriel by pursuing Kyle almost two years ago. Kyle is off-limits. And it shouldn't matter anyway, because Darrek has Gabriel to satisfy him. But now that Kyle no longer has Ben to balance out the equation, and four has become three—two submissives and one Master—part of Darrek worries about the profound absence of affection that leaves in Kyle's life. Kyle needs to know he's cared about. Every time Darrek looks at his old friend, all he sees is the loneliness, the pain and the overwhelming sense that Kyle is lost, yearning for something, anything, to keep him tied to the world, to give him purpose and reason to hope.

That should be all. That's where it should end, and before, maybe it would have ended there.

Not anymore. Now, knowing what he knows, having experienced things physically the way he has experienced them, when Darrek looks at Kyle, he sees him as a submissive, someone to take control of and bend to his will. In his mind's eye, he sees Kyle's magnificent, naked body, bound and spread, ready to be manipulated and used. Kyle is small—much smaller than Darrek, shorter and slimmer even than Gabriel — and that smallness excites Darrek, how physically powerful the size difference makes him feel. The golden, all-American blond shine of Kyle's hair used to do nothing more than remind Darrek of how much women loved that, as Kyle used it as a lure to attract companions that Darrek now knows were all part of the act.

That silken blond hair triggers Darrek in different ways these days, like a constant visual reminder of how angelic Kyle can look. He's sweet and good and it makes Darrek want to soil that, to make Kyle dirty, to remind Kyle just how dirty Darrek knows he is. When he hears Kyle's voice, calling instructions to his crew, Darrek remembers the desperate sounds he made when he was penetrated and opened with the speculum, and how thick Kyle's cock swelled during examination, the lickable pink flush to his skin. Darrek salivates, nurses a raging hard-on and blue balls, suspecting that there'll be no relief until he can live out the bad thoughts stirring in his brain.

Even as he acknowledges that reaction, he knows how evil it is. It's not him. It feels apart from him somehow, and the contradiction makes him want to scream from frustration.

All day, Darrek watches out for his charge, becoming protective of him when one of the guys they work with looks too long or in a way he doesn't like. He ushers Kyle around with an arm draped companionably over Kyle's shoulders or with a hand flush to the center of Kyle's back, acting like a bodyguard in the way he intimidates everyone else out of wanting to get too close.

The whole time, for hours, Kyle says hardly a word to Darrek, but allows his presence, and every touch, every glare at the people pretending not to watch them. Darrek sees Kyle as fragile, delicate, and Kyle knows that he does, but isn't sure if it's true, or if it becomes true solely because Darrek wills it into such. The more vulnerable Darrek views him as being, the more vulnerable Kyle feels. All of the power, all of the control seeps from one into the other until Kyle knows there is no fighting back. There is only surrender.

They drive home in silence. They eat dinner outside, watching

Sierra run and play in the yard. When it's time to retire, Kyle is allowed to retreat into the bathroom and lock the door, hiding himself away in there for as long as he likes.

Moving like he's just going through the motions, suffering a deep, primal panic so intense that it leaves him feeling fuzzy-headed and numb, Kyle emerges from the bathroom and goes to lie on the table in his chambers, staring at the walls, the ceiling, anywhere but at the only other person in the room—his best friend in the world since he was in grade school.

Darrek turns on the video camera.

"Restraints?"

"Please," Kyle says through gritted teeth. Wearing only a pair of boxer shorts, he closes his eyes as Darrek fits the straps around his wrists. He wants more than that—a tight collar around his neck, a strap over his chest at the very least, but he doesn't get it. Darrek doesn't like to bind Kyle down with leather. He prefers, Kyle thinks dizzily, to do so with his own hands.

The shrillness of his fright begins to crawl like a million ants scurrying under his skin, so Kyle pleads, "May I have a blindfold?" Each word bursts like a popped balloon.

Sighing with resignation, Darrek frowns and acquiesces; slipping one over Kyle's closed eyes, leaving it held there with only a strap of elastic pulled tight around the back of his head. It helps, for a moment. The tension in Kyle's form eases marginally. But then Darrek traces the healing wounds on Kyle's chest, carved there by Gabriel's knife. Then, the tension comes right back.

"You wanted this?" Darrek asks, clearly incredulous.

"Yes," Kyle spits. "It made me feel better, Sir."

"You don't have to call me Sir."

"Then what should I call you?" Kyle dares. "You think I would prefer to use your name when you're doing this to me?"

Since Darrek has no comeback for that, he quietly checks Kyle's upper body for visible injury. It doesn't take long. Kyle's ankles need to be secured for his own comfort, but in order to do that they need to cross another line. After brief hesitation, Darrek curls his fingertips under the elastic waistband of Kyle's boxers and slides them down, exposing his genitals, guiding the underwear down his legs and off, setting them on the metal tray laden with supplies at his side. Kyle makes a soft, strangled moan, the muscles in his arms bunching as he pulls on the leather cuffs for comfort. Quickly, Darrek closes Kyle's ankles up in their cuffs, pulling the straps tight, checking the snugness of the buckles.

They're being recorded by the camera. Gabriel will be judging Darrek on his technique and treatment of their captive later, so Darrek makes swift work of the exam. As Kyle fights against the restraints, muscles corded from his neck to his calves, his skin heats up with blood raised to the surface, coloring Kyle's face as well, causing his corn silk hair to shine that much more brightly. Darrek's fingers move over him—his arms, chest, legs, and feet. All the while, Kyle is painfully erect. When Darrek begins gently manipulating Kyle's genitals, Kyle loses control completely. Grunting, sweating, he pulls so hard at his legs, trying to bend them at the knees but prevented from doing so by the ankle cuffs, his feet begin to turn blue.

"Hey," Darrek admonishes. "Relax. I'm not going to hurt you. You hear me?"

"Yeah," Kyle croaks.

Swiftly, without warning, Darrek pulls off the blindfold. "Get out of your head. Look at me. Come on, look. It's just me. You know me better than anyone."

"Oh, you know that's not true," Kyle mocks, but obeys, looking up desperately into Darrek's eyes. His temporary Master's hands are off the table, not touching him at all. Hands balled into fists, Kyle waits for it to finish. "Just get it over with already."

"This isn't supposed to be a punishment. Think of it as a massage. No pain, just me taking care of you. That's all I want. I swear it."

"It's different for me than it is for you. I have different triggers. I can't just turn them off."

"Part of you must like this, or else you wouldn't be here. You wouldn't have given yourself to Ben and Gabe all these years. Try to enjoy it like you do with them. I'm gonna touch you again, okay?"

Kyle wants to laugh in his face, but then Darrek holds Kyle's gaze as he folds his big hand around the soft flesh of Kyle's sac. Rubbing a thumb gently over it, rolling his testicles in his fingers as he checks for injury, he can feel Kyle's response, the twist of his body, the surge in defiant energy. Kyle's eyebrows tilt, beseeching wordlessly. Darrek's hand shifts and strokes once up the stiff column of Kyle's penis. The pad of his thumb sweeps over the head, through warm, slick pre-come.

"Dare," Kyle begs, but it sounds like 'don't'. Darrek pumps him a few times, and Kyle shivers with something besides horror. His flesh jumps inside Darrek's grip. Looking down at Kyle's lap, Darrek does his cursory visual inspection, sweeping the flat of his hand up the underside of Kyle's dick.

"Better?" he asks. Kyle's nostrils flare as he inhales in shallow gasps, because Darrek is still fondling him.

Not wanting to answer, but helpless not to when his training is so ingrained, Kyle rasps, "Yes, Sir."

Kyle sees Darrek's focus sharpen. Because they do know each other so well, Kyle suspects that Darrek senses the truth in his answer. Darrek is more likely to get truth from Kyle when he's submitting like this, and now he knows it, and that's a dangerous thing. Instinctively, Darrek begins to act on this opportunity. "Did you want to hurt yourself at all today?"

His expression twisting with anguish as he fights not to answer, then does, Kyle gasps, "Yes, Sir." Darrek guides Kyle's dick perpendicular to his body, checking for marks, then releases him, the flesh springing back, snug to his pelvis, and combs his fingers through his pubic hair. His callused fingertips graze over skin; circle the base of Kyle's shaft, playing with it.

"Did you?"

"No, Sir," Kyle says a little breathlessly, moving restlessly on the table, but not fighting like he was before. Now it's different. Darrek strokes down Kyle's thighs, up the insides. Kyle makes a sharp inhale when the side of Darrek's hand drags against Kyle's testicles.

It's decadent in that the intimate, gentle touch is something at once forbidden and necessary. The more Darrek touches, the easier it seems to get for him to do it... and the more he wants. Or maybe, Kyle thinks, I'm just projecting. Maybe it really all is just in my head.

"Good. I'm glad."

The camera beeps. Darrek straightens and glances back at the device, mounted to the wall. "Shit, that's probably the memory card. I forgot to check it before we started. I'll be right back."

Darrek strides from the room, looking for the extra memory cards. He comes back with a fresh one and places it into the camera, setting the full card aside.

"Okay, I need to flip you over now. How do you want to do this? Should I take you to the bench or can we try to do it without? I'd really rather do it without, but it's your call."

Kyle looks at him, then quickly away, up at the ceiling, breathing rapidly, sweating lightly. "It might be less scary if I can see you. For the internal exam."

Kyle's voice is hoarse and he struggles to get the words out, his eyes remaining half-lidded and sleepy. He feels so small on the table—built to accommodate Darrek's much larger size. It makes Kyle feel as small as a child. When he glances up at Darrek's eyes, he sees the way Darrek is looking at him. Darrek is getting hard and is going to get to violate Kyle in mere moments. His head spins. The bad/good tension in the air makes it difficult to draw breath.

"Okay," Darrek nods. "We do this our own way then."

He unfastens the ankle cuffs and finds some straps. Guiding Kyle's legs up, leaving him on his back and folding his legs up toward his chest, Darrek opens him up without disturbing Kyle's view of what's going on. Darrek ties the straps to the underside of the table, brings them up and over, beside either side of Kyle's head. He uses them to keep Kyle's legs in place by winding them around his knees, making sure there's no slack to allow movement. Kyle isn't surprised at all that Darrek knows what he's doing; this isn't the first time Darrek has tied someone down.

Kyle tries to regulate his breathing. The thought had occurred to him that if he was bound to the bench, like Gabriel has done before, it would put him in prime position for Darrek to take advantage of what he might perceive as a ripe opportunity and decide maybe the best way to calm Kyle down would be a nice slow reaming of his ass, since it would be so perfectly presented anyway. That's why Kyle chose to ask to keep Darrek in view. At least this way, flat on the table, it would be less likely for Darrek to let it go that far without full-on climbing on and mounting him on the tabletop. Kyle plays the odds and hopes for the best, even as he marvels that *this* is somehow his best option. Vaguely, he tries to figure out, once more, probably futilely, how in the world he got here, and whose fault it is that he has. He can't work it out anymore, but maybe it's better that way.

Unfortunately, he's left on his back, legs in the air, unable to move much at all. The straps make a V that comes to a point behind his head. He can't press down but can lift his hips if he wants, though it strains the muscles in his back to do so. On his right side, Kyle sees Darrek working to gather supplies on the tray. He ties his hair back and pulls on a pair of latex gloves, the speculum shining and ready along with the lube. Kyle's heart begins to beat wildly in his chest.

In a low murmur, Kyle begins to talk to himself, just to get a handle on the terror. He needs to do something to fill the space between old, lurking monsters and new threats. Really, it's just the panic talking. Kyle's sense has fled.

"I hate this. God, I hate this. How the fuck did I get here? Why? Why is this...? Why does this happen? It's my fault. It has to be my fault. I deserve it. I need it. It has to be... be this way. No options. No way out. Cover... cover it all and build on top of it. No one will know. Not even you. Not...."

But then Darrek is there, leaning down over him, looking immensely concerned and attentive, even if his pupils are blown huge and black, his strong jaw set with determination. He caresses the side of Kyle's face with a latex-sheathed hand, the smell of it tickling Kyle's nose. "Hey," he hushes. Kyle turns his face into the touch automatically, needing comfort of any kind.

"They used to dose me like this, you know," Kyle admits a little dazedly when Darrek drags a thumb through the hollow of his cheek. "For the videos. Gabe and Ben. He didn't tell you that part the other day. Coincidentally left it out. But I know. I remember. Always have. It was part of the whole 'gay for pay' act. They'd get a tight shot of Gabe pushing a pill inside me to get me a little stoned and make it easier for them to butt-fuck me with toys. I was always so tense. Scared. Scared for," he laughs, bitterly. "For no reason. What's there to be scared of, right, Dare? It's just sex. I guess Gabe thinks that maybe I'd try to keep getting stoned like that to calm my nerves."

"Did you ever do that on your own?"

"Yeah," Kyle sighs, catching movement out of the corner of his eye, seeing Darrek shift his stance, but Darrek holds his gaze right where it is, not letting him sit up to look at what's going on. That's an instinctive reaction, too. Protect Kyle. Shield Kyle. He's seen it all before. For years it's been like this. "They told me the drugs get absorbed faster into your system that way, so...." His voice breaks on a sharp whimper as a finger enters him. He throws his head back and sucks in a harsh breath, his mouth working around an unvoiced cry. His hands thump against the table, beating it. Then he lifts his head and smacks that against the table as well. The thick, lubed finger buried deeply inside him pulls slowly — very slowly — back out only to twist and push back in, starting a rhythm.

"I want you to enjoy this, Kyle," Darrek says to him, his voice a husky rumble of sound, a storm filled with violence and destruction. The finger plucks free, rubs firmly over his opening, spreading lubricant, awakening the nerves, drawing blood there to engorge the tissues. "I know what it's like for someone I care about to be scared of giving this. I've had two years of practice at making it feel too good for you to care if you're scared or not, at knowing that I need to remind you how much I love you and that it's okay to want this. It's okay... It's okay to like it. You hear me? I want you to like it."

Getting more lube onto his fingers, Darrek presses both his index and middle fingers through the tight ring of Kyle's sphincter, coaxing the muscles loose so that he'll be able to get the speculum inside without pain. He rubs deeply into Kyle's rectum, then scissors the fingers apart. Kyle chokes off a little cry, tears roll down the sides of his face. He pulls his hips up as Darrek's fingers tug out. Darrek holds Kyle's head down to the table so that he doesn't try to smack it again. As much as Kyle wants to slip away, Darrek keeps him right there.

Fighting through the fog of his lust, his balls aching with mind-numbing need, Darrek tries to stay rational.

"This is gonna happen either way, so try to relax and let yourself feel how good it is." The words come easily to Darrek, along with a faint sense of déjà vu that he writes off as products of loving Gabriel, a trauma victim, scared to be vulnerable. He thrusts deep, driving his fingers into Kyle's body, feeling him clench and hug around them, so tight, silky soft and hot, all Darrek wants in that moment is for it to be his tongue instead of his hand. The filthy inappropriateness of that desire makes him salivate.

In a whisper, Darrek hears himself confess, "Wanna taste you here. Right here. Would you let me?" He tugs out, pushes in, over and over, as Kyle rocks against him, urging him on.

"Yeah. Yes, Master...." Kyle purrs, his eyes unfocused and glassy. His back bows slightly on the next inward thrust, his cock jumping at the stimulation. Darrek sees pre-come weep from the slit and wants to taste that too.

"Look at me, Kyle. I want you to know it's me doing this. Not Gabe, not Ben. Me."

Kyle wrenches his gaze over to Darrek. The saddest little hint of a smile curls his lips up on one side. "I know it's you, Dare."

Only slivers of blue show before Kyle's eyelids flutter closed. Darrek pushes into Kyle and watches his lips part and go soft in beautiful anguish, his scarred chest rising and falling with each gulped breath. The question sits on his quivering lips, in the damp shine of his eyes, so lost and hurt.

"I want you to enjoy this," Darrek says again. "No more fear, no more secrets...."

Kyle sobs softly.

Darrek frees his fingers, watching Kyle's sphincter, flushed pink, clench shut once it's no longer stuffed full. He takes the speculum, already lubed, from the tray and begins to slide it inside. Kyle gasps sharply, and whines like it hurts, so Darrek closes Kyle's erection in a tight fist and pumps him as he inserts the metal instrument, then, once it's seated, as he opens it wide. Kyle's hips thrust desperately into the air. Darrek slides three fingers into him, his opening stretched wide with the device in place, leaving him unable to do anything but allow the violation. Kyle feels Darrek's fingers exploring his inner walls, playing in his ass, filling him up so full he releases a long, broken moan. Jacking him even faster, squeezing up over the slickly wet bulbous head of his cock, Darrek feels Kyle push into the touch and writhe on the end of his hand. When Kyle's eyes roll up, Darrek growls his name. With no choice but to obey, Kyle turns his face to Darrek, as another tear slides down his cheek. Darrek breathes against Kyle's skin as he thrums, twitches, whimpers and ejaculates over Darrek's hand, the milky fluid pulsing from him.

For a long while, until Kyle's racing heartbeat slows and returns to normal, they don't move or speak. Kyle's face loses all emotion, except, maybe, a futile breed of lament. All there is between them is Darrek's breath coming as rhythmically against Kyle's cheek as he's just done in Darrek's grasp. Eventually, Darrek's lips close in a soft kiss to the side of Kyle's face. He hisses with what sounds like regret, "Kyle...."

Two more tears slide down Kyle's face, leaving invisible trails. They mark his silent, heartbroken defeat. He tried his best, but he has lost, and Darrek has lost, too. They've lost everything.

Chapter 17

The Solace of the Forsaken

"We should do a second take," Kyle says almost robotically. "Go and erase the memory card. He'll punish both of us if he sees that."

Slowly Darrek becomes fully aware of where his hands are, and lets go of Kyle's cock, pulls his fingers out of Kyle's ass. "Let me make you comfortable first...."

"It doesn't matter."

"It *does* matter," Darrek snaps.

Kyle bites down on his tongue, hard enough to hurt. "Yes, Sir."

Darrek removes the speculum, even though it's going to have to go right back in anyway, and unties Kyle's legs. He even unfastens the cuffs on his wrists. Then Darrek goes to get a warm washcloth and carefully, methodically, tenderly, cleans him. The tenderness hurts the most. When that is done, Darrek visibly deflates a little and wraps Kyle in an embrace that he does not yield or submit to, but remains stiff and guarded.

"I don't want you to be punished. You didn't do anything wrong. But I agree we should do another take if you're okay with that."

Numbly, watching Darrek's face for any sign of recognition, certain that there will be some, frowning as he tries to find it, Kyle makes note of the fact that Darrek didn't admit to doing wrong himself. He skipped right over that part entirely.

"I'm fine, Sir."

"*Stop*," Darrek starts, angry. Biting off the word, chest puffed up like a bull, he continues in a barely controlled fury, "calling me Sir."

"Yes, Sir." He's looking directly at Darrek now. All fear is gone.

All shyness with it. Kyle is empty, a void without affect.

"That's how you want to play it, huh? Fine."

Wordlessly, Kyle dares Darrek to snap and hit him, hurt him, and badly. Darrek goes to the camera, presses a few buttons. There's a low whirring and a few beeps and then it's done. Returning to the table, Darrek plants his hands on his hips, looming hugely over Kyle who sits on the edge of the table. "We won't mention it to Gabe."

"Mention what, Sir? Nothing happened. You did your exam to my front and now I'll flip over so you can finish."

Snarling like a dog, Darrek gets even angrier, if that's even possible. All the while Kyle looks impassively up at him, inviting harm. Which, of course, only adds to Darrek's fury.

"I'm taking it as a sign of your progress that you're managing to be such a complete pain in my ass."

"Sorry," Kyle says with all innocence. "Pain in whose ass, Sir?"

And then, for the briefest moment, fear does flicker in Kyle's cool blue eyes as Darrek briskly spins on a heel and stalks quickly from the room. But Kyle surmises a minute later that Darrek walked away just to clear his head and get a handle on his temper. He returns composed.

"You ready?"

"Yes, Sir," Kyle says dutifully. He turns to get on his hands and knees on the table. "If it's all the same to you, Sir, I don't think I'll need the restraints."

"What the fuck are you doing?"

"Cooperating. That's the goal, right? To get this done as quickly and painlessly as possible?"

"Are you mad at me," Darrek demands in a growl, "Or upset or what?"

With an unreadable expression, but an air of wisdom and calm, bittersweet surrender, accepting his fate, to do battle with it rather than cower in the face of it, Kyle says, "What would I be upset about? Nothing happened, Sir. And, you know, this isn't the first time something has happened to me that hasn't happened to me. *Sir*. I know how to keep my fucking mouth shut. My Masters have taught me well."

Darrek's reaction is slow-building, but it does catch Kyle by surprise. He flinches violently away when Darrek suddenly moves to embrace him. "Don't," Kyle warns. "Don't you even fucking *think* about it."

In a powerful way, Kyle misses Ben—really misses him. He misses Ben so keenly that the emotion grows denser and denser in his heart until it's a dead weight in his chest. Ben understands how intimacy fucks with Kyle's head. He understands it perfectly, like he wrote the rules himself, even if he doesn't know the whys or the whens or the hows. And for all of the ways that Ben has hurt Kyle, mentally, physically, emotionally, he never hurt him like this. Ben would know how to make Kyle feel better, feel *safe*. He could save Kyle from this, this endless cycle of torture and humiliation, and take away the fear, take away everything and leave nothing but the knowledge that nothing and no one but Ben will ever hurt Kyle again, as long as he lives. And that's all Kyle wants.

The next hour or so passes without trouble or much notice on Kyle's part. He barely feels it when Darrek inspects him, inside and out, and recedes into his head so completely that even if Darrek decided to fuck him bareback in the middle of it all, he probably wouldn't even detect it. They get through it, they record it, then, when Kyle finally becomes even slightly aware of his surroundings, he discovers that he is lying in bed, TV on, blanket covering him, and Darrek is holding out a drink for Kyle before he's left alone to rest.

Kyle takes it, drinks his fill, and says, "Thanks Dare," without inflection or eye contact. "You're a swell friend."

"So you're just going to hate me now?" Darrek says with audible hurt.

"Hate you for what? Nothing happened."

It was one step too far, Kyle realizes too late. He should have kept his damn mouth shut, but he'll never learn when it comes to that. It's just how he works.

Darrek is there in a flash, bearing down on Kyle. He wraps a hand around Kyle's throat, rasps in his face, with all of the passion of more than a decade of love and devotion of all different kinds, "Don't even try to pretend that you didn't enjoy it! You got off right in my hand and rode my motherfucking fingers like they were the best cock you've ever had so don't play your pathetic fucking mind games with me when I know you well enough to see what's behind them! You're not brave! You're not as clever as you think you are! You're a scared little boy and I've *had you* now. And I know just how to play it *next time* to give you what you've got coming to you."

Kyle chokes on a sob, it fills his chest and gets caught behind the hand Darrek has wrapping his windpipe. Shuddering, he squeezes his eyes shut, gives up and waits for more hurt. There's always more. He's learned that well. But Darrek leaves, and Kyle falls apart.

An hour slips by. Kyle's tears dry on his cheeks. Darrek has left the house entirely. The door slammed shut a long time ago, leaving Kyle all alone. He can't even bring himself to care that Darrek is upset or wonder what might be going on in Darrek's head. He finds himself staring at the padded wheel with its leather straps, affixed to the far wall. At his own house, they have one just like it in the garage, and Kyle remembers back to the last time he and Ben used it.

It was a few months ago, and that particular session lasted barely a half hour. First, Ben strapped Kyle in tightly, arms and legs stretched in an exaggerated X shape, his back to the wheel's leather padding. With a spin of the wheel, Kyle was turned upside down. All of the blood rushed to his head, making it feel too-full and ready to pop, but then Ben, wearing a leather glove, stroked Kyle until he had a massive erection, drawing blood back upward to do the job. It was hot. Kyle enjoyed it. When he started to get a little too red in the face, Ben turned him right-side-up again, but immediately had his tray of toys at the ready to get to work on Kyle before the dizziness went away. With the room spinning and the beginnings of a brutal headache starting, Kyle focused all of his efforts on looking at what Ben picked up from the collection of toys and tools.

It was a knife.

"No. *No.*" The terror was so profound, it came out more breath than sound, as his lungs refused to work and he began to hyperventilate. Kyle was certain that Ben wouldn't even bother carving Darrek's name in his skin; he'd just slit Kyle's throat from ear to ear and be done with it. Damaged goods. Worthless trash. Expendable.

"I promise to be gentle, kitty," Ben soothed. "Just a little scratch...."

"No!" he shouted, roughly. All Kyle could think of was that man, Gabriel's *step-father* for fuck's sake, being carved up like a Thanksgiving turkey by Trace, Ben and Micah, with a knife very similar to the one currently in Ben's hand. It glinted, catching the sunlight, and Kyle imagined what that man must have felt in those moments, not understanding the why or who, but only that the three strangers meant him harm, possibly even murder. The man Kyle loves was a *murderer*. Somehow it didn't matter that the man they intended to maim or kill was a kiddie rapist and pederast, only that he was a family member of the man Ben loved like a brother and Ben was capable of such a thing. Ben cast his judgment. Kyle, in that moment, guilty of unconfessed crimes of passion and still waiting for his sentence, wanted nothing to do with that knife or the man holding it. "Don't touch me. *Don't touch me!* Get away. *Get away*, Ben! Varese! VARESE! Get away from me, you sick fuck!"

The memory of his own voice rings in Kyle's ears, and the regret is there, thick and strong. But there is no taking it back, and maybe he shouldn't want to. Maybe it was good for Ben to know how his actions had changed how Kyle saw him. Another piece of Kyle's soul rots away, leaving what remains smaller and poorer, and his misery only grows.

When Gabriel gets home from work, it's very late. The first thing he does is collect the videos from Kyle's room (Kyle doesn't so much as blink when Gabriel appears. His eyes are glazed over) and complete the home drug test with the sample of his urine left in the bathroom. Fast forwarding through the footage in parts, Gabriel looks for certain particular things, and when he sees something that raises a red flag, he stops and reviews that segment more closely. After he's gone through the whole thing, he fixates on one aspect — the moments just before the first tape ends, and the second one begins — studying them over and over and over again.

Then he goes to where Kyle awaits. The tear tracks are thin crusted films on his cheeks and under his eyes and nose. Kyle stares out, unseeing, at a spot in mid-air, and doesn't flinch or react at all when Gabriel lifts the edge of his blanket and, with a hand, weighs his testicles. As he does this, he keeps his gaze locked to Kyle's face, and sees what moves behind his eyes, understands it as clearly as if it was a shriek.

With a washcloth, Gabriel cleans Kyle's face and pats it dry. Leaning over him, Gabriel presses a single kiss to his forehead and tries to caress the worry lines away that have formed in his brow. "I can make this better," he offers quietly. "I can bleed it out."

"*Please*," Kyle begs, his voice catching, oozing desperation. "Gabe, please...."

The surge of emotion surprises Gabriel. He nuzzles against the side of Kyle's face, waiting for it to pass as a few of Gabriel's tears dampen Kyle's so recently dried skin.

"I am *so sorry*," Kyle whispers. "For *everything*." His voice is hoarse after hours of crying, scraped raw.

Gabriel moves with the swiftness of an old pro, setting a large, shallow basin on the floor beside where Kyle lays, sterilizing the blade. With that done, he grips Kyle's wrist tight enough that he feels the bones grind. He slices once, and again, shallowly in horizontal stripes, seeing the pain reflected in Kyle's face, his sharp inhales through gritted teeth. Kyle pulls violently at the arm, but Gabriel has it, and holds it in place, watching the blood seep from the wounds and drip in crimson trickles slowly down Kyle's hand, over his fingers to drip into the basin below.

Kyle releases a helpless, wild cry and convulses slightly. Gabriel folds his own body over Kyle's, transferring warmth and strength. "That's it, baby. Let it out. Let it all out. It's okay."

Mouth opening wide as he tries to find the air, Kyle fights as hard as he can, and when he feels the strength of Gabriel's grip and the reality of his vulnerability, Kyle slowly begins to relax again. To help him along, and give him more that is concrete to battle rather than the demons in his head, which he can't fight, Gabriel opens the rubbing alcohol and pours some over the slices he's made in Kyle's forearm. The burning makes Kyle scream until there's no air at all in him. Silent tears slip from his eyes and softly he hiccups. Gabriel presses the sides of their faces together and holds him until it passes, whispering tenderly to him all the while.

When it is done, Gabriel tends to the wounds, bandaging them cleanly. Kyle is paler, but more present, and the unsettling death wish in his eyes is gone, for now. Pulling up a chair, Gabriel holds Kyle's hand, his thumb dragging soft arcs along Kyle's skin.

Kyle begins to speak, unbidden, unafraid. "He fingered me until I came," he tells Gabriel. "He said he wanted me to enjoy it instead of being so scared... wanted to help me get past it like you did. Don't be mad at him. He was only trying to be a good friend and a good Dom. Erasing the tape was my idea. I told him you'd punish me if you knew the truth."

Gabriel doesn't say anything at all, only presses his lips against Kyle's shoulder and drags those small soothing, arcing strokes over his skin.

"I can handle Darrek, Sir," he assures Gabriel. "He knows he crossed the line."

"You need to keep being honest with me."

"Yes, Sir. I love you, Master."

Gabriel, frowning, kisses the corner of Kyle's mouth, caresses his cheek. He takes a small white pill from the tray nearby and slips it between Kyle's lips, offers the cup of water and straw to help him wash it down. "Get some rest. That'll knock you out for the night."

Gabriel covers Kyle with the blanket. When he turns off the light and exits the room, Kyle is already asleep.

There is no sign of Darrek or Sierra in the house, and the first place Gabriel checks is where he finds them both. They are in the garage. Darrek is at his workbench, sanding down the edges of a miniature chest. He's wearing headphones and the music must be turned up loud, because he doesn't hear Gabriel open the door. Sierra is curled up under the workbench at Darrek's feet but out of his line of sight, because he doesn't see when she lifts her head and gives Gabriel the briefest glance before settling back down with her head on her paws. Gabriel watches Darrek from the shadows for a while, the flex of his back and arm muscles, the sweat on his skin, the focus of his efforts and concentration, before retreating and going back to the house.

Roughly twenty minutes after Gabriel is washed up and ready for bed, he is lying in the darkness, under the covers, listening to the crickets chirp outside and the wind blowing through the trees. As tired as he is, sleep won't seem to come. The restless workings of his mind spin and spin and spin. Finally, Darrek comes to bed. He's naked. Even in the pitch blackness, with only some starlight to highlight the span of his broad, bare shoulders, slick with perspiration, Gabriel can read him well enough. The energy, the *need* bakes from him, a human oven. His eyes are black onyx, cold and hard and beautiful. Pale light shines dully in his long hair, which hangs in his face, further obscuring his expression.

Darrek slips into bed, under the sheet and up to Gabriel's side. With the backs of his fingers he caresses the side of Gabriel's face, trying to wake him if he's asleep. For a long moment, Gabriel hesitates, thinking of what Darrek has done to Kyle, trying to analyze the sharp edge of Darrek's keyed up energy. But when Darrek presses his face to the junction of Gabriel's neck and shoulder, breathing hot and harsh, Gabriel can feel his pain as well as confusion so strong Darrek can't see past it. Darrek needs him. He needs comfort and tenderness to get him through, and Gabriel can give him that much.

"Okay," Gabriel murmurs. "Okay, come on."

Darrek pulls impatiently at Gabriel's cotton sleep pants, drawing them off of him and throwing them aside. Then Darrek is on top of him, straddling his hips and sucking on two fingers. Darrek strokes Gabriel to get him hard while simultaneously twisting the saliva-coated fingers into his own body, his arm reached down between his legs as his thighs clench and quiver.

Then, whining softly, Darrek is pressing himself down onto Gabriel, impaling his large, muscle-bound body on his Master's cock. Biting back a low moan, Gabriel reaches up to Darrek's face, wanting to soothe away some of the frown lines turning down his mouth and painting anguish over his features. Darrek won't look at him. His head stays bowed as he starts to move, rearing up and pressing back down in shallow movements, setting the pace. His breath comes unevenly as he holds it until he can't, trying not to get upset, or at least to show it. Gabriel succumbs to the pleasure Darrek gives him. It feels like an apology, a plea, but as Darrek pulls him steadily towards orgasm, moving faster when Gabriel grabs his hip and urges him on, meeting Darrek's downward thrust with an upward flex of his hips, Gabriel knows it's as much as Darrek can give him. There are no words or explanations. Only this. Darrek gives himself because it's all he has.

Gabriel caresses, fondles the chiseled, defined beautiful muscle along Darrek's arms and shoulders, his chest and sides. When he grips Darrek's right nipple between his fingers and twists, Darrek exhales sharply and a dribble of fluid weeps from his thick, dark shaft, jutting up between their bodies.

My present, Gabriel thinks. *My anniversary present*. Thick muscle, like iron, bears down on him. Hard and guarded on the outside, soft, hot and vulnerable on the inside, Gabriel can feel his lover's torment. As strong as he is, and as physically powerful, it's not the sort of strength Darrek truly seeks or needs to find his peace. That's the type of strength that can only be found within and it has slipped from Darrek's grasp. He can put on a good show of having it together, but he doesn't. He's as lost as he's ever been.

So, he rides Gabriel, taking him in deeply, swallowing up his flesh and giving the gift of pleasure to the only person who is capable of saving him. Rubbing hard down the front of Darrek's body, Gabriel opens his hand and wraps it around Darrek's shaft. Pivoting his wrist, Gabriel tugs sharply on him as he simultaneously grabs Darrek behind the neck and draws him down. "C'mere."

"Don't," Darrek asks, as Gabriel starts to bring him off. His hand slips and slides in the warm pre-come on the silky, steely column in his grasp. Even as he pushes into Gabriel's hand instinctively, Darrek's eyes flash from under his curtain of hair.

"Shh." Gabriel gazes up at him, bringing Darrek closer, their chests almost touching as Gabriel plants his feet and snaps his hips, driving the breath from Darrek as he plunges his cock into him to the hilt.

"More," Darrek begs roughly. "Please."

Keeping hold of Darrek by the back of the neck, Gabriel pumps him and fucks him with abandon, using what little strength he has left after such as long day, giving it to Darrek since Darrek has given so much to him in turn.

It goes on and on. Gabriel orgasms with a groan through gritted teeth but keeps moving, fucking up into Darrek as he sees Darrek try not to come. But Gabriel knows just how to play him and with a curse, Darrek finally spurts, his mouth falling open as he gasps for air. He rocks back on Gabriel as he shivers with the aftershocks.

Palming the side of Darrek's ass, kneading the thick, rounded muscle, Gabriel whispers, "Enough. Sleep with me."

Darrek sits back, possessing Gabriel fully, clenching around him, and staring down with haunted eyes.

"Enough," Gabriel repeats, because he can see the fight is still there. It's not enough. But it has to be, at least for now, because Gabriel doesn't know what else to do.

Darrek pulls off of Gabriel and lies down beside him. He turns them so that Gabriel is held tightly in his arms, both of them radiating heat and laying on their right sides, Darrek's over-large body fitted around Gabriel's smaller one. They both fall quickly asleep without bothering to clean up or even pull the sheet back over them.

Chapter 18
Surrender

Morning arrives, bright, stark and blinding. Every sin is laid bare. Darrek wakes to find Gabriel already gone. There's a note saying that, since he'd decided that Darrek and Kyle both needed to rest, Gabriel let them sleep but that he and Darrek would talk privately later that night. The note implicitly states, also, that Sam is on her way over to stay with Kyle for the day, and that Darrek isn't to go anywhere near Kyle without Gabriel present.

The turmoil in Darrek's heart and mind cause him to be both glad and upset about this. He's been granted a reprieve from having to try to explain, but that also means another long day of feeling rattled, ashamed, and worried. When Darrek is alone with Gabriel, things are better, clearer. But when Darrek is alone with Kyle, or with Kyle but he has Gabriel telling him what to do to Kyle for Kyle's own good, strange feelings rise to the surface in Darrek, fast. Instincts that Darrek doesn't understand, or want, barrage his system. In those moments, Kyle doesn't feel like his friend, he feels like something of Darrek's to take and defile at leisure.

Even before Darrek can get out of bed to shower the dried semen from his stomach and thighs, he finds himself thinking about Kyle, naked, in the next room; Kyle, obedient and submissive. Without understanding the impulse at all, Darrek realizes that he feels like it's his duty to fuck Kyle into acquiescence. If Darrek gave Kyle a good, hard fuck, Kyle would fall in line. He'd know his place and snap out of his depression.

Pushing the terrible thoughts back, since they refuse to go away completely, Darrek tries to rationalize it. His instincts to dominate

Kyle come from Kyle's innate submissiveness. Kyle wants it, so Darrek is compelled to give it to him.

That's as far as Darrek is willing to self-analyze. He gets out of bed and goes to shower. After that, he stops trying to think everything through and act on his instincts. That feels good, feels right, so he goes with it. Darrek knows Kyle in ways that Gabriel doesn't. Because he senses that the strangeness between himself and Kyle will only continue to grow unless Darrek gets to the source of the issue, Darrek ignores Gabriel's order to stay away from Kyle for the day. Darrek knows why Gabriel chose Sam as Kyle's temporary sitter. Lilianna, who knows the whole situation, inside and out, is busy. Trace and Micah are busy with Diadem. Ben is still off-limits. That leaves limited options. Sam probably doesn't know many specifics of the dynamics at play between Darrek, Gabriel and Kyle. Darrek plays the odds and bets on this.

After showering, he brings the phone into Kyle's room and goes to coax Kyle from bed. First, Darrek throws off the blanket covering Kyle and stares at his naked body, helpless as can be. Then he notices the new bandage on Kyle's right arm.

"He cut you?"

"Yes, Sir," Kyle admits without inflection, unmoving, eyes unfocused. "Master knows how to take care of me."

No, he doesn't, Darrek thinks automatically. *But I do.*

"I want to take care of you today," Darrek says, sitting on the edge of Kyle's bed. "We can stay home or go to work. Your decision. But first, I'd like you to make a call for me. Gabriel arranged for Sam to come over to watch you. She's probably on her way."

Tenderly, Darrek caresses over the bandage on Kyle's arm, down to his hand where his fingers weave between Kyle's, holding on to it.

"But if you'd rather I leave...."

"Gimme the phone," Kyle sighs.

Darrek hands over the phone. Kyle dials and places the phone to his ear. Darrek continues to hold Kyle's other hand, his thumb gently brushing the skin and, after a few moments, goosebumps rise along Kyle's wounded arm.

"Hey Sam, it's Kyle. My cousin Tom is in town and I'd rather spend the day with him, catching up, than sitting around here or at Diadem. No offense or anything. I just need a change of scenery." There's a pause. Darrek waits as Sam responds, unable to hear what she's saying.

"Yeah, I know you'll have to let Gabe know. That's fine. Tell Gabe I'll have Tom drop me off at the photography studio later and that I know what the consequences will be. Yeah, Dare's already left for work. Okay. Thanks. See you later."

He hangs up and sets the phone down on the bed.

Protectiveness flares big and powerful in Darrek's expression, waking Kyle up fast. Darrek turns slightly to face Kyle more directly, gazing blatantly up and down Kyle's naked body. Darrek is barechested, wearing only a pair of jeans, and so much bigger than Kyle that he's practically a human wall barricading Kyle in place. Kyle is half-hard just from the scrutiny, and embarrassed by it.

Darrek's hand slips free of Kyle's and slides, instead, over Kyle's thigh, up the inside of it. Kyle blurts, "I'd like to get ready for work, please. Sir."

Darrek murmurs, "That's not what you want. I can see that much."

Kyle's stomach swoops. "Oh my god," he breathes. A chill that races up his spine pebbles his skin from head to toe. That's not Darrek talking. He's reciting someone else's words, a script drawn from their past, without knowing he's doing it. But Kyle knows. Darrek hasn't figured it out completely—not quite—but he's close. Dangerously close. It's there in his face as vague distaste and bewilderment, under the lust.

Trembling as Darrek leans closer, the backs of his fingers brushing along Kyle's swelling hard-on, then wrapping it snugly inside a loose fist, Kyle feels woozy, wishes for a gag, wishes for Ben.

He could say no. He could use his safeword, but he doesn't. This is his part of it. This is the role he fills. He gets hard, enjoys it, and lets Darrek take what he wants. They've already gone this far, so there's no going back. Kyle lies there as Darrek strokes him, watching his hand work, and Kyle's breathing quickens, his flesh responding eagerly.

Silent, still, just trying to breathe, Kyle does nothing to prevent it as Darrek leans down, opens his mouth and lowers it onto him. Tongue pushed forward, Darrek cradles Kyle on the hot, wet muscle and closes his lips, suckling the head. Darrek's hand strokes up and down along what he doesn't take into his mouth. Moaning at the taste, the sound vibrating up Kyle's cock, Darrek feeds Kyle back, inch by inch, until he's halfway in Darrek's mouth. He sucks hard as he pulls off. Kyle whimpers and tries not to move, to pretend it isn't happening, but the urge to thrust is strong and he forbids himself that. He's completely erect and Darrek's mouth feels better than it ever has. It always felt good, but now Darrek has had plenty of practice, and knows how to give more pleasure.

Kyle's control slips when Darrek takes him back into his mouth, fitting all of him by letting his throat relax so that Kyle can lodge there. Helplessly, Kyle makes a pleading sort of purr and shivers, pulsing pre-come as Darrek pulls off with a slurp. He strokes Kyle a little, watching him enjoy it, watching him pretend not to enjoy it. Rocking in stuttering, shallow thrusts against Darrek's hand, helpless not to moan with pleasure, feeling shameful and dirty and fevered with lust, he chases release. Underneath it all, it does feel nice, but, then again, Darrek was always eerily talented at making it feel good for Kyle, no matter what.

When Darrek goes back to using his mouth, sucking the protests right through Kyle's dick, Kyle comes right up off the bed, curling forward. His hips thrust upward against Darrek's lips and tongue, his knees come up. With room to maneuver, Darrek slides his hands back and around Kyle's bottom, cupping his cheeks. He pulls them apart and Kyle cries out, with the foreknowledge of what follows. Get Kyle hard by sucking him then finger him loose. That's where salvation lies, but only for one of them. Darrek's middle finger creeps over to Kyle's crease, stroking up and down it, settling over his knot, tickling it as he moans around Kyle's cock.

"I don't want it," Kyle gasps deliriously. "I don't want it anymore. Not like this. I swear I don't. Dare, you don't have to. You *don't....*"

The finger wriggles, working at the pucker, teasing it open. Kyle lets out a wild moan and thrusts hard. His balls draw up tight, ready to shoot. Pulling off, Darrek watches Kyle spurt a thick stream of semen, smearing it down his length, twisting his hand as Kyle keeps coming and begins to slowly soften.

The finger comes away from his hole, but it's just for now. It might take hours, or days, but they've started it. They'll need to finish. Of that, Kyle is certain. Darrek will chase his demon right through Kyle's willing body.

Darrek stands, takes a step back so that Kyle can get to his feet, but Kyle is boneless.

"Let's get you showered," Darrek says gently, in a lust-roughened voice.

Darrek helps him up, steadies him by holding his arm, and guides him to the bathroom. Once Kyle is inside, his face in the mirror flushed, looking used and dazed, he pushes as hard as he can against Darrek's chest, snapping, "Get the fuck out."

Before Darrek can stop him, Kyle slams and locks the door.

It's the beginning of the weirdest day of Kyle's life. Long after Kyle is washed and dressed, his bowels emptied and belly full, the strangeness lingers. It's there in the quiet willingness behind Darrek's eyes, but Kyle knows if he yields to it, both of them would spiral into a place that's to be avoided at all costs.

They get in the truck and Darrek drives them to work.

The day passes in a blur. Right after they get to work, Kyle pays a stranger walking by the job site twenty bucks to get on the phone when Gabriel calls to say that he's Tom, that they're playing a round of golf and Kyle is doing fine. Gabriel calls Darrek not even a minute later. And Darrek, walking amongst the boisterous, busy crew getting their tools and supplies ready, confirms that he's alone and hasn't seen or heard from Kyle.

Now and then, throughout the day, Kyle sends Gabriel texts to check in and let him know he's having a great time with Tom. As he works, surrounded by his crew and plenty of tasks to keep his hands, if not his mind, busy, Kyle thinks of Ben, and Gabriel, and doesn't have the slightest thought of hurting himself. He only ponders what he wants and what he's grateful to already have—namely

Ben's blind devotion and Gabriel's loving care. With effort, Kyle strives to not think of Darrek at all, but the problem is, Darrek is the key to everything. Plus, he's right there, all day, watching Kyle like a hawk.

After the workday has ended, when Kyle is able to look back on it and study it dispassionately, he knows that Darrek decided how it was going to end early on. Darrek, Kyle concludes, knew before he even set eyes on Kyle that morning what was going to happen before the day was out. It's all there is left to do, and perhaps Darrek realizes the only way out of this is by doing all there is left to do. They each have their roles to play; all that is left is to carry it out to the unavoidable conclusion.

"This isn't who you are," Kyle wants to say to him. "You're not this guy."

He imagines Darrek would reply, "Today it is. Today this is who you and Gabriel and Ben need me to be. It's who I need me to be, too."

So, they finish their shift. It passes too quickly. After, they go with a bunch of the guys to a nearby bar. Kyle calls Gabriel to say that he'll probably be over in an hour or so, knowing he can always continue to lie and draw it out if needed. Kyle drinks a few lagers to take the edge off, and would have more but he sees how much his chaperone is imbibing, so cuts himself off in order to act as the self-appointed designated driver. Darrek, who has never gotten the chance to develop a tolerance for alcohol, drinks nearly an entire bottle of tequila and stays right by Kyle's side all night though each of them remain heavily in conversation with other people rather than each other.

Night falls. Their company leaves them in dribs and drabs, until there's barely anyone left and it's clearly time to go. Kyle leads the way back to the Tundra, walking briskly, glancing over his shoulder to ensure Darrek follows behind. Taking the keys and starting the truck, proud that his hands are only trembling a little bit, he waits for Darrek to fold his body into the passenger seat, spares him a glance to make sure he's not about to puke on the floorboards, then shifts into drive.

The town falls behind them and the roads open up into empty, rolling fields of wild grasses without a house or building in sight. The solitude is heavy upon Kyle, and he wonders if it's late enough that Gabriel will be calling again to ask where the hell Kyle is and why Tom hasn't dropped him off yet. The same type of thing may have occurred to Darrek because he mutters, "Pull over," and sits up straighter in his seat.

"You gonna hurl?"

"Just pull over!"

"Dare...."

"There. In the grass," he instructs. Kyle sighs and does as he's told, even as his heart starts to pound, beating a wild rhythm. They swing off onto the level shoulder of the narrow country lane without a car in sight. "Go a little farther. Between those trees. I want to get off the road."

"Darrek, what the hell, man?"

Kyle drives through a cluster of trees, following a dirt lane, but when he begins to fear blowing a tire, he stops and parks, refusing to go further. Turning off the ignition, hand falling to his lap, Kyle bows his head and says with hollow acceptance, "You don't have to hurl, do you?"

Darrek sits there, letting his silence speak for him. After a beat, he opens his door, gets out and closes it behind him. Kyle tracks him as he circles the truck and comes around to the driver's side. Opening the door wide, he holds out a hand for Kyle to take. His stomach a nauseous riot, Kyle wonders if maybe he's the one that's going to hurl as he places his hand in Darrek's and lets him help him down. The phone lies, forgotten, in a compartment beside the driver's seat.

Wrapping a hand around Kyle's back, pulling him close then spinning him quickly around so that his back rests against Darrek's solid chest, Darrek breathes him in and says, "I didn't want to do this at the house. If you tell me to stop, I will. Promise. This isn't a Master/slave thing. This is about you and me."

"I know. Stop talking," Kyle hears himself say from what seems like another world entirely. "And use a condom."

Darrek exhales heavily against the side of Kyle's neck, making goosebumps prickle there and downward, along his spine, his nipples stiffening then his cock following suit. Smelling of booze and sweat, towering over Kyle, Darrek yanks his best friend's jeans open and pushes a greedy hand down inside his boxers, while, at the same time, slipping two fingers of his other hand between Kyle's lips for him to suck on, needing them wet, knowing Kyle will understand why. Moaning while he licks Darrek's fingers, curling his tongue around them, Kyle feels his pants get pushed down, puddling at his knees. Darrek palms Kyle's dick, letting the stiff line of it slide against his palm for a luxurious moment as Kyle grabs Darrek's wrist and purses his lips around the digits filling his mouth.

Then Darrek gets impatient and moves them, pushing Kyle down to his knees, then forward so that his hands get planted in the grass beneath, with Darrek following right after, folding over his back. The fingers slide wet from his lips and Kyle gasps for much-needed air, surging forward instinctively at the weird, startling sensation of Darrek rubbing over the knot of his hole, then roughly impaling Kyle on the two fingers that had just been in his mouth. Kyle is pulled instantly back by a strong arm looped in front of his hips, holding him there as Darrek digs deep. "*Fuck*, Dare...."

"That's right. Gonna fuck you. Need to fuck you," he growls.

The fingers bend and pry and Kyle cries out but Darrek sucks a kiss to his jaw, lighting up the nerves from the top of Kyle's head all the way down to his toes. Feeling the reaction, Darrek snarls and sucks another kiss, this time below Kyle's ear while corkscrewing his hand up into him.

When he wriggles away, Darrek draws him right back, making him take it, take it all. Then, too soon, the fingers yank free, leaving Kyle empty. There's the crinkle of foil. He hears Darrek spit into the hand that was just inside him and a moment later, a broad, hot, throbbing pressure fits itself against Kyle's hole, demanding entry.

Chapter 19
Innocence Lost

Kyle feels so incredibly small in Darrek's arms, and it seems impossible that he'll be able to get inside. Grabbing hold of him by the hip, steadying his cock by the root, Darrek pulls Kyle back onto him while keeping steady forward pressure. Staring down at the junction of their bodies, his eyes adjusting quickly to the light of the stars and moon, Darrek watches Kyle's little pucker spread around him then swallow him up, gripping Darrek so tightly that he lets out a low groan, countered by a soft whimper as Kyle shifts his legs wider and adjusts the angle of his hips, his head rolling forward on his shoulders as he fights against the deep ache from being entered with saliva as the only lube and minimal prep. Darrek pushes a little harder after his crown pops through Kyle's outer ring, driving a startled, gruff little shout from him.

Glowing in the moonlight, Kyle turns his head, glancing back over a shoulder, his eyes half-closed.

Darrek caresses up the gentle curve of Kyle's spine, feeling him arch like a cat in heat. Draping his body over Kyle's back, Darrek takes hold of Kyle's mouth, turning it to the side so that he can catch it over his shoulder. Their lips brush lightly together as Kyle makes sweet, soft little gasps while Darrek presses into him, entering him more fully.

Darrek thought he had never stolen anything in his life, but this, this moment, and Kyle's innocence, is something he has stolen. With a rough grunt, he sees a vision of himself — different but the same — forcing his dick into Kyle, thinking how tight he is, that he'd never fit. Darrek thrusts hard, driving in further. Kyle's lower lip quivers against his, and Darrek angles his head to kiss him more fully. Kyle says his name on the exhale, and it's beautiful and anguished.

Their tongues touch, and it sends a thrill rocketing through Darrek's body, right to the tip of his cock. He nudges, rocking into Kyle and then back as Kyle suckles Darrek's tongue, then opens wider for him, giving him permission, letting him get inside in whatever ways he wants to. Maddened, animalistic sounds erupt from Darrek as he surrenders to the need and just does and takes and fucks and licks and plunders. Using Kyle's mouth with deep, dirty kisses, kissing him breathless, he moves in sharp needful pushes, staying nestled, trying to get impossibly deeper. Kyle's hand reaches down under his body and he jacks himself counter to Darrek's thrusts until Darrek takes that hand back, pins it to the grassy earth and denies him the relief, wanting all of his attention, every part of him, attuned to only the feeling of Darrek inside him, owning him, filling up his empty places.

It becomes more fevered, and the kiss breaks. Darrek's lips move over the back of Kyle's head, through his silken hair, longer than it used to be, as he gulps down air and pounds Kyle's ass, fucking him wildly. Kyle cries out his name, becomes restless, writhing, purring. Darrek finds his sweet spot and drives into it over and over until Kyle is keening, shuddering. Cupping a hand over Kyle's erection, fingering it lightly, Darrek holds him as he shudders and shoots. Semen jets in an arc, soiling Kyle's shirt and splattering over his belly. Darrek straightens to his knees, with Kyle fallen down to the grass before him, ass-up and totally relaxed. Slowly, he withdraws until only the head of his cock is inside, then savors the view as Kyle takes every inch, swallowing it hungrily. Another moment stolen — utterly forbidden, perfectly destined. Working himself faster and faster inside Kyle, watching him take it and invite each push, Darrek fucks his best friend, and remembers.....

We had only been kissing. It was a sleepover, because Kyle's parents were away. We were in my room, in my bed and we had the sheet pulled up over our heads. He pecked a kiss, quick, square on my mouth and looked so

nervous. It looked like he was about to apologize or laugh it off, so I kissed him right back. I kissed him with a smile. I was so happy to kiss Kyle back. We shifted closer, wrapped our arms around each other's backs and kissed again. That was all. That was all it took.

The sheet was ripped off of us.

He didn't say anything at first. He just stared, his eyes popping like he couldn't believe it, but it was the way his mouth looked that frightened me more. It was a tight, straight, hard line.

Then, Daddy started to take off his belt.

"Please, Daddy," I begged. I was just a kid, barely thirteen. "Daddy, I'm sorry!"

"Perverts! Deviants!" Jerry Grealey, my father, the preacher, grabbed me by the arm and pulled, jolting me, nearly yanking it out of the socket. When he let go to wind the buckle of the belt around his hand, I moved on top of Kyle to shield him with my body. The belt swung in a wide arc and found its target, lashing across my bare back. We were only wearing pajama pants, to sleep in. "Tell me. Admit it! Admit what you are!"

"No. Please! Don't! We weren't doing anything bad! We didn't mean it!"

I'd just gotten the cast off of my arm a few days earlier. It was still sore and weak. Daddy grabbed me by it and dragged me to the door, calming down. But it always got worse once Daddy seemed to be calming down, so I started to cry. He got behind me and stuck my sore arm out against the doorframe so that the hand and wrist were in the way if the door should close. This was how he broke the bone in my wrist before, so I knew. He didn't need to say anything. All he had to do was grab the doorknob with his other hand and wait.

"You know better than to talk back to your father. 'He that curseth his father shall surely be put to death.' Exodus 21:17." I moaned with dread, remembering how it felt when the solid wood door crushed that arm, the sound of the snap. I stopped speaking, biting down on my lips to hold in my crying, too. Though I tried to be still, I did pull back toward the bed slightly. He must have felt it, because he whispered to me, loudly, "You want to go and touch him some more, don't you?"

"No, I don't. I don't, Daddy. Please. I'm sorry...."

"You love Kyle, son?"

I had no answer for that that he would approve of and would not be *untrue.*

"You're going to prove your sin and show God that you are indeed a deviant and a pervert and a homosexual. Take your penance or prove your sin. I can hold your hand, right here, and make it so that you are unable to touch Kyle with these fingers in unclean ways. Temptation will be removed, praise Jesus. Or, you can perform your filthy acts, there on that bed, and choose to let God Himself be your judge."

"God! I choose God!"

He threw me across the room, at the bed. My kneecap slammed into the wood of the side of the bed and I swallowed my shout of pain. With a perfectly composed expression lit with righteous fire, Daddy said, "Prove it. Take his pants off."

It was the only choice. He would have done it, slammed the door and crushed my fingers. And it might not have stopped there. Kyle was a part of it. Daddy might have decided to punish him the same way, and I believed I was making the choice that would hurt Kyle less.

On the bed, hearing everything, witnessing everything, Kyle was pushed hard into a breed of terror that few people ever get to experience, and even fewer children.... So he started for us, to show me that he was complicit and wouldn't endanger me by protesting. He pulled down his pants. Kyle liked me a lot. He even loved me a little. If taking his clothes off would spare me physical trauma, Kyle would do it, no question.

But it only instigated Daddy. He called Kyle such horrible names. Told him he wanted it, so he'd get it. Shaking badly, naked and crying, I climbed onto the bed, onto Kyle, and Daddy shoved my face against Kyle's genitals.

"You wanted to use your mouth on him? Then do it. Use your mouth."

Kyle didn't understand. Even when he felt me lick him, he didn't understand. As Daddy ordered me to push Kyle's legs apart and stick a finger up inside him, and Kyle saw Daddy rub the front of his pants while I sobbed with fright, Kyle didn't understand. Then again, he was still a child.

Whimpering, Kyle gasped, low and quiet, like a secret, "It's okay, Dare. I know you have to."

When it was only fingers that I had in Kyle, he looked mostly scared, uncomfortable and shocked. Once I had moved Kyle onto his hands and knees, draping my larger body over Kyle's to shield him from the belt, and Daddy had me stick my pecker in Kyle's dirty hole instead, then it was more

than blank fear. Then, Kyle cried out in pain.
"I'm hurting him, Daddy."

"I'm hurting you," Darrek whispers, hearing the echo through time, knowing the truth of it as much as he wants to deny it. Grimacing against rising memory, he closes his eyes and grits his teeth, but there's no keeping out something that comes from inside. Jerry taught them that.

"'If a man lies with a man as one lies with a woman, both of them have done what is detestable.' Leviticus 20:13. 'I let them become defiled through... that I might fill them with horror so they would know that I am the Lord.' Ezekiel 20:25-26."

"Daddy, please!"

Darrek squeezes his eyes shut against a vision of Kyle, so very young and naked and frightened, on his knees on Darrek's childhood bed, crying little boy tears as Darrek moved inside him, driven by the lashes of Jerry Grealey's belt leaving red stripes across Darrek's back.

"Submit yourselves for the Lord's sake," Jerry shouts in both their minds. *"Submit yourselves to your masters with all respect, not only to those who are good and considerate, but also to those who are harsh!"*

"Daddy, what did you do?" Darrek whispers into nighttime air.

Hearing, understanding, Kyle moans.

Darrek pulls out, strips off the condom and gets to his feet with tears burning his eyes, blinding him.

He remembers. He remembers everything.

It comes back. All of it. The sweetly innocent first kiss. Being discovered. The belt. The threats. Kyle crying softly. Kyle whispering, telling Darrek with his eyes that it was okay, to do it, that there was no choice. He remembers Kyle getting stiff inside Darrek's hand, inside his mouth. He remembers sticking his dick into Kyle and hearing Kyle say that it hurt, begging with small pleas that Darrek was punished for. One lash of the belt for every protest from Kyle.

He remembers feeling how scared Kyle was, and succumbing

to terror like he had never known over his own actions. Even as his small hips pumped, he closed off parts of his mind, not wanting to know what he did, even as he did it. Darrek remembers being sent away after that first time, to bible camp. He didn't see Kyle for weeks.

When he came back, Darrek had lost the memory. But then, it happened again. Darrek's parents invited Kyle to stay over whenever Kyle's parents took off on one of their frequent business trips. As an only child with no other family, Kyle parents always said yes to these invitations. Kyle kept sleeping over. Jerry kept teaching them their sins, their place. It kept happening, and each time, afterward, Darrek would push it down, down, down in his head, until it was like it didn't happen at all.

More than that, Darrek thinks of everything he's done to Kyle the past few days, the things Kyle has submitted to and endured for years upon years, because of what Darrek did to him in that bedroom. Kyle submits because Jerry taught him to.

Groaning sickly, murmuring disgusted little 'no's, over and over again, Darrek tries to get away from Kyle, stumbling away, into the wild grasses. Kyle isn't safe around him. Jerry saw to that.

Darrek fumbles his phone from his pocket and speed dials the only person in the whole of the world that he can.

"Where are you?" Gabriel demands as soon as he picks up.

"What have I done?!" Darrek cries, a wreck, barely intelligible. "Oh fuck, Gabriel. What have I done?! *I raped him.* He was so young. He was just a little kid! All of those times.... We just kissed and Daddy found us. He found us and he forced me on him. He got off on it," Darrek sneers with disgust. "God, I didn't know. *I didn't know!*" The phone drops and Darrek doubles over, retching, a long, throat-tearing sound of horror ripping from the core of his being as his stomach voids its contents — tequila, mostly. The stink of it fills his nose.

He finds the phone in the brush by listening for the shrill shouts coming from the tiny speaker, and nearly drops it again as he puts it to his ear.

"Darrek?! *Dare!*"

"What have I done? God, Kyle...."

"You listen to me. Are you listening? Are you?!"

"Yes, Sir," he slurs, speaking automatically.

"Tell me where you are. Now."

Darrek recites the route number and mile marker. He'd noted both before asking Kyle to pull off. Then he describes, in a hollow voice, where they are.

"Darrek, you still hearing me?" Gabriel growls in a wavering voice, fearing, perhaps, what Darrek has done not so much as what he still might do.

"It doesn't matter. Nothing does. There's no forgiveness. Not for this. There's no point. I've ruined Kyle's whole life. *His whole life*, I... God. God is cruel. I see that now. I thought it was just my father, but no, it's bigger than that. I— it'll be better this way. But you'll need to come and get Kyle. Kyle needs help...."

"Stop it! Stop it right fucking now!" Gabriel yells. Darrek barely hears him, thinking of the knife he has taped under the driver's seat in the truck, for protection, and cries softly into the phone. Knives aren't the danger. He is. "There's nothing I won't forgive you for, baby. I love you, so much."

"No, not after this."

"Shut up! LISTEN!" Darrek has never heard Gabriel this rattled, not even when he was raging at his mother last year, the mother who had so profoundly forsaken him. "Sit down. Wherever you are. Sit your ass right there and wait for me. That's a motherfucking order. Don't you move or touch Kyle. Is that understood?"

"Goodbye, Gabriel. I love you with all my heart. You've been the best thing to ever happen to me and I really am sorry." He hangs up the phone.

Chapter 20

Salvation

"The fuck are you doing!? Darrek, stop! STOP! FUCK!"

Nearly tripping over his own feet in the slick grass, Kyle runs at Darrek. Darrek has wandered away from the opened driver's side door of his truck with something shiny and catching moonlight in his hand. It's a knife. Kyle knows one of those when he sees it, and Darrek is raising this knife to his throat, chin tilted up and jaw clenched against an onslaught of pain.

Kyle gets to him just as the blade starts to part skin.

Not thinking, just knowing it needs to stop, that Darrek needs to be stopped, Kyle grabs the knife. Darrek's big hand takes up the whole handle, though, so Kyle's fingers sip around the blade, which kisses his palm. Darrek's grip loosens in confusion, allowing Kyle's hand to fit between his neck and the metal's edge.

An instinct to fight back hits Darrek, who draws the knife instinctively back toward his throat, slicing deeper into Kyle's palm in the process.

With a startled gasp, Kyle renews his grip.

He grits his teeth, determined, and pulls. The knife embeds itself deeply in his flesh. Making an agonized whimper, Kyle cocks his free arm back.

The punch is thrown sloppily but it's effective enough, hitting Darrek square in the temple.

The knife drops.

Kyle cries out, mouth fallen open around the white-hot pain, staring at all of the dripping blood.

Darrek staggers.

"Asshole!" Kyle yells, and hits him again, in the side of the head with all of his fury and desperation behind the punch.

Darrek crumples, falling in a heap to the ground.

It's a miracle that Gabriel doesn't crash on the way to Darrek. It's not even a five-minute drive, barely long enough to dial Ben's number and spout some barely coherent plea for help and directions. Gabriel finds the spot with tire tracks leading off the road, veers into it, hits a ditch, jumps out of his Discovery and goes running towards the truck in the distance, screaming Darrek's name, tripping over his own feet.

"Here! Over here!"

It's Kyle. Gabriel follows the sound. In the grass, he finds Darrek and Kyle, both with their pants undone and pulled hastily up. Darrek is collapsed backward in the long grass, Kyle is sitting with his legs drawn up, cradling his left hand in his lap.

"What the sweet fuck...?"

Kyle is shaking violently. Blood, too much blood pools in his lap, over his unzipped jeans.

"I punched him," Kyle confesses. "He had a knife. H-his throat. And I grabbed it from him, with my h-hand. I need... a-a hospital. Gabe...."

Gabriel reacts, twisting the shirt over his head, ripping off a long piece and falling to his knees before Kyle. Kyle holds out his hand, sliced across the palm down into the muscle. A sense of disorientation washes like cool water over Gabriel and he bites hard down on his tongue to snap himself out of it. Using the piece of shirt, he binds Kyle's hand, making it tight.

"You're gonna be okay. They can stitch that up, give you a transfusion. Okay? Kyle, look at me. Okay?"

Kyle searches Gabriel's face, and he seems more solid than Gabriel has seen him in almost a year. Despite the bloody chaos all around them, Kyle is okay. He's calm and weakened, but mentally he's more collected than ever. Gabriel understands that instinctively. Kyle's focus helps to sharpen his.

"Okay," Kyle nods. Mainly to stop him shaking so badly for a moment, Gabriel pulls Kyle to him, hugging him, rubbing warmth back into his body.

"I gotta get you both to the car... but Dare's so big...." He cuts off that train of thought before it can go further, knowing it's useless, that getting Kyle to the hospital has to be priority. "Hey. Tonight, was it consensual?"

A muscle in Kyle's jaw twitches, his eyes huge in his face as he gazes up at Gabriel, listening, slowly understanding. He nods tightly. "Tonight. Yes."

"On the phone, Dare said he raped you."

Kyle stops breathing, his thin frame vibrating in Gabriel's embrace. At first, Kyle doesn't deny it. At first, he's only quiet and scared.

Gabriel clutches Kyle to him and makes a small, keening sound of pain, willing it not to be true. He rages inwardly against it, letting out a raged scream, then trying to get a handle on it, trying to get control before it can spiral away from him. They hear an engine, see lights swing off the road. Gabriel sits back and looks at Kyle with the tortured gaze of one who has been there.

"Look, it wasn't his fault," Kyle tells Gabriel urgently. "None of it. Don't be mad at him."

Leaning forward, Gabriel presses their foreheads together, grounding himself to Kyle, trying to get it together, smelling the blood, knowing that Kyle needs help, but unable to think past the blossoming revelations staring them in the face.

"Okay. Okay. We need, you need to... your hand. Come on. That's Ben," he says, and the hope in Kyle's eyes, instant, heart-stopping hope, gives Gabriel such sudden peace and gladness, that in that moment, he knows it could still be okay. All of it, the hell, secrets and cruelty, they can survive it, because Kyle has survived it.

"Ben? Really?"

"Yeah, baby. Come on." Gabriel stands, finding he can force a smile, because Darrek is alive, and Kyle is alive, and they will be okay if he has anything to say about it. He helps Kyle up, and zips Kyle's pants for him. Supporting him, keeping him upright when he staggers, Gabriel leads him to where Ben's truck screeches to an abrupt halt.

Ben and Trace jump from the cab, looking frantic, freezing where they stand when they see all of the blood.

"*Kyle*," Ben cries in fear, bolting for him. Kyle stares at the wreck of Ben's face, all splotchy purple bruises, and lets Ben take his bleeding hand. Lovingly, Ben holds the side of Kyle's face.

Gabriel explains, digging deep to find an inner reserve of strength but unable to focus on any one thing for long. "He was trying to take a knife from Dare. He needs to go to the E.R. Now. Go. Take care of him and I'll deal with the rest of it."

"You take him, Benny. I'll stay with Gabe," Trace says.

Together Trace and Ben get Kyle loaded into the passenger seat of Ben's truck. They back out to the road, swing onto the asphalt, and peel off in the direction of the hospital.

As if in a trance, Gabriel turns from Trace and begins walking back to Darrek. Jogging after him, Trace catches up as they get to the clearing of trampled grass where Darrek lays unconscious. His pants are unzipped, with a damp patch around his bare groin. There's a thin, shallow cut on his neck, but it's hardly bleeding. A small glow shines in the grass from Darrek's dropped phone. The bloody knife lies by Darrek's feet.

"What the hell?" Trace says with shock.

"He fucked Kyle. Then went for the knife. Kyle took it from him, and cut his hand in the process. And clocked him a good one, I guess."

"Darrek was hurting Kyle?" Trace asks, trying to understand.

Gabriel looks at Trace, the man who took care of him when he had no one; his skin baked brown from the sun, his salt and pepper hair, momentarily hidden under a bandana. Trace, for Gabriel, is everything safe, solid, sure. Trace is his family.

"Dare was gonna off himself. Maybe all the talk of suicide lately gave him the bright idea it would solve all his problems."

Gabriel stares at the center of Trace's chest as he says this, then his knees give out, but Trace catches him before he goes down, folding him in his arms. Gabriel sucks in a rough breath and lets it back out as a whine of pain. Trace sighs and holds on to him.

"Hey, it's done," Trace tells him. "They're both gonna be fine.

They're strong and they've got us to help them. We deal with *now*. One thing at a time, okay? First, we need to get him off the ground. I bet seeing your pretty face'll do him a world of good when we wake him up."

In the grass, Darrek stirs, rising from blackness into awareness. Hearing him, Gabriel disengages from Trace and stumbles over to him, falling to his knees, pulling Darrek into his arms before he even knows where he is. Darrek gazes, disoriented, past Gabriel at Trace.

Things start to come back, slowly. When he speaks, Darrek's voice is paper thin and flat. "He hit me," Darrek says. "Kyle."

"TKO," Gabriel agrees, and holds Darrek at arm's length, sniffling. He blinks, draws in a breath, and then says, "Don't you ever... *ever*... do that again."

"Which part?"

Gabriel snarls, desperate for Darrek to get his meaning, struggling for the words. "I know that it hurts, and that it's a *lot*. But I am here with you and I will do whatever it takes. Okay? I forbid you to leave me, Darrek. I need you with me. Do you hear me? Huh?"

Darrek blinks back tears and turns his face away. Gabriel lays a hand on Darrek's cheek and leans down, touching his face to Darrek's, breathing through the storm of emotion as it rises with strength.

"I love you," Gabriel hisses, holding on to him.

Darrek takes a rough, hitching breath and reaches up, grasping at Gabriel, keeping him there. He grunts thickly, moaning in horror. Darrek's hand becomes a claw as he fights through multifaceted hurt of crippling intensity.

"It's gonna be okay," Gabriel promises softly. "I'm taking you home. And Kyle... he's gonna be okay. Ben's taking him to the hospital. Are you hurt anywhere else? Do you need help, too? We could go to the E.R. first, get you checked out. Dare? Talk to me. Talk to me, baby. Come on...."

Darrek stares at him, dumbfounded, gripping Gabriel's arm like he's afraid if he lets go, he'll tumble into an abyss.

"Okay," he croaks. "Home. No hospital."

Things keep occurring to him, and the weight of Trace's stare works on Darrek like truth serum—possibly a psychological holdover from the first time they met, in the dungeon as Master and slave. "Kyle grabbed the knife. The *blade* of the knife."

"Yeah. He did," Gabriel says. "He'll be okay once they get a doctor to look at it."

"The things I've done. What I've put Kyle through...." Darrek struggles to say, the words too poignant to come out clearly.

Darrek sets his jaw and looks back into Gabriel's eyes, aching to the core of his soul for causing Kyle such profoundly scarring damage.

"It's over now. All of it," Trace calls, his voice booming. "There's plenty of shit to talk about, but not here and not now. Accept your Master's love and let him get you home."

Darrek gazes up at Gabriel, whose face is painted with concern, but no anger. None at all. Once, tightly, Gabriel nods, confirming Trace's proclamation. "Let me take you home. Please?"

"I never wanted to hurt him, Gabe."

"I know, baby," Gabriel says thickly, getting to his feet, pulling Darrek with him. He scoops up the phone and pockets it. "Whatever happened with Kyle... when he got in that truck with Benny, even given the bloody hand, and everything else, he looked better than I've seen in a long time. It's gonna be okay. You'll see."

Darrek hangs his head, folds his arms, then realizes the state he's in. Trying to shrink in on himself, he closes his fly and straightens his shirt, stinking of tequila, vomit and semen.

"Let's get out of here," Gabriel says. He braces Darrek with a hand on his back, guiding him out of the field, letting him feel connected to all of the love that Gabriel has for him.

They walk past Trace, towards the vehicles. Darrek swallows thickly, the tallest of the bunch, but feeling very, very small.

Chapter 21

Tenderness and Trepidation

Micah sees Ben, with his worked-over, pitiful face, through a part in the hospital curtain, and walks right into air as thick as soup. No sooner has he slipped inside the curtain that has been pulled around Kyle's bed for privacy than he feels it. The tension is great between Kyle and Ben, and Micah isn't an idiot, so he realizes it instantly. From the look that Kyle gives Micah, it's also clear that his presence is very much welcome.

Kyle is wearing a hospital gown and sitting up in bed. His heavily bandaged hand lays limp at his side. His unscathed hand is tucked closely against his body, the arm wrapping his mid-section like he's fighting not to be sick. He's pale, thin, and haunted. At his bedside is Ben, whose gaze is locked to Kyle with laser-like precision. Target has been acquired. All systems go.

"Hey. Fancy meeting you here," Micah nods to Kyle.

"Hey," Kyle murmurs, chewing his lip. "You just in the neighborhood or something?"

"Yeah. I hang out here all the time and hit on the nurses."

"Male or female?"

With a baffled expression, Micah frowns, "I have to choose?"

It makes Kyle smile, which Micah is glad to see. If there's ever a person who needed a smile, it's him. As the smile fades, though, an urgent pleading enters Kyle's face, specifically around the eyes. Like they're communicating telepathically, Kyle tells Micah, *'I don't know what to say to him. Help.'*

"Sit," Kyle beckons. The arm wound around his stomach tightens. The injured hand shifts to his lap. His gaze darts everywhere,

169

to the harsh fluorescent lights, the scuffed linoleum floor, and the medical equipment tucked against the wall, waiting to be used.

"So," Micah starts, noticing the way Ben's hand is perched on the edge of Kyle's bed, like he wants to take Kyle's hand but isn't sure if he should unwind Kyle's protective grip on himself to do it. "Are you okay?"

"Mm-hmm," Kyle hums. He's twitchy like a junkie going through withdrawal, and Micah senses all he really needs is someone to take control here, but Ben is frozen, unable to do it and chance destroying his opportunity to repair things with his partner.

"Is it just the hand, or...?"

There are fresh bandages on the insides of both of Kyle's arms, quite visible with his short-sleeved gown.

"Yeah," Kyle blurts, slumping down in the bed, trying to disappear. "Next time I'll try to remember to grab the handle instead of the pointy end. Did you talk to Trace? Are Gabriel and Dare...?"

"They're fine. Trace is taking them home." Because he can see the shrill panic in Kyle's expression, Micah adds, "He didn't give me many details, he just told me to get over here and check on you."

That had been an interesting call. Micah had been at home doing a video chat with his wife, Lilianna, when Trace told him that Darrek, drunk off his ass, brought Kyle to the woods and took him for a ride on the end of his dick before getting stupid with a knife.

A female doctor in her fifties appears around the curtain and plucks Kyle's chart from its holder at the end of his bed.

"Okay, Mr. Roth. We've discharged you with the understanding that you'll see your physician to follow up and contact the hand specialist we've recommended to you." She marks off a few things on the papers in her hands. Kyle drops his gaze to his lap, his jaw tightly clenched. "And because of my concerns regarding your other injuries, I'd suggest you see your psychiatrist at your earliest convenience."

"Yes, ma'am," he mutters.

She looks up at this and waits for him to meet her eyes. "Do you have any other questions or concerns before I go?"

He shakes his head once. "Nope. Thanks."

The doctor glances between Ben and Micah, "You'll get him

home safe?"

"No problem," Micah tells her, reading her wariness, but wanting her to leave for Kyle's sake. As she walks away, Kyle tracks her through the curtain's now wider gap. His eyes get progressively wider the farther she gets.

"Mic," Kyle says softly, his face turning slowly red. Ben silently gathers Kyle's bloody shirt and shoes. "Can I ask you something?"

"Yeah, of course." Ben gives Micah a sharp look of warning.

Kyle feels the heat of it and murmurs, "Never mind."

"No, go on. What is it?"

"Forget it."

"Kyle," Micah sighs. Shrilly, Micah's phone begins to ring. He pulls it from his pocket and answers. "Yeah?" After only a second he holds it out to Kyle. "It's for you."

"Really?" Kyle stares.

"Gabe."

With relief so strong he immediately tears up, Kyle turns on the bed, putting his back to Ben, and presses Micah's phone to his ear. "Hello?"

"Talk to me," Gabe tells him, no question in his tone at all, just the sureness and strength of one who has been there.

"They just discharged me. I can go," Kyle says. Squeezing his eyes shut, he tries to compose himself with effort. Head bowed, he sucks in a rough breath that's audible even through the bad connection.

On the short drive over, he and Ben hadn't spoken at all. Every time Ben glanced over, he'd stare at all of the blood and instantly press harder at the gas pedal. Once they were at the Emergency Room, Kyle was taken by nurses while a frazzled doctor started barking orders. They'd cleaned the wound and gave him a local anesthetic before closing up the slice in his palm. When Ben was allowed to get close to Kyle again they were left all alone until the test results came back and they'd decided whether he needed to be admitted or have his other wounds tended to. Kyle was at a complete loss as to what to say to Ben, or even where to start. Ben, for maybe the first time in his life, seemed dumbstruck—too overwhelmed to speak.

"What do you need? If you want me to be there to back you up with talking to Ben, I will be there."

"I don't know."

"It's your call. I can be by your side as your friend and your Dom if you need that. I'll give it. If you want to go with Micah, get some sleep and talk in the morning instead, I think he'd be okay with that. If you want to go with Ben and do this your own way...."

The power in Gabriel's voice makes the options crystal clear for Kyle. He sees the different ways this could go. It's his choice. Part of him wants backup, and for Gabriel to be there when he tells Ben the truth. If Gabriel is there, Ben might be less likely to hurt Kyle in terrible ways when he finds out. But Gabriel needs to help Darrek. It would be selfish for Kyle to take him away when Darrek needs Gabriel so very much.

"I don't know," Kyle says with growing panic.

That's when Ben snatches the phone from him and declares with no room for argument, "He's coming home, where he belongs."

Caught by surprise, Kyle stares out at a spot in mid-air. He's drained, exhausted, betrayed, lost, but the confidence in Ben's voice has a calming effect upon him.

The volume on the phone is loud enough in the relative quiet of the hospital for Kyle to hear everything, as Gabriel says, "I think that's Kyle's decision to make." That means Ben heard everything Gabriel has been saying, too.

"I'm making it for him. It's the middle of the fucking night. He's going to sleep in his own bed and get some rest."

"Kyle has been through hell—"

"Maybe that's why he looks like he's been hit by a truck," Ben seethes.

"—and he needs to tell us where he feels most comfortable," Gabriel finishes. "Give him the phone back. Now."

The silent frustration and rage color Ben's expression. He doesn't respond or give the phone back.

"This isn't about your fucking ego, Knox. This is about helping that kid!"

"All I want is to help him! That's all I've wanted for over a month! For a *year*! I'm trying everything I can think of, Gabriel, and fuck you very much for thinking you know better than me what Kyle needs. He doesn't belong to you! You're not the one that loves him so much you can't see straight!"

Kyle holds out his hand for the phone, patiently, and murmurs, "Please, Ben."

Ben hands it over, reluctantly.

"I want to go with Ben. I'll call you if I need anything."

"I know it's scary," Gabriel tells him. Kyle is exhausted. He's going with Ben because he's done fighting. He just can't do it anymore. He can't. This is the only option he has left, and Gabriel knows it, senses it. These are his last words of encouragement before sending Kyle off into the unknown. "But you're strong. You're amazing. And he loves the hell out of you."

The call ends. Kyle's arm falls, the phone dropping to his side. Ben takes it from him, and with a flick of his wrist, he tosses it to Micah, who catches it from the air. Ben licks his lips wet, takes a single filling breath and beckons, "Kyle."

Slowly, Kyle turns and looks up at Ben from over a shoulder.

"Time to cut the shit. You need rest," Ben says. "It's late. There are conversations that need to happen, but not until tomorrow. First, you need to get some sleep."

"Yes, Sir," Kyle replies softly.

Ben looks down at the bloody shirt in his hand, then tosses it into the medical waste bin. With a shrug, he takes off his jacket and goes to fold it over Kyle's shoulders.

"Chivalry looks good on you," Kyle tells him.

"Yeah, I'm some big hero. You're the damsel in distress, like always. Get off your ass. This place creeps me out."

"I missed you, Ben."

In the corner of the hospital, with people hurrying here and there all around them, and as Micah diligently pretends not to notice, Kyle stands witness while Ben Knox fights tooth and nail against tears. His brow furrows and he holds his breath, asking Kyle many things at once with no words at all.

173

"C'mere," Ben says, in barely a whisper and a ragged one at that. He holds out a hand, sniffs, and turns his face away from Micah.

Kyle stands, and walks hesitantly up to Ben, who immediately pulls Kyle in to a complete, urgent, but careful embrace. Ben, as always, desperate to find the right way to help, grasps at Kyle's back.

"I'm sorry," Kyle says thickly, for Ben's ears only.

Ben's eyes flutter shut and he presses his lips to Kyle's head, "Stop apologizing."

"I didn't know what to do."

Eyes shut, as much without answers as Kyle, Ben simply kisses the center of his forehead and doesn't let go.

"Need anything else? You good?" Micah asks, getting to his feet.

"We're good," Kyle tells him. "Thank you for coming to check on me."

"Don't sweat it. Take care of the big guy for me. He keeps getting his ass in trouble."

"Yeah, I can tell," Kyle grins, tracing the edge of one of Ben's healed-over cuts with a fingertip. "We'll talk to you tomorrow."

Micah nods and slips out of the curtained sanctuary while Ben keeps Kyle gathered up in his arms with fierce, frightened devotion.

Chapter 22
Solving the Riddle

Homesickness doesn't hit Kyle until the moment he comes back home and crosses the threshold. All of the memories of living with Ben in that house come flooding back. For the most part, they are only good and positive. After being away, not wanting to be back in this place, wanting to be anywhere but here, Kyle is surprised by how very glad he is to be home. It's a place that he's made his own after doing constant maintenance and physical improvements, touching every aspect from the electrical to the plumbing to the moldings. More than that, it's where Ben has showed Kyle time and time again how protected and possessed he is. Kyle isn't alone. He's Ben's. And Ben might not be perfect, but Ben is Kyle's too. They have their problems; everyone does. Kyle believes, as he takes a step, then another, and another, inside and the door shuts behind him, that maybe they can get past it all and start fresh. With a deep breath, he lets Ben lead him upstairs and order him to bed.

But when Kyle is under the covers, changed and lying on his very own pillow, Ben sits at his side and admits, "You're going to have to give me hints about how to make this easy on you. I know how you've been... closely monitored. If I overstep, it might freak you out. If I ask for your input on everything, it's going against how we work. I kind of don't know how to play this."

"Just stay with me. You know me better than anybody."

"Do I?"

Ben searches Kyle's face, the cockiness that defines Ben gone in a way that unsettles Kyle to witness. When words fail them, Ben slides farther onto the bed and lies beside Kyle, facing him. He brushes a strand of blond hair from Kyle's forehead, making Kyle close his eyes with pleasure at being there, with Ben, and being touched by Ben. He's asleep almost at once.

A few hours later, he wakes screaming.

Ben holds him down by the shoulders. In a swift movement, he swings a leg astride Kyle's prone form and uses his body weight to keep Kyle still. Leaning forward, Ben shifts a hand up, clamping it over Kyle's mouth to muffle his cries.

Kyle tests him, trying his hardest to get free, but in the end it seems to be Ben's hand quieting him, limiting his air, and the hard glint in Ben's blue eyes looking down upon Kyle in the dark that get him past the nightmare. Reality gets fuzzy, distant, then Kyle is unconscious again.

Morning comes. Kyle sleeps through most of it. Around noon he wakes. All he wants is a shower but Ben won't let him until he drinks a tall glass of orange juice. When it's drained, Kyle goes to use the toilet, and Ben follows, standing there with folded arms while Kyle voids his aching bladder. As he strips off his clothes and climbs into the hot spray in the tub, careful to keep his stitched hand out of the way, Ben stays right there, watching, examining Kyle's body and its many healed-over wounds without comment.

As he scrubs the dirt, one-handed, out of his hair and spreads suds over his whole body, Kyle wonders what it'd be like to be in a relationship where his private moments wouldn't be so displayed to his partner. He's pretty sure he wouldn't like it. As resistant as he was when he first started seeing Ben seriously to let him observe absolutely everything, Kyle discovers that he's become reliant upon that aspect of their life for a deeper sense of being treasured by his lover.

"We need to talk," Ben says as Kyle dries off.

Running his fingers over his jaw, covered in thick blond stubble, Kyle says, "I need a shave."

"You aren't permitted to shave yourself. You eat. We talk. Then, I'll shave you. No bullshit... do you wish you were dead?"

"No," Kyle answers, feeling small.

"Do you wish you were high?"

"Sometimes."

"Do you want to break up?"

"Fuck, no."

"Good. That's all I need to know."

Ben cooks Kyle brunch. He burns the eggs and over-microwaves the sausage, but the cereal is good and the coffee is better.

"What happened to your face?" Kyle asks before taking a huge bite of food.

Ben rolls his eyes, "I thought Gabe told you."

"I didn't get to ask questions. Especially about you."

"Picked a fight," Ben sighs. "I won."

"Fight with who?"

"Your dealer."

"Goddammit, Ben," Kyle exclaims. "Really? Why?"

"Don't be an idiot."

"Did you kill him?"

Ben stares. "You're serious."

"Yeah, I'm serious!"

"No, I didn't kill him. You think I go around killing people I don't like?"

Kyle shrugs. "You would've killed Harry. Maybe you did kill Harry."

"What does that have to do with anything? He was a pedophile who's been raping boys for decades."

"And who are you that you get to be his executioner?"

"We didn't kill Harry," Ben growls. "We just sent a message."

"How do I know that one day you won't want to send me a message, like you did with Harry? And my dealer? Isn't that what you do? You're my Master. You're in charge. My job is to trust you. Your job is to make choices and carry them out, without consulting me first."

"That's not my job," Ben answers, but without much force, because he's focused on something else. Sitting up in his chair, he leans forward, closer to Kyle across the table and narrows his eyes. "Back up for a sec. You really think I'd hurt you? That's what this is all about? The way you were acting, why you left... this is because of *Harry*?"

"No. Yes," Kyle fidgets.

"Please explain," Ben commands.

"I don't know how to explain! You freaked me out, okay? You always get these crazy ideas, and then you *do them*. You always said you'd find Harry and fuck him over. And then you did. *You did that.* You told me things, really fucked up things, about a foursome with Gabe and Dare, and then you did those too. You made it happen. It's never bullshit. It's never just a fantasy. You get an idea, and then it happens."

"It scares you that I'm not full of shit?"

"I don't know," Kyle lies.

"Yes, you do."

"Fine. Yes, it does."

"But *why*?"

Kyle sets down his fork, sits back in his seat, and drops his gaze.

"WHY, Kyle?"

"I guess because I'm, like, the opposite of that. I am full of shit, okay? Up to my eyeballs. And you know that. You know all about me. You know how to take me apart, a piece at a time, until there's nothing left. And as much bullshit as I throw at you, it won't ever matter. I'll never be safe from you."

"*I would never hurt you*," Ben says adamantly, nearly shouting.

Kyle doesn't respond. He clams up. Then he says, "You hurt me."

"Not like that."

"What's the difference, Ben?! Every time I trust you, I'm making myself helpless and letting you chip away at who I am. One day, there's not going to be anything left."

"You are *such* a fucking drama queen," Ben laughs. "Dramatic fucking *pussyboy*. You really think I can take something from you that you don't want to give? You have heard of safewords, right? You're aware that you can use them at any time? You're aware that I've *never* not stopped when you've used yours?"

Kyle deflates a little, so Ben pushes on.

"Yeah, I know what pushes your buttons. I also know that nothing tickles your prick more than having them pushed. You've got a self-destructive streak in you, that's for damn sure. Why do you think you've gotten yourself into this lovely little lifestyle of ours? That's what we do, Kyle. I find out what scares you, and then I give it to you wrapped in a nice shiny bow. I give it to you until you're pissing yourself with fear and then I take it away and make it all better. It makes you stronger. It's a victory. A little notch on your belt to show all your pussyboy friends and brag about. Yeah, I get my rocks off on it, seeing you squirm, hearing you beg me for it, fucking you senseless. I won't deny it. I can't believe it. That's what all the fuss has been about. You having a bitchfit identity crisis. Did it help? Taking Grealey's cock up your pretty pussyboy ass? You've faced that fear and now it's not so scary anymore?"

Shaken, Kyle pushes off the chair, bolting to his feet, ready to run from the room. Ben is around the table and on him in a blink. He grabs Kyle by the throat and shoves him back down. "Sit the fuck down, slave! You don't get to run off again."

Kyle sucks in a rough breath, trying not to cry and give Ben the satisfaction. He thinks of Gabriel, the look on his face after he'd heard Darrek's confession and Kyle's acknowledgement of the truth of it. Ben is going to find out. If Gabriel, Darrek, Trace and Micah know, it's only a matter of time. Kyle does want to run off again, and the pain starts to come back, along with the self-hatred and misery.

"It's still scary. It'll always be scary," Kyle says, in a dead voice, because he has nowhere to go this time. He can't go to Gabriel and Darrek. They have their hands full. And there isn't anywhere else that would be a sanctuary for him. He wants to stay with Ben, to make him understand the whole, wretched truth so that the lying can stop.

"What does that mean?"

"It means it'll always be scary! LISTEN TO ME!"

Kyle is frightfully pale, almost gray, and nearly convulsing he's shaking so badly. He moans softly as the weakness starts to win out. Scared for Kyle, Ben drops to his knees in front of him and steadies him by bracing his arms.

"Hey. *Hey*! Look at me! Kyle! Kyle, what does that mean? What's scary? Darrek?"

"I can't tell you. *I can't tell you,*" Kyle growls defiantly.

"Why? Why can't you tell me?"

"*Because I can't.* I've never been able to tell you. Ever."

Ben tries to understand. He stares at Kyle's face and reads between the words, deciphering the riddle. Darrek. Sex. Terror. Time. Secrets. Darrek as a threat. Sex with Darrek as a threat. Secrets that Kyle has always had.

"Can you tell Gabriel?" Ben tries.

Kyle's reaction answers for him. Nervous, his eyes jump right to where Ben's phone sits on the table.

"You've gotta be fucking kidding me. He knows, doesn't he? Gabriel already fucking knows what this is!"

Ben grabs for the phone.

"NO!" Kyle shrieks, lunging off of the chair and trying to wrestle the phone from Ben.

"Then say it! Just say it!"

"I CAN'T!"

"Why did Darrek try to slit his throat? That's why you grabbed the knife, isn't it? What could possibly have happened to make him want to do that? He couldn't have been that broken up over having sex with you. Even if you didn't ask for it and he forced you... he... Oh."

"Ben," Kyle sobs, seeing Ben figure it out, trying to compensate for glimpsed truths Kyle never intended to be revealed. "It wasn't his fault, okay? I swear to God it wasn't. He made him do it. And I wanted it. Oh God...."

"I'm gonna rip his head off with my bare hands," Ben says softly. It's a lie. Ben isn't angry, just horrified and trying to provoke Kyle into talking.

"It was Jerry! Jerry Grealey! It wasn't Darrek! Jerry told him that if he didn't admit to his sins and being a perverted little faggot and fuck me like I clearly wanted him to, that God would kill us for our sins. He would have *killed us.*"

"Holy fucking... how old were you?" Ben asks, seeking the answer before Kyle can clam up again.

"Twelve. Thirteen."

"It was more than once," Ben says, filling in the blanks. "Jerry Grealey forced you two to have sex? And that sick fuck watched?" Kyle gets very still. Suddenly, he tries to bolt and get away from Ben, falling over his own feet, chest heaving with the force of his tears. Ben manages to grab Kyle's upper arm and spins him, yanking him flush to his chest and wrapping both arms around Kyle to keep him there. Kyle tries to push off the ground and twist free but it's no use.

"He was so scared," Kyle cries. "Jerry beat him. Whipped him. He was gonna slam the door and break Dare's hand to punish him for touching me, and... I let it happen. I *wanted* to be with Darrek, so I didn't try to fight or stand up to Jerry. Darrek never remembered. He never remembered! It's not his fault!"

"It's not *your* fault," Ben shouts. "Do you hear me, Kyle? *It's not your fault!* Jesus, that's the reason for all of it, isn't it? The cutting, the drugs, and the way you've been acting, trying to kill yourself...." Kyle strains against Ben's hold, his face turning colors as he holds his breath and pushes with all of what little strength he has.

"What're you gonna do?" Kyle chokes out.

Ben hears in his lover's voice the fear that he might hurt Kyle to punish him for imagined crimes against young Darrek, and fear that Ben will go after Darrek and Jerry for vengeance. But Ben knows without being told that he will lose Kyle permanently if he makes Darrek into the enemy. And Darrek would not be able to bear an assault against his parents, no matter what they've done.

"What am *I* gonna do? I'm gonna make sure that you never hurt yourself again, by any means. And you know how I'm gonna do that? Hmm? By showing you that I love you and that you are a strong, incredible man, despite the fact that you're a rape victim. You don't think you are, do you? You think you've been protecting poor Darrek all of these years from his abusive fuck of a father. Darrek the victim. Well, guess what? You went through shit, Kyle! You need to face that. Why haven't you told me?" Ben asks, his voice sharp with emotion. Kyle struggles and Ben just holds him closer, caressing up and down Kyle's arms, kissing the side of his head. "I could have helped you," Ben hisses. "*I could have helped you not to hurt like this.* I love you so much, you stupid little shit."

Once Kyle realizes that Ben is crying, he stops struggling completely. Letting his head fall back against Ben, he gives up the fight to get free and lets Ben hold on as tightly as he wants, taking a deep, shaky breath. Ben feels Kyle's tense fear slip slowly away as his own heart breaks.

"Please don't hurt Darrek," Kyle asks quietly. "He's been through more than enough. Trust me. I was there."

"I'm not going to hurt Darrek."

"But... Harry...."

"Has nothing to do with this. This is different. Gabriel wasn't trying to kill himself over misplaced guilt. Right now, all that matters, *all that matters*, Kyle, is healing this wound. You've been carrying this secret for most of your life. You don't have to do that anymore. It's out in the open. The people that matter know, and that's all that counts. This is something that we'll deal with privately. All I want is to take care of you. I can assume that all Gabriel wants is to take care of Darrek. I almost lost you. All I care about is fixing this, and guess what? Now I know how. Okay?"

Kissing the side of Kyle's face, Ben promises, "I'm gonna make this right for you, *your* way. You trust me?"

"Yeah, I trust you," Kyle admits. "But if you go after Jerry Grealey, I will leave you and you'll never find me. Not this time. That's a guarantee."

Ben sighs, debating his response. He agrees with a muffled, "Yeah. Okay," before kissing Kyle once more.

Chapter 23

Fighting Forgiveness

"We can sit," Gabriel offers.

Darrek shakes his head. He's fidgeting, restless, and chewing on his thumbnail. Hair stringy wet from his shower and fallen in his eyes, he looks wild and lost, especially as he is standing tensely in the middle of the hallway of his and Gabriel's quaint, peaceful home with his arm folded protectively in front of his chest.

Trace is still there, hovering a few feet away in the mostly dark house. His presence lends the moment gravity. Gabriel wishes he would go, but has other priorities first.

"Okay," Gabriel relents. "Then, can you tell us what you meant on the phone? When you called me, you said things I can't even *pretend* to understand. Things about Kyle. Something happened with Kyle. Something bad enough to get a knife in your hand. Can you try to explain some of that? We just want to help you, baby. No judging, just listening."

The tension in Darrek's body ratchets up another few notches, desperation fighting shame and horror. He shakes his head again, like he's fighting with himself. He's not looking at Gabriel, or at Trace. He's not looking at anything tangible. It reminds Gabriel of when he was younger, when he had his own ghosts to fight. There were things he knew then, things he saw that no one else could know or see. Now he sees that same frantic energy in Darrek.

Putting some of the pieces together, trying to draw Darrek out, Gabriel continues, "You said you raped Kyle, Dare, but Kyle said *tonight* it was consensual. You said something about being *kids*. You mentioned your *Dad*. Do you remember telling me that stuff?"

183

"It's true," Darrek blurts, his voice hoarse from crying. "I said it. I remembered stuff after having sex with Kyle. It hit me, out of nowhere, like I was getting memories of someone else's life, but it was me. It was *him*. And Daddy."

His eyes rise to Gabriel's face, slide over to Trace and back again.

"Say it," Gabriel whispers. "Go on."

"He forced me on Kyle. He made me do it, got off on it. When I misbehaved, or if we resisted, I'd be punished. I mean, you know, I've told you what he was like."

"Your father," Gabriel clarifies.

"Yeah."

"He beat you. Hurt you."

"Yeah."

"So he threatened you?" Gabriel guesses, recalling the threats made against him, by his own father figure.

"Yeah. If I didn't go through with it, he would have hurt me. He would have hurt Kyle. He made me choose. And I chose... I chose—"

The words break off. Darrek claps a hand over his mouth as his expression crumples with sorrow. He sucks in a rough breath, tears falling again.

Gabriel goes to him, and hugs him. Darrek fearfully wraps Gabriel in his arms.

"I chose Kyle," Darrek sobs. "*Oh god.*"

"Hey," Gabriel hushes, clutching Darrek to him. "It's okay. You're okay."

"He was specific," Darrek sneers. "He told me *exactly* what to do to Kyle. And when I hesitated, he'd whip me with his belt, so I tried... I tried to shield Kyle. I tried...."

"Jesus," Gabriel moans. "More than once?"

"Yeah. More than once."

"Kyle knew," Gabriel realizes, replaying the night in his head, remembering the way Kyle reacted to questions, the way he looked. "Kyle knew the whole time. The whole...."

"What?"

Darrek pulls out of the embrace, steps back, looking at Gabriel with terrible shock.

"I think Kyle knew," Gabriel explains. "He didn't look like you do. He looked *relieved*. You buried the memories, but he had them. He always had them. Oh my god. *Oh my god.*" He tries to imagine what it'd be like to suddenly recall all of what he'd suffered because of Harry at once, and can't. He can't begin to wrap his head around it. More so, he can't fathom how Kyle functioned as Darrek's closest friend for most of their lives, living with this knowledge of their past, and of Jerry Grealey.

Shaking, holding Gabriel's shoulders, eyes beseeching, Darrek quakes with this new revelation. Acting swiftly, needing to not make things worse, Gabriel says, "Hey, it's gonna be okay. I need you to trust me in that, baby. Kyle is... well, he's a survivor. He's *survived.* He stuck by you for all of these years, knowing what happened to both of you and loving you all the way through it. I'm going to do the same thing. And Kyle... he's gonna be okay. Kyle never blamed you and he's just saved your life. That's all I need to know. You are a *good man*, Darrek. Speaking as someone who was forced to do things, sick things, or pay the price, I know how bad it is right now for you, but I promise it won't always be this way. I plan on being with you and loving you for a long, long time and that's all that matters."

"The things I've done to him," Darrek hisses, disgusted.

"You don't have responsibility for that," Trace says from the shadows, voice booming as he proclaims Darrek's innocence. Gabriel sees it help begin to pull Darrek from the hell churning in his mind. "You were both victims."

"*No,*" Darrek groans, "I did it. It was me. *I* forced him. I — "

"No. Hey!" Gabriel says forcefully. "You don't get to carry the weight of what happened any more than I do! Look at me and tell me that I'm responsible at all for Harry touching me or raping me or giving me orders."

It's too much. Darrek rubs both hands over his face, crying, hanging his head. He turns from Gabriel, and Gabriel steps back to give him some space.

"Leave."

Trace glances over at Darrek, hooking a thumb at him. Darrek is still withdrawn, silent, and lingering in the hall like even the burden of committing to a room or a seat is too much to bear.

Trace says to Gabriel, "You know you can't fix this all on your own."

"Leave, dammit," Gabriel repeats stubbornly.

"I was there, remember? I was there every bleeding day. You hate doctors and therapy. I'm the one that dragged your little ass there on a regular basis. And now you're supposed to be the expert at fixing abuse victims? You need help. Both of you."

"Darrek is mine," Gabriel replies, with much less bravado and confidence than he wishes he had. It's all wearing on him, but he's determined to power through for Darrek. "This is my problem. I'll handle it. It doesn't concern you, so please...."

"Oh, it doesn't 'concern' me at all. My job is to help my boy. It's not like I want to be your therapist either, I just want to hear you admit that you will do what's best for that kid over there, and not what's best for *you*. You might think you can, but you can't do this on your own."

Overhearing everything, Darrek's nostrils flare. The tension in his body somehow grows, but Gabriel understands why—Darrek can't stand between Gabriel and Trace; he can only wait for them to finish.

Defiance floods Gabriel's system. Trace already said these things to Gabriel while Darrek was in the shower, after Gabriel relayed what Darrek had said over the phone about Kyle. Gabriel didn't want to hear it then, either, and chose to call to check on Kyle at the hospital, via Micah, rather than endure the lecture. But now, Trace won't leave until he's satisfied that Gabriel is going to be the man he needs to be instead of the child he's behaving like.

Gabriel releases a frustrated shout, his voice torn apart by pain and weariness. He sucks in a rough breath and when Trace steps closer, beats on Trace's chest with a closed fist. It helps to lash out at something solid when so much of what they're fighting is devoid of substance.

"I'm not an idiot! I get it, okay?! Just... *listen to me.* Please."

"I hear you, babydoll," Trace says tenderly, easily pulling away Gabriel's next swing, brushing a thumb over his clenched jaw. "I always hear you."

When Gabriel pleads, shaking, desperate, "Get *out*," it's not as a friend, or a son, but a lover. One who knows he can't make Trace leave and let his boy, Gabriel, stand on his own two feet any more than Gabriel could have stopped Darrek from having sex with Kyle. "I'll do the right thing. I promise." Beseeching, Gabriel pushes at him and says, "Go."

"It's not your fault any more than it's theirs, you know," Trace tells him. "And I hope you can find a way to get your behind into the therapist's office again, too."

More of Gabriel's pride slips through Trace's fingers, melting into nothing, leaving less of the strong Dominant and ever more of the broken boy. If he defies Gabriel any longer, he'll be the one to break him, so Trace nods. He presses a tender kiss to the bow of Gabriel's lips and turns to leave without another word.

There's space for one breath between when the door closes after Trace and when Darrek comes forward and falls to his knees at Gabriel's feet.

Though he intended to say a lot of things once he was there, kneeling, all that comes out is a moan of pure regret and desolation. He grasps Gabriel's ankle, presses his mouth to the top of his shoe, his body folded in half, as low to the ground as it's possible for him to be. Utterly pathetic, Darrek knows he has done wrong. He recognizes it, owns it and will try to make amends with no thought to himself, only those he's hurt. Gabriel, who Darrek loves so much, trusts so much, is his beacon. Once things shake loose, he knows that much at least.

Still as a statue, Gabriel is frozen, but brittle. He says, "*Stand* up." The first word is loud, a burst of frustrated fury; the second is a ragged whisper, barely heard. That's exactly how long it takes Gabriel to fall apart.

Startled by Gabriel's vulnerability, and instinctively drawn to it,

Darrek gets to his feet and towers over his Master.

"I brought this down on you," Darrek realizes. "After every-thing you've been through, I come and lay this mess at your feet and expect you to clean it up for me. *I did that. I—*"

"Shut up," Gabriel hisses as a heavy tear slides down his cheek.

"Hurt me," Darrek invites with maschocistic greed. "Hurt me for bringing Kyle to that field and having sex with him. I *need* it." Cupping Gabriel's face in both hands, pressing his lips to the shell of Gabriel's ear, with heated breath, Darrek repeats more forcefully, "*I need it*, Gabriel."

"I forgive you," Gabriel says. It's thick with emotion, and he's smiling slightly. Another thick tear falls.

"Don't you *dare*," Darrek growls, his fingers making indents in Gabriel's skin. "Don't you fucking dare!"

"Too late. It's all too late. All of... all of it...." Gabriel's lips part, wet with his tears, hot with his fevered sorrow and they chase Darrek's mouth. When finding it, Gabriel moans, shaking Darrek to his core, awakening an animal, previously hidden, now loosed.

All thought and reason is gone because Darrek devours it as he devours Gabriel, worshipping his mouth, bearing down on him until he has to hold the back of Gabriel's head in order to keep him there. Jaws working, taking shallow, frantic inhales of needed oxygen through their noses, they tangle and blend, melding into one anoth-er. Darrek lifts Gabriel without deciding to; just *needing* and needing Gabriel to need him back. Wrapping Gabriel's legs up around his waist, Darrek stumbles forward and carries him to the sideboard. Gabriel's ass settles down onto the piece of furniture. Darrek presses him back against the wall, drawing Gabriel's legs higher.

It's not about sex, for either of them, but ownership, devotion, passion, commitment, obsession. Together in the storm, feeling it rage and tear and shriek around them, it's only in each other's arms that they feel steady and sure. Gabriel's need shines in his eyes, is spoken in the fevered heat of his kiss and the claw of his fingers over Darrek's skin. Love is pledged with every pore.

Feeling Darrek's heartbreak, Gabriel heals it by giving himself. He makes a soft, grunted plea, "Take it off," while pulling at Darrek's shirt. As he twists it over his head, Gabriel fumbles at his own fly, popping the button, digging at the zipper. Darrek, leaning against Gabriel to keep him in place, balanced atop the sideboard, gets the idea and yanks roughly at the back of Gabriel's pants, getting them down, fast, with a small tearing sound as the fabric gives out before Darrek's impatience does.

Darrek swears, "This is all I need. This. All I'll ever, ever need. Just this. Just you. This makes everything feel okay."

If he'd intended to say more, Gabriel swallows it, catching Darrek's lips, kissing him roughly as Darrek works him open, using saliva as lube so that he doesn't cause Gabriel any harm. The passion in the sex is violent enough to make Gabriel shout. Fresh tears — this time, though, of gratitude — fall freely from his eyes. Urging Darrek on ever faster, harder, deeper, Gabriel takes all of it, then demands more. He claims Darrek in ways no one ever could, not in a million years. Not Kyle; not Darrek's father; not anyone. As Darrek gets off on the clenched hug of Gabriel around his stiffened member, drawing Gabriel's legs ever higher, pushing into that perfect soft grip, gasping and growling, manic, Gabriel scratches and bites down on his conqueror. Short nails drag down his bare back. Indentations that will become bruises pepper his shoulder and neck.

With a final snap of his hips, buried completely, Darrek groans and gasps. "Need you," he whispers desperately. "Love you so much."

Pushing Gabriel's head back a few inches, to rest against the wall and give Darrek a better view of his lover's face, he stares into his eyes with total devotion and fretful care. Swiping the pad of his thumb over Gabriel's lower lip as he gasps woozily, Darrek sees that he's sweat-drenched and still hard. His cock, hot and wet, nudges Darrek's stomach.

"What do you need? Name it and you can have it," Gabriel offers.

"Just you. I want to belong to you. Be yours."

"Put," Gabriel grunts, leveraging himself off of Darrek's broad shoulders and the wall behind him, shifting his pose until he feels Darrek slip out. "Put me down."

Darrek obeys and steadies Gabriel as he unwinds his legs and gets them under him. For a moment, Darrek is unsure and his expression says as much. Like a scared little boy, fearing reprisal, he waits for judgment.

But then Gabriel reaches up to caress the tension away. Light and love shine out of Gabriel's eyes.

"You are mine," Gabriel assures him. "Always will be. I need you exactly the way you are, flaws and all. Lie down on the rug."

Darrek hesitates. Then his training kicks in. He obeys the order, walks a few steps and lies on the carpet as Gabriel frowns and scans the room, shoving his hand behind pillows and cushions.

"Gabe?"

"Lube."

"Here," Darrek says, drawing him instantly back just by opening his mouth and pushing his tongue forward.

With a heady moan, Gabriel sighs, "God, I love you."

He straddles Darrek's chest and leans down with a hand braced on the floor as he feeds Darrek his whole cock. With a hungry grunt, Darrek clasps Gabriel's hips and sucks, getting him wet, hollowing his cheeks and sucking hard as Gabriel pulls back out. His expression is serious, desperate, determined to please. Once Darrek licks over him a few more times, lapping at his cock with his tongue. Gabriel loses patience. "Okay. That's good enough."

He doesn't have to position Darrek at all. Darrek automatically draws his legs up and apart, holding his knees as Gabriel slides down his body. He lets out a lustful cry as Gabriel begins to lick him wet.

Spitting onto Darrek's hole, Gabriel rubs it in and twists two fingers inside, spreading them apart in a V to slip his tongue through the middle. The wet wiggle of Gabriel's tongue sends shockwaves of pleasure shooting up Darrek's spine and out through his every nerve. But it's not enough and the darkness starts to threaten to crash down. Gabriel licks him wet, inside and out, sucking on his rim, working him loose with his fingers, but all Darrek can think is that he doesn't deserve Gabriel, that he should do nothing but curl up and hide himself away and let the shattered pieces of his life rain down around him.

Chapter 24

Surviving Destiny

"Wait. Gabe. Gabriel," Darrek sobs. "Stop...."

"Okay. Okay, I'm here." Gabriel stops what he's doing and kneels between Darrek's legs, leaning over him with a hand braced by his head. "Talk to me."

Darrek presses the heels of his hands to his eyes and lets out a growl of frustration.

"Talk to me," Gabriel urges again, more forceful this time.

Darrek shakes his head, grimacing, tears slipping from his eyes.

"Darrek...."

Darrek angrily chokes out a few words. All Gabriel catches is "hate myself" before hissing, "Stop. Fucking stop."

He pushes Darrek's legs back and enters him with a hard thrust.

"I love you," Gabriel growls furiously, angry at so much, certain of next to nothing anymore, only the truth of what he has with Darrek. He snaps his hips, burying himself to the root, grounding Darrek to the here and now. "You believe me? Huh?"

"Yeah," Darrek gasps, stuffed so full, dizzy from it. He's never been so grateful before in his life. "I do."

"You know how fucked up I am. You loved me anyway. You saved me, from *all* of that shit. Now it's my turn. All I need from you is for you to trust me. Okay? Please? Will you trust me?"

"Yeah. I trust you. Forever," he smiles, just a little. But he means it, and it makes the rest easier to endure.

By the time they finish, it's all they can do to climb the steps and pass out on top of the bed.

Hours slide by. Sometime around two a.m. , Darrek wakes. His sleep was dreamless, so at first he doesn't remember. Then, it sinks in. His father. Kyle.

For hours he lays there and watches Gabriel sleep. The first time Gabriel rouses, Darrek brushes his dark hair from his forehead and whispers, "Go to sleep," and Gabriel does.

For a while Darrek loses the battle with consciousness. He comes around near dawn to find Gabriel gazing sleepily at him, his head resting upon a bent arm.

"You should be asleep," Darrek frowns, the words slurred. He sniffs and pulls the blanket higher, over his shoulders.

"Mm-mm," Gabriel hushes. He rolls and tucks himself inside Darrek's arms, letting him spoon up against him. "Perfect," Gabriel sighs, succumbing to tiredness once more, bringing Darrek with him.

Morning comes, arriving with a dramatically changed Gabriel. When Darrek wakes, instead of a sweetly groggy lover, he finds a washed, dressed, chipper Master.

"Mornin' sunshine," Gabriel smiles. "You ready to do this?"

"Do... what?" Darrek asks in a sleep-roughened voice, wiping his eyes clear as he sits upright in the bed. His legs are splayed to keep him steady. He's not even awake yet.

"Toilet. Shower. Teeth. Shave. Deodorant. Breakfast. Coffee. Talk. In that order, precisely."

"Wow."

"I'm waiting, slave."

"Yes, Sir. Whatever you say, Sir."

"Who's in charge here?"

"You?" Darrek says with too much uncertainty. He tries again with a more confident, "You, Master."

"That's fuckin' right. Don't you forget it. You want the collar to remind you?"

"I love you, you know," Darrek says with a small, lopsided grin.

Gabriel's hand shoots out and he grabs Darrek by the balls, through the thin sheet covering him. With a twist of Gabriel's hand,

Darrek yelps and fights to stay still, his mouth working around an unvoiced shout. He grunts out, "I love you for that too, you crazy son of a bitch."

"I am indeed the son of a bitch. I believe I asked you a question, slave."

Gabriel squeezes and pulls. Darrek cries out, "Fuck! Ow. Yes, Master. Please let me wear the collar. Sir."

"Pretty please?"

Darrek laughs through the pain as Gabriel twists his hand the other way.

"P-pretty fuckin' please, Sir."

"I will be supervising each and every step of your morning ritual for the foreseeable future. Is that understood?"

"Yes, Sir."

"If you get weary of my constant presence, I'm sure I can find exceedingly creative ways to pique your interest. You will be quitting your job, as of today. You will be focusing on your carpentry projects and making a few new custom pieces for my business and for our playroom. Is *that* understood?"

"Yes, Sir."

"In your free time, you will be acting as my receptionist."

Darrek snorts, but quickly his chuckle of amusement turns into a shrill gasp, his hips coming completely off the bed as Gabriel's fist closes like a vise around his testicles and yanks on them.

"I'm sorry, is there something about that you find amusing?"

"No, Mr. Hunter, Sir."

"Not cute," Gabriel smiles, coldly, pulling harder. Darrek grunts thickly, his eyes rolling. He thumps his head back against the wall with a low groan. Gabriel releases Darrek's balls. "Let me get your collar and get you started. We've got a lot to talk about."

"Yes, Sir. You're amazing, you know."

Gabriel scoots up to him and draws him in for a soft kiss, letting him see the lust, strength and pride that Gabriel has for him. "No, *you're* amazing."

It works wonders on Darrek's battered soul. He kisses Gabriel back and smiles.

Having Gabriel at his side helps Darrek to get out of bed and get himself together. He's not alone, and he doesn't have to hide how he feels, because with Gabriel, he is safe in every way. Mid-way through shaving the stubble from his jaw, with shaving cream covering the left side of his chin and above his lip, it hits him again. He starts crying, then Gabriel is right there, too, holding him. Gazing at Gabriel in the mirror's reflection, Darrek's angel of absolution, he wants so much. He wants to see a path through the pain, a way to comprehend his life in new ways; he wants forgiveness and solace and reasons for why life can be so vicious.

"You'll get there, baby," Gabriel whispers to him, and kisses him. "I'll show you the way."

Time moves in slow motion. Everything is more challenging with the mental war that Darrek wages just in trying to function normally. But he gets through it. He feels better once he's showered, shaved and freshened up. The collar around his neck is physical proof of his link to Gabriel, and that his Master is taking care of him. That helps, too.

Gabriel makes omelets with fresh vegetables and fruit smoothies to drink rather than coffee as he tries to keep Darrek from getting jittery or tense. It feels a little like being back on vacation, when everything made sense. Darrek likes that.

Then, the talking begins.

Darrek pours it all out and it's like he can't get the words out fast enough. It's a purge of the horrors that filled his senses once he'd released Kyle and broken through the fortified inner walls of his mind.

He tells Gabriel about Kyle's sleepovers, and how it started so innocently, with curiosity, exploration and kissing. Then his father twisted it. He made them feel like they had sinned, that they were blaspheming against God and how he made them finish what they started.

No matter how Darrek tried to explain, that they hadn't done anything wrong, Jerry wouldn't listen. He couldn't hear his son, because he was too preoccupied with his own arousal. Darrek remembers realizing that, and at such a young age—that his father wasn't well, that it was bad what he made his son do, and it was bad that his father enjoyed it so much. It was the guilt, though, that blackened out Darrek's recollection. He loved Kyle dearly before his father caught them, and he loved him after, even more. Kyle was his responsibility from that point forward. Darrek couldn't abandon him and he couldn't face what he'd done to Kyle either. There was no choice but to deny it ever happened.

Darrek talks until his throat is dry and he's coughing. Gabriel tells him to take a break and calm down while he processes everything Darrek has told him.

Gabriel's eyes light up and something clicks into place in his head. He looks right at Darrek. Heart beating faster, Darrek waits.

Gabriel tells him, "Kyle's issues with penetration and being observed in intimate situations by someone getting off on his helplessness all make perfect sense. Of course he feels that way. And if he did love and desire you when you were told to touch him and stimulate him for your father's pleasure, he felt the shame from his reactions to that. He wanted you, but on another level, he knew it was wrong. Misplaced guilt... those issues were established at the core of Kyle's being."

Gabriel grunts and touches his folded hand to his mouth, his eyes scanning invisible puzzle pieces, fitting them together. He sits forward, faces Darrek more directly, hands resting on the table. "Know what else makes sense?"

Darrek shakes his head, feeling defensive and a little nervous.

"You closed off the whole part of you that desires men. You chased Sara and that pristine picture of the wife and kids because you were programmed to. That was the safe road for you. Until you grasped at the thread that Kyle handed you — Diadem's phone number — and felt how good it was when I touched you, you didn't let yourself acknowledge that you might be gay or bisexual. You didn't want to hurt anyone like Kyle was hurt. You felt responsible for that, so you kept far away from what you might have really wanted.

"When I took control of you, and let you experience what you craved — pain, pleasure, trust, reward, tenderness — it opened up new worlds that were off-limits before. And when I was giving you orders regarding how to take control of Kyle for his own good, that put you right back there with Jerry over your shoulder."

Darrek leans forward in his chair, elbow braced on the table, mouth hidden behind his hand, and his gaze slides sideways as he listens to Gabriel attempt to rationalize his choices. He doesn't want to believe it, any of it, but now he has these new, unwanted memories to come to terms with. He doesn't want to scrutinize the ways he's acted with Gabriel and Kyle in the light of his actions as a kid, even if he knows he should.

"You acted out, trying to show yourself everything you'd denied for so long."

"No. Gabriel," he sighs, tensing up, closing his eyes.

"The ways that you've been reacting to Kyle, having him here, pushing back against me when I gave you orders on what to do with Kyle...."

"Stop. Come on. There's no way I... I mean, this *is* my fault, what I did to Kyle. I know that, but it doesn't mean—"

"Listen to me," Gabriel implores. "Darrek—baby—you make sense! Everything fits. Everything about who you are, why you love what you do, why you fear what you do, why you need what you need, how you react—"

"You don't know that! Maybe I'm just a bad guy! Maybe this is all just coming out now so that you know to stay away from me! Huh?!"

Gabriel ignores the outburst and continues anyway, "*It all makes perfect sense.* You, just as you are, right now... you're perfect. There's nothing wrong with you, baby. You're beautiful and incredible and a good man and a victim of awful shit and a survivor and you're exactly who you're supposed to be."

"I don't believe that. I can't," Darrek argues, shaking his head, fighting hard not to cry again, wanting to scream, to run.

"Do you realize that if Harry hadn't done what he did to me, and if Jerry hadn't done what he did to you and Kyle, we would never have met? This is fate. Yes, it hurts. Yes, I wish you and Kyle never had to suffer like you have, but I can't change it. No one can. But it's okay. It's all coming out for the good, and all the pain, the hurt, the guilt... it put us right here, didn't it? We're alive, we survived it. And it's okay. I know you don't believe it yet, but you will. Dare, it's all gonna be okay."

Fighting with all of his strength against the words and suggestions, Darrek feels them hit him hard, nonetheless. He holds in the flood of emotion that wants to rip out of him, covers his face and battles through it a moment at a time. Gabriel comes around to him, pulling Darrek to his chest and holds him there with fingers twined in his long hair as he cries, wringing out what has been bottled up for long, long years.

Chapter 25

Scratching that Itch

Ben passes Gabriel his joint, burned halfway down now. The late afternoon air is crisp and refreshing as they sit on lawn chairs in the backyard of Gabriel and Darrek's home. It's the day after they found Kyle and Darrek in the field, bloody and unconscious, respectively. Gabriel is dressed in jeans and a black sweater which only emphasizes how pale and worn he's looking. Darrek is out on a long run to clear his head and expend excess energy in a healthy way.

With him gone, Gabriel lets down the façade he's been wearing. For a little while, he doesn't have to have it all together for Darrek's sake. He takes the blunt and inhales, holding the smoke in then letting it go, coughing only a little. His head buzzes.

"Stop looking at me like that," he frowns.

"Like what?" Ben says innocently. "You look fabulous by the way. I can see you've got your shit all figured out—"

"Give it a fucking rest, Benny!"

Ben nods, reigning in his frustration with Gabriel's innate stubbornness.

"Is he high?" Gabriel worries, gesturing at where Kyle is kneeling in the overgrown green grass with Sierra curled up beside him. Kyle's hands—one heavily bandaged, one not—are bound in leather behind his back. Earbuds are stuck in his ears, the music playing through them drowning out the conversation. A black mask covers his eyes. Lips parted slightly, peaceful calm painted over his features, Kyle tilts his chin into the breeze and it ruffles his corn silk hair.

"High on life," Ben grins.

"What's that supposed to mean?" It's more defensive than either of them expect. Gabriel is instantly chagrined. Ben narrows his eyes, takes back the joint.

"Huh," Ben grunts, glancing between them. "He got to you, didn't he? You used to hate him so much. He was nothing but manipulative scum, right, Hunter? The trash I liked to bang in my off-time, when I wasn't on my knees for you, that is. Now, when you look at him, you see yourself. Or maybe you saw yourself in him all along, and that's why you couldn't stand him."

A pain shoots into Gabriel's chest, then expands outward in waves. He hunches forward, twisting his face away from his friend.

"Hey," Ben says sharply, making Gabriel turn, with much reluctance. There are tears in his eyes. "You're freaking me out. Are you having a bad trip?"

"No," Gabriel grumbles, holding his hand out for the weed, which Ben gives him.

"I guess you and Darrek had a long night and a longer morning. Is that why you look like cold shit?"

"Gee, thanks Ben. Dare and I are fine. We're dealing with it."

"Oh, no shit?" Ben says with plenty of biting sarcasm. "You fucking liar. You're gonna just sit there pouting like a bitch until I say it for you, aren't you? Fine.

"You and Dare aren't the only ones who had plenty to talk about since last night. Kyle was a veritable fount of information once he realized I didn't intend to carve him up like a roast turkey for having the gall to be a rape victim. Now, I know what that says about his faith in me, and yes, that was a fuck of a pill to swallow, but I'm working on it.

"Passing that by for the time being and acknowledging that I know what a horse's ass that makes me for scaring him so deeply, let me just say that he had a hell of a lot to tell me. Things that made me want to lobotomize myself just to stop from imagining this vile, evil shit that happened to them. But he needs me to absorb all of that so that he doesn't have to carry it alone anymore. And I can absorb it, Gabey, because it doesn't scare me like it does with someone else who's had to live through it. Someone like you. I know you're trying to be the big, strong man for Darrek. Thing is, I can see what it's doing to you."

Gabriel bites his tongue and stares straight ahead, watching Kyle bask in the fresh air and post-confessional bliss.

"Did you know Kyle's a good listener?" Ben says softly. "He pays attention. He's always on. He's always there. He heard you and Darrek together. Hunter, you cannot expect Darrek to be your Dom and you especially can't expect him to be your Daddy. He's your sub and your partner and he's going through a lot, to say the least. If you push him to do for you what Daddy does, it takes both of you to the bad place. Do you hear me?"

Gabriel nods stiffly, not meeting Ben's hard gaze. He clears his throat and angrily wipes at his eyes before dropping his hand back to his lap. He can't argue with Ben, not when he's giving Gabriel a good, cold dose of reality.

"I know what that kid means to you," Ben continues, a little less harshly, but the tenderness makes it harder for Gabriel to bear. "Don't ask that of him. If you ask, he'll give it, because he just wants to obey his Master and make you happy. That doesn't mean he can't bang you—because I know how much you like him to—but you have to keep it out of the bad place."

Gabriel digs deep, rasps, "Yeah," and starts to pick at the plastic of the arm of his chair.

"Now, you also owe it to him to get your shit together so that you can help him through this. Right?"

"Right."

"You don't need Darrek to be Daddy. You have one. More than one, actually. If you need Daddy to scratch that itch, you know he will. Or I will. You trust us. I know you do. We've been scratching that itch just fine since you were seventeen."

"Not like this," Gabriel argues softly.

Ben doesn't refute that. "You can trust us," he repeats.

Gabriel hears this and the truth in it. He can trust Ben and Trace. That's a fact. He becomes hyperaware of all of the pressure built up over the past weeks, his part in the responsibility for what has transpired with Kyle and Darrek, being responsible for both of them. The stress from that, on top of the stress of launching a new business for the first time in his life is monumental. Gabriel craves release, for someone else to be in charge, at least for a little while. He wants to be taken care of and given things he craves without having to go to the trouble of listing out what they would be. With Ben and Trace, and their complex history together, Gabriel knows they would understand instinctively. He would be safe. He could indulge, be purged in more ways than one, and be freed of some of that pressure. It's exactly what he needs.

He imagines it, the fantasy coming to life in vivid colors in his mind's eye, of submitting in every way to these two powerful, caring, skilled Dominants. Nothing would be off the table. He could let them take him in ways he's secretly wanted for years, but been unable to consent to. It would be so freeing, to be able to be made so vulnerable and open the doors to another level of taboo familial intimacy. Flushing with embarrassment and arousal, almost too quietly to hear, Gabriel says, "Set it up. Call 'im."

"What, now?" Ben asks, surprised.

It has to be now. Now that he's opened himself to the idea, he doesn't want to wait for it to happen. Plus, he fears that if he doesn't instigate it right away, it might never happen. He could lose his nerve.

"Call 'im, Benny," Gabriel practically growls. "Tell him to get his ass over here. And bring Micah and Lily to keep an eye on Dare and Kyle."

"Say please," Ben teases in such a way that a shiver of want shoots right up Gabriel's spine and tickles over his balls, making them feel too full, his pants too tight.

"Please," he responds obediently, needfully.

"Good boy."

When Darrek returns from his run, Gabriel is sitting cross-legged outside in the grass in front of Kyle and facing him, with Sierra lounging at Gabriel's side. A bottle of some sort of hard alcohol is clutched in Gabriel's right hand. Its presence is a clear signal to Darrek that something is off and causing Gabriel stress.

With his left hand, Gabriel ever so lightly caresses Kyle's cheek.

Blindfolded, handcuffed and deafened by the earbuds playing loud music in his ears, Kyle detects Gabriel through smell and touch alone. It's kind of fascinating to watch. Darrek stretches out to avoid cramps, seeing Gabriel study Kyle's tranquility, grazing fingertips over his pale skin while Kyle follows each touch, turning into it before it can dance away.

Darrek probably would have continued standing there, puzzling it out, catching his breath and coming down from his runner's high, except Ben comes up to him, lays a hand on his shoulder and says, "Come inside with me. We need to talk."

The trouble is, Darrek doesn't entirely trust Ben. Ben seems to read this wariness in Darrek's tight-lipped expression, so he lifts his shirt, turns in a circle and says, "No weapons, shackles or dildos. Promise. I'm not gonna shank you."

Ben grabs the sweaty front of Darrek's shirt and yanks him down, kissing him square on the mouth. It's a dirty, hard kiss. Ben grunts and sucks on Darrek's lip before pulling away. "Mm, salty," he smirks, licking Darrek's sweat from his lips. "I just need to talk."

Darrek, frowning slightly with bewilderment, glances sideways at Gabriel. "Um, does this have anything to do with what's going on over there?"

"Your drunken pothead seeking the answers to the universe's mysteries in Kyle's nose hairs? Yeah, it does, actually. Come on."

They head into the kitchen. Ben gets Darrek a bottle of water from the fridge and nods to a chair at the kitchen table.

"Thanks," Darrek grunts, sighing as he sits and leans back in the chair.

"Good run?"

"Great run. I forgot how much I love it," he admits.

"Very healthy. I approve."

"Good. So...?"

"Yeah," Ben murmurs. He's taken the chair beside Darrek's, and sits forward on it. "There's not really an easy way to say this."

Darrek tries to anticipate what's on Ben's mind. He knows that Ben was brought up to speed by Kyle, so he assumes it's about Jerry.

"If you're looking for an apology —" Darrek starts.

"No," Ben says sharply, cutting him off. "I'm not. This is about Gabriel."

"Oh."

"You know how crazy he is about you," Ben starts. "He feels he owes you big after the way you've been there for him through the nightmare with his stepfather and the way that's affected him. At this point, just finding out the real reason for Kyle's suicide attempts... and everything with you since last night... He's trying to be everything for you. He doesn't know how to not try to be that. It's just the way he is."

"Yeah," Darrek sighs, turning his head to peer out the kitchen window towards where Gabriel sits. "I know. He wants to save me, but he can't."

"Right. And you have enough to process without having to worry about overloading him, too. You both need to start seeing a professional to talk this all out. That's key. But for Gabriel, there's something else that might help him along. And it's not weed or rum. I, um... I know that he has you dominate him once in a while. The Daddy thing gets thrown in...."

Face turning scarlet, Darrek laughs self-consciously through the torrent of embarrassment. "Wow."

"Bear with me," Ben says. "Hey." He waits for Darrek to look at him, and tells him, straight out, "It's gotta stop, man. It might feel like the most natural thing in the world, to both of you, but it's bad for my brother out there, and it's bad for you. You got me?"

Darrek feels Ben gauge the effect his words are having by measuring the quickening rhythm of Darrek's breathing, and the ratcheting level of his energy. He grips Darrek's knee and squeezes.

"I want to help. Trace wants to help. We can give Gabriel what he needs in a very efficient, safe, loving way that doesn't threaten you or your relationship with him, at all. We're a family now. All of us. That includes me and you. I am here for you. I'm here for Gabriel, too. If either of you needs anything, I will do anything in my power to give it. Be his sub. Be his lover and companion. Be his partner. Hell, be his husband if you go for that shit. Don't be the one that punishes and hurts him. Don't be Daddy."

Curling forward, arms crossed to his chest, Darrek strangles on the force of his tears, fighting them back, hard. Ben is right there, though. He slides forward and hugs Darrek's head to him, folding over him, rubbing his back. Darrek's sobs wrack him, and Ben just holds on tighter. "It's okay. You're okay. Gabriel's okay," he promises.

He grabs Darrek by the shoulders, pushes him upright and, holding Darrek's face in his hands, wipes away his tears.

"Can you trust me with this?" Ben asks, struggling with the words. "I know I'm asking a lot. But I trusted you with Kyle."

Darrek sees the shine in Ben's eyes, hears the waver of his voice, and breaks.

"I'm so sorry, Ben," Darrek weeps. He collapses into Ben, because Ben lets him. They grasp at each other as forces beyond their control rage around them and anguish chews them up from the inside with pointed, needle-like teeth.

An uncertain amount of time later, Darrek is cried out, for the moment at least. Ben seems, to Darrek, the most human he ever has, as his sorrow for his lover radiates from every part of him.

"Swear to me that you'll take good care of him."

Every word is a battle. Proud devotion shines in Darrek's eyes.

Clasping Darrek's hand in his, Ben grips it and swears, "Always have. Always will."

From the periphery of his vision, Gabriel sees Darrek and Ben go inside, knowing why. He raises the bottle and takes a deep drink, savoring the warmth and burn as the rum slides down into his chest. Carefully, he peels the blindfold off of Kyle. He takes the earbuds out.

Face-to-face with Kyle, with only the sky, the birds and Sierra to overhear them, he asks, "How are you?"

"Why?" Kyle's expression is a blank mask, inscrutable. It's the first word he's said since he arrived with Ben.

"Answer the question."

"Is that an order?"

"No," Gabriel relents. "Just. Answer the question."

"You don't have to take care of me anymore," Kyle says, and Gabriel listens for bitterness, but Kyle is just too damn hard to read. However, the fact that Kyle has raised his walls back up to the point where Gabriel is totally blocked out is a bad enough sign to scare him. "And you don't have to be nice or pretend you like me. You've never liked me and now I'm the other man, right?"

Passing right by all of this, because none of it matters—not to Gabriel, at least—he softens his voice and intentionally strips the hard 'Dominant' edge from it to say, "You don't have to stay with him if he still scares you. I'll help you get away, somewhere safe."

"What, Ben?" Kyle actually laughs, but it's cold and his eyes are dead. "Ben's essentially turned into a fucking romantic, falling over himself to impress me. It's uncanny. I can actually tell that he loves me."

"You don't have to pretend with me," Gabriel urges, searching Kyle's face. "I get it, okay? *I get it.*"

"What do you 'get', Gabe?" Gabriel feels the anger, and sees it too, filling up the dead space, painting it a bloody red. "I wasn't raped, like you, I—"

"Weren't you?"

There's a thick, heavy pause as Gabriel struggles to show Kyle what's sitting right in front of him.

Chapter 26
Child Without a Choice

Gabriel isn't being domineering or distant. He's not judging or looking down on Kyle. He's not hiding anything. This is the Gabriel Darrek sees, Kyle realizes. The one that was taken apart by a sick man then taped back together, slowly, over a decade of time, by the family he built carefully around him. It disturbs Kyle more than anything else has, because he sees, in that moment, how similar they are. Kyle can relate to that feeling of being pieced together—that bruised horror at the cruelty of the world.

"The people we love are the ones able to hurt us the most," the new, exposed Gabriel tells him. "I wanted my new father to love me and be proud of me. I *wanted* that."

His voice wavers with urgency, his lip quivers. "Just because you loved Darrek, doesn't mean it wasn't rape. It's because you cared about him, and were attracted to him that made it so tragically damaging for you. You didn't bring that on yourself because you thought you wanted it. The choice was taken away from you. Jerry scared you and he threatened his son. You had no choice. Kyle, you had *no choice.* You're not complicit. You're not responsible, any more than I am for going along with it and keeping my mouth shut with Harry. I didn't say no most of the time. Not at all. I knew better than to talk back. We were just kids. You were a *kid.*"

Kyle's breath catches. He's fine and then he's not. Tears are in his eyes. He pulls at the cuffs restraining him, wanting to lash out, but Gabriel just sits there calmly, out of reach.

"Stop lying to yourself. Just..." Gabriel beseeches. "Stop."

"I'm not innocent," he spits. "I let it happen. All of it. I asked him to do it! Jerry... Jerry was going to..." Kyle makes a sound of disgusted horror. "So I told Darrek... I *told* him...."

"Because you were a scared boy without parents to protect him, or anyone to defend you but yourself. You were acting out of self-preservation, and trying to protect your friend from harm. That's brave, that's incredible, but you were raped. You were *raped*."

Kyle tries to pull free, but hasn't the strength to do it. He inhales but it sounds like a terrified whimper.

"Did you want it?"

"Doesn't matter...."

"Did you *want* it? Kyle..." Gabriel takes hold of Kyle's arms, keeping him steady as Kyle shrinks in on himself. "Kyle, did you?" His grip loosens and caresses upwards until he's holding Kyle's face in his hands, the pads of his thumbs making soft arcs over Kyle's skin. "Did you want it?"

"Not like that," Kyle chokes out. "Not like that." He gazes up at Gabriel, trying to make him understand. He makes a long, low moan of helpless dismay.

"I know, baby," Gabriel soothes. "I know."

Unable to breathe, too aware of Gabriel's nearness and the tenderness of his touch, denying it, craving more pain and punishment instead, Kyle pushes against him. But he's sobbing, from deep down in his chest.

"Don't keep it in," Gabriel whispers. "Don't you *dare* keep it in."

Kyle's wail increases in volume. He digs his feet into the earth and pushes as hard as he can against Gabriel.

"Jerry took advantage of you, because you *couldn't fight back*. The most enticing victims are the ones that have no way to defend themselves. He preyed on you. Kyle, look at me. Look at me!" He holds Kyle's jaw and seethes. "Don't take credit for a predator's crime. You were just a sweet kid, who loved his friend so much."

Kyle whines softly and tries to twist away. He inhales and breathes in Gabriel's breath. Their foreheads touch. Gabriel's fingertips move in soothing arcs over the hollows of his cheeks. Baring his teeth, just pushing and pushing outward against everything locked up inside, Kyle fights the good fight. It's when he hears Gabriel crying softly that his heart turns outside in and inside out and it comes flooding from him—a wash of cleansing but terrible power that carries with it the foundations of who Kyle thought he was.

Kyle loved Darrek in a complete, pure-hearted way. Kyle's family was not always there for him, but Darrek was. He was the best friend Kyle ever had and that was part of his love. It was more than that, though. Kyle thought Darrek was beautiful, and wanted to hold his hand sometimes when they were together. He felt like he would probably never be brave enough to try to hold hands with Darrek, though. It would freak Darrek out. Still, Kyle wanted that. He had secret fantasies of kissing Darrek, touching and being touched by Darrek.

Sometimes, when they had sleepovers, Kyle would whisper "I love you" to Darrek when he was sleeping. Kyle would look at Darrek's lips and want to kiss them, but knew that would freak Darrek out too, so he didn't.

Kyle kept all of these feelings and desires inside, his alone. Until one night, during one of their sleepovers, they were lying under the sheet on Darrek's big bed, laughing and talking about ghost stories.

Each time Darrek chuckled and smiled, Kyle's gaze slipped right down to Darrek's lips. It was so dark under there, with only the light from the nightlights seeping through the thin covering over them. Kyle thought it was probably okay to look.

Then, something funny happened. Darrek kept shushing Kyle, putting a finger to Kyle's lips and trying to keep his own voice down so that Mr. Grealey didn't hear them talking. Each time he did, Darrek would shift a little closer to Kyle. Their bodies were almost touching as they lay on their sides, face-to-face, and Kyle forgot for a second why Darrek would freak out if he knew Kyle loved him, so he, quickly, placed a light kiss right on Darrek's mouth.

Right away, even before he pulled back, Kyle knew he shouldn't have done it, and regretted it. Part of his brain tried to perfectly record how soft and warm Darrek's lips felt against his, and the rest of Kyle's brain scrambled for a joke or something believable to say so they could laugh it off. He started to open his mouth to say something — he didn't know what — when Darrek's eyes widened fractionally in the dark and he leaned in to kiss Kyle back.

It was like a dream. Kyle couldn't believe it was happening. He wrapped his arm around Darrek's side as Darrek's lips brushed gently against his own. When Darrek moved his arm to encircle Kyle, too, Kyle's heart rate skipped up even more. It was the best thing to ever happen to him.

That was before.

The after happened so fast, Kyle didn't understand most of it until it was done, and he was experiencing brand new sorts of pain, both physical and emotional.

Kyle didn't hear Mr. Grealey come into the room, and was dazed with shock through most of the threats and shouting as the sheet and then Darrek were yanked violently from the bed. The strangeness of what Mr. Grealey was shouting made it hard for Kyle to follow or react. All he knew was that Darrek often got hurt, and badly, at the hands of his father. He was beaten. There had been bruises and broken bones that Darrek swore were from riding his bike, but Kyle never saw Darrek riding his bike. Kyle had never witnessed any violence first-hand either, though.

When Mr. Grealey seemed about to slam Darrek's hand in the bedroom door, Kyle knew without a doubt that if there was anything he could do to make it stop, he had to do it, and fast.

Darrek came back to the bed. Kyle told Darrek it was okay without knowing what it was he was agreeing to, only that Darrek seemed to have been given a choice between a crushed hand and Kyle. Kyle wanted Darrek to choose him if it saved him from having his hand slammed in the door. Of course he did.

When Darrek was told to take Kyle's underwear off, with Mr. Grealey staring, Kyle's stomach started to churn sickeningly. He tensed up and Darrek started to protest, but that made Mr. Grealey begin to move to whip Darrek's back with his leather belt, folded over in a hand. So, since Darrek wasn't moving to follow Mr. Grealey's orders, Kyle obeyed for him, and took his underwear off.

Kyle tried to stay quiet to still the belt, but then Darrek's face was shoved against Kyle's penis. Jerry kept shouting orders, threats, bible verses. All Kyle was aware of, though, was Darrek crying with terror, Darrek hesitantly licking him then sucking on him, using a trembling hand to lift the semi-flaccid organ. Kyle had gotten hard during the kissing and he thought that this was happening, that Mr. Grealey commanded it of

Darrek because Kyle was sort of hard. At first, it was so difficult to not say no, to just lie there and do nothing while Mr. Grealey stared at the sight of Darrek sucking Kyle's dick, but Kyle's stark fear for Darrek was washing all of that away, fast.

This was happening because Kyle got hard.

Kyle wanted it.

Now Mr. Grealey was ordering Darrek to do things to Kyle as his penance.

Kyle pleaded, "Please. Please don't. Dare, please don't. I don't want it."

Mr. Grealey told him he did, he could see that much. Because of Kyle's protest, the folded belt lashed across Darrek's back, making him swallow a scream, his lips sealed around Kyle's shaft.

Darrek's lips were something Kyle had fantasized about for a long time. They were touching him now, but it was a nightmare and Kyle couldn't wake up.

Darrek pressed Kyle's knees down at his father's instruction and Kyle tried to push away, to shove Darrek off. When Kyle curled forward, Mr. Grealey gave more instructions, punctuated with whistling arcs of the belt and screams from Darrek. Then Darrek's finger was between Kyle's butt cheeks, pushing through his hole, slipping into his body and, after another shouted command, pumping there.

Kyle groaned and bit back a sob, too scared to move a muscle, too confused to react at first. He heard Darrek's crying, had lost count of how many times so far Darrek had been whipped. But, strangely, when Kyle was still, and silent, the whipping stopped.

Darrek was spared more pain.

So Kyle kept still. When he made any sound at all, it was to tell Darrek that it was okay, to reassure him and show Mr. Grealey that he didn't want Darrek to get hurt anymore. He ground his teeth together to hold in his crying, his protests, and the soft grunts of surprise that unwittingly came from him as he was penetrated, fondled and sucked. Closing his eyes against the sight of Mr. Grealey watching and rubbing himself, Kyle tried to ignore the tongue licking his penis and the finger pumping, soon joined by a second, in and out of his body.

When Darrek stopped and began to move Kyle onto his hands and knees, Kyle told Darrek it was okay again, both of them sobbing silently. Then Kyle was on his knees; Darrek was behind him, holding him down.

Mr. Grealey told Darrek to put his pecker in Kyle's hole.
Kyle knew Darrek didn't want it. Kyle had wanted it, and now he
was getting it, but it was horrible, the opposite of all of his love-struck
daydreams.
Kyle couldn't say no without Darrek getting more hurt. He couldn't
make it stop, for either of them. He could only be still, be quiet, and obey.
Held down by Darrek's hands, Mr. Grealey's will, and his own fright,
Kyle was brutally violated by the person he loved most in the whole world.
That's when he knew the true meaning of helplessness.
But if Kyle diligently followed the orders of the determined, powerful
man standing beside the bed, and let his body be used, probed, groped, and
penetrated against his will, Kyle would be okay. That's the only way that
Kyle would be okay.

The past recedes, lingering at a distance. The present takes hold of
Kyle strongly. He's still restrained. It's different but it's the same,
and it's horrible.

"Take the cuffs off. Take the cuffs off. *Take the cuffs off!*"

Gabriel moves fast. He gets behind Kyle. The leather is only
buckled and not padlocked, so Gabriel wrestles the straps free. Kyle
goes scooting back violently away from them. He wraps his arms
around his head, gripping it as he rocks, weeping wildly.

Gabriel starts toward him.

"Don't touch me!" Kyle cries out. It trails off into a chant of,
"Don't... don't...."

Ben comes running from the house. Sprinting to Kyle, he stops
dead only a foot away as Kyle releases a throat-tearing yell from
deep, deep down. He curls up in a ball, covering his head, hiding his
face in his knees. Moaning with misery, he rocks.

"Kyle," Ben tries, not confident, not assured, just frightened and
hurting for him.

"Ben," Kyle sighs in a thin ghost of a voice, sounding like someone adrift, untethered, and forsaken.

"Here. Right here," Ben says, dropping to his knees, kissing the
top of Kyle's head. Kyle reaches up and hooks a hand around the

side of Ben's face. Overlaying the hand with his own, Ben gives Kyle something to anchor to. "Right here."

From a distance, Darrek watches. Standing at the foot of the steps, leading to the back door, he sees Kyle come apart. With a grimace, Kyle's tears echo back through years and years, cutting into Darrek in ways he had forgotten were possible. Guilt rises up, fresh and powerful. Darrek stays frozen, apart, bearing his earned torment without complaint.

This is my fault. I did this, he knows. I did this to Kyle. It might have been Jerry that made it happen, but it was me that did the touching, that did nothing to stop it. I was afraid of getting hurt, so I shared the burden with my best friend, and this is what's come of it.

Darrek, for the first time, sees Kyle completely, without barriers. He remembers everything now, and the friendship he's shared with Kyle for most of his life has new dimension and mind-rending implications. More than ever, Kyle feels like Darrek's. What they've survived together cemented their bond, long ago. They helped make each other who they are, in ways both of them are just realizing.

Kyle introduced me to Diadem, but it was me that showed Kyle how to submit. I took his virginity, his innocence, his sanity. And I can't fix what's been done. Ever. All I have left is this, the men we've become, the people who have formed our new family. All we can do is go forward. There's no going back. Thank God, there's no going back.

Chapter 27
Gabriel's Submission

Grinding, bass-heavy rock music plays loudly in the garage, echoing off of the walls. At the workbench, Darrek brushes away curlicues of wood from where he's etching a carving by hand into the unfinished piece before him. His hair is tied back and he's wearing goggles to protect his eyes. When Darrek senses movement to his left, he glances up quickly.

Waving and smiling to show he means no ill will, Micah crosses to him.

"You're the babysitter, huh?" Darrek says, turning back to his work. "Shouldn't you be in there making sure he's okay?"

He glances pointedly back to the house where Kyle is asleep on the couch, cocooned in blankets and sound from his iPod and noise from the television.

"My wife is staying with him. I figured if he wakes, she'd be a more soothing presence than me."

"Lily?" Darrek, fleetingly, loses some of the anger he wears like a cloak.

"Yeah," Micah nods. "Why don't we go for a walk or something and get out of here. You don't want to be here for this."

"Yes. I do. I need to be *right here*." He flattens his big hands on his workbench, over the wood he's been carving diligently. "I need to be busy, and I need to be here for him."

"Gabriel is in good hands," Micah tells him with care.

"I know!" he barks, then repeats, softer, "I know."

Darrek picks up a small chisel and bends over his workbench, illuminated by a small lamp above it.

"What are you working on?" Micah asks with what seems to be genuine curiosity.

"A table. Small one, for Gabe's office."

"That's an angel?"

"Yeah." Darrek tenderly traces the extended wing, the details in the feathers unfurled. It's not even halfway done.

"You do beautiful work."

Darrek looks up. Micah seems to apologize with his eyes for what Darrek is being made to endure, but, just the same, it's clear he's ready to subdue if Darrek gets out of control.

"Thanks," Darrek mutters, setting his jaw and tuning it all out, all of it but the music and translating the picture in his head—his angel.

Back in the house, Gabriel is wary and pacing restlessly. Micah, Lilianna and Trace show up on a motorcycle and in a truck, respectively. Up until then, Gabriel had just been jittery, but the sight of a woman amongst the virile men does weird things to his mindset. After everyone is inside, Lilianna senses Gabriel's unease immediately, though.

With Micah gone around to the garage to seek out Darrek, she pulls Gabriel aside and kisses each of his cheeks in greeting. Her soft, curly cascades of black hair frame an elegant and exotic heart-shaped face. Her parents, Gabriel knows, are from Argentina and France. At five foot eight and voluptuous, she has a commanding presence. It's mainly her eyes—wise, self-assured, and a dark chocolate brown, lined darkly with thick eyelashes—that hold Gabriel.

She puts a hand over his heart, feeling his pulse race, and says, "It's good to see you again. Do what you need. I know Trace well and, believe me, I know that every person has their needs. We all do."

Gabriel hears what she doesn't say and the particular look that passes, very briefly, between her and Trace. There's a history there, he realizes, wondering what it is, and how Micah factors in.

"I don't judge, Gabriel. As long as you don't judge me," she grins slyly. "I'm just here to keep an eye on Kyle, like before. He's had a tough day."

"Yeah," Gabriel says unsteadily. "Yeah, okay."

"Go on. They're waiting for you."

She moves like a cat, winding gracefully around the furniture to sit on the floor, leaning back against the couch on which Kyle is lying.

That leaves Gabriel with Trace and Ben.

"Upstairs. Go," Trace commands. He's as stony-faced as ever, and maybe a little pissed off, too. "You hear me, boy? Go!"

Unwittingly, Gabriel's gaze slides to Lilianna and her exotic, dark eyes are already locked on to him. Her hand rests between her bent legs and the way she lets her gaze move slowly up and down Gabriel's body tells him clearly enough that she'd love to be the one disciplining him instead.

"Hey! You don't look at her," Trace snaps. "You look at *me*."

Face flushing, Gabriel goes. They climb the stairs behind him. He pauses at the top. Trace gives their second bedroom, laden with supplies, a lingering, interested look and says, "Bedroom. Get in there and show Benny where the keys are."

While Gabriel walks into the master bedroom. He points to the top drawer of a chest and Ben quickly finds the keys to the supply cabinets. Trace grabs Ben by the arm and whispers to him, too low for Gabriel to make out. Ben nods and goes without a word. Trace walks farther into the room and shuts the door.

Standing at the foot of the bed, Gabriel hears the dull, distant sounds of the television below and the stereo playing in the garage. They expect him to scream, he realizes. All of them do. He panics and channels it into defensive action. Trace moves closer to him, and Gabriel, breathing heavily through his nose, freezes for half a second, then shoves violently at Trace's shoulders and tries to bolt from the room. But this has always been part of their game, and Trace is ready for him.

Catching Gabriel's wrists, Trace draws them down and behind him, spinning Gabriel so that his back is to Trace's chest. Gabriel's wrists are trapped in a brutal, bruising hold behind his lower back.

"You behave for me, now, boy," Trace says with a smile at Gabriel's left ear, popping Gabriel's fly open easily with his free hand, tugging the zipper down. Gabriel hears the closet door slide open in the other room and gear clank around. He swallows a small, scared sound and his knees go weak as Trace roughly pushes his hand inside Gabriel's underwear.

With a small, breathy grunt, Gabriel twists in Trace's grasp, writhing as he's fondled. Trace guides Gabriel's cock free of his pants and lightly brushes over the head with his fingertips. It has always driven Gabriel crazy how Trace takes his time, draws it out, lets Gabriel feel exposed and forces him to face how much he likes being toyed with, as much as he wants to believe otherwise. The more Gabriel fights, the more Trace plays with him, and the harder Gabriel will come once Trace pulls the orgasm from him.

Trace pushes the pants and boxers down a little more on Gabriel's hips and enjoys the view as Gabriel starts to get hard and tries to pretend he's not. Staring up at the ceiling or closing his eyes, he refuses to watch as Trace fingers his dick, stroking up and down the shaft, giving the crown a little squeeze, rubbing with his index finger at the spot just under the ridge on the underside, triggering the bundle of nerves there. At the same time, Trace forces Gabriel's arms higher up his back to limit his range of movement.

"There. Isn't that better?" Trace flattens his hand and pushes Gabriel's cock up flat to his belly, rubbing over it as he traps it. Then he pinches his fingers around the head, squeezing tighter and tighter.

"Ahh!" Gabriel gasps.

"I asked you a question, boy. Don't be rude." Trace hooks his hand around the root of Gabriel's shaft and presses, forcing it to curve down, closing it and his testicles in a tight grip and tugging.

"Y-yeah. B-better."

Trace doesn't say a word. He just gives Gabriel a hard yank.

"Ahh! Fuck! Sorry. S-sorry, Daddy."

"What are you sorry for, boy? You been bad?"

"Yeah," Gabriel says breathlessly, gulping air. Ben slips into the room with gear in hand and Gabriel's panic shoots through the roof. With a whimper he sways in Trace's hold, sagging back against him as his knees start to give out.

Trace lets go of Gabriel's arms and genitals and steadies him with an arm crossed over his hips. With a kiss behind Gabriel's ear, Trace soothes, "Breathe. Just breathe. Daddy's not gonna hurt you. Just gonna remind you of your place. Maybe we should've done this a long time ago. What do you think, boy? When you showed up— homeless, underage, no one to care for you... should I have taken you to bed, then and there? Held you down and made you take my cock like the bad boy that you are? I thought I was doing you a favor by keeping it in my pants, but maybe not. I ain't givin' it to you 'til you ask me for it, though. You ask nice and sweet or you'll get the belt instead of a fuck. Up to you, sweetheart."

Trace beckons Ben from the shadows. He dumps the supplies on the bed. "Put the cockring on 'im. Then get his shirt off."

Wide-eyed, breaking into a light sweat and trembling, Gabriel takes shallow, unsteady breaths and looks away when Ben steps up in front of him and manipulates his cock and balls into a steel cock-ring. The feel of them both looming over him, from the front and back, clothed while his pants are down, is a heady rush. He wants it. God, does he want it. He needs it like air.

The ring snaps into place and clamps around him, unrelenting. Trace goes back to lightly rubbing Gabriel's sac while Ben twists Gabriel's shirt up over his head, pulling his arms up with it. Then he's shirtless and his pants are halfway down.

"On the bed," Trace instructs, not waiting for him to decide. They manhandle him over the end of the mattress, pressing him down onto his stomach and guiding his arms behind his back where Ben starts to secure leather cuffs lined with fleece. Trace yanks Gabriel's pants down, pulls his boots off and takes the rest of the clothes off of him.

Instantly, once he's naked, Gabriel starts to fight it again. He bucks and tries to throw them off, but Ben just pins his shoulders to the bed while Trace plants a knee on the back of Gabriel's thigh.

"What is it gonna be, sweetheart?"

A hand caresses up his spine to his neck, raising goosebumps, then draws right back down, the whole length of his torso to his but-tocks. Pulling them apart, Trace brushes the pad of a thumb over the knot of his hole. Gabriel exhales sharply.

"What's it gonna be?"

"Oh god," Gabriel moans. They weigh him down, the both of them, but all he can feel, the focus of his attention—one hundred percent—is the brush of Trace's thumb over his asshole. He wants to push back and take more, but first he needs to ask. He tilts his hips slightly and clenches the next time the finger drags across.

"You like that?"

"Yeah."

"Feels nice, doesn't it?"

"Daddy...."

"Say please."

"Please." Fingers pry at him, pulling at his hole, spreading him. He grunts hard and moans. "Want it."

"What do you want, boy?"

He hears the snap of latex on skin, the wet squirt of lube and shivers visibly. The cuffs are soft and tight and he loves the feel of them binding him as Trace pulls his ass open.

"Want you in me," he croaks. A finger, wet and slick, rubs around his opening, spreading lube, then it finds the center and pushes. His rim parts around it. The ring of muscle hugs the finger like a kiss as it slides through.

"That's it, Benny. Nice and gentle," Trace says quietly.

Deeper, slowly, Ben's finger buries itself in Gabriel. One knuckle in, then two before it pulls back out, then twists and plunges in again, this time all the way. Gabriel gasps, thrumming on the bed. Ben rubs at the back of Gabriel's neck with his free hand and Trace keeps him spread. It's obscene and he does feel like he's bad. He's not a grown man, with responsibilities and the mental pressures of adulthood; he's just young and horny and wants to be punished for it.

"Oh *god*," Gabriel moans, turning his face into the bedding, breathing hot against the fabric as the finger works in his ass, smearing him with lots of lube, working the muscle loose. Another finger, thicker, rougher, wedges in beside the one already there—Trace's finger. He hooks it in from underneath and pulls, keeping it buried. Gabriel's cock pulses and he gives an involuntary thrust as his cock stiffens painfully, because they're both inside him, and he fucking loves it. "Please, Daddy... I'm sorry."

"That's all done now. You hear me, boy? It's done. You take your punishment, you spread for us and be a good boy, and you're forgiven. Daddy understands. Right, Benny?"

"Right," Ben rasps, sounding so far gone, so hard-up and dominant that Gabriel feels it as a thrill racing up his spine, swelling his aching cock. Ben works another finger in with the two already there and Gabriel's blood surges to the spot, the tissues engorged with it, the nerves there lighting up. Ben's index and middle fingers pump in a slow, steady rhythm, while Trace's middle finger is still and steady, tugging Gabriel open for Ben to work.

"Okay, let's get him up. Up on your knees, boy."

The two fingers Ben had buried in him tug out, and Gabriel tries to hold in a hard moan as Trace hooks three fingers into him, curling them up and keeping them there as Gabriel, with Ben's help, gets up on his knees, upright. Buried in Gabriel's heat, Trace caresses with his left hand up his boy's side, through the light coating of sweat slicking his skin. The hand wraps Gabriel's cuffs and pulls, keeping him in the pose. Gabriel clenches in flutters around him, and hears Trace growl softly with his arousal.

"Thigh spreader," he tells Ben. "And condoms. Grab a handful of 'em."

While Ben makes quick work of shifting Gabriel's legs far apart and clasping the metal bar to his thighs to keep them that way, with one cuff wrapping each leg, Trace thrusts his hooked fingers a little farther up Gabriel's hole, stroking over his inner walls.

"You know how sweet you are in here, boy?" Trace whispers by his ear. Gabriel's head rolls forward on his shoulders. He's impaled on Trace's hand, held upright on his knees and hanging forward by his arms bound behind him, straining inside the cockring, He hasn't needed to get fucked this desperately in a long time. "Don't hold back on me now. I wanna hear it when I feed your ass my cock."

It's the fingers, steady and nestled, that screw with Gabriel's head the most. He feels dirty as Ben quietly binds him, like it's the most natural thing in the world. Ben finishes with the thigh spreader and Trace says, "Good. Now get the collar and rope. I expect princess is gonna fight me once I take my cock out, and I don't want him going anywhere."

Ben picks the collar from the bed and wraps it around Gabriel's neck. He glances back into Gabriel's eyes as he does it. And that's difficult to bear, because it's not a stranger, some random Dom. It's Ben—who's been his closest friend for as long as Gabriel can remember, and their history is written there in his eyes, but it's never been like this. They've already crossed a line and can't ever go back. Not now. With a whimper, Gabriel suddenly can't stand the fingers hooked inside his ass, and surges forward, toward Ben, trying to get away, but Trace still has his bound wrists and Gabriel isn't going anywhere. He's yanked back upright and the fingers in him spread, prying him open wide.

Mouth falling open around a sweet little cry, he falls back against Trace's solid form behind him as Ben gets the collar tight around his throat and feeds a rope through the metal loop in the front. The rope gets pulled down and Ben takes hold of Gabriel's testicles.

"*No*, Daddy...."

"This is the way it's gotta be, princess. You be good and it won't hurt."

Gabriel hums through the panic, eyes closing over, sweating, and gasping. Ben winds the rope around the base of Gabriel's sac, many times, and Gabriel is distracted by the wriggling digits violating him. He's too full, too hard, and starts to move, just slightly, rocking back with little pumps of his hips on the hand, trying to rock and rub off against Ben's hands working on his balls. Delirious, powerfully aroused, shameless, he feels Trace pivot his wrist and begin to rub repeatedly through his crack.

"I know, sweetheart. I know you want it. You like how my fingers feel?"

"Yeah," he groans.

"You want me to touch your sweet spot?"

"Fuck," Gabriel hisses. "Please."

"Tell me your safeword."

"Discovery."

"Good boy." Trace praises. "Benny, bend him over."

With a nod, Ben pushes at Gabriel's shoulders. He bends Gabriel in half, then even more as he presses Gabriel's face, turned sideways, flat to the bed while Trace keeps hold of his arms to make sure Gabriel's ass stays up. Ben yanks at the rope, making it tight. Gabriel whimpers as it pulls sharply on his testicles, stretching them out as Ben ties the knot, making sure there's no slack as the rope goes taut between the collar and where the rope winds around the root of his sac. The skin stretches and Gabriel releases a wild, wordless pleading sound.

"Nope. Tighter," Trace tells Ben. "Just a little."

"Daddy, please. It hurts," Gabriel begs.

Ben reties the knot, pulling the rope even shorter and Gabriel screams as his balls are stretched right up to the point of tolerance. The blood flow cuts off and the organ turns a deep red. Trace caresses the skin, pulled smooth now. Gabriel yells as he gasps for air. Ben checks his work and nods to Trace.

"Good. That's perfect," Trace smiles, rubbing, touching the skin around where the rope constricts like a noose. Gabriel can't move an inch without hurting himself. It forces him into an extreme pose, knees drawn up to his chest, arms behind his back, shoulders planted. Trace grabs him by the hips and inches him back on the bed, right up to the edge. The bed is high, and Gabriel's feet hook around the end of the mattress, his heels nearly touching his ass as Trace examines his work.

"It *hurts*," Gabriel pleads.

"Clothes off," Trace tells Ben. "Wear a cockring if you need it. I'm not in a rush here."

"What's the plan?" Ben asks quietly. Gabriel tries to stop crying out so that he can hear what they say.

"I'll get us started. Then we'll change it up a bit. We'll see how much he can take."

"You mean...?"

"You know what I mean. Take your fucking pants off."

Once he has a condom on, Trace steps up to the edge of the bed and Gabriel, palming his ass. He aligns himself and sets the broad, blunt head of his lubed cock to Gabriel's hole. Folded up as he is on the bed, small and trembling, he could very well be seventeen again.

"You know I love you, beautiful," Trace sighs.

"Trace," Gabriel begs softly.

"Shh," Trace hushes, and thrusts.

It's indescribable decadence, being claimed after so long. Trace let out a thunderous groan of pure pleasure. He works himself steadily farther into Gabriel with shallow movements, but as gentle as he's being, Gabriel sobs like it hurts worse than the rope.

"Take care of him," Trace barks to Ben, who instantly moves to soothe Gabriel with tender caresses. He checks the rope and presses a reverent kiss to the back of Gabriel's neck as Trace fucks him, taking him deep. Trace gets fully seated and groans his satisfaction. Fingering the spot where Gabriel's ass is hugged up around the root of his cock, Trace rubs the rim, caresses the stretched, delicate tissue and holds his hand out for more lube. "Benny," he calls.

"Yeah," Ben answers dutifully. "Got it."

Once his latex-sheathed fingers have a good dollop of lubricant, Trace works the slick in to Gabriel's rim, making it really wet. Trace withdraws until he feels his head catch, then he holds Gabriel's hips and re-enters him in a long, smooth stroke.

Hips tilting, ass flexing, Gabriel pushes back against Trace's cock, like he's trying to push him out, but it only lets Trace in easier. Gabriel gasps roughly and makes the mistake of jolting forward. His balls get a brutal yank and he keens through the pain.

"That's right. You stay right there for me. Nice and still. You ain't goin' anywhere. Damn, you feel nice," Trace says contentedly, moving at an easy pace but with long strokes with the full length of his cock.

Once he's moving easy, Trace quickens the speed of his thrusts, faster and faster until his hips are loudly slapping Gabriel's ass as he pounds his hole. Moaning low and long, Gabriel bears it. His cries sharpen as Trace changes his angle and starts to nail Gabriel's prostate on each instroke. Ben helps hold him still so that he doesn't try to buck forward again and hurt himself more. Pushing against Gabriel's shoulders, he keeps him down as Trace barrages him. Cries become shouts as Gabriel fights the bonds, Ben, the thigh spreader and Trace.

Trace stops moving, panting and biting back his climax. It gives Gabriel a reprieve. With shrill little gasps for air, he shudders as the shockwaves subside, every nerve in his body crackling with the force of the stimulation.

"Flip him," Trace says, catching his breath. "Rope comes off."

"Got it," Ben replies. One second later, he uses a knife to part the cord connecting the collar to Gabriel's balls.

Gabriel hums his relief, breathing roughly, overloaded.

He's tense and out-of-it when they roll him over onto his back. His hands are still trapped behind his back, but when Trace climbs onto the bed and sits so that Gabriel's head is in his lap, it relieves the pressure as his hands dig into his spine.

"I gotcha. I gotcha, sweetheart."

"Ben," Gabriel asks, looking up at Trace.

"That's right." Ben steps up, eyes dark, pulse racing, his dick like hot iron, thick and ready. He rolls on the condom and doesn't waste a moment. Gabriel is already lubed, so he steps up between his legs.

Trace grabs the thigh-spreader and pulls it back to Gabriel's chest to keep his ass pulled open. Gabriel makes a scared little noise. Ben breaches his outer ring of muscle, and Gabriel has a perfect view of Ben's face as his lips curl back, showing teeth as he growls and feeds Gabriel all of his fattened cock in one push. Gasping sharply, writhing at the sudden fullness, he's held still by Trace's firm grip. Ben is too hard to be patient and it feels too good for him to hold back. It's rough and dirty and Gabriel's mouth works around yells that bubble up all the way to his throat.

"Slow it down, Benny," Trace tells him. "There's no rush."

"Shit," Ben snarls, skating the edge, eyes rolling up in his head. He pauses and plants a hand on the bed beside Gabriel's hip. "Come on!"

"*Slow down.*"

Trace carefully unfastens the cockring binding Gabriel and takes it off of him. It gets Gabriel to sigh and roll his hips forward into Trace's hand as it closes around his aching balls. Massaging them, Trace watches Gabriel's pleasure. With a nod, Ben resumes his thrusts, but they're slow and longer. Gabriel throws his head back and lets out a cry of pure, undiluted need, moving his hips in little circles against Ben's thick, sliding cock.

"That's it, princess. I know you love it," Trace smiles. He starts to stroke Gabriel's cock, soaking wet with pre-come, hugely erect and red where it curves up between his legs.

"Daddy," he moans, pleading. "Don't stop. Please don't... don't stop. Yeah... fuck yeah... Ben...."

"Shit," Ben curses, snapping his hips as Gabriel clenches around him and keeps up those damning little rolls of his hips.

"You don't get to come yet, Benny," Trace warns.

"Oh, fuck you," he spits back, growling, then yelling.

Trace pumps Gabriel faster, closing him up in a tight fist, jacking him in little pulses until Gabriel gasps. He keens through gritted teeth as come shoots from the tip of his reddened cock, splashing over his belly, chest and even up to his jaw. He moans behind tightly closed lips and shudders hard with the force of his orgasm, still coming. Trace wrings every drop free, milking the white drops from the slit.

"Good. Good boy. So good, baby...."

Humming happily, Gabriel relaxes at last. Ben still moves inside him, rocking in and out.

"I need to fuckin' come, Trace," Ben complains, his voice gruff and an octave lower than it usually is.

"Pull out then." To Gabriel, he says, "Okay, big finish. Gonna make sure you sleep real good tonight. Okay, my good boy?"

"'Kay Daddy," Gabriel slurs. "Trust you."

"That's what I like to hear."

The thigh spreader comes off. So do the cuffs. Gabriel is too spent to care. All he's left with is the collar as Trace lies down on his back on the bed and sets Gabriel down on the end of his cock, lowering him onto it. They drape him forward over Trace, who holds him in a close embrace, petting Gabriel's dark, inky hair, stuck to his forehead in places. His gray-blue eyes peer out, questioning but calm. Ben works two fingers into him beside Trace's member, and Gabriel understands. He focuses on his breathing and tries to stay loose. It's easy with Trace's arms around him, and purged of his fight as well as his seed, basking in the afterglow.

When Ben thinks Gabriel's ready to try taking both of them at once, Trace says softly to Gabriel, "It hurts too much, you tell us.

Stay nice and relaxed. Nice and relaxed...."

Hands caress his skin. Love and devotion of many kinds wash over him and Gabriel lets it heal him from the inside out. The last of his energy is expended with a desperate shout as Ben gets the thick, rounded head of his dick through Gabriel's rim, above where Trace is nestled. Slippery with lube, Ben's shaft presses gently but demandingly in farther. With animalistic grunts of frustration and bliss, Ben battles back his orgasm, squeezed tightly as Gabriel's ass swallows both cocks at once.

"Holy... holy fucking...." Ben pants.

Gabriel makes frantic, pained, overwhelmed sounds, holding on to Trace as they fill him to bursting.

"That's it," Trace says roughly. "So good, baby. Stay nice and still. Don't move now."

Mouth opened wide, Gabriel tries to draw air and can't fit it in his lungs. He's stuffed too full to manage it. Clawing at Trace, he leaves red scratches in his wake as Ben somehow goes deeper, bit-by-bit, making almost as much noise as Gabriel.

"Easy Benny. Easy," Trace warns, but Ben is gone. He pushes harder, once, then a second time, making Gabriel sob and Ben comes with a rasping cry, filling the condom. Collapsing forward onto Gabriel, Ben sandwiches him between them.

"Sorry, Gabe. Too fuckin' tight. I couldn't.... You okay? Gabey?"

Gabriel just makes a small hurt sound and tries to inhale through his nose, burying his face against Trace's neck.

"Talk to me," Ben beseeches, kissing Gabriel's shoulder, his neck, his jaw. "You okay?"

He nods, weakly, and settles a bit when Ben caresses up and down his side. "'M okay," he says between shallow gasps. Trace brushes the hair back from his boy's pale face.

"You want me out, or should I wait?"

In answer, Gabriel draws Ben's arm up around him as well, weaving their fingers together and keeping it held there.

Time passes, but they stay still. Eventually, Gabriel is able to let them go. He's weeping soundlessly and lets them clean him up and get themselves dressed. Ben dresses Gabriel in a pair of loose drawstring pants and helps him stand. Gabriel steps forward into Ben's arms, whispering words of gratitude as the tears rain down, cleansing and good. But when Gabriel turns to Trace, he can't speak. He can only kiss Trace's lips, his breath hitching.

"You're gonna be just fine," Trace tells him, trying to make him believe it. "You believe me?"

Gabriel frowns, but nods. Trace brushes a finger over Gabriel's lower lip. Gabriel's lips press a kiss to it. He draws up on his toes, his heart overflowing with relief and trust, feeling blessed, feeling lucky to have this kind of closeness with people who care so profoundly for him, and kisses Trace's cheek.

"Thank you."

"You're welcome, baby."

Chapter 28

A Difficult Recovery

It's a slow, torturous recovery for Darrek. After the night with Trace and Ben, Gabriel is steadier, more confident, more hopeful and entirely focused on being present for Darrek in every way, whenever Darrek needs him. Darrek says he's glad of the transformation in Gabriel's mindset, and does not begrudge him the pleasure and joy derived from submitting. He assures Gabriel of as much then seeks, above all else, space and privacy—especially from Gabriel. And Gabriel gives it to him.

It starts with a closed, locked bedroom door the day after Gabriel starts thinking of Trace as Daddy. Darrek leaves a pillow and blankets on the hallway floor. Without argument, knowing he can't tell Darrek what he needs in order to heal, Gabriel silently accepts the new arrangement and begins sleeping on the couch downstairs since it would be too weird to take Kyle's old bed.

Darrek resigns from his construction job. Gabriel spends all day, every day, at his office as the business starts to take off, with clients coming in almost faster than Gabriel can manage them. When it rains, it pours, Gabriel tells himself, and resolves to conquer each task. For the most part, Darrek has the house to himself. If Gabriel calls to check on him, Darrek doesn't answer, but he will send a text reply that everything's fine. Gabriel understands that Darrek is self-conscious about the abuse he suffered, and its effects on him. He doesn't want to be touched, hugged or interfered with, and he's not ready to talk either. As he is, in turn, coming to peace with his own needs and his part in everything that has transpired, Gabriel complies.

Four strange weeks pass.

On a Saturday night, Gabriel picks the bedroom door's lock. Darrek is inside, sitting up in bed, reading a paperback book with the bedside lamp turned on. After one look at Gabriel, he closes the book and sets it aside. Unwilling or, possibly, unable to break the strained silence that has lasted for far too long, marking the darkest period in their whole relationship, Darrek only stares at his partner. Freshly healed emotional scars and sadness are visible behind his eyes.

Shirtless, barefoot, wearing only a pair of drawstring pants, Gabriel unties them, pushes the pants down past his hips, and steps out of the legs. He crawls up the bed as Darrek turns his face away, dropping his gaze. Gabriel gets astride Darrek's hips, covered in a thin sheet, and lays a hand on Darrek's bare chest. "I miss you," Gabriel tells him. "Whatever you want, okay? Whatever you need. I just need you. I'm asking you to let me help. I want to help you through this. Whatever that means."

Brow furrowing, Darrek sighs his stubbornness away and kisses Gabriel quiet. It acts like an electric charge, turning Gabriel on like a switch. A sexually-charged person by nature, after so much time spent celibate, he practically vibrates on Darrek's lap.

"Lie down. Just let me. You don't have to do anything, just let me. Please," Gabriel says breathlessly.

Darrek reclines. Gabriel pushes the sheet away and gets Darrek's loose pajama pants down just far enough to guide him free. Using his mouth, Gabriel gets Darrek hard without much time or effort. It's welcome proof that Darrek has been missing intimacy as well, which only heightens Gabriel's fevered state. Since he'd lubed and prepped himself before coming in the room, Gabriel easily lowers himself onto Darrek's erection. Though trying to play it cool, Darrek is already breathing heavy, his pupils blown black, his hands gripping Gabriel tightly by the hips and guiding him into movement.

Not wasting any time, Gabriel rolls his hips, back and forward, up and down, riding Darrek, making him groan.

"C-cockring."

"No time," Gabriel argues.

"Fuck," Darrek grunts.

For a minute or two, Gabriel bounces on Darrek's dick, and Darrek fights not to come. Then, unprovoked, he stretches his long, toned arms up in a Y shape to the headboard behind him, and grabs onto the rungs.

"Can you...?" he starts, but can't quite find the nerve to ask.

"What?" Gabriel gasps. "Restraints?"

"Yeah."

"Fuck yeah."

Gabriel climbs off, leaving Darrek hurriedly grabbing at and squeezing the base of his genitals, battling back his rapidly approaching climax. It doesn't take long for Gabriel to find some handcuffs in a drawer and shackle Darrek's wrists to the headboard, stretched to either side of the bed. Putting a pillow snugly behind Darrek's head to make sure he's comfortable, Gabriel gets ready to climb back on.

"Wait! Wait. Um... nipple clamps?"

"Goddamn it, Dare! I wanna fuck!"

"I know! Just get 'em. Get three."

"Three? You sprout another one while I wasn't looking?"

"What do you think, smartass?"

Darrek is back to not looking at him, so Gabriel gets the clamps. Staying up on his knees, astride Darrek's thighs, Gabriel clips them on, one and then the other, to Darrek's chest. Once they're secure, Gabriel plays with them a moment, brushing them back and forth, up and down, then twisting them a little. Darrek tenses and flushes hot in his cuffs, heat baking from his body.

Scooting back a little, Gabriel cradles Darrek's sac in a hand and asks, "Is one gonna be enough?"

"It'll do," Darrek grunts. He hums when Gabriel clamps it on, writhing when the clip is pulled, gently, and twisted. "Harder."

Gabriel complies, then takes the clamp off and massages the flesh, getting a rush of heady pleasure at the way it makes Darrek struggle and pant. He puts the clip back on and straddles him again, taking Darrek's cock in hand and feeding it into his hole with a low moan.

Their bodies move together as if dancing. Gabriel pounds down rhythmically, at a frantic pace, possessing Darrek. Feet planted on the bed, alight with pain and pleasure, both, Darrek thrusts up into

Gabriel when he can and, a few minutes later, orgasms with a gruff shout, hips twitching.

Darrek guesses what comes next before Gabriel says or does a thing, and is ready when Gabriel wants him. No sooner has Gabriel pulled off with a wet squelch than Darrek opens his mouth wide, tongue pushed forward. Hungry for relief of his own, Gabriel shifts up Darrek's upper body. With his knees astride Darrek's chest, Gabriel leans down over his lover's head and enters his mouth. Sliding back over Darrek's tongue, feeling it curl around his girth, pushing into the suction Darrek gives him as his lips make a tight seal and his cheeks hollow, Gabriel cries out sharply. Getting a hold on Darrek's head by tangling a hand in his hair, Gabriel steadies him and withdraws only to rock back in, burying his flesh to the root. He feels and hears it when he lodges in Darrek's throat. Holding there, letting him choke on his cock for a long moment, Gabriel thrums with excitement and the hot, wet, gripping hug of Darrek around him. Moving right there, getting off on the friction of his cockhead wedged in the soft, close channel, pulling back only now and then to let Darrek get some air but mainly letting him enjoy the rush of oxygen deprivation, Gabriel chases his release.

Eyes fluttering, gagging slightly and sucking down rough drags of air through his nose when he can, Darrek writhes under Gabriel. His feet kick and he pushes off the bed, futilely. His arms pull at the cuffs and tears stream from his eyes. Gabriel tugs out when he shoots, unloading a huge load of come over Darrek's mouth, chin and neck. He caresses through the mess, coating Darrek with it, working it into his skin.

Once spent, Gabriel slinks down Darrek's long, powerful body and removes the clamps. Sucking on his nipples where the clamps have left indentations, long minutes are spent at the task. Releasing the nubs, he leaves them throbbing, stiff and red. Then Gabriel licks down the center of Darrek's body, making him squirm, skirting around his cum-soaked cock to his balls. Gabriel pulls the clip off, provoking a yelp, but instantly opens his mouth and sucks on both of Darrek's testicles. Calling out hoarsely, legs fallen widely open, Darrek's head gets thrown back, his neck elongated as he drowns in pure gratification. Taking as much time at the task as he did on Darrek's nipples, Gabriel is pleased to see his lover is fully erect again by the time he's done.

Licking the spend from Darrek's shaft, cleaning him thoroughly, Gabriel teases with only his tongue until Darrek is begging and growling like an animal. Then Gabriel gives him a slow, lazy blowjob, drawing it out as much as he possibly can.

Darrek is a satisfied, smiling puddle on the bed by the time Gabriel is done with him and is packing the cuffs back away.

"So does that win me back my spot in bed?" he asks with his back turned.

"Yeah," Darrek mumbles dazedly. "Sure. Whatever."

"And we'll talk about things another day?" Gabriel glances back.

Darrek nods, chewing on his lower lip. "Another day," he agrees.

After cleaning up, Gabriel is so happy, he's positively giddy as he brings his pillow up to the bedroom and slips under fresh sheets beside Darrek.

"Hey. I missed you too," Darrek whispers in the dark, turned on his side to face Gabriel.

"I love you so much, baby. You know that, right? You're a part of me and I'm going to be with you forever, whether you like it or not. The rest of it we'll handle our way, together. But me and you? That's a constant."

"Yeah. We'll talk another day. Remember?"

Gabriel's smile wipes right away. Urgently, he pleads with his eyes and asks, "Do you still love me?"

"Don't be stupid. I'll love you forever. I'm yours, remember? That's a promise."

Gabriel is quiet. He turns and presses back against Darrek, wanting Darrek to spoon up against him. When he does, Gabriel draws Darrek's arm around him, and says, "I want to go away again. I want to be back on that island, when it was just you and me and paradise."

"We'll get there," Darrek assures him, kissing his hair. "'Night."

"Goodnight," Gabriel sighs, holding on tightly.

Almost one week later, Darrek and Gabriel are finishing up dinner on a Thursday night, and they still haven't talked about what happened. Poking at some steamed vegetables with his fork, Darrek pushes his hair back over one ear and clears his throat. "So, um, Kyle's been calling me, like, every day. Since the night he went to the hospital."

"What? Seriously?"

"Seriously," Darrek nods, shrugging. "And he leaves a message each time, saying that he hopes I'm okay, and asking that I call him. I erase the message and don't respond. But he keeps calling. If it's okay with you, I'm going to call him tonight, just to clear the air. Have you talked to either him or Ben since last month?"

"No," Gabriel admits. "I haven't. Trace and Micah have each called me at work to check on how I'm doing, but I haven't talked to Ben. I think he's had his hands full."

"So, what do you think?"

"Clearing the air makes sense. It'd be cathartic for both of you, especially if he's been concerned enough to call every day. But I know it must be scary for you to face him."

"Seeing him again, standing in front of him and looking him in the eye without wanting to tear myself to pieces over how fucking sorry I am — that'll be the hardest thing I've ever had to do. Ever. But I have to try. I owe him a dialogue, and if it's tough for me, what does that even matter? He's looked me in the eye for a decade. He's been amazingly strong and I've just been fooling myself."

"Neither of you have been seeing things clearly, and you know that," Gabriel tells him adamantly.

Darrek watches Gabriel closely as he sips his water. A heavy silence descends.

"I have to ask," Darrek warns. "About the subbing and the sex with Trace and Ben...."

"Yeah," Gabriel says in a clipped, rough voice, eyes still downcast. "It happened. It did what it was supposed to do."

"Are you going to want that again from them?"

"You know the answer to that. It's an outlet for me so that I don't cause you further harm. But... if the sex is what bothers you, I can make sure that future sessions don't include that. It can just be toys, strictly professional, not personal. Daddy—" He blushes at the slip. Clears his throat and tries again. "Trace has taken care of me since I was seventeen. He saved me from homelessness. He probably saved my life by taking me off the streets. He didn't know me from Adam and he didn't owe me shit, but, even still, he gave me a chance. He gave me *everything*. Ben is my big brother, and he did just as much. I love them like family, my *real* family, and I know it's messed up, but it makes me feel better to submit sexually to them. Not to get off, but to feel safe. To feel like I don't always have to be the one in control. I feel so much better since they helped me that night, and so incredibly happy because I walked away from that in a better place up here," He points at his head. "Without breaking my heart over asking things of you that you can't give me without causing yourself harm."

"I want to be enough for you," Darrek tells him softly, choking up. "And I'm not. Do you even know how much that hurts?"

"You are enough, baby. You're the love of my life. You're the first and last man I'll ever love and commit myself to. I've told you I'm never leaving you, Dare. They each have partners. They will never, ever be my partners. Ever. *You* are my partner. I could never love them the way I love you. It's one thing to call someone family; it's another to be in a romantic, long-term relationship with them. You're the one I want to share my life with until we're old and gray. I'll shout it to the world. I'll say it in front of God or a judge and put a ring on your finger, if that's what needs to happen. I belong to you. I'm yours."

He comes around the table, pushes Darrek's chair back. Falling to his knees at Darrek's feet, he lays his head in Darrek's lap, winding his arms around him, giving himself over, body and soul. Darrek combs his fingers through Gabriel's dark hair and sighs.

"C'mere. C'mere," he beckons. Gabriel raises his head. Darrek kisses him passionately.

"Okay," Darrek tells him, looking him right in the eye.
"Yeah?"

"Yeah. Okay." With a smile, Darrek holds Gabriel's chin in his hand and says, "You're kind of irresistible when you're professing your undying love to me."

"Good," Gabriel grins.

Chapter 29

Confronting Kyle

The call is briefer than Darrek expects it to be. He'd gotten all worked up about it, wondering what would happen, or what they'd say to each other. In the end, all Kyle does is ask him to meet after work the following day for a late lunch at a busy pub where they've eaten countless times before. After a curt goodbye, Kyle hangs up. At a quarter after three that Friday, Darrek walks into the pub near their old worksite and sees Kyle sitting at a table for two by the front window.

For almost five full minutes, Darrek lingers by the front entrance, trying to find the courage to walk over there. He's afraid to face Kyle. It's just too hard with the sudden, life-changing weight of guilt and remorse pressing down on him, which Darrek is still trying to process in a healthy way. In the end, it's Darrek's masochistic side that moves him, craving the acute pangs that will come from letting Kyle look him in the eye.

He should be uncomfortable. It should be hard. They've been through a lot. It's because the last thing that Darrek wants is to confront Kyle that he chooses to do so.

Even so, he might not have been able to physically do it, to go, step-by-step, over to that table if not for his collar. Gabriel offers it to him every morning, and every single morning, Darrek kneels, bares his neck, and begs his Master to collar him. Darrek wears the collar now. It's easily visible above the top of his flannel, button-down work shirt. It anchors him to Gabriel, connecting them, and in a submissive, obedient mindset, grounded in the present, not the past, Darrek starts walking.

He weaves his way over and tries to judge what's in store for him by Kyle's appearance alone. Tan and healthy-looking, Kyle has obviously put back on some of the weight that he'd lost, and it suits him. As he's come right from work, he's wearing dirty, worn jeans and a t-shirt, with a heavy jacket hanging from the back of his chair. A turkey burger, an empty beer bottle and a full one sit in front of him.

"Hey," Darrek says in greeting.

"Have a seat," Kyle gestures to the empty chair across from him. "Sorry for ordering before you. I was starving." He waves over the waitress, and when she's in earshot, tells her, "He'd like to order."

"Yeah, um, I'll have the same, but water to drink. Thanks."

She scribbles on her pad and promises to be back in a minute with the water. Darrek waits until she has left and says, "You look good."

Kyle stares levelly at Darrek, reclined back in his chair, cocky and cool as Darrek has ever seen him. The mouth of the beer dances by Kyle's lips, ready to be drunk at a moment's notice.

"How are things at home?" Darrek asks when Kyle stays mum.

"Things are great," Kyle boasts, glancing up and down Darrek's form—at the collar, his casual dress, the tension brought of emotional torment—trying to get a read on him. "Ben cooks me breakfast every morning, and dinner every night. He offered to quit his job at Diadem, and he blows me—enthusiastically—every day. It's the only time I let him touch me. That's the deal, now. If he wants me to live in that house with him, I'm not his sub, I'm his partner and *I* make the rules." Kyle sips his beer, swallows, and adds, "He even spreads for me."

"Ben spreads for you," Darrek echoes with disbelief. "Wow. He's like the girlfriend you always wanted."

"I know, right? Except I never wanted a girlfriend."

They hush up as the waitress returns with Darrek's water. He smiles politely and waits for her to go away again.

"I can't believe you're not subbing anymore," Darrek tells Kyle quietly. "That's who you are."

Kyle measures him, saying nothing.

"Talk to me, man," Darrek frowns. "Why have you been calling every goddamned day if you aren't interested in having a conversation?"

"I needed to know if you were okay," Kyle says at last, setting down the beer and picking at his french fries. "And I figured that if you were clearing out your messages every day, then you were still alive at least."

"Why do you even care? After what I did...."

"Why do I *care*? I've been trying to figure that shit out for decades. That's my favorite topic with my shrink. Why do I care about Darrek Grealey? Why do I love him? Why have I wasted so much time pursuing him? Why am I so concerned about his wellbeing after he repeatedly forced himself on me? Why can't I sleep at night until I ring your number and make sure it doesn't go right to voicemail? I honestly have no fucking clue."

The intensity with which Darrek looks at Kyle, and the intent behind it, shifts so powerfully and dramatically, that Kyle stops meeting his gaze or looking in his general direction. Kyle turns toward the window instead, like he finds it to provide a much more calming view.

"I'm figuring out who I am, I guess," Kyle tells Darrek. "I was so... stripped down... that I've been taking time to build back up."

"Makes sense."

Kyle watches a car zip past, his eyes tracking it. His fingers trace the handles of his silverware, the edge of his plate. He chuckles, "You know, I honestly thought this would be gone. It's amazing how stupid I can be sometimes."

"What are you talking about?"

Kyle looks at him then abruptly away. Jaw set, golden eyelashes catching the sunlight, Kyle is truly beautiful, even in grungy work clothes.

"Don't be a dumbass. *This*." He gestures between himself and Darrek, the air, thicker now with sexual tension, filling the space. "I hated you, you know. You used me and threw me away like a piece of trash. A *cum rag*; and you threw me away before you'd even pulled out, to call your precious Gabriel. I *hated* you. You gave me no choice. It was next to rape, and you didn't even care. Ben would *never* make me feel that worthless. *Ever*."

Kyle is still staring out the window.

"Look at me. Hey. Kyle."

"No. You don't get to give me orders anymore. No one does, not without my permission," Kyle seethes, and Darrek is horrified to see that he's close to tears.

"You should hate me," Darrek agrees, absorbing Kyle's anger willingly.

"Shut the fuck up, Darrek," Kyle chuckles sardonically. "So fucking self-deprecating, it's ridiculous. I *should* hate you. You're right about that. And I've tried. I really have. You're a problem for me — an actual, huge problem in my life — and yet I'm actively seeking you out. It's self-destructive as fuck."

The truth of the confession is written across Kyle's face. Darrek sees it there, and the tears that fall from Kyle's eyes before he angrily wipes them away, sniffling.

Terrified, seeing his life — huge spans of it — in brand new ways, Darrek's blood runs cold, then hot. Because he does need Kyle, and in vastly different ways. He's the best friend Darrek has ever had, but he's also Darrek's conquest. For a split second, Darrek stares right at the terribleness of that head-on.

Kyle bolts from his chair, ready to run away again, but Darrek instinctively grabs his arm and keeps him there.

They both stop and look at it — Darrek's fist around Kyle's forearm. Fear and helplessness spark brilliantly in Kyle's blue eyes.

"Sit down," Darrek says. "Please."

An unwanted but no less real or powerful thrill shivers down Darrek's body from the contact with Kyle, stirring his cock. Because he does feel it. He could bend Kyle over that very table, in front of everyone in the place, and have at it, and Kyle wouldn't say no or even fight back. He could stop Darrek no more than Darrek could stop Gabriel.

"I want to talk to you. That's all. That's *all*."

Kyle gives in and sits, but props his elbows on the table and presses his mouth against the sides of his clasped hands, masking his expression from Darrek.

"I love you, too. You know that. And I am truly sorry for hurting you," Darrek tells him.

There's something Kyle wants to say, it's there on the tip of his tongue, but he struggles with it. Darrek waits to hear what it is, but it won't seem to come.

"What is it? Kyle?"

Kyle's eyes close over. His knee bounces restlessly.

"Kyle...."

His voice breaking in the middle of the question, Kyle asks softly, "Are you okay?"

It's Darrek's turn to look away, because he knows what Kyle is asking.

"I'm getting there," Darrek says carefully. "Gabriel has been trying to help, but this isn't something he can do for me."

"He understands what you're going through—" Kyle starts.

"I know," Darrek interrupts. "But it's something I needed to handle on my own."

They both eat some of their food, and even that small act of normalcy feels like a victory. Kyle fills Darrek in on the gossip from their work crew and tells him that he could have his job back if he wants it. Darrek declines.

Before they leave the pub, Kyle admits to one more thing.

"Gabriel was very kind to me," he says, speaking slowly, choosing his words with care. "Every single way that he's watched out for me, or tried to help... it's meant a lot."

"Yeah, well, like you said. He understands what we're going through, and he'll always be your Master. Stuff like that doesn't really go away. Plus, he cares about you."

"Do you wish he never found me that night you flew back, and brought me home?"

"No."

Kyle rolls his eyes, taps his beer bottle against the table.

"It'd be kind of hypocritical of me to be jealous, don't you think?" Darrek waits for Kyle to look up at him, and when he doesn't, adds, "You're okay with Ben? You feel safe?"

"I'm good," Kyle nods. "I can handle him. It's you I worry about."

Darrek doesn't have a reply to that.

"Thanks for the talk," Kyle says.

"No problem," Darrek replies with a small, grateful smile. "Thanks for... you know. Being you."

Kyle shakes his head, chuckling, then pretends to retch.

"Too much?" Darrek chuckles. "Really?"

"Really," Kyle insists. "My respect for you is gone."

Kyle pays their bill and they walk out to their vehicles.

"So... call me," Kyle winks.

Darrek laughs brightly. "Oh no, you did not!"

"Dork," Kyle snorts. "Go home to your sexy-ass boyfriend."

"You too. Fuck his ass nice and hard for me, yeah?"

"Will do."

Chapter 30

Drawn Deeper

A month's worth of painstakingly accumulated confidence had buoyed Kyle, keeping him afloat enough to get his ass in that pub and endure the conversation with the man who encompasses so much of what Kyle fears and loves. But even with the shine of his submissiveness still glinting in his eyes, Darrek maintained an eerily immense level of power.

As he sits in his car, parked in back of his and Ben's house, Kyle tries to figure it out. It's maddening. After all of it, everything they've both been through—with each other, with their Doms—none of it has made any difference really.

Kyle confessed, not an hour ago, to Darrek, though perhaps not in so many words, the uncanny effect he has on his supposed best friend. It took every ounce of courage that Kyle has gathered to say those things, and, having used up his store of bravery for the day, he's left hollow. Darrek looked right at him when Kyle tried to convey the way he gets in Kyle's head, twists him up, tears him open. There was regret, and guilt, but underneath, there was hunger.

Even after what Darrek has endured after awakening those buried memories of the abuse they suffered because of Jerry Grealey, even after trying to slit his own throat out of sheer horror, he would do it again. He enjoyed pinning Kyle and kissing him on that day which seems so long ago and isn't. He enjoyed having Kyle bound and helpless on that table without Gabriel to watch over them. And he enjoyed the fuck in the woods. Both of them are aware now of why they react the way they do to each other, with Darrek taking control and Kyle submitting to it. Being aware doesn't stop the want.

So, what does that mean? Where does it leave Kyle? Well-used to having the upper hand with his Masters and those close to him, Kyle is suddenly in a very bizarre predicament. As much as he has wanted to slip away and escape his life by whatever means available to him—blood, drugs, sex—he finds himself with the metaphorical hooks of three different people embedded in him.

Ben has him, undoubtedly. Darrek has him, more so now than ever before. Gabriel has him, too, for saving him, and loving him as a kindred spirit. With the way that Gabriel talks to Kyle now, it's like there are two collars around Kyle's neck instead of one. Part of Kyle will always be Gabriel's submissive. That's not even something that causes Ben displeasure. If Gabriel has that level of control over him, that means Kyle is safer in Ben's eyes. He has Gabriel watching out for Kyle, too, and ready to step in at a moment's notice.

The ramifications spin out endlessly. Will Ben want to watch Gabriel dominate Kyle? Ben will definitely continue to dominate Gabriel, possibly with Kyle in audience, possibly with Kyle chained up and enduring everything in tandem with him. Or, Trace could take care of his boy while Ben takes care of Kyle. And where does that leave Darrek, who has demonstrated his instincts to protect and be possessive of Kyle?

Part of Kyle hopes, in a sad, twisted way, that Ben is losing interest in him, and that the murkiness of his and Darrek's past will sour what once was sweet. If Ben releases Kyle, he would be able to try to escape. He could evade Darrek and Gabriel long enough to get away, get lost. The thought of that entrances Kyle. Holding on to the dream of disappearing, letting it wash away the hot tickle stirring his cock, making his skin itch for leather and chains, Kyle closes his eyes and lets go.

Tap tap tap.

Kyle startles, straightening in his seat, eyes popping open wide with the guilt of being caught indulging in a secret fantasy. Unable to yet face the thought of opening the driver's side door, he lowers the window and clears his throat.

"Hey," he mutters.

"What'cha doin'?"

Ben looms big as life outside the car, just like Gabriel did that night he ran away.

"Thinking," Kyle answers, staring out at fields of tall, waving grass.

"'Bout what?" Ben presses, but deliberately and obviously trying to keep things within the boundaries of a normal, equally-weighted exchange between partners. That's why Kyle doesn't look at Ben. It's probably written in his face, how he wants to reach down inside the dark places and squeeze until Kyle gives it up, confessing whatever is on his mind.

"Nothing," Kyle says, then instantly regrets the lie.

"Now, see," Ben tsks, "We both know that's not true. And I would *really* like you to be honest with me."

It's amazing, Kyle marvels, how easily it comes to Ben. Finding that he does have some courage left after all, Kyle manages eye contact. The force of Ben's personality and desire is so dense and strong that Kyle has to fight to endure the heat of Ben's scrutiny. When Ben looks at him like that, Kyle is not in his car, in his grungy work clothes, at all. He's naked, spread, probed and groped. Nothing is sacred — not in his head or in his body.

The car is suddenly a cage, so Kyle blurts, "Back up. Let me out."

"I made dinner," Ben sighs, and not only does he back up, but he turns around, putting his back to Kyle so that he's more comfortable. "Come inside and eat before it gets cold."

"I had a late lunch. I, um, met Dare after work."

As much as it makes him feel better to see Ben trying to do right by him and ease up on the pressure, it's much more strenuous to try to maintain normal discourse. Ben stiffens at the mention of Darrek, but stays turned away while Kyle closes the car's door with a slam.

"What?" Ben says quietly. "You *met him?*"

"We talked about some things. I wanted to see how he was doing, since he's been quiet for so long, and Gabe isn't returning your calls either. It went well. There's nothing to worry about."

Ben laughs and in such a way that Kyle's bladder threatens to void itself.

"Yeah," he scoffs. "I can tell how great it went. You've been sitting out here for an hour."

"No, I..." Kyle starts to protest, then glances at his watch. "Oh." Left with the choice to argue or go back inside the house, Ben chooses the house. He stalks off, going in through the back door, leaving it open as if he expects Kyle to follow, which he does but at a distance.

Once they're inside the kitchen, renovated a year ago with dark, custom cabinetry, courtesy of Kyle's talents, Ben plants his hands on the counter and takes a couple of deep breaths.

"Ben," Kyle sighs, smelling the rich aroma of the food, realizing maybe he can eat after all. "Look at me."

Again, choosing not to argue, Ben does as asked, and turns. Kyle studies, momentarily, the healed scars on Ben's eyebrow and lip from the fight with the dealer. Then he makes the mistake of looking back into Ben's eyes. It's all right there like Ben said it aloud—what he wants to do, how he would play this if he got to make the rules. Wordlessly he tells Kyle how he'd strip him, then and there, tie his hands behind him, get him down on his back on the floor, maybe straddle his head as he hooked his arms under Kyle's knees and bent them back to Kyle's ears, pulling his legs open wide as they had this little chat, letting the heady mind-fuck of being so closely, obscenely observed help to loosen Kyle's tongue. Then, Ben begins deciding what toy he'd use on Kyle to make him really squirm, should he clam up.

"Okay, don't look at me," Kyle says roughly, getting hot as a devious grin flickers across Ben's lips.

"You're hard," Ben notices as his glance lowers. "Is that because of me or your rapist?"

"Both," Kyle allows. "I told him how much he intimidates me, and he kind of seemed to like it. I mean, he's still Darrek, so he was sweet and a gentleman and all, but I could tell."

The funny thing is that Kyle can feel it, can hear it like a shattered cry of un-healable pain. It hurts Ben as much as it does Kyle that Kyle is a victim of abuse and unspeakable cruelty. It kills Ben that Kyle could still, theoretically, let Darrek use and hurt him again. And, given all of that, Ben wants to guide him through it the way they have always gotten through. Old habits die hard, for both of them.

"Come on, kitty, you know you want to let me. Let's play for a little while. I promise to scratch that spot that really makes you purr...."

"Knock it off," Kyle grunts, breathing heavier, turning his face slightly away, and trying to cope without being able to use any of his coping mechanisms. But then Ben comes closer and slowly falls to his knees in front of him, unfastening Kyle's pants. "Fuck. Ben...."

The protest forms in Kyle's head but doesn't get anywhere near his lips, since he can't say no to a blowjob that he knows will be spectacular.

Ben's lips close up around his dick as he tongues at the head, repeatedly rubbing the pointed tip of his tongue through the divot under the crown. Then, with a wide, flat, lick over the slit, devours the salty taste of him, making Kyle swallow a moan.

Hands wrapping Kyle's hips, thumbs fitted snugly in the indentations, Ben draws him into a forward thrust, letting Kyle slide an inch at a time back into his mouth. Lips sealed tight, jaw working to open wider, Ben takes all of him.

Once buried, Ben's beard tickling Kyle's balls, Kyle pulls back shallowly before helplessly slamming back in. Feeling through the tension in Ben's fingers how much he needs to take charge of this and hold Kyle down, Ben's to play with and take apart, Kyle gets off fast. Ben stays arousingly submissive and lets him set the pace. Kyle gets handfuls of Ben's short hair and fucks his mouth with fervor, slamming his cock back into Ben's throat. He gets closer and closer to the edge, then pulls Ben off of him, yanking Ben's head back by the hair, and watches the reddened column of his cock slip, shiny wet with saliva, from Ben's lips. It bobs between them. Ben nuzzles against it. Coated with saliva, Kyle's cock slides against Ben's rough facial hair and Ben chases it with the tip of his tongue and an opened mouth, licking in small strokes up the underside of his shaft, then down to the root where he sucks a kiss. Growling, Kyle feeds himself to Ben once more, who uses his willing mouth in rapid thrusts until Kyle comes with a shiver.

Ben swallows every drop, sucking the spend from him and pulls off, squeezing up through the spit and come. It squelches through his fingers, as Kyle gradually softens in his grasp.

Breathing hot against the hollow of Kyle's hip, Ben inhales his musky scent with greed. Kyle watches Ben claw down the instinct to take for himself, to turn the moment sideways and possibly cause Kyle distress. Fondling him, Ben drags an opened palm up Kyle's shaft, pushing it up flush to his belly, then rubbing down to his balls and rolling them in a hand. When the aftershocks are long passed, Ben reluctantly stops touching and tucks Kyle back into his pants before zipping them up.

"Thanks," Kyle manages gruffly.

Ben won't look at him. He's still gripping Kyle's hips, though now clothed, and the energy thrums from every pore, every muscle.

"Ben?"

The hand on Kyle's thigh shifts between his legs, strokes down then up the inside. Kyle's breath catches as the hand opens and hooks up against the junction, fitted to the crease of his ass, thumb wrapped around, pointed toward his balls. Ben massages him, making Kyle want to spread.

"Please," Ben asks, with noticeable effort to be rational. "I'll be gentle. I swear."

"Why would I want you to be gentle?"

Me and my fucking mouth, Kyle thinks distantly as Ben is suddenly on his feet, looking as wild as an animal. The subsequent fright has teeth like razors made of ice as Ben rips down Kyle's pants, spins him and gets himself free. There's a wet sound as Ben spits thickly into his palm. Two fingers prod between Kyle's butt cheeks, find his hole and enter him with a twist of Ben's wrist, smearing the fluid inside. Kyle starts to fight it instinctively, tensing up, making the stretch burn and ache until he groans from it, but Ben loves the fight and jabs a little deeper, holding Kyle by the nape of the neck as he writhes on the end of Ben's right hand, with Ben breathing hot and fast by his ear. The fingers scissor apart inside him and Kyle shifts his legs wider.

"How do you want it?" he hears Ben ask, sounding wrecked, sounding gone.

Kyle, trembling, gets to his hands and knees on the tile floor, struggling to get hard again as Ben is at his back in a second, the broad head of his heavy cock pressing firmly at his opening, squeezing through. Kyle pushes out as he's breached with a rough yell, letting Ben slide right in.

The ache engulfs him, and for a moment, he's back there, in the woods, but Ben is simultaneously much gentler and much more needful than Darrek was. Ben has needed this for long months, a longer time span of restraint than either of them can remember. He desires it more than Darrek ever did, and as he stuffs Kyle full of his cock, Kyle is engulfed with heat from the fire of Ben's passion.

Bending close to catch every grunt, every purr, Ben tugs back out, and holds Kyle still as he presses back in, rasping, "Love you. Missed you," so sincerely that Kyle finds he can't breathe, the emotion chokes him so completely.

Ben is tender with him, moving deep inside but carefully. Kyle is his instrument, strung tight, reacting to the slightest provocation. Wrapped in Ben, filled with him, used by him, Kyle is immensely satisfied when Ben empties into him with a heady moan. Kissed over and over, down his neck, along his jaw, the shell of his ear, Kyle tingles from head to toe.

"What do you want? Just name it," Ben pants, sated and sounding happier than he's been in a long time.

"I want to get cleaned up, and think about fingering you open and fucking you sloppy later in bed after we eat."

"Always a slut for some denial," Ben smirks, feathering his fingers over Kyle's erection, slick with pre-come.

"You know it."

Kyle rushes through his shower and hurries back to the kitchen. All of the food has been laid out on the table and, appetite reawakened, Kyle serves himself heaping portions.

After they've each taken a few bites of food and are less famished, Ben asks, "So what's the verdict after the little sit-down you had today? I know you're thinking about something or else you wouldn't have been out in that damn car for so long."

Kyle spears some vegetables with his fork, working out the answer in his head before voicing it. "I don't know. He was different. He's had a slow recovery from the mental shock and kept Gabe out of it for the most part. I really thought he wouldn't give two shits about me, since he didn't try to get ahold of me at all this whole month and be all about Gabe this and Gabe that, but there's something weird between us. I tried to be the good guy, you know? Be his friend—just his friend—and come clean so we could both move past it and get back to being buddies, but he..." Kyle sighs, and shrugs. "I don't know."

"Yeah, you do," Ben coaxes. "He's not done with you. Is he? He looks at you and he's not your buddy. He's the guy pinning and fingering you."

"It sounds paranoid," Kyle murmurs. "But I tried to go and he grabbed my arm and told me to sit down like it was an order. He didn't even think about it. That's just who I am to him now. And I don't know what to do with that. But Darrek isn't a stupid guy or a bad guy. He gets it. He knows it's wrong, and sincerely doesn't want to cause me further harm, so I really don't think he would do anything to hurt me. Not really, but.... Maybe I'm imagining it. Maybe I'm crazy. What do you think?"

"What do I think?" Ben stabs a slice of meat and rips it with his teeth. After he chews and swallows the piece, he gazes across the table at Kyle with lowered brow and clenched jaw, and says, "I think I don't know whether I want to take his balls as a necklace or drive him to the damn shrink myself, but let me make this clear for you. *No one* gets to lay a finger on you without my say so. Even if you're not my sub, you're my partner, and I won't let anyone scare or intimidate you. You're safe."

"Okay," Kyle nods.

"No more meeting with him alone."

Kyle nods again. "Do you have to go into work tonight? I thought you had an appointment."

"Not if you don't want me to. I can reschedule."

"Yeah," Kyle says, bashfully.

"Then it's done."

"Just, you know, for tonight. I don't want to be alone."

"You don't need to explain," Ben insists. Since Ben is looking intently at him again, Kyle finds he can't raise his eyes, but just the feel of Ben's heavy stare, his fierce love and adoration clears some of the weight and worry from Kyle's shoulders, leaving him lighter.

Ben showers first, Kyle second, and when he emerges, towel-dried but still with dampened skin beaded with water droplets and stringy-wet hair, Kyle finds Ben in bed. Lying nude on his stomach under the sheet, Ben's gaze is affixed to his lover. An absence of sexual paraphernalia has strangely always disturbed Kyle. When the whips and chains come out, so do the rules. If everything is stripped away but the emotions and trust, and nary a rule in sight, Kyle is left floundering in a scary place. Maybe that's why Ben looks at him with such forthright confidence and calm. With his dark eyes and scruffy beard, the dark dusting of hair over his arms and the bare expanse of his muscular back, Ben oozes masculinity and exactly the kind of self-assuredness that Kyle feels he lacks.

Patiently, Ben waits for Kyle to climb out of his head and join him. Without a doubt, it's only because their roles to play that evening have been already so firmly established that Kyle is able to walk from the bathroom door to the mattress. Dropping his towel, he fights a nonsensical blush as he slips under the sheet and moves to lie atop Ben's back. Winding both his arms around Ben's, pressing his lips against the back of Ben's shoulder, Kyle lets body heat and full body contact warm him, drawing the chill away.

Sadness, regret, apologies, and formless yearning tense Kyle's body, and roughen his every breath. Ben could still lose Kyle. That's a fact, and because it scares Ben more than anything else in the world, he gives. He gives everything, all of him, even though that scares him, too. It's a sort of silent surrender that moves Kyle in a profound way.

Kyle's stiffened flesh is cradled in Ben's buttocks. He draws back and drags forward, sending an outward-radiating wave of goosebumps that pebble Ben's skin. Ben is a man of many conquests and plenty of casual, dirty sex, but Kyle is the only person that Ben has ever permitted to make love to him. As Kyle opens the lube, spreading it over his fingers, letting them warm before moving to intimately touch Ben, a spark of shyness, highly uncharacteristic, hits Ben. As if to mask it, he says, "I got you something today. Made the arrangements and all, but I can't pick it up until after tomorrow."

Kyle doesn't reply verbally. He doesn't want to talk, but only to enjoy this, and savor the gift Ben has given him already. After teasing Ben's opening with his fingertip until he's practically begging for it, Kyle presses two fingers inside. The discussion is thereby ended.

Kyle works him open without hurry, dragging heated, open-mouthed kisses over the back of Ben's neck, upper back and shoulders, watching him react, writhe and breathe roughly. There is already a pillow under Ben's hips, since he knew what was coming, and how he wanted it to come. He lies as still as he can as his skin flushes pinker and hotter, his eyes defiantly opened but lips tightly sealed to hold in his grunts. A proud man by nature, and a difficult one, Ben had been Kyle's pet project for years as he tried to wrap him around a finger, seducing the un-seducible.

Astonishingly, it happened. Ben was not only seduced, but, just as Kyle tried to use his new emotional weapon and hold it over Ben that he cared, Ben turned it around on him and forced Kyle to admit that there was mutual love there, or he'd leave.

And he would have left. Kyle knows that. Ben would rather break his own heart than let someone else do it for him. But Kyle stayed, and Ben drew him deeper. And deeper. And deeper. Now they've gotten to a point where Kyle has given all he has, and it's left to Ben to fill him back up.

Once the prep work is more than done, and Kyle is just fingering Ben lazily for the sheer enjoyment of it, Kyle finally draws free and watches Ben's face, his body language. This man — powerful, fearsome, strong — trembles bodily under Kyle. He spreads his legs wider, bends his back to tilt his hips further, inviting, and the rest is easy. All it takes is a push.

Steadying himself with one hand at the root, grasping Ben with the other, and a moment later they're joined. Ben swallows a growl as his body stretches to accommodate Kyle's girth, gripping it tight, breathing sharply through his nostrils. Burying his face against the side of Ben's neck, Kyle nudges farther inside, knowing all paths to life, warmth and hope lead through Ben.

Fitted so completely, held so intimately, Kyle scratches down Ben's biceps, leaving pink trails, gasping. He draws back, thrusts back in, feeling Ben's arms flex as he absorbs the shockwave.

Betrayed by finding true, pure love in someone who was supposed to be incapable of such emotions, Kyle uses his small anger by funneling it into his passion. It stiffens his cock, drives his movements even faster. He doesn't know where they go from here, but it doesn't matter. In that moment, all that matters is the perfect sensations and sweetness of their lovemaking, Ben's selflessness and the soft, "I love you, Kyle," that he gasps.

Moaning against the admission, Kyle bites down on the junction of Ben's neck and shoulder, leaving deep dents with the points of his teeth, driving ever faster, ever harder.

Riding him to completion, once spent of seed and no less empty, feeling full-to-bursting, Kyle holds on to Ben and whispers in accusation, "It wasn't supposed to be like this. I wasn't supposed to love you back."

"I know," Ben says quietly. "Tough shit."

Kyle gives one last, firm push, so that his flesh is buried in Ben to the hilt, claiming his stake, letting Ben feel it.

"Fuck you, Ben."

"Yep," he groans.

Chapter 31
Ben, Betrayed

For Ben Knox, it has been a long and brutal day. He had interviewed possible candidates for their open Dominatrix position, had two client appointments, one female and one male, and the subsequent paperwork from all of that to deal with after.

It's now past midnight. The stars are out, he notices, as he lets the infinite expanse of the glittering velvet night press down on him from above as he crosses Diadem's property. Taking a page from Gabriel's book, he raided the cupboard in the kitchen and now has a nearly full bottle of rum in hand to help him come down and relax. The quiet is thick in his ears, broken only by crickets, the distant barking of dogs and the crunch of twigs and gravel under his boots. Diadem is locked up and dark. The only light for miles comes from the building directly in front of him—the barn. Heading right for it, as he nears, new sounds spice the previous stillness. Intrigued, Ben approaches with stealth.

Through the opened doors, above hay and hanging from the rafters is Micah, trussed up in thick rope. Arms crossed behind his back and tied tightly, suspended by ropes wrapping his chest, waist and thighs, his legs bent up under him and bound by many loops, Micah is naked, gagged and helpless. With a swig from the bottle of rum, Ben leans against a nearby tree and watches for a few minutes.

Trace is there, too, and has a wide array of toys on hand to choose from. He cycles through more than a few while Ben bears witness. There's a wide wooden paddle, a leather whip with metal barbs tied to the tails, forceps, and other complicated gear that Ben can't make out too clearly given the distance. Micah is positioned sideways relative to Ben's position, facing into the barn so there's no chance that he is even aware of Ben's presence about fifteen yards away, under the star-speckled sky. His olive-colored skin covered with sweat and his dark brown hair plastered down with the same perspiration to his head, Micah is restrained so effectively that he can't even struggle against the bonds, but only endure the bite of the rope, the pull of gravity and his own reactions to Trace's gifts of pain and pleasure.

When Trace progresses from the paddle to the forceps, Micah's muffled shrieks sharpen to a pitch so exquisite that they instinctively cause Ben's attention to perk. Gaze locked to the figure hanging in the barn, Ben's every muscle is tensed and ready to spring him into action. The cries fade into roughened breathing. Trace walks in a wide circle around Micah, holding something that looks like a short baton in his right hand. The gag is removed. Slicking lubricant over the toy in his hand, Trace lets Micah see him do it.

Ben turns away. He drinks rum and steers his thoughts deliberately away from the spectacle before him. He has better things to be concerned with anyway.

Both Ben's greatest flaw and his primary talent is his tendency toward extreme decisiveness. It's a quality that has shaped his every relationship, both professional and personal. Kyle has used it to weave their lives together, irrevocably. Gabriel has benefited from it by finding a home, a new family, and a friend devoted enough to be willing to commit violent criminal assault against a pedophile for the sake of his honor.

Ben is aware of how he is and who he is, that people either love him or loathe him. He has lost family and lovers for being so pigheaded, but he can't change even if he wanted to. Luckily, for the most part, decisiveness has brought Ben good things. It has worked in his favor, taking his life in directions that he couldn't have foreseen and at speeds that cannot be affected without producing major damage should anyone reach for the brake.

As he leans against the rough bark of the tree, swirling the rum in its bottle, Ben, for the first time, feels real fear at seeing glimpses of the direction he's currently pointed toward. He has won back Kyle, and against high odds, but it's not the same as it was. No, not at all. What they have now is much more of an equal partnership between two lovers than Ben thought he would ever be capable of being involved in. There is give and take, and it works for them. The empty horror behind Kyle's blue eyes is fled, and he is stronger than ever before. There's also a healthy amount of new fear in him for his dear friend Darrek, and love for Gabriel, whom Kyle had always despised out of jealousy and misperceptions. The new status quo with Kyle, the leveled playing field, has given Ben access to new avenues, new possibilities and he's moving so fast that even as he sees what's approaching in a crazed blur of color and noise, he knows at the core of his being that it's too late to stop even if he wanted to. Basically, he's fucked. His own rules have turned against him, giving him a good ol' sucker punch to the gonads.

The rum chases back the tight, clenching, cold terror and shame, warming him from the inside out.

From the barn, a wild, pleading shout from a deep, scraped raw, male voice calls, "No! Oh God, please! NO! *Stop!*"

It's followed by a sharp, loud gasp that Ben hears perfectly, even from so far away. Momentarily distracted as his body reacts to the sounds, wickedly familiar as they are, Ben starts to get hard, remembering all of the times, years of sessions during which he had dominated Micah and produced a similar effect. Sipping his rum, Ben wrests his thoughts back to Kyle. It's surprisingly easy. Kyle is big as life in Ben's head and heart these days.

Ben can't go home, because he'd be faced with the problem, head-on. It's easier to stay and avoid it all a little longer.

A darkened figure of a man slowly approaches from the warm, flickering glow of the oil lamps in the barn. Backlit, Trace is still easily recognizable by his tied-back hair, his beard, and his heavy, confident footsteps.

"Good evening, Sir," Ben says pleasantly, tilting the rum bottle toward his friend in tribute.

"Benny-boy," Trace grunts in welcome. He digs in a pocket for his lighter, flicks it into life and cups his hand around a pristine cigarette dangling from his lips, nestled in the recesses of his thick beard. It takes a few tries as the wind threatens the flame, but Trace gets it lit and takes a deep drag as he straightens up, stretching to work a kink out of his spine.

Letting his head fall back to rest against his tree, Ben asks conversationally, "Do mine eyes deceive me, or are you sodomizing our Micah with a billy club?"

"Mm," Trace grunts, nodding and taking another greedy suck from his cancer stick. He blows out the smoke through gritted teeth and turns to look back at the barn. "Role play. Rape fantasy."

"Aw, sweet," Ben replies without much surprise. Micah's issues have always led him down some very dark roads in search of solace. It's not Ben's place to judge, just to help in a safe way, letting Micah explore the dark and be there to pull him out of it when Ben sees he's had enough. Part of him struggles to give those reins over to Trace, but Ben has seen proof of Trace's intense breed of commitment to Micah and it's not his job anymore to fill the Dominant role in Micah's life. "So, you're the cop, or...?"

"He is." As always, Trace is remarkably unfazed by his reality, causing Ben to wonder, not for the first time, what on Earth happened to the man to make him so eerily blasé. It's one of the reasons why Ben is so very fond of Trace and how they've worked together so long in such an intense profession.

"That's some pretty fucking method shit he's got going on. One might almost suspect he was actually scared of you."

"Yeah, well," Trace shrugs, squinting at the amber glow painting over his submissive's flushed, glistening skin. There's an extra loop of rope now hooked under the butt-end of the black billy club, keeping it lodged deeply in Micah's rectum as he dangles from the rafters and struggles for breath. "There's a lot of honesty in our relationship."

"I see that."

Trace turns to Ben, giving him a long look. Ben tries to be as cool as Trace, but, really, no one is as cool as Trace and he's fairly sure some of his turmoil is evident. The likelihood that Trace would be able to pinpoint the issue given how little he knows about what is really bothering Ben Knox is very, very slim.

"You wanna join?" he asks Ben, nodding to the barn and his captive. "We could double-team. You know, for old time's sake."

"Hmm," Ben hums, playing at considering the offer. "Pass. But tempting. Definitely tempting. Rain check, maybe? Do you want me to skedaddle and give you two lovebirds some privacy?"

Stretching out his arms widely, as if inviting the heavens to fall down upon them, Trace beams with a huge, white, shark-like smile and says, "It's a free fuckin' country. Don't leave on our account."

"Right."

"So, you hangin' out, or...?"

"Pretty sure Micah's the only one hanging tonight, but I'll stick around. Give 'em hell, tiger! Just don't kill the poor bastard."

"Will do," Trace grins, the cat that caught the canary. He gives Ben a salute, which Ben returns in kind.

"Sick motherfucker," Ben murmurs with a chuckle, upending his bottle.

An hour later, Trace emerges again, this time carrying Micah, who is close enough to unconsciousness to make the difference inconsequential.

"Hey," Trace rasps, frowning with concentration. "Gimme a hand, huh? Sit with him inside while I get things cleaned up."

"Yep. Sure thing, boss," Ben sighs. Trace is bearing most of Micah's weight on an arm slung around the man's lean, sweat-slick back, so Ben gets him from the other side and Micah hangs between them as he'd hung from the barn's beams.

They get Micah inside the east-facing recovery room, wallpapered with a quaint blue-flowered print. Micah is laid out on the narrow bed and covered with a sheet. Ben brings a couple of bottles of water in from the kitchen and settles into the chair beside the bed. Trace hooks a hand under Micah's jaw, turning his head — limp with exhaustion — this way and that. When they open a crack, Trace lifts each of Micah's eyelids to test the responsiveness of his pupils with a flashlight. Ben sees Trace's thumb drag in a gentle arc over Micah's cheek and quickly averts his gaze when Trace leans down and places a soft kiss to Micah's brow.

"Go on. He's asleep. Finish up and you two can get out of here," Ben urges.

"Yeah," Trace grunts, leaving very reluctantly.

"Go on, ya big softie."

With a brief glance at Ben, possibly to do a visual check of Ben's sobriety, Trace relents and goes, promising to make it quick.

Though Ben expects Micah to be out for the night, he rouses not five minutes later, glancing with a groan at his surroundings, clearly oblivious to how he got to where he is. When he sees Ben at his side, sipping from the bottle of rum, his vision clears a little more and some dull coherency floats there.

"Drink," Ben urges, touching the mouth of an opened water bottle to Micah's dry lips.

Micah frowns and tries to turn away, but Ben insists, "Drink it."

Hearing the disapproval in his own voice even before Micah glances up at him, wordlessly calling him on it, Ben bites it back with effort. Micah sips the water and takes the bottle from Ben, gripping it with an unsteady hand. He extends a closed fist to Ben, which Ben touches with his own.

"She's on a business trip to Hong Kong," Micah says hoarsely, without a drop of fight left in him, referring to his wife, Lilianna. "No need to worry about hiding marks or bruises." He gestures down at his body, stiff with pain and soreness, with red marks laced back and forth down the length of it from the ropes and from Trace.

"You need another massage?"

Micah shakes his head. Ben had watched Trace carefully knead the blood and life back into Micah's poor form, laid out on the hay, after he'd been let down and untied.

"But she knows about Trace, doesn't she?"

"Not *all* about him," Micah admits.

"As in, she's unfamiliar with his uncanny ability to bake a perfect soufflé?"

"Mm," Micah grunts, sipping more water with a grimace. He gestures for the bottle of rum instead, but Ben shakes his head and keeps it out of reach.

"Uh-uh. Water. Hydrate, you kinky fucker."

Micah rolls his eyes, completely resenting Ben's care and concern.

"Deal is... she gets to take a female lover," Micah tells him in his worn-thin voice, ragged from screaming. "I get to take a male lover. And I've told you about the threesomes. It's supposed to be about sex, and that's it. It's not supposed to get serious."

"And the subbing?"

Micah's head moves subtly back and forth.

"Fuck."

"Exactly. Far as she knows, I'm just a Dom here. If I sub, it's only to her. It's... complicated."

Quietly, Ben asks, "You ever think you'd be getting serious with someone here at Diadem?"

"Did you?" Micah counters.

Ben laughs a little at that, shaking his head in the darkened room. "We are in some spectacularly deep shit, aren't we?"

"Well," Micah says thoughtfully, "We can always reminisce about the good ol' days when it was just you and Gabe, pissing on me in the dungeon."

"Business as usual," Ben grins.

After a pause, Micah tells Ben softly, sincerely, and straight from the heart, "It doesn't make you weak to care, you know. Hold on to him, no matter what the world tries to throw at you in the process. The easy path is not always the best one. Trust me, I know."

They stare at one another, each of them worn out in different ways.

"Need anything?" Ben asks.

Micah holds out a hand, palm up, the arm laced with rope burn. Ben places his hand on top. It gets folded inside of Micah's fingers.

"Nope. Just this."

Chapter 32
Accounting for Kyle

The following day, after a very late night, Ben sleeps in. When he does wake, it's with a throbbing head that feels ready to burst, courtesy of his hangover. He showers, grabs a towering mug of coffee and goes to hide in his office while Kyle is busy outside with cleaning and fixing gutters on the house. Ben keeps the stereo turned up and a wary eye on the garage door, which he can just barely glimpse through the hall, hoping that there's no reason for Kyle to go in there, since Kyle has been keeping his tools and equipment in the detached shed. The only thing left in the garage at this point is the BDSM gear, and Kyle has been avoiding that like the plague. But still, Ben's pessimistic streak warns him that his luck won't hold when there's this big a secret waiting to be discovered.

The package that he'd ordered for Kyle was ready the day before, so Ben picked it up and brought it back to Diadem with him, tucking the box in the room with all of the video equipment. He would have liked to have left it there, but they're closed today and this package is not one that would do well sitting unattended. So now it's here, *in the house*, and Ben feels like the world's biggest jackass.

He begins to tweak on too much coffee just as Kyle comes in from doing his chores to get a drink.

Pale, puffy-eyed and sullen, Ben hunches blearily over his monitor and pretends to be occupied so that Kyle doesn't bother him.

It doesn't work.

Leaning curiously in the doorway, a little sweaty, a little flushed, and very much the living embodiment of all of Ben's temptations, Kyle says cordially, "Mornin' sunshine. Need some aspirin?"

Ben rubs a hand roughly over his face, through his beard; trying to will his head clear. It really doesn't help that Kyle is doing the doting partner routine, playing Ben's nursemaid. That thought sparks a sudden, uncomfortably vivid fantasy of Kyle in nurse's scrubs, lying on a gleaming, steel operating table, his pants pulled down, legs spread invitingly, and all kinds of useful instruments at Ben's disposal to provoke colorful reactions.

"Ben?" Kyle calls with a smirk, drawing him back to the present. "Where'd you go?"

"Don't ask," he grumbles. But with the briefest glance at his blond tempter, Ben gets another flash, seeing Kyle slink across the floor towards him on his hands and knees, purring. In the fantasy, Kyle rubs against Ben's leg, nuzzles the inside of his thigh, pulls down Ben's zipper with his teeth and starts to lick with a wet, rough tongue....

"Fuck me sideways," Ben moans, burying his face in his coffee mug.

Miraculously, Kyle appears—standing—at Ben's side with two aspirin in his palm. "What does that even mean?"

"Hell if I know," Ben scowls, throwing the pills back in his mouth and dry-swallowing them.

"I thought you bought me something."

Ben cringes miserably. He closes his eyes and, in his mind, sees Kyle, completely naked, shaved, oiled, collared, and lapping up a shallow bowl of hot come.

Grabbing and adjusting himself, Ben forces his eyes opened just to make the fantasies stop.

"Changed my mind. I'm keeping it for myself. You can't have it."

Kyle circles Ben's swivel chair, coming up behind him. For a long moment he just massages Ben's neck and shoulders, causing him to lean back into the touch and moan. Once Ben has relaxed slightly, Kyle rubs with one hand down Ben's chest, over the gentle swell of his pectoral muscle, down the firm ripples of his abs, under his pant's waistband. Getting a handful of Ben's swollen cock, Kyle offers seductively, "If I take care of this, *then* can I have it?"

"Hands off," Ben snarls, too on-edge and annoyed with himself to be nice.

"Oh, is that the game? Okay. No hands then."

One hard push at the side of the chair gets it to spin and Kyle is on his knees between Ben's legs before he can gather the sense to protest. Ben's fantasy—one of them, at least—miraculously comes to life before his eyes. Kyle takes hold of Ben's zipper between his bared teeth, and pulls it slowly down. Next he nips at the elastic band of his boxers and pulls those out of the way, too. Luckily, Ben is hard enough to spring free as soon as the clothing is moved aside, so Kyle has full access and begins to lick. With a few swipes up the underside of Ben's shaft, Kyle presses the flesh up against Ben's pelvis with long licks, then a few more swipes of his tongue from tip to root, up the top, pushes Ben's member down against the straining fabric of his underwear.

Ben white-knuckles the chair's arms, almost too turned on to be able to watch. Kyle's hair spills over his blue eyes. His pink tongue curls out, petting Ben wetly, his hot breath warming already fevered flesh. All he wants is to grab Kyle's head and plunge himself into that mouth to feel it close, hot and soft, to suck around him, which is why he grabs on to the chair as tightly as he does. When Kyle begins to purr—intentionally—Ben slides forward in the chair, leaned back to give his determined submissive better access. Seeing how much Ben is enjoying the tongue-action, Kyle keeps at it like the dutiful sub that he is. He positions Ben how he wants him with his chin, cheek and nose, dragging filthy kisses, trailing long straight strokes with the flat of his tongue, making swirling paths with just the pointed tip. When Ben gets close, panting and shuddering slightly, Kyle sucks a few intense kisses around the head, taking it a little more into his mouth each time, then lets it go and licks quickly, repeatedly, firmly up the underside of the shaft, pressing it flat to Ben's body until he comes with a sharp, guttural moan.

As Kyle licks him clean, clothes and all, Ben finally lets himself touch Kyle, tangling his fingers in the short strands of his silken hair, caressing the sides of his angelic face.

"So..." Kyle asks slyly, all sparkling cornflower-blue irises and bruised, swollen red lips. "Where's my present?"

Ben rolls his eyes. Kyle scrapes his teeth playfully over Ben's abs.

"Gimme."

"Don't go anywhere, and don't follow me," Ben snaps. He pushes Kyle gently out of the way and leaves the room in a hurry.

"Is that an order, Sir?" Kyle calls after him, smiling.

"You bet your sweet ass it is!" Ben roars from two rooms away, making Kyle burst out laughing.

"God, you're so tense!" Kyle says, sitting himself comfortably in Ben's chair and twisting back and forth in it in little half-circles. "What the hell happened at work last night to turn you into such a raging—"

The word sticks in his throat as Ben reappears in the doorway. With much less volume and bravado, Kyle finishes lamely, "Bitch."

Without breathing or moving a muscle, Kyle hisses, "What the fuck is that?"

"His name is *Kyle*," Ben says defensively.

"Kyle," Kyle repeats.

"Yes. Kyle. I call him Junior."

The white cat is covered in pale grey leopard spots. With startling blue eyes, the male feline looks right at Kyle and mewls as Ben scratches behind his pointed ears. Curled up comfortably in Ben's arms, it nuzzles his chest.

"He's a Bengal. I got him because animals are proven to be good stress relief. They use them in therapy all the time."

All of the humor is long gone from Kyle's expression and posture. At first he's completely frozen, but then bolts up out of the chair, fast, fuming. The cat becomes startled and jumps from Ben's arms to prance over to the chair in the far corner, bounding up onto the cushion.

Breathing heavily, chest rising with quickened breaths, Kyle isn't just angry, he's *pissed*. Blinking his eyes clear, his voice suddenly thick with emotion, he glares at Ben. Ben stands his ground, face hardened to protect his injured pride. Kyle takes two steps and crosses to him. Laying two hands flat on Ben's chest, Kyle shoves him backward.

"You need more than this," Ben explains through gritted teeth. "The D/s shit, the job, the twisted friendship with Darrek—*that's* your problem. You'd never see it on your own, so I have to do it for you, just like everything else. You can't ask for it, or admit that you want it, so I have to throw it in your motherfucking face to make you see it."

Kyle chokes back the beginnings of a sob and hits Ben again, this time forcefully enough to knock Ben into the wall. The cat meows at them, watching the whole exchange with rapt attention.

"Stop," Ben tells him tenderly, making it worse. He grabs Kyle's forearms loosely, the muscles hardened with tension as Kyle fights against Ben's hold.

"*How could you?!*" Kyle rages. "You named him *Kyle*? You couldn't even call *me* Kyle! For like a fucking YEAR you refused to say my name! I was just a slave! Your *kitty*. Your *toy*."

"I know. And I'm sorry for that," Ben says slowly, levelly, infuriatingly calm. The display of Kyle's wrath brings out Ben's composure at last, showing him his role to play. "The past is fucking with your head. Isn't it? It doesn't take a genius to figure out what the solution is, and it isn't suicide. You need hope and comfort. There *is* more than this, Kyle. I want *us* to have more than this. I may be a proud son-of-a-bitch but I'm man enough to admit how much I love you."

Kyle looks at the damned cat. A tear slides down his cheek and the cat tilts its head sideways, meowing curiously at him, staring with those eerily colorful eyes. It's a gorgeous creature, and smart, lithe—perfect. The cat isn't what is upsetting Kyle, though. It's that defensive look in Ben's eyes, like a very big, life-changing decision has already been made, and without Kyle's permission or consent.

Ben knows what he thinks Kyle needs. Like everything else, when Ben has it in his head to do something, he does it. Ben wanted to show Kyle that he needed Ben in his life, so he did. Ben wanted to show Kyle that he knew all of his deep, dark secrets, so he did. Ben knew that if he let Kyle go and explore his obsession with Darrek and Gabriel, that it would only drive Kyle right back into Ben's arms, so he did. Ben wanted to give Kyle an animal companion to love and be loved by, so he did.

If that was all, it would be infuriating, but it would still be okay. The trouble is that it is very, very far from all. It's that look — the one in Ben's eyes, right now, and the way he'd stayed out late getting trashed and hid all morning in his office — that tells Kyle in clear, plainspoken language, that he is well and truly fucked.

Kyle tries to violently yank his arms free of Ben's grasp. He can't, as hard as he tries to, enough to make the veins stand out in Ben's neck. Kyle tries to rage against his captor, wanting to beat on Ben's body until he hurts too. It feels good. It's cleansing and empowering to be able to get angry at something other than himself.

Heart-stopping affection floods Ben's expression then, scaring Kyle more than anything in his life has thus far. Because Kyle chose Ben as a Dom, and as a lover, for his inability to be tender, affectionate, and sentimental. All Ben ever wanted was someone to take apart and fuck with — a human sex toy — or so Kyle let himself believe. That's all this was supposed to be. That's all this was *ever* supposed to be — shallow, superficial, temporary, convenient.

"What did —" Kyle gasps, heart beating too fast, his lungs squeezing the oxygen out, forbidding its subsequent intake. "What did you — Ben, let go. Let go of me!"

"You care about things so deeply," Ben tells him. "That's not a fault. That's amazing. And nothing I could ever do to you — nothing Gabe or Dare could ever do to you, either — could ever take that away, as much as you want it to. You can't stomp it out by being cruel to yourself. You can't carve it out with knives or purge it through the end of your cock."

"You," Kyle spits. "You son of a bitch! You liar!"

Kyle snarls and puts all of his weight into pushing back against Ben, because Ben is all there is. Ben is everything that's worth struggling with and battling against. And Ben is the ideal focus of Kyle's formless outrage, since he's not going anywhere. That's why Kyle is so furious. Ben has decided. Ben is staying, right here in Kyle's arms, for the rest of his life.

Sending Ben crashing back into the wall a second time, Kyle manages to drive the wind from him. For a minute or so, they wrestle there, with Kyle trying to hurt or be hurt, and being completely denied the satisfaction.

"Hate me. Go ahead. Doesn't change anything, and you know it."

And Kyle does know it. If Ben wants this, he'll hold on, hold Kyle's heart in his hands, forever. Kyle might want to run away, but even if he did, Ben would still own his heart. That's the bitch of it. Ben waits, watching Kyle fall apart. He's exceedingly patient as Kyle decides for them both how this is going to go. Kyle's heartbeat *thump-thump-thumps* under Ben's palms, evidence of the vitality in his body. Slowly, the fight dissipates, and Kyle surrenders, his breath hitching as he hiccups softly, his cheeks wet and eyes bloodshot.

After letting go of Kyle's left wrist, Ben wipes away some of the teardrops chasing down his lover's face. The tenderness of the gesture wrenches free an anguished cry and Kyle falls against Ben, exhaling against his neck then finding his mouth, kissing him even as he struggles to suck down air. Ben turns them, propping Kyle against the wall, holding him there as he kisses every newfound breath away, and Kyle lets him.

Chapter 33

Push and Pull

"Good morning, you've reached the offices of Daring Angel Photography. I'm Dare, how may I direct your call?"

There's a pause. "Mm-hmm. Nope. No, I don't think so. I see. Well, I'm sorry I couldn't be of more help. Have a fabulous day!"

Gabriel waits for it, doesn't get it, so, from the back room where he has hundreds of negatives laid out in front of him on the light table, he calls, "Babe, who was that?"

"Wrong number!"

A lie. It's more than a wrong number. It's bait, and it almost works.

Darrek has been cheerfully talking the ear off of anyone that calls, including the wrong numbers. Gabriel resists the urge to divert his attention from the negatives and goes back to work. For a good twenty minutes he has no distractions, as long as he doesn't give in to the temptation to glance out through the opened door at his receptionist.

Then, the office's front door opens. Instinctively, Gabriel's gaze flicks up and he slides sideways to see who it is.

A delivery guy brings a shallow box over to Darrek and sets it down on the desk while tapping a few times on the electronic gadget in his hands. With a barely noticeable upward glance and what Gabriel considers to be a huge display of self-control, the middle-aged black man holds out the device for Darrek and says, "Mornin' um... Sir. Signature please." Darrek scribbles on the electronic line and beams a wide smile. "Last name?"

"Grealey," Darrek responds warmly. "Though I'm thinking of changing it to Hunter. Or possibly a combination of the two. But,

266

wait. That'd probably be Grunter, wouldn't it? Never mind. We'll just stick to one or the other."

"Whatever, man. Thanks. Have a nice day."

The deliveryman quickly heads back out the way he came in as Darrek replies, loudly, "You too! Have a great day! Thanks for the mail!"

The baited hook snags. Gabriel doesn't fight it and lets Darrek—his warmth, his charm, his ridiculousness—reel him in despite how exhausted and overworked Gabriel may be. For Gabriel, his love for, and devotion to, Darrek wins out over everything—logic, responsibility and his own tiredness.

Sighing, Gabriel leaves the light table and goes straight to the front desk. He leans down and plants his hands on the top of it. Darrek's natural scent starts to act on Gabriel as much as the sight of him and the damned flashes memory—vivid and debauched—of the decadent sex acts they indulged in hardly more than two hours earlier, when Gabriel's focus last slipped.

With forced calmness barely conquering strong, wicked, primal instincts, Gabriel asks with genuine curiosity, "Is this because of the pigtails?"

"Is what because of the pigtails?" Darrek replies, suddenly timid and unsurprisingly feigning ignorance. The last time Gabriel had Darrek wear his hair in pigtails was during their vacation when Darrek had no choice but to play by Gabriel's rules. Something as insignificant as a hairdo had pushed Darrek hard, into a kind of shyness that fed Gabriel's libido like few things have. On vacation, the pigtails were just the beginning, a first step toward true submissiveness and long, glorious, hours of play.

Now, at work in Gabriel's office, Darrek is clearly fighting with himself—needing to submit completely, wanting more from his Master, and hating the humiliation all at the same time. The struggle manifests fascinatingly as Darrek covers over profound self-consciousness with feigned cheerfulness that they both know won't take much for Gabriel to break through.

Indeed, as Gabriel yanks the dark sunglasses from Darrek's nose, revealing eyes shining with defiance, Gabriel detects his slave's vulnerability and arousal in his shortness of breath and the rising color under his skin. "Take these off."

"But they complete my *ensemble*," Darrek protests jokingly, indicating his black skinny jeans, a half-unbuttoned, black silk shirt and leather boots. The pigtails bounce as Darrek glances down at himself, then back up at the front door like he's watching to make sure the conversation stays private.

Gabriel sees right through all of it, and it's clear that Darrek knows he does. He won't meet Gabriel's hard gaze and he fidgets restlessly in the wooden chair. Darrek is already more nervous than if Gabriel had him strung up and shackled from the ceiling, naked. Fascinated by this and feeding off of it, getting high off of the power of managing to do so much with such little effort, Gabriel stares Darrek down, waiting.

When Darrek finally surrenders and looks up directly at Gabriel, a tendon in Darrek's thick, long neck jumps under the studded collar wrapping it. Gabriel's gaze goes instantly to the spot. The desire to bite is almost too great to overcome.

Catching the look and reading Gabriel like only a devoted submissive can, Darrek tilts his head to the side and playfully tugs the collar out of the way, offering his neck to his Master. "Though I do live to please you...."

"What would please me is for you to be more *obedient*," Gabriel responds in a tone both cool and hard as granite.

Darrek leans back in the desk chair, his thickly muscled arms braced on its sides. His unbuttoned shirt pulls open wider, revealing more of his bare, waxed-smooth chest. His pecs flex as he struggles to overcome his body's reactions to Gabriel's display of dominance. Biting timidly on his lower lip, made uncomfortable by his arousal, Darrek shifts on the wooden seat of the chair, one he handmade and painstakingly crafted.

"Is there anything else you require of me, Mr. Hunter, Sir? More paperwork, maybe?"

Darrek's eyes are full of hot, churning invitation and willingness to tease Gabriel into compliance. Darrek doesn't want to sit alone with his thoughts and poisonous memories, answering phones and doing busywork. He wants Gabriel to strip him naked, freeing him of the tormenting outfit, and fuck him into compliance—wants it badly enough to do absolutely anything to get it, certain, though, that asking outright would be the surest way not to get it at all.

The black lipstick Darrek had been wearing when they left the house that morning is now smeared mostly off, thanks to the slow, lazy blowjob Darrek eagerly gave Gabriel once commanded to do so. At the time, Gabriel was sitting at the same front desk, the blinds raised and the spectacle of them on display for anyone who might bother to look. Darrek hadn't really fit in the foot well of the desk, but it didn't matter. Gabriel held on to the pigtails, pulling them gently, letting Darrek feel their presence every second he was made to swallow Gabriel's cock. In no time at all, Gabriel rode Darrek's wet, wriggling tongue and hot, tight throat to orgasm, but Darrek was left unsatisfied and hard up.

Bound only by Gabriel's keen scrutiny, desperate, probably, for something to keep his hands and his mind busy, Darrek pulls a wooden ruler from the desk drawer. He slides it in a smooth, long stroke over his palm, fingering the edge while trying to unflinchingly hold Gabriel's gaze.

"I have *a lot* of work to do. A client is coming in an hour from now and she's expecting me to have — Stop it. Hands on the desk. Now."

Darrek, holding Gabriel's stare, had moved to slyly adjust himself in the constricting pants.

Jaw clenched, gaze dropping, Darrek sets the ruler down and plants his hands on the desk's wooden surface but doesn't apologize.

More bait.

This is a game they've been playing almost non-stop for days. Sometimes Gabriel is too busy or tired to attend to Darrek as much as he would like to. He'll let Darrek seduce him into screwing around just a little, transforming fast into Darrek's Dominant, not intending to take it anywhere. But, then, temptation builds in Gabriel until responsibilities are forgotten and they've found themselves in the middle of pure, wanton depravity.

"You will behave. You will obey me, *explicitly*, or you will be punished."

"Mr. Hunter," Darrek replies without smiling. "That's no way to speak to your secretary."

He's calling Gabriel on the fact that he is already, again, breaking his own rules about keeping work and sex separate.

Darrek sits forward in the chair, hands still glued to the top. He spreads his legs inside the foot well and rolls his hips slightly, seductively, to try and relieve pressure, the large bulge of his crotch more than noticeable.

Gabriel's control breaks.

"Get in the back room. *Now.*"

After Gabriel locks the front door, he follows Darrek into the back. Detailed plans and ideas are already forming as Gabriel realizes the lesson that must be taught here. This isn't about keeping sex out of the workplace, like Darrek might think it is. This is about something else entirely; an imbalance in their relationship that calls more urgently for a response. Darrek is pushing Gabriel for what he thinks he needs and trying to subtly shift the power dynamic in his favor, and that in itself is the problem.

Once in the back room, Gabriel turns on some of the lighting equipment, angled toward the raised platform where he does his still-photography work. In the clear, no-nonsense baritone of a seasoned, expert Dominant, Gabriel says, "Okay, take your clothes off. All of them. Slowly. Leave the collar on. You don't touch the collar."

A clean white drape is spread over the platform before Gabriel goes to the tripod holding his favorite digital camera. He switches it from still to video mode. Not needing to be asked, Darrek steps into the pool of light, onto the sheet on the platform. He slowly finishes unbuttoning his shirt, letting it slide from his broad shoulders and onto the floor. His fingers, trembling slightly, go to his fly, popping the button, slowly inching down the zipper. He pushes at the fabric encasing his hips, letting it tug his briefs down with them as he gets them to mid-thigh. Then, having already kicked his boots off, he steps out of each leg.

Gabriel throws him body oil once he's done.

"You wanted my attention? You've got it. All of it. Give me a show and make it good. You hold out on me and you bet your ass I'll know it."

Chapter 34
Daring Darrek

Darrek stares darkly at Gabriel, but Gabriel isn't looking at him, at least not directly. He's watching through the camera, adjusting the zoom and focus. Squirting oil into his palm, Darrek begins to spread it over his chest, rubbing it into the skin, over each muscle. His palm rolls over his left nipple, drags up to the inside of his shoulder, and over the base of his neck. The suntanned skin glistens everywhere his hand goes.

His left hand kneads his right pectoral muscle, twisting the nipple as his right squeezes oil up the shaft of his cock. Taking his time, Darrek tugs himself slowly, giving Gabriel time to adjust the camera's focus again, getting himself completely hard.

The attention, the spotlights, the solitude as he stands there alone, lets Darrek revel in the attention, all on him. Flushing with heat, guilt, lust and sorrow all at the same time, Darrek loses his ability to look at the camera. Eyes closed over, he blocks it all out and centers his attention on the slick slide of the oil over his skin, and how it eases every stroke. The stimulation gets him fully hard, despite his embarrassment and conflicted emotions. He lets go of his cock and it curves up, tight and stiff. Rolling his balls in his hand, pinching his nipple sharply enough to hurt, Darrek's breathing roughens.

"Lay down. On your back. Plant your feet and keep 'em spread wide."

Darrek lies down with his groin toward the camera. The position keeps his face mostly out of the camera's range, so it helps him relax. He spreads his legs, giving Gabriel a great shot of his balls, drawn taut, his thickening erection and his little pink hole. Smearing oil over the insides of his thighs, Darrek waits for the next command.

"Go ahead, don't even pretend you don't want to," is all Gabriel says.

Unable to see him, only to hear him, Darrek gazes blankly up at the ceiling's rafters and reaches between his legs. Inching his feet a little farther apart, he rubs over and behind his sac, through his cheeks. He pulls them apart, flushing with a new wave of heat at making such a spectacle of himself here, in Gabriel's sanctuary — his safe, secret, private place. His index and middle fingers trace through his crack, rubbing in tight circles around the wrinkled knot of his hole. Circling it, getting it wet, teasing himself open, he takes his time then adds pressure. He parts around both fingers and he moans. They slide in to the first knuckle, spreading the wetness inside.

When Gabriel speaks, Darrek is at first startled, because he's right there, standing over him, not even a foot away and with the camera cradled in his hands, the lens pointed down at Darrek's face. Eyes sprung open, breath coming quick, his blush growing rapidly, Darrek stares up into Gabriel's cool, avid gaze.

"This is just for us. You and me, no one else. I want to save this and always have it — have you, like this — you're so incredibly beautiful, and nervous, but trusting me. I love it. Push them in, all the way. Good. Now tug them out. All the way. That's it. Fingers out. Now show me how wet you are, Dare."

He closes his eyes and palms his ass with both hands, pulling it open.

"More than that," Gabriel urges, panning down Darrek's body, stopping and focusing between his legs. "Don't be shy. Every part of you is beautiful to me, but especially this part."

Darrek lays there, jittery; part of his sense memory from his abuse lingers, preventing him from enjoying this moment with Gabriel as completely as he might otherwise. Part of him wants to feel bad about needing Gabriel like he does, and needing Gabriel to need him in return. The little boy he used to be expects to be punished for the forbidden things he desires. A broken arm, a vicious beating, mindfucks, brainwashing and being subjected to the secret, perverse desires of a sick man — it's all part of Darrek's identity; he can't escape it or deny it. The only hope is in moving on and growing from the suffering. That's what he strives for. He strives to be stronger—for his true love, his Gabriel, and himself.

He tries to own all of it, the bad and the good. For a moment, he's back in the dungeons of Diadem, that first time when it was Trace between Darrek's legs and Gabriel giving the orders, breaking down walls Darrek didn't even know he had yet. Gabriel has been Darrek's salvation, his savior, saving him from self-delusions and lies, giving him truth, honesty and trust in return. Gabriel, who is proud of him, who loves Darrek exactly the way he is.

Kneeling between Darrek's feet, getting a close-up shot, taking his time, Gabriel lets Darrek know that he's seen. Every part of him, the secret parts, the dirty parts, the hidden beauty, it's all Gabriel's and it's all exactly the way it should be. It's perfect.

"Three fingers. Now. Come on."

Breathing heavily, Darrek shifts his hand between his legs once more and does as asked. He pushes three fingers through his rim, past the outer ring of muscle, savoring the full feeling and the small ache of the stretch then tugs them out a few inches before pushing right back in. The friction stiffens his prick.

"How's it feel?"

"Good," he rasps.

"How good?"

"Really good."

"Know what'd make it better? Grab your balls. Hold 'em by the base. That's it. Squeeze right there. Don't move."

Gabriel steadies the camera with one hand and produces the ruler with the other.

"Shit," Darrek groans, before it even touches him, his dread and excitement alike crawling up his bowels. His three fingers keep pushing and pulling in his ass as Gabriel slaps his balls, held tightly in a hand. The flat of the wood smacks the sensitive organ, tapping lightly, just enough to sting a little and cramp him up. Getting off on the pain, Darrek's dick weeps pre-come and he holds his breath, wanting more.

In a second, he gets it. A harder slap is delivered directly to Darrek's left testicle, making him flinch and grunt. He exhales sharply, gulping down air then holding it again with a frown as Gabriel slaps the spot with the ruler again and again. Face on fire, balls throbbing, stomach in knots, he feels the ruler rub in a caress over the stretched skin of his scrotum.

"Beautiful. Keep your hand out of the way. Stick those fingers in all the way and keep 'em there. Good. Let your legs fall open."

"I can't."

"Sure you can."

Darrek fights his instinct, though dull and conquerable, to curl up around his aching balls. Staring up at the ceiling, chest rising and falling in shallow gasps, brow furrowed with tension and anticipation, he gets very still and waits. The waiting is almost as much of a delicious torment as the bite of the ruler, and Gabriel knows it, playing it for all it's worth, catching as much of Darrek's reaction as he can with the camera.

"Do it," Darrek begs.

Gabriel runs the flat of the ruler over Darrek's inner thigh, across his knuckles, over the pulled-tight skin of his sac, then swats his balls.

"More," he moans wantonly. All he can feel is his own hands on his body, his nerves jittering from head to toe. "Please. Gabe. Master...."

He opens his eyes and lifts his head to look. Gabe has set the camera down by Darrek's head, facing him, and he's gone to the far end of the room. A closet with a padlock is opened halfway and Gabriel is standing just inside it. He searches for something and, having found it, brings it back to Darrek, lying in the light.

"You keep that in the closet? Why?" Darrek blurts.

"Emergencies," Gabriel answers with a sly gleam in his eyes.

"What kind of emergencies?"

"Cases of extreme boredom. I keep a selection of my favorite videos of you on my laptop, so, you know... if it's a slow day, or I need a pick-me-up...."

"Hell of a pick me up," Darrek murmurs, eyeing the thick dildo, with a narrow, indented ring just before the flared base. He imagines Gabriel at work, a suit and tie much like the one he's currently wearing, inserting the wide toy into his slim body, maybe fucking himself with it, maybe just leaving it in while he jerks off to home-made porn. "You've used it?"

"Of course," Gabriel scoffs. He picks up the camera, turns it to aim between Darrek's legs and settles there on his knees. "Fingers out."

Darrek withdraws his hand and shivers with outwardly radiating goosebumps as Gabriel aligns the fake cock with his hole and adds just enough pressure to get Darrek's ass to begin to swallow it, feeding it into him unhurriedly, checking the sharpness of the picture and angle of the shot. When he has taken about four inches of the phallus, Gabriel begins to work it in and out, each slide pushing it deeper. Darrek moans thickly, legs fallen wide, his one hand still locked up around his balls. He squeezes them to spice the pleasure with a little pain and his dick twitching, dark, hot and wet against his belly.

Gabriel stares at him, the way he hungers for the fullness of the plastic cock, drawing his legs up even more, presenting his ass for fucking. His cock twitches on the next inward thrust, begging for attention.

"Good," Gabriel praises. "Gorgeous."

He gives the base of the toy a hard push and buries it completely in Darrek's body, pressing at the end with his fingers until he's sure that it's not going to slide back out.

"That's it. Hold it in. Got it?"

"Yeah," Darrek pants, his brow glistening with beads of sweat. "Thank you."

"You're welcome, baby. Okay. Stand up. Get dressed."

"What?" Darrek blinks.

"You heard me."

"But...."

"Now."

Silently, Darrek struggles to his knees, then his feet and gathers his pants first, moaning long and low when he stoops and the large toy shifts inside his rectum.

"Not a sound, you hear?" Gabriel scolds. "Just get dressed. Quietly. Obediently. I don't want to see it on your face that you feel anything, or there will be consequences that you will *not* enjoy. Feel that collar?"

"Yes, Sir," Darrek murmurs.

"Then act like the well-behaved slave that I know you can be."

"Yes, Sir," he smiles, and means it completely, wanting nothing but to make Gabriel proud of him.

He gets his feet in the legs of his briefs and jeans, and shimmies them up over his hips. When he tries to stuff his hard-on inside them, he glances at his Master. Gabriel's arms are folded stubbornly, the camera back in the tripod.

Darrek presses his stiffened flesh down against his leg and gets the jeans closed after a solid couple of minutes of struggle.

"The shirt. Then the boots," Gabriel orders sharply.

When Darrek has to bend over to grab the shirt, he feels the groan bubble up in his throat as the fat plastic cock moves and the denim squeezes painfully around his swollen genitals. Biting the inside of his cheek to stay quiet, he grabs the silken fabric of the shirt, straightens, and slides his arms into it.

"Button it up. All the way."

Darrek manages to slide his feet into the boots without needing to bend again, for which he is silently very, very grateful.

Taking his time, Gabriel gathers the sheet on the platform, turns off the camera, and flicks off the lights. Without turning to Darrek, he says, "Go back to the desk."

Walking awkwardly and stiffly, each step a special kind of agony, he shuffles to the front desk.

Gabriel walks to the blinds and opens them back up.

"Sit down. In the chair."

Darrek almost whimpers in complaint just at the thought, but he knows he can't protest. Drawing out the chair, he lowers himself into it, trying to keep his legs as straight as possible. When his ass connects with the wood, a lightning bolt rockets up his spine, bursting in tongues of fire that lick outward into his body. His dick is smashed against his leg, inside rough, constricting denim. He regrets the tight jeans very, very much. Unseeing, barely hearing, unable to use any of his senses over the screaming of the nerves in his body, Darrek isn't really aware of Gabriel walking in a circle around the desk, to get behind his seat, but he feels it when Gabriel pushes his chair, getting him pinned between it and the heavy wooden desk, and, in the process, forcing him to sit perfectly upright. The cry is torn from his chest. His hands splay widely on the desk's surface and he breathes shakily through his nose.

"I thought I asked you to be quiet," Gabriel hisses with deadly severity, right by Darrek's ear.

"Please," he begs through gritted teeth. His whole pelvic area is enflamed with throbbing, gripping, brutal, spectacular torment.

Looping a finger through the back of the collar, Gabriel yanks on it once, letting Darrek feel it constrict his windpipe, though gently. "You still think the *ensemble* is cute? I told you to wear the pigtails to remind you that you are my *bitch*. You hear me, slave? You're mine. I own your ass. I own every part of you. I decide when you get fucked, when you get off, when you get hard, what you wear, all of it. You submit to me. You obey. You sit here, looking pretty and carrying out orders to the best of your ability. That's all. Got it?"

Darrek grunts, unable to find his voice at first, finding the display of dominance unspeakably, dizzyingly hot. Gabriel twists the collar tighter and Darrek's cock throbs wetly in his jeans. Writhing in the chair, trying to get comfortable, Darrek is stopped by a hissed, "I asked a question."

"Got it, Sir," he manages. "I apologize. Thank you, Master. Please forgive me, Master."

Gabriel lets go and walks back around the desk. To Darrek's shock, he unlocks the door to the office. Standing there, his hand on the handle, he says, "You may unzip your pants. Go on."

Darrek glances furtively at the opened blinds, but the binding clothes are more of a concern than his privacy, so he unzips and pulls his cock out, moaning in huge relief.

"Now, if you stay pulled in nice and close to the desk, no one will know. Right?"

And with that, Gabriel turns, his demeanor changed utterly in the blink of an eye. All smiles, charming and debonair, he opens the front door and extends an arm into the office. "Marguerite! You're right on time. Can I get you anything? Coffee, tea, water?"

An elegantly dressed woman in her later fifties glides into the office and Darrek feels all of his fevered, hot, pulsing blood rush upward from his cock to flood his face in a wave of extreme self-consciousness, shocked beyond sense that Gabriel would bring a client in *now*. Like a statue, Darrek sits there, unmoving, trying to be invisible. He can feel the head of his exposed dick brushing against the underside of the desk, smearing warm fluid there. Never before in his life has he blushed so fiercely.

"Bottled water would be divine, Gabriel, thank you so much," she grins, holding her clutch purse in both hands. Then she notices Darrek and gives him a glance tarnished ever-so-slightly with mild disapproval at his hairdo. "Oh, you hired help?"

"Yes," Gabriel smiles with satisfaction and aloofness. "He's a temp. Darrek, this is Marguerite, Marguerite, Darrek."

"Pleasure," Darrek mutters shortly. "Excuse me." He picks up the phone and pretends to make a call. Because he can't think of anything else to do, he calls the house, lets it ring, then starts to talk to the answering machine, feeling like a total, complete ass.

They gather around a counter that runs all along the far wall, lit prettily with discreet overhead lighting and begin to review proofs for a series of portraits that Marguerite had commissioned Gabriel to create for her.

It goes on forever. The chilly air of the room tickles Darrek's cock, and he wills it soft, but the fat toy up his ass, thicker than Gabriel, keeps him unbearably stiff. The alluring sight of Gabriel in his suave, disarmingly seductive, professional photographer mode, and wearing a full, perfectly-tailored suit to boot, doesn't help at all. Darrek just stares helplessly at Gabriel's firm ass in his snug cotton trousers and prays for Marguerite to get the fuck out already.

An eternity — or an hour — later, she does go, with a polite nod of goodbye to Darrek and a lingering handshake coupled with a brief kiss on the cheek for Gabriel. As soon as she's through the door and it closes behind her, Gabriel locks the door again.

"Fuck you!" Darrek growls.

Gabriel laughs.

"Baby, this is your game. I'm just playing along," Gabriel says with a faint smile so sexy that Darrek has to look away or explode.

"Please, Master," he beseeches, without an ounce of dignity left.

"Soon," Gabriel promises. "First, I want you to show me the immaculate self-control that I know you to have, just for a little longer."

Expression strained with the thinness of his patience, sweaty of brow and shaky of knee, Darrek can only nod.

Gabriel slinks around the desk, peeling off his suit jacket, loosening his tie, and unbuttoning the top two buttons of his shirt. He turns the desk chair and slips easily into the foot well as Darrek gapes at him with equal parts utter devotion and clawing horror. Gabriel is just small enough to fit under there, sitting on his heels. "Raise your hips."

Darrek lifts his ass off the chair an inch or two and waits, breathing roughly, as Gabriel pulls his pants down for him, taking them all the way to his ankles. Gabriel pulls him back down onto the chair, then wraps a hand around his shaft to steady it. He licks a few times over the head before suckling it. Darrek sputters out a colorful stream of curses and grips the arms of the chair almost tightly enough to snap them off. Gabriel's soft, warm lips close around him, just behind his cockhead, in a wide O. Sucking the pulsing, hot flesh, wet with the body oil and pre-come, Gabriel uses his hand to lightly stroke up and down Darrek's shaft, teasing him towards madness. Then he takes more of him into his mouth, letting him slide back over his tongue to lodge in his throat.

"*Fuck*," Darrek rasps, thrusting hard and slapping the desk with an opened palm.

Gabriel moans, humming as he pulls off and plays his fingers over the tip of Darrek's cock.

"What do you want, slave? Do you want to take revenge on your Master, or do you want to continue to be very, very good for me?"

Understanding the question and all of its facets instantly, Darrek grunts thickly with the strain of physical self-control as he tries to decide on his honest answer.

Gabriel nuzzles Darrek's erection. It slides, wet, against his shaved-smooth cheek. Gabriel drags his parted lips over the shaft and his tongue darts out to lick over Darrek's tightly drawn up sac. It gives Darrek no relief, only furthers his lust and the ache in his balls.

"It's not a trick question, you know. I'm asking you a direct, simple question. What do you want? Do you want to make me cry? Make me hate myself and hate you a little, and that little will grow every day, in increments, until it destroys me and destroys what we have together? Because it will. I could still turn into a monster; repeat the cycle, oldest story in the world. You could still turn into that, too. You wanna be Daddy? Think about it. Do you?

"Or do you want to be *mine*—my slave, gorgeous, trusting and safeguarded with every breath that I have left in my body."

"Yours," Darrek gasps strangling on sorrow, almost in a cry of passion. But the sorrow brings certainty. "Yours, Master," Darrek begs, making his choice, for better or worse, for richer or poorer, 'til death do they part.

Gabriel sucks him a few more times, taking him so close that Darrek begins to whine back in his throat.

Pulling off with a slurp, Gabriel tells his slave, "You will always have a safeword, but I set the rules."

"Yes," Darrek moans, giving over, and completely.

"Lean back. Put both your feet on the edge of the desk. Now!" The blinds are still open, though neither of them cares. Darrek leans back in the solid chair, feet on the desk, legs spread, pants down. Gabriel oh-so-slowly tugs the dildo from his ass while jacking him fast with a tight fist. Darrek gasps sharply, strangling on the force of his climax.

"Yes! Yes, please! Want it... Gabe... God. *Fuck!*"

Gabriel works the toy in the clenched vise of Darrek's ass as he comes, filling him with it until he's so full he yells through the pleasure, watching him come in hot, dripping jets of semen that ruin his black shirt. Then he swallows Darrek down. Darrek palms Gabriel's head with both hands and devotes himself anew to the devilish, talented man with an angel's name, there in his grasp.

Chapter 35

Dangerous Desires

Between the bite of the chill in the air, nipping with sharp teeth at Kyle's nose, cheeks, ears and neck, and the warmth of the paper cup filled with coffee cradled in his hands, he tries to lose himself somewhere in the middle. The cold pulls at his exposed skin and the drink burns from inside out. The concrete sensations ground him, keeping him tethered when so much else threatens to send his thoughts spinning off into the ether.

He's sitting at a small table outside of a local coffee shop, down the street from his shrink's office. It's getting late. The sun is setting behind the tall, brickface buildings along the road lined with shops, reflecting in fiery colors in the windowpanes.

He should be walking back to his car. He should be going home. He should be doing a lot of things.

His phone rings in his pocket. Suspecting, initially, that it's Ben, Kyle hesitates. It gets to the fourth ring before he mutters a curse and digs it out. He has already answered before his brain catches up and informs him that the screen had flashed Gabriel's name, and not Ben's. The lag time in information comprehension leaves him unable to form a sensible greeting at first.

"Uhh," he grunts, trying to figure out why Gabriel would be calling and what to say, but too mentally exhausted to do either.

"Kyle? You all right?"

"Peachy."

"What's wrong?"

Kyle sighs, sips his coffee and huddles farther into his woolen coat. "Nothing. Long day."

"My ass. You wanna talk about it?"

Regretting the last-minute decision to answer, Kyle asks, "What can I do for you, Gabe?" without answering the question.

"If this is a bad time...."

Some of Kyle's instincts kick in. He notices, finally, that Gabriel sounds weird, too. He almost sounds... nervous. Gabriel doesn't do nervous.

"Nah. I'm downtown, having coffee. Just got done baring my soul to my trusty head shrinker, so I'm kind of sick of talking about me. If you're free you can always come down and join. They've got great lattes here."

"Yeah, I think this is more of a phone discussion than an in-public, across-the-table one. How's your hand?"

"Better," Kyle says, flexing it inside his glove.

"Good. How are things with Ben?"

"You haven't talked to him?"

"No, not since... you know. I don't really know how to go there yet. That's kind of one of the reasons why I'm calling. I want to talk to him, but I need to see where you stand first. I don't really know how everything with Darrek affected you and Ben. And your relationship is not really any of my business, but...."

Kyle lifts his head and stares out into space, his heels hooked on a wrung of his chair and his toes tapping against the concrete of the sidewalk. There's so much to say, but he's paralyzed.

"Look," Gabriel says when Kyle stays silent. "This was a bad idea. I'm sorry for bothering you."

"I miss you," Kyle admits. "Things with Ben... They're better than they've ever been, but they're also just so fucking weird. Things have... things have happened since I last talked to you and Dare. When I was with you, my biggest problem was Dare's hard-on, and that feels like another lifetime. Shit's moved to a whole other level now. You sure you can't come down for a drink?"

"Bad idea."

"Why?"

Gabriel chuckles tensely, making Kyle frown into the phone and strain his ears to catch every sound.

"Why's it a bad idea, Gabe?" he presses.

"Because part of me wants to apologize to you for things that I feel responsible for, and the way that I've always apologized to people I love is with more physical expressions than verbal ones. That's not fair to you and I know that. My goal is to make sure none of the inappropriate line crossing happens again, with anyone. I'm striving for honesty. Even if it means making a total ass of myself."

Kyle can hear Gabriel's self-effacing embarrassment over the crappy connection. The cold of the air is forgotten, as is the coffee and the pedestrians milling around. Kyle's world has temporarily shrunken down to the tinny sound of Gabriel's gruff voice.

"What are you talking about?"

"You know what I'm talking about," Gabriel says, exasperated. "Sometimes when I think about you, and how much you're going through, I just want to touch you and try to make it better. And I can't. I'm not the person that can fix you, Kyle. I used to think I could be, but that's not my job."

Kyle's reaction to this fascinates him. That Gabriel has just confessed to loving him, to wanting to touch him, and for feeling guilty about it, instantly makes Kyle want to touch Gabriel, too. Kyle knows all about feeling guilty over desiring affection with another man. And the more he learns about the complicated man at the other end of the phone line, the more Kyle sees the similarities. The idea of being affectionate with Gabriel, kissing Gabriel, hugging him, feeling the beating of his heart under his hand, those things feel like gifts he'd be giving himself, too. He takes a moment to study these emotions, and recognizes the toxicity in them. It doesn't do much to sway him one way or the other. Hovering in limbo, between here and there, Kyle continues to listen.

"We haven't talked about what I'm starting to explore with Trace and Ben, and using them to get a handle on my shit. What I've asked of Ben and what he has offered doesn't matter if you aren't game. Ben can be very accommodating when it comes to dominating someone that's asking for it. I think we both know that, but you...."

Kyle takes his feet off of the chair's rungs and wraps them around the legs of the chair instead, spreading his legs wider and sitting more on the edge of his seat. Closing his eyes, the town, the emotional heaviness that's weighted him down—it all disappears with the urgency in Gabriel's voice in his ear.

All of the things that Kyle has felt subjected to—his past, the men in his life, his own choices—are mirrored in Gabriel. Gabriel gets it. He's been through worse than Kyle, and that niggling guilt is there, just as it's been for a year. Kyle feels guilty for keeping the secret from Gabriel about Harry, Gabriel's stepfather, and what Ben, Trace and Micah did to him behind Gabriel's back. As much as Kyle feels like the victim, a screw-up, and damaged or unworthy, he could never hope to comprehend what Gabriel must go through on a day-to-day basis. But the bitch of it is that Gabriel handles his shit. He got out of Diadem. He's got his own business, and is doing his best to maintain a functioning relationship with Darrek.

"I've never been selfish with Ben," Kyle tells him. "I know he has sex with other people, but that his heart is with me. If he can help you, I'm fine with that."

So many things that have been at the forefront of Kyle's mind start to fall away, getting smaller and flat—overpowered by the hugeness of Kyle's reality. Worrying about sex and submitting, foursomes and fetishes, it's child's play. It used to be everything to him, but now there's something more.

"Kyle?" Gabriel says when the silence stretches out.

Kyle imagines being able to tell Gabriel. He would just open his mouth and say it. What does it even matter if Gabriel wants to have sex with Ben when Ben has committed himself to Kyle more permanently than any priest or judge ever could. For just a flicker of a moment, Kyle is angry with Ben again, so much so that all he wants is for Ben to be there having coffee with him so that Kyle could push him out of his chair.

His nose starts to run and he sniffs. That's when he realizes he's crying.

"Kyle?"

"I'm okay," he says softly. "Call Ben if it'll make you feel better."

The answer isn't immediate. When it does come, Gabriel's voice sounds tight and hushed. "I'm coming down there."

"No," Kyle says sharply. It doesn't matter. None of it does. "It's just been a lot. I'm dealing. It's a process."

For as long and as hard as Kyle tried to get Ben to do what he wanted, Ben owns him, inside and out. The desire and drama with Gabriel and Darrek suddenly don't matter at all, really. All that matters is the swelling hope of possibility, against all odds.

Stay upstairs, Ben had told him. And for a little while, Kyle does. From the bedroom window he watches Gabriel walk back away from the house with Ben, through tall, knee-high grass. Gabriel's body language is all wrong, though, and Kyle begins to forget why hiding from their guests had seemed like such a great idea.

So, Kyle walks downstairs, through the empty house, with Junior at his heels. After stopping to grab a beer from the fridge, he exits via the back door to find Darrek sitting on the stoop.

"Stay," Kyle tells the cat, who just gives him a snide mewl and turns his tail up as he pads in the direction of his water dish.

"You have a cat?" Darrek asks, surprised as Kyle appears and carefully closes the door, then stands idly a few feet away.

"Yep."

"The spots are cool. What's its name?"

"Kyle," he sighs.

Darrek laughs like it's a joke, but one look at Kyle's face tells him it's not and the chuckle dies.

One assumption quickly leads to another and another. Kyle sees it happen in Darrek's face, then Darrek says, "I don't know how you're in a relationship with that guy."

"We each pick our poison," Kyle responds. "You want a beer, or...?"

"Nah. I've given up the stuff. Staying sober. Wanna keep my wits about me." Darrek watches the two men in the grass sharply. "But thanks. How are you?"

"Breathing. You?"

"Same."

"Are we going to acknowledge why you guys are here, or pretend we're clueless?"

Darrek glances sideways up at Kyle, and enough of that mag-

285

netic pull between them kicks in that Kyle feels it show in his face. When Darrek briefly glances down Kyle's body before returning to the task of keeping a close eye on what happens between Ben and Gabriel, Kyle begins to wish he'd stayed inside.

"Sit down."

Sickeningly, Kyle obeys. Like he's not in control of his own limbs, he takes a step closer to Darrek and sets his ass on the stoop.

"Let me see your hand," Darrek says gently.

Kyle rolls his eyes and holds the hand out. Darrek takes it, turning it palm-side-up. His callused thumb brushes over the healed slice, sending small wriggling, unsettling snakes of arousal chasing up Kyle's arm and straight down to his dick.

"Did you stop cutting?"

"Yessir," Kyle murmurs, his face red and hot. *This is Darrek,* he screams inwardly at himself, though it does no good. The reflexes are there now. Logic is inconsequential.

As much as Darrek may intend to remind Kyle not to use the honorific, he doesn't actually say it. Instead, he asks, "Is Ben cutting you?"

"No, Sir."

"Is he hurting you at all?" Darrek asks, and more forcefully than he had asked the other questions, like he's feeding off of Kyle's submissiveness, getting stronger.

Say 'fuck you, Dare.' Say it. Spit in his face.

"No, Sir."

You pussy. God, you're such a pussy!

Darrek still has his hand. He's not letting it go. "Look at me."

Stubborn, simultaneously guarded and laid bare, Kyle obeys, letting Darrek look to his heart's content. It feels like another examination, only worse. It goes on longer than he wants it to. Darrek reaches up to touch Kyle's face. It's a tender brush of fingers and he briefly holds Kyle's chin as he says, "I'm glad he's taking care of you."

"He's a good man. We're in it for the long haul. Both of us."

"I can tell."

Kyle gently tilts his head out of Darrek's grasp and takes his hand back. "I guess this is weird for you. Ben and Gabe." Kyle nods toward the field and the dark forms moving through it.

"It helps Gabe. He's my Master. All that matters to me is making him happy."

Kyle nods.

"You told Gabe you were okay with this."

"I am," Kyle agrees.

Long, awkward, strained minutes pass. Just to break the tension, Kyle turns to face Darrek, ready to make a joke or something to lighten things up, but the words melt under the scorching intensity of Darrek's stare. Just like that, they're right back there, in that truck, driving into the woods. Or, worse, back in that long lost child's bedroom in the Grealey household, with Darrek pinning Kyle down.

Kyle stands, putting his back to Darrek. He's unsurprised when he feels movement behind him. A shadow falls over him as Darrek presses up against Kyle. A huge hand wraps Kyle's shoulder. It's gentle, but heavy.

"Kyle," Darrek sighs.

Stop.

But he can't say it. He doesn't even really want to. Twisting out of Darrek's reach, Kyle climbs the couple of steps to the back door and goes inside.

Darrek follows. Then they're inside with the door closed. Kyle plants his hands flat on the counter, watching Ben and Gabriel's tiny forms in the distance through the window, and does nothing—says nothing.

Standing a couple feet away, Darrek says, "We should probably talk about this... or try to...."

But Kyle doesn't want to talk. He doesn't even want to be there, but it's *Darrek* and they've been through so much that being with him is as right as it is wrong in Kyle's head. He turns and goes to Darrek, hugging him.

Those huge, callused hands move against Kyle's back as Darrek returns the hug and kisses the top of his head. It makes Kyle look up, tilting his head back and his hips forward. Instinctively, Darrek's hand cups Kyle's ass and Kyle's lips part softly when Darrek dips his head to kiss them.

With a pained whine, Darrek breaks the kiss almost immediately after it starts. "You need to get away from me. Go."

"I still love you," Kyle says in a small voice. "I wish I didn't. I wish I hated you. Make me hate you, Dare."

"Go," Darrek says more forcefully. "Go upstairs and lock the door."

Clapping a hand over his mouth as a sickened groan escapes him; Darrek pushes outside, yanking the door closed behind him and hurrying to his Tundra. Once he gets there, he sits inside of it, putting as much of a barrier between himself and Kyle as he can, praying for Gabriel to get back, and soon.

Gabriel walks at Ben's side, his hands pushed into the pockets of his leather jacket, which is zipped up, his neck wrapped in a scarf, his head covered with a black knit hat. His gray eyes are starkly light, contrasted by all of that dark, as he keeps a foot or two at least away from Ben at all times. Ben is less bundled, wearing only an old flannel over a white tee shirt, and the cold doesn't seem to touch him at all.

Whenever Ben moves closer, Gabriel backs up. It's a dance they've been playing ever since Gabriel showed up at Ben's doorstep. So far all they've mainly talked about is the state of Gabriel's old company, Diadem. They've caught up on office gossip and Gabriel has filled Ben in on his new business venture and some of the success he's had with it so far.

"You know," Ben says, squinting up at the cloudless sky as the sun sinks ever lower. The grass shines golden in the dying light. "I can't help but notice *this*."

"This what?"

Ben stops walking, turns on a boot heel and takes a deliberate step toward Gabriel, who in turn, takes a large backward step, the grass crushing under his feet, thereby proving Ben's point.

"Since when do you avoid me, Hunter?"

"Since we crossed a line."

"It's not like I snuck up and put my dick in you when you weren't looking. You asked us to. So... what? You're intimidated by me now? We can't be friends anymore without it being weird?"

As Ben likely intended, Gabriel can't argue any of that. He can't change the way he's reacting to Ben since they had sex, and can't explain it either. Silent, heated anger flashes in his ice-colored eyes. "I think this was a mistake," he says once he composes himself.

Flustered, Gabriel moves to go around Ben, but then Ben just steps in his way, blocking the path. Gabriel tries the other way, and Ben just does it again.

Gabriel snaps, "What are you trying to prove?"

"If you didn't want to be here, you wouldn't be here. Am I wrong? Hmm?" Ben raises his eyebrows and gestures at the property. "See, here's the thing. Kyle and I have been actively trying to move past all of the bullshit. And so far, so good! It's awesome. There's honesty and a total absence of suicide attempts. Then you go and call him the other day. It fucked with his head. He came home in a bad mood and didn't want to talk about it. That's a big step backward, and that makes me unhappy."

Sarcasm drips from every word as Ben unleashes his frustrations and anger at Gabriel. "Now here you are, waving Darrek in his face to fuck with his head some more. That also makes me unhappy. So, what do you want, Hunter?"

Defeated, Gabriel bites his tongue and folds his arms.

"Look, I can tell that a lot is going on with you two," Gabriel says. "Kyle's demeanor on the call said as much, but this wasn't the right time to come here. I see that now. Darrek and I will go and leave you both alone."

"Get over here," Ben growls, pointing at the ground right in front of him. "Now. Or I'll fuckin' make you come over here."

Instantly chagrined, Gabriel drops his gaze to his feet, bites his tongue and does as Ben says. "Look at me when I'm talking to you."

With effort, Gabriel wrenches his gaze upward.

"You tell me what this is about right now, or so help me, I'll take you over my knee and spank it out of you like you're a willful child and not a grown-fucking-man."

"God, you're sexy when you do that," Gabriel smiles, breaking the tension.

"Oh, come on!" Ben complains with the perfect mix of disappointment and humor. "You're supposed to keep being a bratty little bitch so I can spank you. Don't you know how this goes? You're ruining my chance to get a piece all on my own without Daddy around."

"You can still get a piece."

He's still smiling when he says it, but he's not kidding at all. Vulnerability oozes from Gabriel, instantly awakening all of the predatory instincts in Ben.

"Have I told you yet how awesome this new little arrangement is? Because it's completely awesome," Ben says. "Prove it. Go on." Gabriel's gray eyes shift, scanning Ben's carefully controlled expression.

Gabriel hesitates. The smile vanishes.

"*Prove it,*" Ben repeats fiercely through gritted teeth.

Just like that, Gabriel is breathing heavy. His gaze drops. Slowly, he turns so that his back is to Ben and, eyes rolling with a wash of heady desire, he fumbles at his clothing. The jacket is unzipped. He slips it off and fumbles at his fly. Swallowing thickly, he raises his chin. His eyes glisten proudly, but it's the only part of him that holds any pride as Ben moves so that he's flush to Gabriel's left side.

Gabriel just stands there, fighting not to moan as Ben slips his right hand inside the back of Gabriel's loosened pants, caressing downward. After a moment, as Gabriel shifts his legs apart, exhaling sharply with a frown, Ben pushes his left hand into the front of Gabriel's pants, too. Groping him from both sides, he holds the evidence of Gabriel's lust in the palm of his hand, indisputable. The first two fingers of Ben's right hand tease at Gabriel's opening, rubbing over it repeatedly. Gabriel breathes out a quiet, desperate, needy sigh. He turns in Ben's hold, putting his back to him and hooks an arm up around behind his head to grab on to Ben, combing his fingers back through Ben's thick hair. Ben's mouth draws closer to Gabriel's neck, the bristles of his beard tickling.

Still fondling Gabriel's cock, Ben gets his right hand free temporarily, sucking the first two fingers wet. He pushes them back down inside Gabriel's underwear and twists the digits up into his ass.

Gabriel grunts, breathlessly, "Please."

"Please what?"

"Please, Daddy."

Growling, Ben bites down on Gabriel's earlobe, tugs the fingers back then pushes them in farther, spreading them apart more the deeper they go. He also pushes Gabriel's briefs out of the way in front, guiding his cock free and stroking it slowly.

"He needs me to be strong. I have to be strong, not selfish. I have to do the right thing, but sometimes I want to do the wrong thing," Gabriel confesses, letting it all come out. It's much easier to admit while Ben is violating him. The act feels dirty, so it's not so very hard to speak about things that he's ashamed of. "I can't do the wrong thing with him, so I wanna do the wrong thing with you."

"I don't have a condom," Ben admits.

"Jacket pocket. Left side."

"Damn."

Grinning, Ben reclaims his hands and bends to snag the discarded jacket and find the rubbers. After digging in the pocket and discovering the lube Gabriel stashed in there, too, Ben straightens.

"My dirty boy came prepared," he says, turning back to Gabriel while getting his fly down.

Gabriel is already falling to his knees, pulling his underwear down in back, and bending sharply forward to the grass so that his bare ass sticks up in the air, waiting and ready.

"God, I really, really love this arrangement," Ben says adamantly.

Condom and lube on, Ben positions himself between Gabriel's legs, behind him. Smearing lube roughly in and around Gabriel's hole, he works slowly to pry him open, getting him loose and Gabriel savors every second of it. Ben fits himself there and draws Gabriel gradually back onto his sheathed member. With his hips held in Ben's iron grip, Gabriel is made to yield and open to it.

Very slowly, Ben impales his best friend on the end of his cock. Mouth fallen open, Gabriel cries out as Ben makes him take his whole length, stretching him as he goes, making him really feel it. Tearing handfuls of the grass, Gabriel doesn't hold anything back. He yells and shudders as Ben fucks him hard, slapping his ass with his pelvis, then his hand, roughly kneading his buttocks, leaving bruises.

"Tell me you love it," Ben orders.

"I love it," Gabriel gasps. "Harder. Please, harder."

"Touch yourself. I know you want to."

"Yeah," Gabriel moans.

Hand pumping fast between his legs, Gabriel climaxes before Ben does, shooting onto the earth beneath them. Hips twitching into his fist, grunting hard, body clenched up from head to toe, Gabriel rips Ben's orgasm from him with a surprised shout.

Raising an opened hand, Ben lets it fall, delivering a hard, loud smack to the thickest part of Gabriel's right butt cheek. "Good talk!"

He pulls out with a groan and tosses the condom, chuckling when Gabriel doesn't move and just stays like that—ass up, stretched loose, spanked, rubbed raw, spent and utterly relaxed as he lets out a long, low moan against the dirt.

"I really do feel much better," Gabriel says with a tired, delirious sort of surprise.

"Of course you do," Ben scoffs. "That's why they pay me the big bucks. You need some help there or are you good?"

"No, I'm good," Gabriel sighs, still not moving at all.

"You know you stay in that position too long, I'm gonna have to fuck that again."

"Yeah, I'm, uh... I'm okay with that."

Chapter 36
New Orders

Sometimes life grants flashes of hyperawareness, letting you realize the actual profundity of your current moment, all of its implications going forward and all of the instances that have led up to it. You see yourself and your companions in the light of truth and honesty, flaws and all. Kyle has one of those moments as Gabriel and Ben walk back to the house through the long grass and he stands at an upstairs window as a hawk swoops and circles in the air over their heads.

This is my life, he sees. *These men. This place. This is where I'm meant to be.*

The smile in Ben's eyes, without judgment; the hunch of Gabriel's shoulders betraying the fact that, even still, he carries the weight of the world on them, and maybe always will, despite the confidence in his stride and the contentedness in his expression; standing by the side of the truck, Darrek's heartbroken stare resonates with Kyle, and it feels like they're falling back through years and years into younger bodies and more innocent souls. It all hits him at once. Choking up without being able to say why, he lays a hand flat on the glass and hugs the cat to his chest, seeing how they're all wrapped up in each other in such far-reaching ways.

Ben stands by the house, hands in his pockets as Gabriel and Darrek get in the truck, and slowly reverse away.

After Ben visits the bathroom to freshen up, he finds Kyle right there, at the window in their bedroom, crying.

"What happened?" Ben demands. He's instantly defensive and angry, rightfully suspicious of Darrek.

Kyle walks a few paces, letting the cat down, and winds his arms around Ben's neck. Breathing in the comforting, familiar scent of him, it's like coming home. He turns his face into the side of Ben's neck. He can't explain why or what. Ben guides Kyle's face back, wanting to see it and reason out the tears. Kyle can't meet his eyes and only overlays Ben's hand with his own.

Pulling back, embarrassed, Kyle's face clouds over.

Stepping towards him, trying to close the gap that Kyle puts between their bodies, Ben gets nearer as Kyle backs off.

"Don't look at me."

"What happened?"

Kyle sighs, wiping angrily at his face. He stares, glassy-eyed, at where the truck was, behind the house, before it drove away. "Nothing's ever easy, is it?"

"What are you talking about? Is this about Gabe and Darrek? Did Darrek do something...?"

"No. Yes." Kyle shakes his head.

Frowning, Ben leads him by the hand over to the bed. Ben moves to stand behind him, and circles his arms around Kyle, embracing and holding Kyle's arms tight to his chest. "You're okay. Take a deep breath."

Kyle nods, inhales and holds it before letting it back out. He does it again, and feels his heartbeat slow and the anxiety fade. But the demonstration of how Ben knows just how to make him feel better hits Kyle anew. Sighing softly, he leans back against his lover's solid presence.

"Talk to me. I don't know how to help if you don't tell me what's wrong."

"Okay," Kyle murmurs. "I admit it, all right? You were right."

"About what?"

"The only thing that matters. Us. The future. Looking forward instead of backward."

"So, this isn't about the two jackasses that were just here?"

"No, it's about them too. We can't change who we are. How do we live as a healthy, normal couple when this is our life? Huh? I feel like it has to be one or the other, that we need to give something up, but I... I don't want to! I need to submit to you, and I want you to take care of Gabe as his Dom. But we can't have it both ways, can we?"

"Who says we can't? It's our life. We make the rules and decide what works for us. If anyone doesn't like it, they can fuck off."

Sadness overwhelms Kyle, dragging him down. Ben strengthens his hold on Kyle's body.

Gazing out through the back window at the growing darkness and deepening shadows, Kyle asks quietly, "Don't let go, okay?"

"Never," Ben promises.

As he sits on their bed, Ben pulls Kyle down after him so that he's straddling Ben's lap, facing him. Ben's hands wrap Kyle's thighs. Temptation is literally spread over Ben and Kyle sees the effect he has. Ben's desire, his dominance, his strength—it soothes Kyle's aches, makes him instinctively surrender to his need to submit.

"You know what I really want? Hmm?"

Arousal roughens the question, and hearing it feels like fingertips tracing lightly up Kyle's spine. Skin tightening with a shiver of pleasure, Kyle responds with, "No. Tell me."

"Should I tell you, or should I tie you up and let you find out the surprise after?"

"Tell me," Kyle asks, sweetly, pleading, scratching lightly back over Ben's scalp, through his short, light hair. He swallows a moan when Ben lowers his mouth to suck a spot under Kyle's jaw, the stiff hairs of his beard raking against the skin. "Please."

"I don't think I want to," Ben teases.

Kyle rears up on his lap, rocking forward in a slow, firm drag against Ben's groin. Both of Ben's hands move to cup Kyle's ass as he sinks back down.

"Please," Kyle says with more vigor, adding, "Master."

"I want to tie your hands together, right to the headboard. Use the thigh spreader and pull your pants down to your knees, get you kneeling there. Maybe use a blindfold and a gag. I'd get out a prostate stimulator and a glass dish and I'd milk you fucking dry. Then, once I'd emptied you, I'd suck you so hard, get you screamin'. You couldn't even come, but you'd try. Then I'd fuck you and watch you lick up every single drop of your cream."

Twin spots of color burn high on Kyle's cheeks. His breathing has roughened. As he goes shy, he begins to twist away, but before he can so much as flinch, Ben has him by the wrists and yanks him back down close.

"Behave," Ben scolds.

"Yes, Master."

"Hands."

His wrists are released and Kyle slowly moves his arms, drawing them up, bending them so that his hands lace together behind his head. Ben pushes up Kyle's shirt, rubbing up the taut plane of his stomach, unfastening his pants while he does it. Then he pulls Kyle's dick free of them, tugging on it hard enough to force him to follow, hips lifting, thighs clenching. Pushing the pants down past Kyle's ass, Ben eases up, letting him sit back down, though spreading his own legs wider to force Kyle's farther apart.

Kyle's head falls back as Ben eye-fucks his slave's body and plays with it. His fingers tease between Kyle's legs, over his balls, through his crack.

"Were you with Darrek while I was with Gabriel?"

A muscle in Kyle's jaw twitches. He realizes that Ben might be feeling for stickiness, proof of an *incident*.

He nods. "Yes, Sir."

"He touched you?" Ben asks quietly, possessively, reading between the lines of Kyle's tension and emotional upset.

Kyle grunts as Ben squeezes lightly up his shaft, up to the head, trapping it against his palm.

"Yes, Sir," he admits, feeling ashamed. Undulating on Ben's lap, he pushes up into the hand and tries to draw back, though Ben holds the end of his dick tightly and doesn't let go. "It was just a hug, but then it wasn't. We kissed. He touched my ass. It was turning into something else before we realized it. Darrek told me I should get away from him. So, I came up here. It was... terrifying."

"He initiated it, or you did?"

"I started it," Kyle mutters. The ingrained instinct to feel ashamed of his nakedness and the way Ben ogles him, toys with him, gnaws at Kyle's gut, especially because of what he's admitting to.

"Would you have stopped him if he didn't stop first?"

"Ben, please," Kyle groans, uneasy, nauseated by his own behavior.

"Would you?" Ben demands, getting angry. He squeezes hard enough to cause pain and watches Kyle's mouth fall open, his lower lip quivering. Ben yanks and draws a small, beautiful cry.

"No, Sir."

"Look at me!"

Kyle wrenches his eyes over to Ben's face. Ben lets go of Kyle's penis and gently touches Kyle's face instead.

"Why would you let him do that? Why?! You don't deserve that!"

Kyle grits his teeth, grimacing. His eyes fill with unshed tears.

"I am making a commandment, right now. Set in stone. You hear me, slave?"

"Yes, Master," Kyle murmurs sheepishly.

"Darrek Grealey does not touch you in a sexual manner, ever again. Do you understand?"

"Yes, Master."

"You do not permit it. If he tries anyway, you scream or bite or kick or punch and I will find him, and break his fingers, one by one. If he tries to put his dick in you again, I burn it off, slowly. I will let Gabriel know. I mean it. Darrek does not fucking touch you."

Kyle is shocked beyond the ability to respond at first. He stares at Ben, seeing how adamant he is, as serious as he was about finding Harry, Gabriel's pedophile, and fucking him up. When Ben says something like this, he means it absolutely.

He means this, *absolutely*.

"C-can I still be friends with him, Sir?" Kyle manages.

Ben sneers, mentally tearing Darrek a new asshole or some damn thing. "Friends, yes. That's *it*. That's fucking *it*, Kyle."

The emotion sneaks up on him. Kyle sucks in a rough breath and it comes out as a sob. He trembles on Ben's lap with increasing violence, until he's overwhelmed and lets his laced hands fall as he crashes forward into Ben, struggling for breath.

Ben wraps his arms around Kyle, soothing, breathing heavily

with fury. Kyle sobs in Ben's arms for a long time, until it's all wrung out, every drop. Once it's all gone, he sniffs, rubbing at his eyes and nose, unable to let go or sit back, just holding on to Ben.

"Thank you," Kyle prays. "God, thank you." Another cry from deep down inside is pulled from his chest. His body tries to give more, somehow, but can't. Kyle's hands clasp to Ben's body, and he feels like only a scared, forsaken boy, clutching to a father who has moved to protect him, at last. "Thank you."

"You're safe," Ben assures him. "And I'm going to keep you safe—from your enemies, your friends, and yourself. No one hurts you. Not anymore."

Kyle presses a soft, urgent, salty, tear-damp kiss to Ben's cheek, so grateful he nearly drowns in the tidal force of it.

Chapter 37

Ingrained Instinct

A quiet week passes, marked out for Kyle in regular beats — get up, get dressed, go to work, come home to an empty house, fight the temptation to go to Diadem and find Ben, wait, welcome Ben home greedily with opened arms, and open legs.

When they make love, Kyle can sense it — Ben's passion, his silence and fiery determination to draw Kyle out of the dark past and into the promise of the present.

That fight inside Ben, emotional proof of his devotion, is Kyle's miracle. It's so big, in a private but heartfelt way that it changes Kyle's heart, and subtly alters their every waking moment. The rest of their troubles — the what-ifs and used-to-bes — all fall away in the face of the could-bes and the solidity of their relationship. Everything is surmountable. Life, itself, is bearable.

Standing out of the way at his jobsite, supervising some menial task on a gray, foggy day, Kyle daydreams about his last visit with his shrink. He had decided to say it once he got there. After he'd walked in, sat down and before even saying hello, he blurted it out. Looking down at his feet, he told Dr. O'Malley, "I'm a victim of rape and abuse and a survivor. It's made my whole life harder for so many years, but I want to be able to accept it somehow, and move on. Ben has showed me that he's committed to me and he's not leaving, no matter what. He's been supportive of me since he found out, and he's doing his best to protect me from things or people or behaviors that can hurt me. We're a family. He's my family."

Tense and relieved at the same time, Kyle had touched the toes of his sneakers together and waited for the response. From the edge of his vision he could see Dr. O'Malley shift forward in her chair, felt the weight of her silence.

Then, without casting judgment, she'd asked him, "How does that make you feel?"

He'd laughed. Thinking of everything they usually cover in their sessions — the self-harm, his adolescence, Darrek — Kyle almost doesn't recognize himself. He's a new person, entirely different in make-up from who he was.

With a carefree smile, he'd looked right at her and said, "Happy."

Happiness is not something he's used to feeling. Standing in the dust and noise, with the men of his crew bustling around him, Kyle marvels at how fast things can turn around on you.

His phone rings with a buzz in his pocket. A glance tells him who it is, and he debates for a fleeting moment before walking a few paces away to answer.

"Yeah?" he half-shouts over the din.

"Hey, this a bad time?"

"Depends, I guess," he replies noncommittally. "What's up?"

"I, uh, just wanted to talk to you. Can you swing by the office after work?"

"I don't know if I should. Ben...."

He hears Gabriel sigh.

"Call him then. Ask permission."

"Gabe," Kyle starts.

"Just a conversation. That's all I'm asking for."

Yeah right, he thinks. "Lemme call you right back."

"Thanks."

Kyle hangs up, stares at his phone, debating, then dials Ben.

"What's wrong?" Ben asks as soon as he answers.

"Not everything is an emergency, you know."

"With you it is," Ben counters. "You never call me from work. You know better."

From the other end of the line, in the background, Kyle hears a long, drawn out moan and flushes. "You have a client," he apologizes.

"I'm doing the video. What's the problem?"

"N-no problem," Kyle says, rubbing his eyes and trying to mentally carve out a space in his head somewhere between his work-life and private-life, with burly, sweaty men busy in both halves, but for wildly different reasons. "Sorry, Sir."

"Spit it out! I've only got a second here."

"Gabriel. He called. He wants me to stop by his office to talk," Kyle explains. Lowering his voice so that he's not overheard by his workers, he asks, "So, can I?"

"You've gotta be fucking kidding me."

"Please," Kyle asks. "Just to see what he wants. You trust me, don't you?"

"*You* don't even trust you!"

"It's *Gabriel*," Kyle hisses. "He's not going to molest me in the supply closet or some fucking thing. You trusted him to take care of me for weeks."

"That was before."

"Before," Kyle echoes, incredulous. "Fine. Sorry for bothering you."

"God fucking damn it," Ben growls. "No fucking, you hear me? No groping. No sucking. No licking. No touching whatsoever. *Whatsoever*, Kyle. You talk, you leave, and when you're done, you come straight over here so I can look in your eyes to see for myself that nothing happened."

"You're being insane and overprotective."

"Do you want to go? Do you think it's a good idea?"

"I think it helps me understand what's happening in my head when I talk to Gabe. We're a lot alike. That's all."

"Go then. But remember my terms. Get back to work. Love you."

The line cuts out and Kyle redials Gabriel's cell.

"Okay. I'll be there at three."

The day chugs slowly by. The visit to the shrink is forgotten. Kyle tries to distract himself with work, and it helps for a while. But as three o'clock nears, his nervousness cranks up and up.

When the workday is done, he drives to the glass-front studio with the large sign above for Daring Angel's Photography. The bell on the door tinkles as he pushes through. A woman in her thirties is seated in one of the chairs in the waiting area, talking to no one. After closer scrutiny, he spies her Bluetooth earpiece.

From the back room, he hears, "Kyle? That you?"

"Yeah!"

"Come on back, I'm finishing up!"

"Okay!"

He walks back through the doorway. A small baby boy, less than a year old, is seated on a soft, mottled grey backdrop and dressed in a ridiculous sailor suit. From behind the camera, Gabriel rolls his eyes for Kyle's benefit and nods to the child.

"Hey, can you turn him a little to the side and get his hand out of his mouth? I keep trying to do it myself but he just squirms out of position by the time I get back to the camera and my remote broke this morning and *someone* isn't being the biggest help right now." Gabriel nods back to the front room to clarify.

"I thought you do video." Kyle slowly approaches the baby, stepping carefully over cords and around directional lights.

"Yeah, well, glamour shots and portraits help pay the bills. Just get his hand down and step back a little so I can get the shot."

"Um..." Kyle hesitates. He crouches by the little boy and says, "Hey, buddy."

He gently tries to tug the chubby little fist out of the boy's mouth. The baby's attention snaps to Kyle. Huge brown eyes lock on to him and the harder Kyle pulls at the boy's arm, the farther the baby leans over to get back the clenched fist until he tumbles right over and rolls onto his back with a happy squeal.

"Okay. Up we go," Kyle says as he lifts the baby and sets him back on his bottom. With a piercing shriek of delight, the boy grabs with surprising strength at Kyle's bottom lip, yanking on it. "Ow!"

Gabriel laughs and Kyle frowns. Extricating himself, Kyle quickly scoots back and a series of flashes tells him that Gabriel must have gotten some shots.

The baby tries to crawl in Kyle's direction, chasing after him, so Gabriel calls, "Greyson! Hey, look at the birdie! Greyson!"

Squeezing a squeak-toy, Gabriel gets baby Greyson's attention shifted back onto him and takes another couple of quick shots.

"Awesome. Okay, I think I got what I needed. Thanks for the

help."

Gabriel moves around the camera and walks over with a small smile. Kyle stands and pushes his hands in his pockets as Gabriel scoops up the baby and sets him on a hip. Greyson dives for Kyle, burbling with joy and almost falls out of Gabriel's arms.

"Whoa there, guy," Gabriel says as he rights the baby.

Kyle sees the stupid little sailor hat on the floor and stoops to pick it up. Gabriel doesn't move to take it from him, so Kyle plops it on the boy's head. Before he can get out of range again, Kyle's hand is grabbed and the baby latches on, biting down on the side of it.

"Ahh! Christ! He's got teeth!" Kyle yanks his hand back, seeing little baby teeth-dents in at the junction of his index finger and thumb. "That's... not sanitary."

"Teething," Gabriel clarifies. "He screamed for a half-hour straight until he just started gnawing on his hands. You can wait here if you want. I'll be right back." Gabriel leaves him, taking the baby back to his mother.

For a while, Kyle mills about, listening in on the conversation as Gabriel finishes the transaction and promises to have proofs by the end of the week. Then he gets distracted by some of the developed negatives hanging on the far wall, and goes to check them out.

A flattened hand touches him suddenly on his lower back and Gabriel is there at his side before Kyle even hears him approach. Jumping quickly away, he says, "No touching! Ben said no touching."

Gabriel raises his hands, palm-out, and says, "Sorry. Okay. No touching."

Feeling like a freak, Kyle is instantly embarrassed by the force of his reaction, but just as surprised that he was able to speak up for himself. Heart beating more wildly than it should, and feeling backed up to the wall, he tries to move sideways, putting the room at his back instead to help him calm down. "I'm heading over to Diadem after this. He's going to...."

"Make sure you're okay?"

"Something like that." His eyes are drawn magnetically to the bite mark on his hand, which he rubs absentmindedly.

"I didn't do that," Gabriel smirks. "And I'm not gonna jump

you."

"I know," he scoffs.

It hangs there, between them. Part of Kyle feels restrained, naked and helpless again before Gabriel's calm confidence. Another part of him can only think of how selflessly attentive Gabriel has been to him, and how kind.

"Ben called to tell me about you and Darrek, in the house. After."

Kyle tries to dissolve and melt down through the cracks in the concrete.

"He touched you, kissed you, while Ben and I talked." Gabriel waits for Kyle to respond as Kyle's embarrassment and shame only grows. "He shouldn't have done that."

Restless, Kyle removes his hands from his pockets and rubs his arms instead, hanging his head, wishing that he wasn't wishing for cuffs and chains, trying to stifle the instinct to get down on his knees for Gabriel.

"It was my fault," Gabriel continues. "I told Ben as much. Dare and I were only there so that Ben could relieve some of my stress, and I wanted to apologize to you in person, without Dare around. I should have known better than to expect the two of you to completely avoid each other without anyone there to mediate or keep an eye on things. Not after everything that happened between you two. I feel like an enabler, like I'm the one causing you pain, and *I need that to stop.*"

Hearing the emotion and urgency in Gabriel's voice, thick and hoarse, Kyle is also hyperaware of how his dick is hot and hard against his thigh. There is raw want for Gabriel who makes him feel safe, and cared for. The ingrained instinct to try to sexually please a more dominant man for his own wellbeing is difficult to overcome.

It's too much. He doesn't know how to do this like civilized men, or platonic friends. He wants Gabriel to forcibly restrain him and drag a blade down his chest like he did in the parking lot that night so long ago. As good as things have gotten for Kyle, part of him craves that outlet and to be purged again of everything that gets bottled up. It's nice when it's all out of his hands and all he has to do is take it. Now it would be a sweet indulgence, rather than a need, but the distinction doesn't seem to matter when Gabriel is standing right there, and anything is possible.

"It's so fucked up," Gabriel hisses. "I see you, what it's doing to you to be here with me. The door is locked. We're alone. You want to obey me, don't you? You want me to hold you down? You want to surrender to me?"

"You're my Dom," Kyle rasps, his head spinning. He backs up to a pillar and rests against it, grasping it with both hands.

"Which means you trust me. You're powerless when you're alone with me like this. I could do anything to you. And you know what I want to do to you, Kyle? *Everything.* I wanna touch you and taste you and fuck you, in the name of making you feel better, even though *I know* that it wouldn't do that, it would hurt you. I want to do such twisted things to you, even though Ben told me not to, especially because Ben told me not to. You're so sweet and helpless. You know what that makes me? *Do you know what that makes me, Kyle?*"

The last question is a wrenching scream of pain. Kyle's eyes open with realization, and he looks at Gabriel—Gabriel who was victimized for so very long.

"It's not the same," Kyle argues, leaving the safety of the pillar, leaving his resolve behind as well. He steps up to Gabriel, whose expression is equal parts horror and lust. "It's not. It's just because we understand each other."

"Bullshit! It is the same. *I'm turning into him.*" Gabriel jabs his own chest with a finger. "Even now, I'm trying to figure out how to get you to let me fuck you. I'd do it right there," he says, pointing towards the pool of light where all the cameras are focused. "And film it. Then I'd have to think of a way to scare you into not telling Ben for your own good."

He's shaking, Kyle sees, and all of the blood is draining from his face. So he takes hold of Gabriel, trying to soothe. "You're not Harry, and I'm not a child anymore. It's different."

"He turned me into this," Gabriel gasps. "I'm a fucking monster, just like he was!"

"You're not like him!" Kyle yells, helping to repeat the cycle in his own way by trying to defend the man who just admitted to wanting to hurt him, even against his will. "He was raping little boys! Lots of little boys! For years! He raped so many that he didn't even remember you were one of them! *It's different!*"

"...what?"

Shit.

"What did... what did you say? Why would you...? *How would you know that?* I—"

"They found him," Kyle hears himself say. Gabriel grabs a handful of Kyle's shirt and steps closer, right in his space. His breath moves as a gentle heat over Kyle's skin. "Harry. They tortured him, trying to make him confess what he did to you, but every name he said... none of them were you. *None of them.* They used a knife to carve the boys' names into his skin, rubbed ink in the wounds. They marked him so that everyone would know what he did, that he raped children. It was last year, when you went to see him and your mom. You were never supposed to find out. They made me promise not to tell you or Darrek. I was so scared. I was scared of them getting caught. I was scared of Ben because he had it in him to do something like that. It's one of the reasons why I left him, but I couldn't tell you. I couldn't tell you! I'm sorry, Gabe. Please don't tell Ben. You can't tell any of them."

"Who," Gabriel snarls.

"Trace. Micah."

Fury engulfs him. Kyle sees it happen. Gabriel's hand splays wide, then tenses into a claw that rakes over Kyle's chest violently enough to draw blood before twisting sharply in his shirt. Teeth gritted, grunting and whimpering, Gabriel fights not to lash out.

"They... they had no right. They had no right!"

"You couldn't have stopped it. And it happened a long time ago. It's done. Ancient history. You have to let it go. Please let it go. I'll—" Kyle tries. "I'll do anything you want, okay? Anything. Just don't tell. Please? *Please*, Gabe.... It'll fuck up everything between you and them and I don't want to be responsible for hurting you, too."

Something in Kyle's words clicks in Gabriel's head.

The fury dies.

Gabriel becomes aware of himself, and what he's doing. Looking down at his hold on Kyle's shirt, Gabriel says, "Oh god. *Kyle.*"

His body decides before his brain can catch up. Kyle chases

Gabriel's mouth for a kiss that starts slow and soft, but turns dirty and hard just due to sheer force of emotion. Gabriel's tongue enters Kyle's mouth, his hand holding Kyle's head so that he can go deeper and take and take and take. But when Kyle finds himself palming Gabriel's erection through his pants, it changes the dynamic completely.

Gabriel shoves him roughly away and for a fleeting second, there's something so primal and uncaged in his gray-blue eyes that Kyle goes very still with a cold, tight fear. He could do it, Kyle sees. If pushed, he would. Gabriel would take of Kyle whether he consented or not, even knowing it was wrong. And Kyle wouldn't say no; not to Gabriel, and not to Darrek.

"I'm going with you," Gabriel says roughly. He turns his back to Kyle and composes himself.

"I don't think that's a good idea," Kyle starts.

"I don't fucking care! I'm going with you."

"Gabriel...."

"I'm not having you lie for me, and I'm not letting this be your secret anymore. Understand?!"

"Yes, Sir," Kyle says meekly.

"I'm so sorry," Gabriel urges without turning back around. "Even when I try to think around it, and head things off before they can get worse, it's too late and it gets away from me. But I won't turn into him. I won't. I'm a better man than that."

"I know."

Chapter 38

The Gift of Honesty

Sitting at a red light, Kyle taps away on his phone as they drive to Diadem, sending a text message to Ben telling him that he's on his way, leaving out Gabriel's accompanying presence entirely. It's mind-boggling that Gabriel knows now about Harry, and what Ben, Trace and Micah did to the man down in Texas. After over a year of secrecy, Kyle doesn't know how to incorporate Gabriel's awareness into his reality. At the same time, the relief he feels at not having to hide that incident anymore is palpable. It's the second biggest secret Kyle has ever had to keep, and knowing he's free of it is wonderful, no matter what the consequences might be.

The traffic light turns green. He sets the phone aside and glances in the rearview at Gabriel in his Discovery. Emotions swirl confusedly in Kyle—fright, sadness, guilt, and even love. Gabriel pegged him, all right. Kyle would let Gabriel hurt him if it was what Gabriel needed. Before, Gabriel was the Other—the enemy, the competition. Somehow, he's gotten into Kyle's heart, more keenly even, maybe, amazingly, than Darrek. Darrek will always be both a bad and good thing for Kyle, but Gabriel has become something Kyle has difficulty fearing or mistrusting, even if he should. How it happened, Kyle has no idea.

The phone rings. Without looking at it, he answers, and keeps driving. Hand on the wheel, headlights burning the fading daylight, tires rolling over asphalt in the town that's his home and life's blood, Kyle sits alone in his car and says, "Hey."

"You okay?"

The softness in the question, the care, is like a caress.

Shivering, aroused and grateful he's alone, Kyle controls the pitch and tone of his voice as well as he can and answers, "Yes. Just a little freaked. It's my fault, you know. I came to you."

"No. It's my fault you were there, and it's Ben's fault that you had to lie about Harry," Gabriel retorts, bristling. "He made you lie to cover up his mess. That was wrong."

"We all lie," Kyle says calmly. "Especially to protect people we love."

It hangs there, in the air. Neither of them speaks for a long time. There's only the rumbling of the tires, the purr of the engines, the whistle of the wind.

Self-awareness of a powerful sort settles on Kyle. Gabriel isn't a monster; he's a survivor of abuse, trying to be a better man. The same goes for Kyle. He's not a monster. He's not the one who hurt Darrek; he's just another survivor of abuse, trying to live with that fact, and trying to overcome it, in every possible way.

"Not anymore," Gabriel tells him. "No more lies. No more secrets. Honesty is the only thing that can save us."

"You're a good man," Kyle tells him sincerely. "I don't want to have to lose you."

"You're better off without me. Ben will take care of you. You're safer if I keep my distance."

"Gabriel," Kyle begs, without argument, only sentiment.

"I love you too much to put you in danger. You deserve better than that."

The call ends. They roll up the long, winding drive, over crunching rocks, through tall grass as they leave the road and rationality behind and enter wilderness. There are two cars, a truck and a motorcycle parked around the main building of Diadem. Gabriel and Kyle park side-by-side, turn off their engines, and step outside, slamming their doors closed. A dark figure sits on the front porch before them, a paper coffee cup in hand, with steam wafting from the top.

"What's this?"

Kyle doesn't know what to say, so he says nothing. Putting one foot in front of the other, he circles the truck and walks to the front steps, climbing them slowly and feeling eyes on his every move. Expression impassive, body language loose as he can manage, he approaches Ben, with Gabriel at his heels. His foot has barely touched the top step when he reaches for his shirt and lifts it, showing his chest, waiting for Ben to look and see the long red scratches. Then he lets the shirt drop back down, covering him.

"I kissed him," Kyle admits, eyes averted, jaw clenched. "But that's it. Sir."

Ben takes two quick steps forward, reaching out to cup the side of Kyle's face in a hand. Kyle leans into the touch, and anguish flickers, tightening his lips. Then it's battled down and hidden.

"Why is he here?" Ben asks quietly, then repeats it for Gabriel's benefit. "Why are you here?"

Gabriel stays on the packed earth and gravel, his feet planted like they've taken root there. "Come here. This needs to be a more private conversation."

"My ass it does. Say what you need to say. Why the fuck did you scratch him up? Huh?! Why did you kiss him?"

"I'm sorry," Kyle hisses.

"Kyle, you stay out of this," Gabriel says sharply. "None of this is your fault. You have nothing to explain. I shouldn't have gotten you alone. I shouldn't have touched you. That was wrong. The rest of it is between me and Benny."

Trying to catch up, to put the pieces together and failing, Ben looks between them, but can't seem to bring himself to leave Kyle's side when the frantic energy emanates from him so plainly.

"How about you let Kyle be my concern, huh, bitch? What's this all about? 'Cause I don't like the smell of it one goddamned bit."

"He knows," Kyle says in barely a whisper, for Ben's ears alone. Raising his eyes, he reinforces his words with unspoken meaning. "Harry."

It may be the first time Kyle has ever seen Ben look scared and guilty. His eyes widen fractionally, and he gets very, very still. Kyle nods slightly, then inclines his head toward Gabriel. "Go."

Explanation seems inconsequential. For a moment, all there is, blocking out everything else, is the pain in Gabriel's eyes. Kyle sees it reflected in the glass of the front door to Diadem. Kyle's torment and desires, the scratches on his chest, the confessed shared kiss, they will be dealt with once Gabriel is away and Kyle is in Ben's arms, where he should be. First, Ben needs to deal with Gabriel.

"Stay right here. Don't leave the porch."

"Yes, Sir," Kyle agrees. Ben walks away from Kyle and goes to Gabriel.

Kyle can see it happen clearly enough in the reflection without even turning around. Ben jumps down the steps, and goes right up to Gabriel, who takes a backwards step that Ben only follows. But then Gabriel stops his retreat and slams both hands against Ben's chest, his mouth twisted in a grimace as he roughly sucks in air.

"I swore," Ben says in a toneless voice. "To you. Now it's done. It's *done*, Gabey. He won't hurt anyone anymore."

Gabriel searches his friend's face, with wide, childlike eyes. Betrayed, scared, helpless all over again, he's left at a loss. Kyle knows how that feels.

Gabriel flinches, fighting an inner battle that Kyle is quite familiar with, probably wanting to strike out at Ben again, wanting to scream, wanting to break apart into a million pieces just to put an end to it all for good. The years fall away before their eyes and Gabriel's only a teenager, homeless, with nothing and no one, not even faith in the goodness of humankind. Standing before Gabriel, catching him by the arm when he continues to grunt and growl and fight the good fight, is the one person in all the world who chose to save him, and for no reason other than it was the right thing to do.

The words won't come at first, though they see him struggle to find them. Gabriel tries to shake off Ben, but it only causes him to grab for a tighter hold. "He was mine to deal with. Not yours. This was *mine*. How dare you? All of you! You had no right!"

Ben says not a word, but the face that stares back at Gabriel is the one Ben must have worn that day, when they carved the names of Harry's young victims in his flesh, so that he'd always remember his crimes. The fright and awe in Gabriel's expression tells Kyle as much. Ben patiently lets Gabriel rage at something he can't change or take back.

"GODDAMMIT, BEN," Gabriel screams, voice shattering.

Unmoved, hard as a statue, Ben stands counter to Gabriel's formless, wild horror. Gabriel punches at Ben, doing nothing, growls at him, to no end. Ben holds Gabriel's face in a hand and leans in to place a tender kiss to his forehead. His hand falls away, and he steps back, arms spread wide. "It's done."

Diadem's front door opens, and Trace and Micah step out. One look at Kyle, at Ben and Gabriel, and some understanding passes between them. Outnumbered, broken and struggling to breathe, Gabriel surrenders. The past is right there with them, a ghost, a crime, a promise. The future is there too, in Kyle and in Gabriel's conquered desire to take advantage of someone incapable of defending himself. In anguish, Gabriel turns his back to Ben and goes to his vehicle, wiping his face dry on his sleeve, his head hanging. Trace bounds down the steps and goes after him, catching him by the door to Gabriel's Discovery, his jangling keys the loudest sound for miles.

His deep voice rumbling like distant thunder, Trace talks to Gabriel, whose gaze remains downcast; his posture slumped and drained of fight. Leaning close, Trace explains.

"Once you became part of our family, this became our problem, too. You don't get to keep it for yourself. We didn't do it only for you. We did it for Harry, and everyone he hurt, all of those kids who would have been hurt next, too. Benny, Micah and I, we volunteered to carry this. You're carrying enough. It's on us, us, babydoll, not you. Be mad. Go ahead if it makes you feel better. But it happened. I ain't sorry. The world is a safer place, now."

They catch the reactions in Gabriel's face—the way his brow tightens in furrows, the continued screaming behind his eyes.

"You did this behind my back!" he yells. "You didn't even tell me! You never would have told me, would you?!"

"No. We wouldn't. It's our job to protect you."

"What you did was *wrong*," Gabriel urges, trying to make Trace see.

"So be it," Trace shrugs. "Can't change the past. You know that. Harry knows that. Boy, does he know it."

He waits for Gabriel's response, holds his arms out.

"You wanna hate me? Hit me? Free shot. Go on. Get it out of your system."

Gabriel is too tired to let anger take him that far.

"No? Okay then. If you change your mind, you know where I am," Trace says.

"Damn it, Trace," Gabriel sighs.

He folds Gabriel into a love-infused hug that Gabriel doesn't return, but doesn't fight, either. "I love the hell out of you, kid," Trace tells him. "I'll always watch out for you, even when you don't want me to. That's what family's for."

They break apart. Trace nods, tightly, to Micah, and glances sideways at Ben.

And then that's it. Kyle's skin tightens with a brief inner chill as Gabriel quietly gets behind the wheel and guns the engine. Trace watches him pull out of the parking spot and swing around before driving slowly away. When Gabriel is on his way, Trace turns back to the others and strolls toward them with an inexplicable knowing look that passes between him and Ben, then him and Micah.

Feeling like a cub in a lion's den, Kyle knows he's outmanned and will never be quite as strong or confident as those around him, who have devoted themselves to the cause of protecting him and Gabriel and Darrek, who they love dearly. And maybe that's okay. Maybe that's the new balance that will keep them all in better reach of their own definitions of happiness and inner peace. They all have their battles to fight, but no one can win the war by fighting alone.

Lost in his head, Kyle doesn't see Ben approach, which is why he nearly jumps out of his skin when a hand curls possessively around his arm.

"Hey," Ben soothes, sensing Kyle's keyed-up, nervous energy. "It's fine. See? No sweat. We're not the bad guys. We'd never hurt you, or anyone we care about. We just know how to take care of ours."

"I'm glad he knows. I hated keeping that secret."

"Mm. Is that why you told him?"

"I didn't tell him," Kyle says defensively, naked under Ben's close scrutiny. "It slipped out. It was an accident! I swear it! Ask Gabe. He was saying that he was afraid he's turning into Harry, but I know he's not. He's nothing like Harry. Gabriel knows right from wrong. He admitted to being attracted to the vulnerability he sees in me, and that he wanted to act on it, but he didn't. He stopped. Gabe realized what he was doing, and stopped himself."

Ben seems sad as he hears this, and pulls Kyle into a hug. "I'm glad he stopped. But I guess I need to keep an even closer eye on you than I thought. It's good that Gabe knows about Harry. It'll help him sleep at night. It'll help you sleep at night, too."

Putting a little more space between them, Ben lifts Kyle's shirt and examines the scratches. Kyle wants to twist away and push the fabric back down. It takes all of his self-control not to. His face colors, turning red and he discovers he's holding his breath. When Ben's fingertips trace the marks, Kyle's nipples stiffen almost painfully. Closing his eyes over, he endures it as best he can.

"I have one more appointment today. You'll stay here, in my office, until I'm done."

"Yes, Sir."

"Look at me."

Kyle wrenches his gaze upward, lets Ben have at it.

"That's all that happened? You aren't lying to me?"

"No, Sir," he says awkwardly, sounding like he's half-swallowing the words.

"Tell me the truth."

Kyle sighs, wanting to look away, hating how he feels like Ben sees right through him, "I wanted him. I would have let it go farther. He's the one that stopped. He says he didn't want to hurt me. Gabe's a good guy."

"Like I don't already know," Ben says, satisfied, and visibly proud of Kyle for his honesty. "Come on. I'll get you something to eat while you wait. You look like hell."

The sound of tires crunching over the driveway draws Darrek out from the opened garage. Wiping his hands on a rag, he squints up into the bright sunlight after leaving the dark of his workspace. Gabriel, crying and exhausted, emerges from his Discovery and heads slowly over to him.

"What happened?" Darrek says immediately, meeting him halfway. "Gabe? What's wrong?"

With a thousand-yard stare full of resignation and heartache, Gabriel folds himself into Darrek's embrace, the smell of sawdust strong on him.

Darrek doesn't linger in the hug, but pulls back to study Gabriel's misery and physical condition.

"I'm okay," Gabriel assures him. "Can we sit somewhere? We need to talk."

"Yeah, of course."

In the kitchen, just through the garage and up a few steps, they find seats. After sipping from a glass of water, filled from the tap, Gabriel starts explaining. The first thing he tells Darrek about is what happened with Kyle at the office.

"I wanted to keep him there, Dare. I wanted things from him that I had no right to want or expect, and he would have gone along with it if I'd pressed the issue. It's fucked up. It's really fucked up. I told him he's better off staying away from me. Safer."

Darrek's initial reaction is silence, his expression filled with a heavy sort of sorrow. "That's not all, is it?" he asks. The look on his face tells Gabriel that Darrek feels he's no longer capable of being shocked or surprised, by anything. He expects the worst. He's ready for it.

"No. It's not. Kyle let something slip. We drove to Diadem to straighten things out, and sure enough, I found out we've been lied to for a year by Ben, by Trace and Micah, by all of them. They never would have told us if not for Kyle. They didn't want me to know."

He shakes his head, takes another drink, then holds his head in a hand. "Back when we went to Texas to confront Harry and my mother," Gabriel tells Darrek. "We weren't the only ones down there. Trace, Ben, Micah... they made the trip, too. They went to find Harry, and must have gotten to him after we did. They attacked him in punishment for what he did to me, made it so Harry couldn't go to the cops after, not without explaining things he'd never want to explain. They uh, forced him to give up names of the boys he molested. They carved and inked them into his skin."

"Holy fuck," Darrek gasps.

"Then they let him go. A *year* ago. A whole fucking year! Kyle knew about that, too, this whole time. The shit with Harry, the shit with Jerry — that damn kid had all of this evil rattling around in his brain for so long. No wonder he went off like he did! My god.

"At Diadem, they admitted it—Ben and Trace. Owned up to it. And the worst part is I'm not even mad. I'm not mad at all. I feel like I should be, and at first I was, but I think mostly because of the lying. So much fucking *lying*."

"I won't lie to you," Dare says softly. "Promise."

Gabriel glances around their quiet, darkened house. The curtains are all shut. Sierra is curled up at his feet. As Darrek processes the news, Gabriel gives him time. He knows it's a lot, and that it will all have repercussions.

"I need a break from it," Gabriel tells him, feeling stripped down and floundering. He hasn't felt this lost since he ran away from home, darting out into a dangerous world, alone, just to escape; just for a chance at life. That's still all he wants—a chance to make things better. At least now he has earned the wisdom to see where his best chances lie. "You and Sierra, our life here, the photography business, can we just focus on that for a while?"

"Yeah," Darrek agrees, urgently. He reaches for Gabriel's hand, holds it and gives him an encouraging sort of smile. "I'll do whatever it takes. Whatever you need."

"I need the break," Gabriel repeats.

"Then we'll have a break. We'll keep it simple. It'll be good for us."

"It will," Gabriel agrees, latching onto Darrek's confidence in the suggestion. "Trace and Ben will always be there if I need them. But with Kyle it's different. It's gotten really dangerous. For all of us, but mostly for Kyle."

Darrek shifts in his seat, straightening, and his expression hardening. He's steeling himself, but for what, Gabriel isn't entirely sure. He knows that what they need is something Darrek might not be able to give. It'll be painful and terrible, but it will also be the first real step toward healing.

"Come with me to therapy," Gabriel says. "I'd like to start there. I'd like *us* to start there, while we figure things out."

Jaw clenched, body stiff, Darrek holds Gabriel's gaze. He nods. "Okay."

Some of Gabriel's tension melts. He manages a small smile.

"Thank you. And Dare... about Kyle...."

He squeezes Darrek's hand, watches as he battles momentarily with a crippling wave of emotion. Once the brunt of it passes, he clears his throat, then asks, "I need some closure. Is that okay? To see him one last time?"

"I'm sorry, baby," Gabriel says, struggling with the words as the tears start again. "I'm so damn sorry."

Darrek tries to smile, to show that it's okay, but he's crying too. Gabriel overlays their joined hands with his palm, knowing what Darrek is letting go of and how big it is.

Darrek nods, takes a deep breath, and blows it out. "It's the right thing to do. It's the least I can do."

"I love you," Gabriel swears, with his whole heart. "So much. Time to take the next step. Both of us. Together."

"Together," Darrek agrees.

After a moment, Darrek stands from his seat and goes around to Gabriel, drawing him up. Arms encircling Gabriel, Darrek takes another deep breath. Gabriel can feel the rigidity in Darrek's body gradually softening. He hopes, prays, that they're past the worst of it, and that it will get better, that the burdens of their hearts will become easier to bear. At least they're not alone. It will be a journey they can take jointly, helping each other if they stumble and fall, being there to celebrate the victories and give encouragement whenever doubt might creep in. To love and be loved, with honesty, patience and devotion, are the best gifts they can give each other. It's more than they've ever had before, and Gabriel knows it's enough to get them through.

It's a long night. Kyle sits alone with his thoughts for most of the evening in Ben's office, picking over the food Ben orders for him. They're there even after the sun has set and the stars have come out. By the time Ben is finished and they get home, all Kyle wants is sleep. Wrung out, he's out as soon as his head hits the pillow, before Ben can join him in bed.

Morning comes early, like it usually does on workdays. Ben is still asleep, so Kyle creeps around, getting ready, grabbing breakfast. As soon as he's at work, he dives into it, using the distraction to regain a sense of normalcy, basking in the dullness of his routine.

When Kyle gets home that afternoon, he finds that Ben must be there, too. Ben's truck is in the driveway as Kyle pulls up in front of the house. The sight makes Kyle smile all the way down to the core of his soul.

Excited to see Ben—the man he loves, who understands him and his needs so well, and loves nothing more than to take care of him—Kyle knows how lucky he is as he parks and locks his car. He catches sight of Ben out of the corner of his eye, standing in the house's front entryway with the door opened.

After he steps away from his car, Kyle is almost instantly stopped. He comes face-to-face with Darrek, big as life, standing right in front of him. Gabriel's Discovery is parked in the road, with him waiting behind the wheel and the engine running. He must have pulled up right after Kyle did.

Kyle hears Junior meow softly, far away and held in Ben's arms. The clouds continue to sweep across the sky, but everything in Kyle's immediate vicinity comes to a standstill.

He sees plainly in Darrek's face that he's had a sleepless night with Gabriel, discussing newfound truths. Sorrow and regret fill Darrek to brimming. It spills over through his pores, tainting the air around him.

Responsibility for his part in causing Darrek and Gabriel's pain weighs on Kyle. Tucking his car keys in his pocket, he stands his ground.

"He told me everything," Darrek says, implying a lot.

Kyle tries to reason it out, and guess at the amount of truth in that.

"I can't believe you didn't tell me, after all this time," Darrek says. "We talked to you constantly during that trip. I just... it seems impossible, but it's true. You really are great at keeping secrets."

That hurts, and he knows that it was intended to.

"Harry deserved it," Kyle begins, defensively. "You might have been comfortable letting that son of a bitch go free, but we couldn't. He had to pay. And he did. It's justice."

That hurt too, Kyle sees, but doesn't feel the pleasure from it that he wanted.

"They won't go after Jerry," he tells Darrek quietly. "Not if you don't want it. It wouldn't be the right thing to do, because it would hurt your mother and your siblings. But I do think they need to know. They need to know what kind of a man he is. If you want help with that part of it, Ben, Trace, Micah... they'll give it."

Darrek looks at him, really looks. Kyle feels it like a touch, his skin pebbling with goosebumps.

"You'd be better off staying away from us."

"Maybe," Kyle allows.

"You've been my best friend since we were kids," Darrek tells him, anguished. "You're the closest thing I've ever had to a real brother. If *I'm* capable of raping you, then what exactly do you think Gabriel is capable of? He was your Dom and your enemy before he was your friend and whatever he is to you now. We're bad for you. Both of us."

"You may be my best friend," Kyle answers. "But you never really knew me. Gabriel understands me better than you ever will. Maybe you're right. I mean, I can't change who I am, and I don't want to, anyway."

"Gabe's different now. I guess he knows he could never hurt me like he could hurt you. I could never be scared of Gabriel, and I don't think he would ever take advantage of someone to that extent. I mean, I guess he kind of started to go that way when I first met him. He had sex with me even though he knew I wasn't looking for that. It was more of a selfish thing, like he wanted to have sex, so he did. I don't know. It's all screwed up." Darrek takes a deep breath, reaching down inside to find his courage again, looking squarely at Kyle. "You seem different."

"How do you mean?"

"I don't know, more confident or something. It's good."

"It feels good to be honest. About everything. It's the first time in my life that I haven't had to hide shit. I mean, I'm still scared of stuff, but I can tell the truth about it. I don't have to bottle it up anymore."

Darrek nods.

"Um," Darrek starts, straightening and taking a few steps away.

"I am sorry. For what it's worth. You know."

It feels like they're back there, in the field, struggling over the knife, with Darrek wanting to spill his own blood for the crime of hurting Kyle, and Kyle willing to shed his blood too, to stop Darrek from doing so. But when it comes right down to it, there's always someone bleeding. Someone has to pay the price. Kyle can see it in Darrek's face that he would take it back, all of it, ever since Kyle was just a young boy trying to be brave, kissing his best friend that he loved so well under the covers, and Darrek kissed him back.

"I forgive you," Kyle smiles.

"You've been taking care of my sorry ass for a decade. Thank you for that."

Kyle is unable to reply, the words are too big to voice.

"You and Ben are great together. I didn't always see it, but I do now. He's good at knowing what you need. I'm happy for you both."

It's too much. It's like some sort of goodbye, some monumental shift that he can't affect in any way, he can only endure. Clawing down his rising emotions, Kyle clears his throat and says, "I'm... I'm gonna go."

"Can I hug you?" Darrek asks quietly, and when Kyle looks up to respond, sees the tears on his best friend's cheek, the sincere apology in his eyes.

"Christ, Dare," Kyle gasps and goes to him, putting himself in Darrek's embrace.

Then he feels it. Darrek lets him go. He's right there, holding him, but he's really gone.

Kyle cries silently and pushes him away, his breath hitching. "Go."

Nodding, Darrek says thickly, "Yeah. Yeah, I should go. See ya around, Kyle."

"Yeah. See ya."

Darrek walks back to the SUV, with Gabriel waiting patiently inside. Ben waits on the stoop, holding their cat, watching out for Kyle, as always. Wrapping his arms tightly around his chest, Kyle holds himself and watches his first love walk away, knowing it will never be like it was, that maybe it'll be the last time he ever sees

Darrek Grealey. But maybe that's okay, after all. Without denying the pain that comes with the ending, Kyle sinks in, accepting the heartache. He knows the cleansing power it has, and the gift of sincerity. There are no more lies left to hide behind, no secrets left to keep him down. Slowly, unavoidably, he rises back up, untethered and free.

If you enjoyed this story, you can sign up for a free membership at ForbiddenFiction.com and discuss it with other readers and the author at the *From Temptation* story page
at http://forbiddenfiction.com/library/story/LK1-1.000026.

We do our best to proof all our work, but if you spot a text error we missed, please let us know via our website Contact Form
at http://forbiddenfiction.com/contact

Author's Notes

It's been quite a difficult journey to bring this book to fruition. It was years ago that I first wrote *Deliver Us*, and I always intended to write a sequel but it took longer that I would have liked for the right inspiration to strike. Once I had written the first draft, it quickly became clear that there was still a ways to go. Perhaps because of how much of blood, sweat, and tears went into the crafting of this story, of everything I have endeavored to write, I am most proud of this one. The finished product and Kyle's journey toward conquering his demons make it all worthwhile. He's part of me, always will be, and it has been a pleasure to fight for him. This book couldn't have happened without the guidance of two people in particular–my editors, Rylan Hunter and D.M. Atkins. I extend huge, heartfelt gratitude for their patience, their vision, and their determination to keep pushing this story to do justice to Kyle's spirit.

Kyle is a self-made mirage. He appears one way on the surface–clever, cocky, and focused–yet there are many hidden layers to his true identity, constantly working against him. No matter how clever you are, or how honorable your dreams may be, life finds ways to make you fight to achieve them. Sometimes, as with Kyle and Darrek, it's an attempt to move past a horrifying, seemingly insurmountable obstacle. The purpose of this book and this arc of the *Deliver Us* storyline was to show that fight. It's mostly a secret struggle, as is similarly true for many others, but that much more glorious in its hard-won, bittersweet triumph.

I've borrowed Kyle's passion and bravery to get me here, to the end of this book. I sincerely hope you have enjoyed reading it. My wish is for you to be inspired to take from it the diligence to question who may be presenting to you a self-made mirage that doubles as a shield to keep the dangers of the world at bay, the courage to believe in yourself, the trust to accept the love that is given to you, the fortitude needed to never give up the fight, and the knowledge that it does get better.

About the Author

Website: http://lynnkelling.com

Five years ago, **Lynn Kelling** spontaneously started writing and hasn't stopped since. It all started with the desire to take a closer look at behaviors and ideas lurking at the fringes of life — basically anything that people may hesitate to speak of in mixed company, but everyone wonders about anyway. She is drawn to that which some may consider to be taboo — the darker and wilder the better — in order to expose the humanity within it. Our most telling moments are conveyed through intimacy and that which makes us feel vulnerable, powerful, or both, and so what could be more intriguing? Lynn is an artist and lover of any form of creative self-expression that comes from a place of honesty and emotion, whether it's body art or opera. She works as a multimedia designer in the Philadelphia area where she lives with her husband and two children.

About the Publisher

ForbiddenFiction.com is a publisher devoted to writing that breaks the boundaries of original erotic fiction. Our stories combine intense sexuality with quality writing. Stories at Forbidden Fiction.com not only arouse readers through sensations, but also engage them emotionally and mentally through storytelling as well-crafted as the sex is hot.

ForbiddenFiction.com is also designed to be a social reading environment. You'll have fun even if just reading the latest post each day, yet you will have the chance for so much more. Readers and authors can be part of ongoing discussions of specific works and individual authors as well as more general topics.

Sign up for a FREE Membership today at ForbiddenFiction.

www.ingramcontent.com/pod-product-compliance
Lightning Source LLC
Chambersburg PA
CBHW070211260626
47160CB00002B/519

* 9 7 8 1 6 2 2 3 4 0 7 7 4 *